Turkoise

Joan M. Sargent

Parendi Press

SONOMA, CALIFORNIA

TURKOISE

ISBN-978-0-615-30143-3

for BAW

Hereafter, in a better world than this,
I shall desire more love and knowledge of you.

As You Like It, Act I, Scene II

ONE

Emily

The day was uneventful up to 12:25 PM, just a solo run on the foggy beach and a late breakfast on Montana Avenue. Then, I drove straight down Seventh instead of taking the left turn home.

After a week of tight deadlines and last-minute revisions, I was in no mood to return to my desk. Besides, the weather showed signs of improving. I'd go up to Will Rogers Park, watch some polo, lower my mental thermostat for a while.

As I wound through the maze of streets in the canyon, I opened the back window enough for my dog Fizzy to hang her head out. At the park entrance I ran my card through the kiosk then coasted into a space, just as a squirrel leaped across the lawn. In a nanosecond, all hell erupted in the backseat. Before I could snag her leash, Fizz propelled herself out the window.

I was chasing her without success when an old black motorcycle roared past. Its rider cornered Fizz under a tree and scooped her up. We met in the middle of the parking lot.

Between his lanky frame and his untamed hair, the overall effect was Romantic poet—in a battered cowhide jacket. I guessed screenwriter. Or worse, entertainment lawyer.

He pushed his sunglasses to the top of his head. His eyes were brown, with very long lashes. "What kind of dog is this?" he asked, grinning.

"Jack Russell. Mostly," I said. Then, to be polite, "What kind of motorcycle is that?"

His grin morphed into a smile. "Vintage."

"Very nice." I stepped back to leave.

"I think so," he said, without taking his eyes off me.

"Well, thanks very much," I said, then waved a final good-bye to him and strolled off with my dog to the glade overlooking the playing field. Behind me, I thought I heard the revving of an engine.

The match had been underway for a while and the horses' hooves thumped the turf as they huffed up and down the field. The clouds were burning off and the sun was warm. I slid the loop of Fizz's leash over my ankle and lay back. I was just dozing off when I heard footsteps crunching the grass beside me, then a voice.

"The thing is, I just realized I didn't get your name."

I squinted up through my fingers. It was him, the motorcyclist. He hadn't left after all.

"Hi," I said as I sat up.

"I should have introduced myself." He extended a hand out. "Nick Turner."

Having no choice, I shook his hand. This close, and without the dog between us, he smelled of bar soap and sun-warmed leather.

"Emily."

"Emily—?"

"Reidell."

Above the field, one last ribbon of gray vapor slid out toward the ocean.

"Mind if I watch the game with you?" he asked.

"No, no, of course not." It occurred to me that I was not doing a good job of getting rid of this guy.

He sat himself down cross-legged next to me.

"Great day, isn't it?" he asked.

"The warmth feels good after all the fog."

"You from this area?"

"The other side of the canyon." I gestured in the general direction of my apartment on the San Vicente bluffs.

"Ah, I'm right over the hill here. Galloway."

The polo ball sailed through the goal at the far end. I heard a shout, scattered applause, saw two players high-five each other.

"So, what do you do when you're not out chasing your dog?" Nick asked.

"I'm a science writer."

"For a magazine or—?"

"I freelance; magazines, newspapers, websites."

"What do you write about?"

"Health and medical news, science topics."

"Sounds like our lines of work overlap."

"How is that?"

"I'm a psychiatrist, here in the Palisades."

I looked over to him. I had to admit, those brown eyes looked intelligent under their arched brows. "Oh? What type of therapy?"

"Well, talking, of course, and some Recovered Memory Therapy."

One of his top incisors was slightly chipped. His hands were long and smooth; his fingers, perfectly articulated. I pushed my hair behind my right ear, then clasped my arms around my knees. "I've never heard of that type of therapy," I said.

"It's done with hypnosis, or just deep relaxation. So far, I've used it only for stubborn cases, to free up the patient's mind, get them to open up."

"About their pasts?"

"Sometimes way past."

"You mean, like repressed childhood memories?"

He watched me for another moment before replying. "Yes, and for some, memories from 'past lives.'"

"Really." I reached over to pull up a ripe dandelion then blew its seeds over the field. Although I knew many so-called "therapists" used such New Age-y treatments in their work, I'd never met a real MD who believed in that nonsense.

"Careful. We shrinks can read body language." There was the grin again.

"It's just, well, you know. Everybody thinks they were Cleopatra. Or Napoleon."

He shrugged. "They could be."

"That doesn't matter?"

"Not at all. Their stories could simply be what we sometimes call 'healing fictions.'"

"Healing fictions."

"Stories which make their own cures."

"So a patient comes to you, is hypnotized, tells some tale about their supposed past and just…gets well and goes home?"

"That's how it works sometimes." He looked down at his boots, then back over to me.

A finger-thick wave of hair twirled around his ear, just teasing his jaw line. His face was a bit wind-burned and there was a tiny wound on his lower cheek; perhaps he'd cut himself shaving. I imagined him standing at a steamy mirror earlier, leaning forward, bath towel wrapped around his waist, pressing the spot with a washcloth.

I cleared my throat. "Do you give interviews?" If this guy was the real deal, I might end up with a good story myself.

He smiled broadly. "Only to beautiful journalists from Santa Monica."

After Jonathan, and all our disagreements over whose career got top billing, I wasn't interested in anything resembling a date. "Thank you. But it really was just a professional request," I said.

"No problem with that."

After a moment or two, I asked, "So, did you go to school around here?"

He slid a look to me, then chuckled. "Are we on or off the record now?"

Before he had to leave, about half-an-hour later, I found out he'd been born in May of 1966 in a small town near Chicago, where his dad had owned a plumbing supply business. After studying physics at the University of Michigan, he'd gone to UCLA Med, then done his residency at Cedars-Sinai. In addition to his private practice, he also did outpatient counseling one day a week at Marina-City Hospital, which gave him a chance for frequent visits with his younger sister Valerie and her husband, who lived in Marina del Rey. He volunteered the fact that he'd lived with a woman for several years in his late twenties and early thirties, but said their relationship had not survived the transition from medical school to medical practice.

I had, it seemed, bumped into a shrink who loved to talk. We made an appointment to meet at his office at four on the eighteenth, the first time he had available due to an out-of-town conference, and exchanged cards just in case there was a problem.

Back home that evening, I checked him out on the Internet only to discover he'd entered UCLA Med just a few years before I started my own undergrad education in biology and English at UCLA. Since his residency he'd presented, at various conferences, a number of papers relating to identity disorders of one type or another, but none on Recovered Memory Therapy, which was considered so controversial it had yet to be accepted as a curative treatment in diagnostic manuals.

* * *

Though I tried not to, every time I thought of our appointment during the next ten days I wondered what exactly he was doing at that moment. Caring young doctor. Cool old motorcycle. I could just about hear the groupies swarming. Okay, as long as he didn't expect me to join them.

Even so, by the time our Wednesday appointment rolled around, I was so nervous a casual observer might have thought I was the one being interviewed in the shrink's office. And, between my sweaty hands and hammering heart, maybe I needed one. But when Nick opened the door, smiling broadly and asking if I'd like some tea, my anxiety faded.

Part of the calming effect came from the welcoming atmosphere of his office. The late-day sun streaming through the ficus at the window splashed light and shadow across the hardwood floor. A Diebenkorn lithograph floated above a cloud-colored sofa, a Twombly print nearby. One entire wall was occupied with books. Yet another was covered by an impressive collection of framed degrees and honors. Though Dr. Turner might be a bit unorthodox, his work certainly had the respect of his peers.

We sat down; he on the sofa, me on the Eames chair, and discussed the mechanics of hypnotherapy for a while. Then he answered my questions while I took notes.

"How do you approach hypnotherapy sessions?" I asked.

"Well, you don't always start with hypnosis right away, because it doesn't work with all patients, and it's not always necessary. We always talk as much as possible first. Beyond that, well," he paused, "it's a feeling I get as to when or if hypnosis might be useful."

"What is your view on the past lives stories? Do you think any of them might be real?"

"Well, as a medical practitioner, I find I have to view them as healing fictions created in a hypnagogic state. Otherwise, the patient and I might get sidetracked into history."

"But do you—I'm asking for my readers now—as a scientist, do you, based on your work, believe in reincarnation?"

He leaned back against the sofa. "To tell you the truth, I didn't at all, until—"

His tone had changed. I looked up from my notes. He was staring out through the big, south-facing window, biting his lower lip, pensive.

He looked back at me. "Until I encountered a rather extraordinary case that made me think—"

I held my breath.

"—but I can't discuss it. I'm sorry. You know the rules." He looked apologetic.

"Of course, I understand." And I did, having interviewed a number of physicians in the past.

"You know, the list of people who believed in reincarnation is pretty impressive," he said.

"Like who, specifically?"

"Pythagoras, Socrates, Voltaire, Goethe, Thoreau, Whitman, Huxley, Tolstoy, General Patton, Henry Ford, Benjamin Franklin—"

"I'm impressed."

"But not impressed enough to believe it without proof."

"Well, no."

He smiled at me. His gaze was gentle, and unfaltering.

"So," I asked, pen hovering over notebook, "is there anything else you think I should know?"

"Hmmm." He scrunched his brows in mock thought. "Well," his voice was sly, "maybe this." He walked over, sat down on the ottoman before me and placed his hand on my cheek, scrutinizing my face. "Your eyes," he said, "they have gold flecks in the green."

"Is that a medical condition?"

"A rare one. Chronic beauty."

"Thank you, Doctor." I leaned down to put my notebook into my tote. My hand was trembling.

"There's only one way to approach this." His voice was serious.

"How?" I looked up.

He bent forward and touched his lips to mine, for more than just an instant.

"What are your girlfriends going to say about this?" I whispered.

"You mean my former girlfriends?" he murmured, and his breath tickled my ear.

He sat back, drummed his fingers on his knee. "Speaking of that issue, am I going to have to tear you away from a jealous boyfriend?"

"He tore himself away. To Boston."

"Cold," he said.

I laughed and said, "I think so." When I was actually thinking, *Jonathan who*?

Nick Turner and I kissed even more that night after dinner. Within weeks, he was driving with me and my wildlife spotting scope up to Big Bear and out to the desert. He bought me a helmet and we spent Saturdays riding his motorcycle two-up all over Southern California; our favorite route, the Coast Highway from Malibu to my family's home in Carpinteria. Every Sunday, we jogged together on the beach.

On the surface, much about us didn't seem to jive. I was a morning person; he was a night owl. He didn't care much what he ate; I was a fresh food nut. His world was elastic, theoretical and often, it seemed to me, governed by the ephemeral; mine rested on fact and substance. But we often laughed over these paradoxes and, despite any differences in points-of-view, we meshed perfectly. In fact, it was as if we completed one another. And so it was, on a clear summer evening above Camp Nelson, exactly two months after our first meeting that, beyond words, we made love for the first time during the height of the Perseid Meteor Shower as white fireballs rolled through the heavens and fell like glittering fireworks to earth.

. . .

Four months later, just before Christmas, 2002, he held out a palm-size globe and said, on bended knee as I sat on the sofa in front of him, "I want you to share the world with me."

I turned the globe around in my hands. "You want to travel?"

He looked annoyed. Then he squeezed my knees with his hands. "I want you to marry me!"

I stared at him. "Marry? Oh, Nicky!"

He pulled me to him on the floor, where we wrapped ourselves around each other and kissed and kissed, laughing, with Fizzy jumping around and barking like a lunatic.

We drove up to Carpinteria and he and Dad held a "private conference" in which Nick properly asked for my hand—the old-fashioned way—and we all celebrated with a champagne dinner at the best restaurant in Santa Barbara. We flew back to Chicago so I could meet his parents. His mom and I were joking with each other almost instantly, like old friends.

We spent the next several months planning our future together; hiring an architect to design a second floor for the little house on Galloway, taking inventories of housewares, linens, enrolling in gift registries. We decided to be married at my parents' home, in the garden bordered by the orange trees, just family and fifty-or-so guests. I bought a wedding dress, ivory silk in a simple style as a surprise for Nick, who loved seeing me in dresses. In the spirit of the moment, Nick volunteered to wear my brother Michael's old bee-keeping helmet with protective netting, an offer I vetoed, to his faux dismay.

· · ·

And then, July 27th, last Sunday; wedding preparations completed, I watched, perched on the upended plastic egg crate in his garage as he reassembled a wheel on the vintage bike I'd first seen him on the year before. The sea-breeze ruffled the jasmine outside. A light plane droned overhead.

How I loved seeing his long fingers patiently fitting parts together, his quiet absorption, that crooked smile making me smile as he looked up in the middle of a task.

"I read that article on Wolfgang Sennheiser's 'Frontiers of Therapy,'" I said. "I guess he's pretty convinced regression stories usually come from another source, like hidden memories." I took a swig from my bottle of Power Water.

"Yeah, old Sennheiser; they always drag him out when they want an 'opposing view.' The problem is, his views are a bit dated."

"Oh, so he's an old guy?"

"Well"—he fit the wheel back on the bike and adjusted the chain—"let's put it this way: there are rumors he went to grammar school with Freud."

"But that that doesn't necessarily mean he's wrong, does it?"

He spun the wheel, then wiped his hands on a shop rag and laughed. "No, Ems, it doesn't."

I sat back against the big red tool chest. "Didn't you say this bike had some nickname?"

"'Two of Everything': two carbs, two magnetos, two double oil pumps; everything works better in twos, don't you think?" He patted the rear fender. "Only six of these babies ever made. Could you pass me the wrench, love?"

I laughed, walked over to him and, delightfully intoxicated from the combination of jasmine and motor oil and the thought of actually being his wife, put my arms around him and nuzzled the side of his neck. He held me there as he lay the wrench aside then picked up all five-two of me and sat me down on the most romantic place in the garage, the tailgate of his Land Cruiser.

. . .

We were to have been married tomorrow, August 2, 2003, Nick and I.

Instead I sat, head bowed, surrounded by mourners and banks of white chrysanthemums in the dim light of Glenwood Memorial Gardens, where the Hall of Love met the Hall of Remembrance.

Never again would Nick and I make love under a starry sky. Never again would I feel my arms around him as we rode in the sun. Because Nick had died at 2:15 PM on July 28th. He'd stepped from the curb in front of his office for a late lunch across the street at the exact moment a drunk driver careened off Sunset. The car's impact had thrown him twenty feet into a cinderblock wall. Before any of us could get to the emergency room at St. John's, he was gone.

And now his body was at a crematorium, enclosed within a drawer of fire, jets of flame reaching up to engulf him. When his flesh and sinew had been consumed, his bones would be ground into ashes. The ashes would be placed inside an urn. The urn would be buried.

His sister Valerie, hanky held over her eyes as her shoulders shook, reached for my hand. His parents, Jim and May, sat to her left. May, black veil over a small hat, sat slumped forward, staring straight ahead in a stupor. Nick had been her firstborn. Her only son.

Someone had placed a program in my lap. "In memoriam . . ." it read, "Nicholas James Turner . . . loving son of . . . pioneering work . . ."

I had seen his colleagues arriving; associates from UCLA Neuropsychiatric, the Institute for Depth Psychology, the Laguna-Newport Clinic. Even those who had expressed doubt about his methods were here.

The chaplain's eulogy filtered into my consciousness as if an echo from a place far away. Now he was describing Nick's work; how his patients had trusted him, how the medical community respected him. Someone in the family must have given him Nick's resumé. He could read the words, but he could never really know the love Nick had for his work or his courage in trying new methods of healing. And how could he know what amazing love Nick and I shared? That no one could ever take Nick's place, in any of our lives?

A white marble statue of Lady Time stood behind the chaplain, her face cast down; a secular *Pieta*. On one arm she held a spent hour glass; on the other, a single palm frond. All around me the walls were lined floor to ceiling with marble drawers containing ashes, one atop the other; last testaments to a myriad of lives spent on earth. At the end of the Hall of Love the sun glowed through a clerestory stained glass of a serene mountain landscape. A single candle threw flickering light and shadow from the pendant cutwork lamp above.

There was a brief silence, then friends began coming up to the podium to speak.

First, a fellow I remembered as Martin, from Nick's residency at Cedars, telling how, after forty-eight hours straight tending to suicide attempts and drug overdoses, an exhausted Nick had sat the entire night with a frightened young cancer patient facing more surgery the next morning and…

Nick and I were going to have children.

Now Gil, his biking buddy, talking about the day he'd met Nick at the Long Beach Convention Center, the vintage motorcycle show, then driving with Nick down to San Pedro Harbor two weeks later to pick up the bike that had led him, one beautiful Saturday in June, to the girl of his dreams.

I sensed the eyes of my old friends Margo Maine and Olivia Delgado watching me from across the aisle. Someone in the back was crying.

My mother's steadying hand came around my shoulders. I lay my head against her lapel, felt the solid twill of her jacket against my cheek, the strands of her pearl bracelet rippling together as she stroked my arm. The familiar fragrance of her Shalimar surrounded me. I huddled closer to her shoulder to try to keep myself in one piece as my entire body quaked.

The chaplain delivered more prayers, a soloist sang "Amazing Grace," mourners began filing out behind us. I stood in the aisle, supported by my father's arm. People I had never seen before pressed my hand. Kind strangers spoke words of pity. "So sorry… is there anything I can do?"

then shook their heads in disbelief as they left the chapel.

And then, my father at one side of me, Michael on the other, I was walked outdoors, into the stinging glare. The afternoon was heating up, a hot wind gusting in from the east. If it continued, the smog would shift west over Santa Monica Bay and tomorrow the ocean would be flat as a mirror and the now-blue sky over it a sickly yellow-brown. The season of the Santa Anas was near.

Michael and Dad settled me gently into the back seat of a car. I pulled my legs up under me and my pumps fell from my feet onto the floor mat. I leaned my head against the window. The air was so hot and dry my breath left no cloud on the glass.

After the wake was over, my family brought me home, Mother brewed a pot of tea, opened a box of cookies she found in the pantry, and insisted I go right to bed and I knew she was probably right. I hadn't slept much since that terrible phone call on Monday.

She set the tea and cookies on my bedside table, helped me put on a nightshirt, made me take the Diazepam my doctor had sent over, then tucked me into bed. Then she sat beside me, running her hands over my hair as she had always done when I was a child. "Strawberry blond—so pretty in a bob." She touched my cheek and smiled. "And those sweet freckles." She gave me a long hug. "Are you sure you wouldn't like me here tonight? I really think it might be best."

She would sleep more comfortably at Michael's house up in Topanga. And, she had been by my side all week. Now I just wanted to be alone. "Oh, well. I'll be fine," I said, pulling the comforter closer.

Mother and Michael exchanged a worried look. "All right. But we'll be back early with breakfast," she said, and kissed me.

Michael added, "And if there's anything . . ." He held up his cell phone and pointed to it. "Okay?"

The front door closed, the sound of their footsteps grew faint on the street below, and the engine of Michael's car started up. Then, silence.

I dragged the sheet over my head and curled myself into it like a shroud. Fizzy jumped up next to me, pawed the covers, gave a little whimper and burrowed into the crook of my leg.

TWO

Emily

August 3-10, 2003

Mother wanted to stay for another week. I promised her I'd be fine on my own, but after she and Dad left I wandered about, unsure whether I was awake or asleep, one of the living or the dead, unable, even in my one-bedroom apartment, to keep track of common, everyday things: detergent, dish towels, ink pens. At one point I lost my glasses completely and had to wear my prescription sunglasses day and night. Later, I left some canned soup in a pan on high and, smelling smoke, found the whole mess fused together on the burner. Fizzy disappeared and I realized too late I'd left the door ajar. Too confused to look for her I sat, head in hands, unsure what to do until a jogger in the canyon brought her back.

. . .

Valerie called a week after Nick's memorial service. She was on her way to his house and needed some help.

"We just found out," she said as she dropped her bag and keys on my sofa, "that Nick died, as the lawyers said, 'intestate.'" She took a deep breath. "Meaning, he didn't have a will."

She sat at my dining room table. I sat next to her.

"Someone has to take care of the mail and bills." She wept as she spoke. "Dwight's been doing it, but he had business in Phoenix this week, so…"

We drove slowly, a thread of quiet between us, through the green lanes of the canyon, then up Sunset to the Palisades and the little house on Galloway. The driveway was empty. Nick must have walked to work that Monday instead of driving, as he usually did.

The mailbox on the porch was filled to overflowing and when I pulled the mail out a note from the carrier fell to the mat. *8/5. Mail held at post office.*

"Oh," Valerie said absently as she opened the front door, "there's the e-mail, too."

The blinds had been drawn and inside the house was dark and chilled. A layer of dust had already settled on the mahogany console in the entryway. The once-bright flowers of the mixed bouquet there—the one I'd brought over from the farmer's market our last Saturday together—were slumped colorless over the edge of the dry vase. In the front room a copy of the *New England Journal of Medicine* lay face down on the plaid armchair and a half-empty mug of coffee remains sat cold on the end table.

While Valerie sat on the sofa, separating bills from junk, I ventured into the kitchen, coffee mug in hand. I opened the refrigerator where I found a deli box of chicken salad and the half-full bottle of fruit juice we'd shared two days before the accident. I tossed them out and stared down at the running water as I washed the mug then, beyond caring, dried my hands with a mildewed dish towel from the kitchen hamper.

I tiptoed slowly into the back of the house and peered around the doorway into the bedroom, but couldn't… Instead, I stepped out onto the covered patio. The second story we'd planned above it would have had a new master bedroom with a view to the ocean, and a little office space for me. I looked up the back yard to the garage behind the house. Nick had installed a smaller door within the main door. I walked up the gravel path to the garage and tried the handle slowly; for once, it was unlocked.

There was the Land Cruiser, its tailgate down as we had left it Saturday before last. My bandanna was still lying in the wheel well where I'd dropped it. The beautiful old motorcycle I'd first seen him on sat in the corner, away from tools or equipment that might fall onto it.

I glimpsed the back of the house through the garage window. The sliding glass door to the bedroom was closed, reflecting the orange trees in the back garden, a single, disc-shaped cloud above. With what trace of courage I had left, I marched down the path back to the patio and pulled the door open.

Some of Nick's clothes lay where he'd left them on the wing chair in the corner: the frayed khakis spattered with motor oil, his faded Bruins tee, and his favorite work shirt. I held the shirt up to my face, buried my nose in its softness, smelled Nick, and the sweet scent of the vetiver grass in his aftershave.

The tweed jacket I'd given him for his birthday in May was in his closet, as were several pairs of jeans, draped casually over their hangers. I ran my hand over a pair of the now-precious, unwashed jeans, touched them to my cheek, enfolded them in my arms, remembered how I'd rested the side of my face against his thigh as we sat with friends in the living room just three weeks ago, his hand stroking my hair as he spoke, remembered looking up at him. His leathers were there too, including his vintage jacket, the one he had been wearing the day we met.

So many objects of Nick's everyday life, their meanings distilled by his death.

As I waited for the computer in his study to boot up so I could download the e-mail, I saw the bottle of Perrier-Jouet we'd bought the night we'd gotten engaged, sitting on the windowsill above. Scattered about the desk were the mementos of his last days: a couple of Motrin tablets, a tall box of tissues, the August issue of *Cycle World*, a book called *Physics of Mind*. They all sat waiting for him to return and pick them up or use them, as if he had only gone down to Gourmet Corner in Palisades Village for a few groceries. I picked up the book and thumbed through it, staring vacantly at its diagrams of waves and nerve synapses.

An alarm chirped and up came the screensaver, a see-through mechanical clock, its gears and wheels moving, then a prompt for a password; one I could not remember. Perhaps he had written it down somewhere.

I opened the top drawer of the wooden file cabinet next to the desk, hoping to find it there. Cables, connecting wires, an old modem. CDs. Several reams of paper. But no hint of a password. I found the key for the bottom drawer where he'd always kept it, taped under the left speaker, then shuffled through the drawer's contents: hanging files of conference information, printed downloads and, at the very back, nearly lost behind the reams of paper information, a thick manila envelope with my name on it.

My name.

I eased the hanging files back, pulled it out. Yes. *For Emily Reidell* it read, in Nick's rounded script, underlined diagonally across the front, folded closed, and secured with a button-and-string infinity knot. Stuck under the flap was an unaddressed white envelope and a card with a photo of surf bursting over rocks at sunset.

Stuck to the front were two Post-It notes, also in Nick's hand. One read: *Cleared w/ patient and CC law office.* The other, underneath, read: *Check w/CC office before giving to E. 8/1/03.* The day before our wedding.

Reflexively, my fingers touched my earlobes and the one-carat diamond studs he'd given me. Was this to have been a second wedding gift?

The drawer slid on its rails and clicked shut as I stared at the fat envelope in my hands, wondering what could have been so important he'd kept it hidden under lock and key, to be given to me on the eve of our marriage. Then, without thinking further, I sat down on the big sofa next to the desk and, like rolling dice from a cup, emptied the envelope onto the cotton blanket next to me.

A small mountain of micro-cassette tapes fell out, along with two smaller envelopes, one business-sized, and the other a smaller manila. I reached over with my thumb and index finger and picked up one of the little cassettes. On its tiny white label read, CN, 9/22 thru 10/07/98. On another, CN, 10/15-22/98. Eighteen in all, encompassing a six-month period from late summer 1998 to the winter of 1999.

The business envelope contained a three-page business document from a law office in Century City, dated July, 2002, less than one month after Nick and I had met, releasing all contents of the tapes to Nicholas J. Turner or his assigns for the purpose of advancing medical knowledge. The other large envelope held three pages of notes.

The notes, in Nick's handwriting, described a young woman who had come to him for help. She was twenty-six, bright, serious, thoughtful. Her father, a systems analyst, and her mother, a librarian, had moved to Southern California from the Midwest in 1972, shortly after they'd adopted her. Her adoption records, Nick had noted at the bottom of the page, had been sealed.

She was a graduate student in architecture and urban planning. Her name was Clare. According to Nick's evaluation, Clare, with her intelligence and motivation, should have been an excellent candidate for treatment, yet none of the therapists she had consulted had been able to help her decipher the meaning of a troubling dream. In it, a faceless stranger materialized from half-shadows extending his right hand out to offer her an opaque, blue-green stone.

Night after night the vision returned, evading all attempts at explanation. Compounding her unrest about the strange dream was another issue upsetting Clare: She was lonely, and afraid she would never find love. Like many of Nick's clients, she'd been referred to him as a last resort by her previous therapist, who'd given up on her case.

Apparently, Nick had tried traditional "talking therapy" with Clare, including discussion of her dreams. But after several weeks, during which time the dream of the stone appeared yet again, making it obvious that Clare's unconscious was resisting this first-defense line of healing, Nick began to try alternate routes. Filed behind the notes were the results of Clare's Myers-Briggs personality indicator test dated September 10, 1998, labeled, like the other documents, only with the initials "CN."

Clare, it seemed, showed a strong bent toward intuition, with thinking and feeling second and third. Sensation—grounding to the physical world—was almost completely absent from her personality profile. Little wonder she was haunted by a dream that more fact-oriented people like me might have thought about only briefly.

I heard Valerie calling my name and looked up to see her standing in the doorway. She was only thirty-one, but today she looked twenty years older. She'd been on the phone with credit card companies, finding out what needed to be done next.

She took a deep breath and let it out, then, seeing the pile of tapes on the sofa, asked, "What's that?"

"Tapes and notes of some kind." I held up the big envelope. "It had my name on it."

"How about the e-mail?"

"Do you by chance know his password?"

She shook her head. "I checked the answering machine. Just the shoe shop telling him his boots were repaired."

Silence fell over the room, save the hum of the CPU. Then Valerie pulled a crumpled tissue out of her pocket as I helplessly watched her tears. "I talk to him. Like I used to. My big brother, like he's beside me. Silly, huh?" She tried to smile, swallowed more tears, ran the now-limp tissue over her eyes. "Can we go?"

"Do you mind if I take these?" I held up the envelope.

"If he'd written your name on them they'll be yours sooner or later.

Besides," she shrugged, "who knows what will be left after the lawyers get finished?"

I gathered the tapes into the envelopes and we walked out of the house arm-in-arm, each lost deep in our own memories.

. . .

It took me a while after I got home, but I finally managed to find the micro-cassette recorder I'd used in college at the back of the hall closet. I sat down at my desk with a notepad and pen and slipped the first cassette in, hoping for some sort of explanation from Nick as to what the package was about.

My heart flinched at the sound of Nick's voice marking the date and session, the first time I'd heard him speak since the call he'd made to me on the afternoon he died. But, after visiting the house this morning, I had realized something important: These tapes were not just a mystery to unravel, they were now, like every other material thing from Nick's life, part of his legacy. Whatever the cost, I needed to know what they were about.

I concentrated and put pen to notepad, determined to listen and understand the best I could. A brief pause followed—I thought for a moment the tape had actually been erased—then a click, then Nick again, gently guiding another person into deep calm.

"You are warm and comfortable, safe and secure. Your only sensation is of utter tranquility, deep peace. This peace will allow you to remember events and places you have no memory of in your conscious state. You may speak of anything you wish. Here you know you are safe and secure, always safe and secure." The cassette continued to roll silently for several minutes. Then a second voice made what sounded like an attempt at a word. "Hummm."

"Where are you, Clare?" Nick's voice was gentle, muted.

"I don't know. Strange. Warm."

"What time in your life is it?"

"Not this life."

Silence again, save the squeak of leather shifting under someone's weight.

Then, Nick's voice again. "What year is it?"

"The time of the Sea People."

"Can you see your feet, Clare?"

"Mmm, yes."

"Are you wearing any shoes or footwear?"

"Sandals, tied onto my leg."

"Can you look around? What do you see around you?"

"Flowers, like bougainvillea. White walls. Winding street, narrow."

"Do you know the name of this place?"

"It was made by a sailor."

"How did a sailor make this place?"

"Ah, he gave his lover a piece of the earth; she threw it into the sea."

"So, you are on an island?"

"When she threw it into the water it made the islands."

"So this is a group of islands?"

"Yes, circles inside circles."

"So the earth thrown into the water made circles and the circles became land?"

"Mmm, yes."

I pushed the pause button. Concentric circles of land in the ocean. I could think of no such place in the world. Except the one described by Plato.

Somewhere I had an anthology of classics. I finally found it on the bottom shelf of the bookcase, its edges yellowed and dusty. I turned to "Timaeus and Critias," Plato's unfinished treatise on a sophisticated society of traders and artists dwelling on a multi-ringed island. Hadn't I just recently seen a program on cable about this topic? No, not "Atlantis": Santorini in the Greek Cyclades. Once known as Kalliste, before the cataclysm that all but wiped its memory off the face of the earth. I had made a brief visit there during my junior year abroad. Nea Kameni, the tiny volcanic isle at heart of Santorini, still burned; I had changed my vinyl-soled shoes for leather ones before stepping out onto its smoldering surface.

I returned to the tape, soothed myself by the familiar sound of Nick's voice as he encouraged Clare to continue, moving her along when she came to difficult places so as not to traumatize her, holding her attention in the places that illuminated her understanding. As I soon discovered, the tapes' content did not present itself chronologically, and the chronology of the tapes stretched across nearly 3,500 years. Often, as details surfaced, Clare would revisit episodes or leap ahead to a later incident. In several stories she even used languages she claimed were foreign to her. As in almost all "past life" regression cases, she claimed to have either very little or no knowledge of the times and places she spoke of under hypnosis.

Clare's sessions also included talking therapy and in these, she told of a place she found herself in her between-life "rotations." Like others who had had near-death experiences, she referred to it as "The Other Side," a parallel world of peace and beauty to which the spirit repairs between lifetimes. It was a place where, as she described it, "everything is made of light," a way station of sorts where the soul floats on a gentle, rippling motion created by expanding waves of yet more light. It was here, on the other side of death, that she knew she would have another life to come.

I listened to the tapes for the better part of two days. When I had finished at the blue hour of dusk on the third day, I sat meditating on their contents in my big chintz armchair facing the canyon and a wedge of the sea. Although I had listened as carefully as I could, I still had no idea what I really had. Or even why a package full of a stranger's medical records would have my name on it.

"Healing fictions" Nick had called his patients' regressions. So a woman named Clare had come to him, undergone hypnosis and been healed, presumably, by a series of stories. Still, why, *why*, of all the records Nick must surely have made of his clients' sessions, many surely including such regression work as this, did he save these in particular for me? On first listening, my sense of them was of two people, Clare and a lover, coming together, then parting, only to return to each other, like waves on a beach, breaking against the sand, retreating, then coming back again, one life after another. Theoretically.

Then, suddenly, I remembered. That first day in Nick's office, the special case he could not discuss, the one he had wanted to tell me about. Could these by any chance be a record of that hypnosis? Were they, somehow, proof of reincarnation?

At that moment, I knew what I must do. Difficult as the task might be under the burden of my own despair, I needed, like the archaeologist presented with pottery shards from a dig, to reassemble Clare's stories in comprehensible form to try to uncover whatever truth they represented not just individually, but as a whole. Only now, I did not have Nick to show the way to mend together an analysand's words into the fabric of a life story. I would have to find the path, and the answers to this unexpected mystery, alone. The task seemed impossible. But I owed Nick, and the memory of our love, no less.

Because of the fragmented character of Clare's regressions, it took me months to investigate the contents of the tapes. I was looking for patterns, clues to prove that what sounded like eyewitness stories of six historical periods were not actually evidence of dissociative identity disorder or cryptomnesia—hidden memories—or even out-and-out fraud. Making something of this patient's story was the one thing I had to do to honor Nick's work without, I hoped, distorting any of the truth.

On many days, I worked bound in my own cloak of dark sorrow. Other times, I nearly gave up on the work, and myself. I was on my own "night sea journey," the passage I knew I must take, without knowing where it would lead. My guide was Clare's voice; my atlas the tapes, with their stories of a voyage through Love's labyrinth of light and shadow, where love confronted its greatest foe: the Minotaur called time.

So I began writing down Clare's healing fictions where the tapes be-gan, with the story of a teenage girl named Acasia and her last days on a mythical island shimmering in the ancient light of thirty-six centuries past, at the heart of Homer's wine-dark sea.

THREE

Clare/Acasia

1628 B.C.
Santorini, Greece

Sunlight touches white stone, then a winding path.

On my feet are sandals, on my leg an anklet of bronze. Before me are villas stacked on hillsides, shorebirds wheeling below, the great interior ocean all around.

I stand on an island like no other, an island born of a nugget of clay plunged to the deep. We call her Kalliste, "most fair," earth child of the Bull God Poseidon, who rules beneath the waves.

Across the outer rings, the bright beam of Helios glances off the bronze ramparts of the god's sacred temple on the central isle of Pyrgos, then turns west to ignite the finials crowning the Temple of the Goddess Atana. Now the warm dawn spills like a tide over the Palace of the Golden Axe, terrace built on terrace in blazing red, blue, and yellow. Behind the palace the volcano slumbers, cloaked in benevolent green; the most peaceful place on the island, despite what the oracle once said.

Just below me on this, Thera, the external island enclosing Pyrgos and the inner rings in its palm, the Agora and storehouses at the harbor are busy with labor: fishermen hauling in the day's catches, farmers unloading baskets of vegetables and grain-filled *pithoi*, keepers of wine, hoisting the heavy amphorae into their stands. And of course the ships, great and small, setting sail to harbors around the sea, even to the Pillars of Herakles at the very end of the earth, where begins the Ocean Stream.

The countries of the world call us the Sea People because we live by ocean trade, and in this our most valued friend is the great isle of Krete, one days' sailing to the south.

One of the most sought-after trade items we offer is our famous pottery, thin as the eggshells of birds, and prized as far away as Sumeria. I have special pride in our pottery, for my own pottery work has been traded across the sea.

As on Krete and in Aegypt, the women of Kalliste are free to work as men do and, in the last year of my childhood, I was apprenticed to the Harbor Workshop. There I learned to hold the wheel level and true, to throw small jars, and make vessels for use at table. Before long my wine bowls were requested at the palace, which helped to spread my name. Later, I assisted Nephthys, the most famous painter in the Kyklades, who taught me how to grind pigments and make brushes using reed, wax, and the fur of the civet cat. For a time, I spent most days painting frescoes in the villas of Therasia village.

And then, last spring, the great earthquake came, killing my parents. Now my two half-brothers, Chrysos and Leksi, run our inland farm and I must do all the spinning and weaving for commerce. Many days now I work from sunrise to sunset just to complete the tasks they heap upon me. I know that with fewer hands we must each bear a greater share of the burden, but their mother was not mine; they are a bit older, the children of my father's first wife, and some days it seems I am a house servant to them, instead of family. But I do not complain. Unlike others after the great quake, I still have family with me, however removed their sentiment may be.

But now, having stayed up late to finish my tasks last evening, I am on my way to paint a fresco at the great house of the trader Deukalion before my brothers return from the farm with more wool. I only need one more tool to finish my work: new sponges to color the background. For these I will exchange several klews of wool with the sponge-diver Ephites.

Helios travels closest to the earth this season and everyone is working hard before the heat drives us inside. Ephites is just climbing naked from the sea, a dark young boy whose wet hair glistens silver as he shakes the sponges from his net.

"Acasia! I have many sizes for you today!" He reaches into a nearby basket. "Look! A very large one, and more of the small ones you liked before!" He holds two handfuls out to me, smiling.

"And for you, Ephites, the angora, your mother's favorite!"

"Thank you, Acasia. Any time you need more sponges . . ."

Our small trade finished, I begin my hike back up the beach toward the warehouses and workshops on the strand. The clatter of iron chimes across the harbor. Cauldrons of pitch used to save ships' keels from the ocean salt boil high on tripods and the shoreline shimmers in waves of melted air.

In the midst of all this activity stands a remarkable-looking man, a man I have not seen in Therasia before. He is lean and of modest height, and seems to be a bit older than my oldest brother Chrysos. His sun-burnished skin hints of a life spent at sea. His mouth, perhaps from some Aethiopian blood, is full. But it is his eyes, eyes the color of the clear water at the shore's edge, that hold mine.

He must sense me watching him, because he looks my way. I hurry up the hill, wrapping my mantle closely around my head as I go, so he will not recognize me again.

* * *

Deukalion waddles into the central hall of his villa and greets me, a broad smile on his face, with a hug and a kiss to my cheek. "The paint will dry quickly today, will it not?" He is a jovial man with a talent for mixing business and pleasure, a talent that has brought him much wealth. "And what is the island's most beautiful young artist creating today?" He swiftly surveys my sketches. "Ahh, excellent!" He pulls playfully at the dark curl on my forehead. "I shall see you this evening."

I pick up my flake of obsidian to make several more drawings on the plaster, line up my clay pots and begin: a flotilla of ships in full dress, oarsmen at their stations; revelers in the village waving from windows and rooftops; the sea and the sky as one upon which play leaping dolphins and birds in flight. So complete is my concentration that I do not notice even when midday is long past, and only when I can no longer mix colors in the fading light do I look up.

As I do, Deukalion's hearty laugh echoes throughout the house, followed by another man's laughter. Putting my brushes aside, I hurriedly wrap my hair in its pins and fix my apron. Deukalion steps through the doorway and behind him, the man I saw at the harbor this morning.

"Acasia!" Deukalion calls, "May I introduce Kalliste's most accomplished mariner, Theion of the Petras clan, from the village of Exomiti, on the southern shore."

The man named Theion steps forward and bows. As I return his greeting I feel the floor falling away, my knees crumpling under me.

"Acasia!" My patron and his companion both rush forward. Lifting me by the arms, they lead me to a low couch on the outer arcade just as the sun slips into the sea.

Duekalion calls, and Hypatia, his serving woman, places a bowl of wine into my hands. I take a sip and see both men leaning over me, frowning.

"I am afraid I forgot to eat," I admit, recalling the fragrant lamb meat still in my sack.

"Now, Acasia," lectures my patron, "you are going to make me look bad in front of your brothers. You must not neglect to eat, even on my meager measure." He smiles at his guest and sits down next to me. "Of course, now you will have to join us for dinner."

"No." The faintness still lingers as I try to sit up. "We have a wool order from Medon and tribute due the storehouse. If my brothers—"

"Do not worry." Deukalion gently pushes my shoulder back to the couch. "I will have a word with them."

"And I have a freshly-built villa whose walls need adornment. Perhaps we could discuss it," Theion adds, smiling down at me.

"There. That's two of us. Now you can't refuse," Deukalion says, arms outstretched.

The men help me to my feet and Hypatia walks me to the bath, where I remove my apron, turn the brass dolphin valve over the stone basin, and dip my hands in to wash them. But the moment my hands touch the water I cry out. It is hot, hotter than any water I have felt at any house in Therasia and I rush to add cool from the jar below. Deukalion's cistern must have had sun all day today.

After replacing my corselet, I braid my hair across my head and pull my curls to fall over the front of my tunic. Hypatia returns with a shawl, which she drapes across my shoulders against the night air.

The fountain is singing as I enter the garden on the rooftop and the fire bowls sputter brightly on their tall stands among the jasmine and lilies. Deukalion's other guests have arrived: old Rhexenor the politician in the place of honor; Byreos, the shipbuilder of wide repute; his exotic wife, Chione, cooing to a miniature pet deer on the pillow at her feet; the trader Ixion of Cyprus, swathed in Tyrian-purple robes.

We recline on couches covered with leopard skins around a table hewn, Deukalion says, by his grandfather, from the burl of a single cypress. The torches are set alight and as their flames unfurl, the servants enter, bearing bronze platters heaped high with fruits of the earth and sea.

While the steward kneels at the krater bowl to mix and serve the wine, I steal a glance at Theion. How perfect his profile—more god than earthling.

With the arrival of the musicians, the notes of double pipes skip through the air, the strings of the zithera trill. A pair of acrobats perform a crane dance around us, whirling above their heads sheer lengths of linen as they dip and sway to the rhythm of the rattle, and the eunuch Cleobis sings with a voice sent from the goddess herself. Our wine cups are never allowed to be empty and the fire bowls burn on as stars of a thousand colors gather to light the sky.

While the others share stories, Theion leans toward me and says, in a near-whisper, "And what might you have been doing among us seafaring brutes this morning?"

So he does recognize me. My face flushes and to hide it I look at him sideways, hoping he does not see my embarrassment. "Ephites, the young diver. We exchange goods, my wool for his sponges, which I use for my painting." Why should he care about Ephites or sponges? What can I say to a man who looks like a god?

"The goddess has bestowed on you a great gift for art." He is smiling at me, probably as one would smile down to a younger sister. Fortunately, as I am trying to think of something to say, the room falls into a brief silence and it is then that we all hear old Rhexenor at the head of the table telling, for the benefit of the visitors, the history of Kalliste.

We natives of Thera knew it well: the story of the early days, of the ancient men who worked hard to tame the land, the sacrifices to the goddess Atana and the great Poseidon, who in turn gave our ancestors knowledge of the seasons, where to dig canals, plant olives, graze goats. Those early Kallisteans had learned well how to build strong ships, to trade wisely. Small flocks had become many. The trees had blossomed and fruited. Our storehouses had become full.

"And," Rhexenor finished, "think how safe we are, with no need of battlements, the sea our fortress." He sighs, shifts heavily and calls for his man, "Ah, but it is past time for old Rhexenor to be in bed. Cassios! Help these bent bones to their rest!"

In honor of Deukalion's most important guest, the entire party stands as one, including me, though a little slowly out of confusion, not knowing the etiquette of the moment.

Theion bends toward me. "May I walk you to your villa? The young moon gives little light tonight."

At first I do not know how to answer; we have just met. But when I see Deukalion watching us, smiling, I smile back to him, then say to Theion, "Of course. Follow me."

The baton streams bright behind us as I lead him down the path to my family's villa. He lifts the torch into the standard on the outer wall; its pine resin warms the air as its light flickers softly through the bougainvillea blossoms, bathing us rose-gold against the darkness.

"Your brothers?" he asks.

"Chrysos and Leksi."

"Might I ask their permission to show you my ship? It is a steady vessel, and my oarsmen are strong and long-rowing."

No man has ever asked for my company before. "Yes, I would like that," I say, scarcely able to breathe as I speak.

The Aegyptians say the Sea People do not dream. But we do. And all my dreams this night are of this man.

. . .

At table the following morning, Chrysos confronts me about a message he has received from Theion asking if I might join him on his ship. "Who is this fellow?" he demands as he sops the last of his beer with a hunk of bread. "A sea trader? What does he want with you?"

"Could you not spare me for part of a day, brother?"

"No, Acasia." Chrysos is unmoved. "Your hands are needed here. And stay away from him, this Theion character. You are much too young to be trotting off with a man. When the time comes for husband-hunting, we will do it for you, as it should be. And it will be someone closer to your age, and a man of the earth, not . . ." he mutters as he rises from the bench, "some sailor!"

Morning at my loom passes very slowly, partly because every few minutes I look out my window down toward Therasia harbor. Is Theion there now? Has he received my brother's reply and forgotten about me already? The waters of the rings glitter in the sun. I can almost hear the echo of work and voices from the harbor. Theion, talking to a shipwright; Theion, talking with the harbormaster . . .

So much work! Carded wool to be spun. Lengths of wool to be woven. And of course my many household tasks.

A shadow crosses the loom: Chrysos stands at my back. He is on his way up to the farm to bring down the last of the baled wool, which must be on the ship for Delos in four days' time. "And don't get any ideas about sneaking away to find that sailor," he calls on his way down the stairs in the light-well "because I hear he's on the other side of the island."

I wonder if Theion still has family there. Or a woman. Probably some-one beautiful and clever, a woman of the world who knows everything about what men want and who could have any man she wanted.

* * *

Although I have never seen Exomiti, I have been told one can see it from the highest point on the island. The next morning, very early, even before I begin work, I take a ride in the back of a donkey cart up above Therasia to the old footpath that runs up the spine of the island. The terrain is steep and several times I nearly lose my balance on the loose pebbles, but by the time the sun is rising over the eastern shore I am standing at Thera's highest point, looking down toward Exomiti, where daylight is just touching its little harbor. Unlike our village of Therasia, the villas of Exomiti cluster around a broad, crescent-shaped beach of black sand. Here there are waves washing ashore from the great sea. So that is where his family is from. If only wanting could make dreams happen. Slowly, I make my way down the pathway and am back at my loom at the start of another work day.

The evening brings a welcome visitor, my old aunt Euphemia and her two big hounds, who live in a small villa nearby. After a little meal of bread, cheese, and olives, I confide my troubles to her about how strict my brothers are being. Then I tell her my story about Theion.

"My dear niece, you must always follow your heart, and don't tell me the farm couldn't survive without you. It survived for many years before you were even born. If you have feelings for a man you must follow them, because so often it is the woman who truly knows both their feelings, not the man. I hear some parents are following the Aegyptian custom now, and trusting their children to find their own mates. A wise idea." Then, suddenly, she puts her hand on my arm and asks, "How old are you?"

"Fourteen," I reply, sitting up straight and wondering at the same time if Theion knows exactly how young I am.

"Hmmm. Young yet, but old enough to choose." She looks at me directly. "Old enough for babies?"

"Yes." I blush.

She gives my cheek a soft little slap. "Then find your love, whomever he may be. What are you waiting for?"

I throw my shutters open to the sea at first light the following morning. The day is brilliant, sky and water so perfectly joined in color that the ships around the harbor seem to glide upon an ocean of blue air. I wrap a light cloak around me and, buoyed by Euphemia's words, follow the steps I took the day I met Theion, through our district of close-set villas to the meeting place we call Kyklos Square, then down to Therasia harbor.

Wasting no time, I walk past the market stalls and directly to the docks, searching for Theion.

Seeing no sign of him, I stop to ask the harbormaster. No, he tells me, Theion is not here today. He checks the shipping schedule. "Didn't I hear he was going to Rhodes, let me see, tomorrow?"

"And you have not seen him today?"

"Sorry, miss, that's all I know."

Could Theion be in Exomiti? Could he have sailed already for Rhodes? I buy some barley bread and leeks for dinner, then walk around to the north side of the market building where the shipbuilding operations begin.

And there he is, quite a distance from me, but recognizable all the same. He is talking to someone, laughing. He is talking to the widow Xera. She is several years older than I, darkly beautiful. She is known across the island as the woman who refused to cover her breasts after widowhood, as is expected. But no wonder: Her breasts are round, her hips curvaceous. The tiered flounces of her skirt, adorned with flecks of gold and silver, sparkle in the sun's light. She smiles up to Theion, and as I watch, stunned, Theion takes her hand. She looks as if she is trying to make a decision.

I do not know what passes between them next, because I run up the hill, dabbing my hands across my cheeks to brush away the tears as I run.

My brothers are on the farm tonight, Euphemia at her villa. I remove my clothes and stand before the polished brass mirror in the corner of my alcove. To my eye, my figure still seems that of a girl; legs long as a giraffe, skinny hips, small breasts. Not nearly curvaceous enough to take Theion's attentions away from a woman like Xera. I need to eat more goat cheese, plump myself up in the right places. I toss on my cot all night. Sleep comes late and I wake too early, tired and jumpy from what bit of rest I have had.

The pile of wool my brothers have left seems even larger than it was yesterday. I prick my finger on the distaff, which brings blood and more hot tears. Wool, wool, wool! Was that all that mattered? I look out the window yet again. The whole world lay stretched out before me, and here I was, tied to my small room by a klew of wool.

Early in the afternoon I hear harness bells and the slow clop of donkey's hooves below. The bells jangle to a stop, and Chrysos' voice calls up the light-well. "Acasia!"

"Yes, brother?"

"We need your help."

Leksi is with him and waves up to me. The younger of my half-brothers has always been the more sympathetic of the two, perhaps because he and I are closer in age. I sit behind the two of them as we zigzag our way through the afternoon traffic down the winding streets and toward the harbor.

Chrysos pulls the cart up on the quay as close as he can to the dock. Leksi jumps down and the two begin unloading the bales in front of an enormous wooden crane now offloading the last of a cargo of copper from an open-decked trader. While I wait holding the donkeys, Leksi runs up the plank to the ship to tell the cranesman to pick up the bales and Chrysos confirms the manifest with our king's agent.

And then suddenly Theion is beside me. He bows politely. "Acasia," is all he says.

Goddess Atana, help me. I try not to cry.

"And how are you today?" he asks.

"Well, thank y—"

My words are interrupted by a ghastly crash, and a scream. The crane operator has lost control of the crane. Ingots of copper scatter across the deck, and the huge arm of the crane swings wildly about. Men are shouting.

The scream was Leksi's and everything on the boat is now chaos. Leksi has been knocked off the deck by the crane. All I can see is a ring of waves where he has disappeared.

"Goddess! He cannot swim!" I cry, dropping the reins and starting for the dock.

Theion stops me. "Wait!" he shouts, and is gone almost before the words are completely out of my mouth to dive from the end of the dock. Loading comes to a halt and the waterfront goes silent as Theion drags the unconscious Leksi through the water. I tie the donkeys to a piling and run to my brother.

With Chrysos' help, Theion pulls Leksi up onto the sand. Chrysos and I watch as Theion turns Leksi over onto his stomach and pushes his hands hard, again and again, into Leksi's back. Chrysos pulls on Theion's tunic to stop him, but a pair of fishermen drag him away.

"Let him do his work!" they shout.

To my amazement, water sputters from Leksi's mouth. He coughs and gulps a breath.

Chrysos, facing Theion, stares. "Thank you. I am indebted, but I do not think we have met. I am Chrysos, of the Dodona clan of Therasia."

"Theion, head of the Petras clan, from Exomiti. Is this man"—he points to Leksi—"a relation of yours?"

"He is," Chrysos answers, watching Theion closely now.

"Give him a mixture of honey and wine, and a day's rest. He will be well. The effects of salt do not last long, but he must be watched." Saluting my brother with hand-to-chest, Theion disappears into the busyness of the dock as I help Leksi up.

. . .

As I tend to my brother that evening and the next day, my mind is again flooded with images of Theion and Xera. The two of them on his ship. The two of them dancing happily at a festival. The two of them in bed together, laughing. Then—oh, I can't think about that.

As unassumingly as I can, I ask Leksi, "Have you heard of the widow Xera?"

My brother looks at me strangely. "Xera? I've heard the sailors talk about her. Why?"

"Oh," I reply as I try to concentrate on my loom, "I thought I saw her at the harbor the other day."

"Probably looking for another dupe to pay for her jewelry while she sports around." He shakes his head, then laughs until he breaks into a fit of coughing, and I run to give him another draught of honey-wine.

Though I doubted the "dupe" could be Theion, I could not, however hard I tried, purge the picture of them from my mind. Even in between sleeps at night it haunted me.

After the sophisticated Xera, what could I ever be to him but an unworldly child?

•   •   •

But my daydreaming has taken its toll on my work. I am already behind with the spinning and the orders are coming in to the king's office from distant markets. Autumn is near and with it, the unsettled weather that brings sailing to a halt until the spring, when the traders can once again make their circular trip around the eastern ports under safer and more predictable winds. The last orders have to be delivered soon. Many nights I am spinning wool by the light of my lantern.

One afternoon, just as I am near collapse with exhaustion, the message boy Jiri appears downstairs at our door. Although Chrysos had not mentioned it to me, he has at last given Theion permission to take me for a viewing of the rings and Pyrgos. Would I like to join him tomorrow? He had a delivery to make to Exomiti. If my answer was yes, we could meet at the fountain at Kyklos Square.

I fly through my work the rest of the day, ignoring tired eyes, pricked fingers, tangled yarn, even the dangerous Xera, and am awake even before dawn the next morning to crimp my hair with the heated tongs. After trying on nearly all my little wardrobe, I dress carefully in the cream-colored tunic with blue embroidery at the arms and hem.

Theion and I arrive at the little square at exactly the same moment. He is even darker brown than the day I first saw him. And twice as handsome.

As we walk, he tells me something about his ship, the plans for which he had been willed by his grandfather, a builder of trade vessels in Epidauros. Then he tells me of the places he travels, from Corinth to Krete. As he recounts his adventures, I see how often he smiles, how white his teeth are against his sunburned skin and the crinkles at the corners of his remarkable blue-green eyes from squinting across bright waters.

"Here." He stops at what must be the most splendid bark in the harbor. Her name is the *Pheidas*. Her stern curves up and out in a graceful arc, then loops back to face the blue-painted prow. High above, a cedar mast crisp with fragrance holds two spars and a web of forestays. On the oiled deck, a small pavilion tented with quilted vellum protects the steering man from the sun. Her rowers, no less than twelve Nubians in working skirts of linen and hide, stand at attention. Theion takes my hand to help me board. His hand is strong, worked-hardened and smooth as leather against my wool-softened skin.

Oarsmen at their stations, time-beater at the drum, Theion gives the order and the sturdy little ship glides out of the harbor and across the bay. Turning past the Gates of the Guardians we enter the waters between the first and second rings. We turn starboard and the inside of the inner ring comes into view. Its many villas, some in white stone, others in patterns of black, white and red, peer out above the low hills dense with palm, cypress, and oak. Theion points: two overfed lionesses doze, legs dangling as they straddle in their half-sleep the broad limbs of a great old fig. I hear the distant trumpet of elephants, a gift to our king, Theion tells me, from the Hyksos ruler at Avaris.

Now we come to the waters of Pyrgos Island to see the Temple of the Bull God, a robust ziggurat of white tuff cut from the hills of Thera, crowned with bronze horns glinting high in the late-morning sun. Nearby across a narrow channel rises the Temple of the Mother Goddess, its six sky-touching columns carved in the style of papyrus reeds and tipped in gold. Beyond is the Palace of the Golden Axe. Its red, blue, and yellow inverted pillars and stacked cubes glow brightly above its leafy grounds where I glimpse one of the sacred bulls allowed to roam freely there until captured by the Bull Men for the games. He watches us silently, then snorts at our passing with scorn and gallops away, a great squared body with tail held high, into the forest dark.

I had no idea how grand Pyrgos was. I look over to Theion. His eyes laugh and his words in their kindness seem to invite. "Have you been such a stranger to the pleasures of Kalliste?"

"I am so little traveled. And with the death of my parents, and so many extra tasks . . ."

"Well, for today, you must forget your cares." He motions to the Nubians and calls to them in their language. With a flap like the wings of a great bird leaving earth, the foresail flutters down, then fills full.

Pushed ahead by a light breeze, we glide south past Skaros Point then emerge at the tip of Thera's western arm and plow cleanly into the rolling sea. The sun stands high overhead when we come upon Theion's home off the port bow. Its small harbor is as busy as Therasia, and I watch as the stevedores fit the cargo, tens and tens of small amphorae of wine, neatly, base-to-neck, below deck.

As we leave, Theion singles out one of the white villas perched on the low hillside above the harbor, his home as a child. He tells me of his mother, a Rhodian, tall and graceful with gray eyes and a love of poetry, who taught him the worth of a woman's heart and of his father, who died of grief after his mother was taken by mortal illness.

It was the words of his ancestors that had guided his life, he said. He had been taught by his father, as his father was by his, that it was wiser to be a poor man than an indentured one. He had brought Theion to know the sea young, how to build fine ships so he might, with his knowledge and his hands, make his way as a free man in the world.

Moved out of my bashfulness by his candor, I open up to him, telling him of my father, who set great olive groves on Thera; of my mother and her creative hands and then, finally, of myself, and how favored I am, living where I do, that I may live and do work that will please the mother goddess, although my burden seems heavy now.

He watches me carefully, as if making a study of my face, and I wonder what he is thinking. Perhaps, *"She is so young." "She is so untraveled."* Or even *"She is not worth the trouble of negotiating with her brothers for."*

Soon, much too soon for me, dusk comes over the western sea and the enchanting day comes to an end. Cressets of sweetwood blaze above the Therasia shoreline, spreading soft fragrance over the harbor. The moon rises full on the water. Theion takes my hand, thanks me for joining him and bows deeply in farewell.

That evening as I dine with my brothers I cannot stop talking about how kind Theion is, how hard-working and honest; how he, too, lost both his parents and has no one. By the time the constellation of the ship has risen in the sky, both my brothers, perhaps out of exhaustion from listening to me go on or perhaps, as Chrysos points out, to give us another pair of working hands, agree I may invite Theion to join us at the farm for the harvest. After the ritual sacrifice of thanks at the shepherd's altar, we would all be rewarded with a great feast of kid and wine.

. . .

Early two mornings later I welcome Theion to our farm, where I show him how to pluck ripe figs from the trees. They are plump in their soft skins as we spread them down before the sun and will be covered with their own sugar within days. Soon my brothers and I will harvest the olives, which are ripening early this year, and press their fruit to make oil. It is a big task, the harvest, but dried figs and rich oil are always in demand and ours trade at high value in Saqqara.

After the evening meal, Chrysos offers Theion a cot in an empty corner of the storeroom. For myself, I have difficulty sleeping, knowing he sleeps so near. How I want to lie down with him, to feel his body close against mine!

I awaken well after sunrise to the knock of the shutter against its frame. The Meltemi autumn winds are up and the sails of the little windmill above the house rise and fall, turning light to shade and back as they bring water down from the big canal.

My brothers are working to mend the olive press, whose lever has broken. Chrysos' wife Galea and I watch the men from the stone bench outside while I have my bread and wine. Time must now be spent cutting and carving a new bar and fitting it into the wheel, so Theion asks if I might show him the wild lands at the border of our farm.

Though much of the big plain has been divided by the king's council into a neat patchwork of farms, most of Thera is wild and, as we follow the canal that encloses the farms to its origins in the low hills behind the growing lands, and walk their undulating fields, we crush herbs under our steps and smell their mingled fragrance. Pheasant and peacock call our arrival; pretty-faced gazelles look up from rock pools. When the sun is high and hot, we rest on a flat boulder beneath the gnarled limbs of an olive. Theion watches me intently as I unknot the wineskin.

"I am sorry to stare so, Acasia, but I was just trying to decide which is more beautiful, the untamed places of the island, or you in the sunlight, pouring wine with your hair free and the color in your cheeks."

He reclines on one arm, the indolent god of all around him. Then he motions to me, "Come, Acasia, and sit beside me."

I hand him his cup of wine. As I do, his hand embraces mine, bringing the cup to his lips. He sets the cup down then, like the dream I have had night after night, he places his hand upon my cheek, leans forward, and kisses me.

The silver leaves of the old tree swirl with the wind while shadows and sunlight dance weightless around us. A pair of bumblebees circle each other above.

"Acasia?"

"Yes?" I have trouble speaking, because I have never been kissed by a man, let alone one as wonderful as this one, and my heart seems about to jump from my chest. Either that, or I may faint again.

"Are you promised to another?"

"No, there is no other," I confess, looking down at the rock.

"Good," he says, kissing the palm of my hand and pressing it to his cheek.

"But what about Xera?"

He frowns, and a look of confusion crosses his face. "Therasia's most notorious widow? When did you—oh, the other day, at the shipyard." He laughs, puts his hand back on my cheek. "Why would I want a woman who has had almost every sailor on Kalliste, when I can sit under the shade of a lovely old olive tree with the freshest, most beautiful young woman on the island?"

"Who?" I realize I am being teased. "Oh, you mean…? It was just that…"

"It was just what?" His voice is tender.

I cannot even look at him as I admit, "I saw you taking her hand. At the shipyard."

For a moment he seems absorbed in thought. Then, a smile crosses his face. "Oh, yes. We were discussing her son, whom she wishes to be apprenticed to a cousin on Krete. The harbormaster had told her I make frequent visits there, and she wanted a message to be carried to him. And that," his smile returns, "was all. Why?"

"I thought perhaps . . ." Now what to say? I had already made a fool of myself.

"I know her reputation. And please, believe me, she is of no interest to me." He is watching me carefully now.

"Oh," is all I can reply, rather dumbly.

"Yes, my sweet Acasia. Yes." And he kisses me again, then pulls me close, resting my head against his chest and stroking my hair. His skin is smooth and sun-warmed and smells of sesame, and my hand glides across it as I reach around to embrace him. Hand-in-hand, we walk together back through the wild lands to the road leading down to the harbor, and he bids me farewell, for he must be away for several days to ferry amphorae to Krete. Just before he walks out of view he turns back, touches his heart, and extends his hand toward me.

Evening is quiet at the farm and I sit for a long time facing Therasia, thinking of Theion there as I watch the sun's last light slide across Cape Tripiti to illuminate with red-orange fire-glow the hills and temples of Pyrgos.

· · ·

The goats bawl me awake just before dawn. My bed on the ground floor of the farmhouse is swaying gently. The swaying turns to shaking. *Goddess Atana, make it stop!* I clutch my rug and the wicker frame for what seems like an endless time but the earth just keeps rolling. A jar smashes heavily against the floor. Plaster sifts from the ceiling onto my head. Someone screams, "Stay here!" Then, as quickly as the temblor began, the earth goes still.

With daylight we can see the damage. The windmill stands firm and the olive press and its repair have held, but the goats are crying pathetically and some have actually jumped from the little enclosure Leksi had built for them next to their night-hut. Only a few containers of seed and grain have broken. It is agreed that I should return to the family villa to see how well it has withstood the quake. Leksi gives me a cup of wine to calm my blood and I wrap my shawl closely around me in an attempt to steady myself for the walk.

I arrive to find the little house looking reasonably sound on the outside; only a bit of plaster fallen from an exterior overhang, and the stone terrace slightly buckled.

Inside the house, however, chaos reigns. Maia, our servant girl, has been working with Euphemia all morning, first at her villa, now at ours, yet still more remains to be done. Crockery and household idols lie in pieces, thrown from their niches in the small prayer room. The lustral basin for pre-sacrifice cleansing is cracked. The cooking pots in the alcove on the rooftop are scattered. But this time the god was kind; no one has been hurt. When everything has been cleaned, I offer my most beautiful clay figure of Atana Potineida at the hearth shrine in thanks for our safety, with prayers that this disturbance does not portend more, or worse, to come.

I return to my weaving, in which I have fallen behind during the harvest days at the farm. Between that and overseeing the cleanup and repair work on the villa, plus organizing the woven wool for baling, I scarcely have time even for sleep. Even so, I manage to make time after my regular tasks are finished each day to make a coat for Theion from our best wool. Eleven days later, I am overjoyed to hear his voice greeting Maia below and run to him as he enters the first-floor garden.

"Everyone at the harbors, here and Malia, was talking about the quake!" We hold tightly to one another for a long moment, then he places a knotted cloth of fabric like none I have ever felt before into my hands. "Perhaps this will comfort you a little."

The bright red pouch glistens, strangely cool in my palm. I stroke it with my fingers, a wonder.

"It is new, brought by my Canaanite traders from lands far to the east. They say it is made by worms that spin it from the leaves of trees."

Cloth this fine spun from leaves? I knew of cotton-wool from that shrub grown in Aegypt, but this felt completely different, like nothing I had ever touched before.

"I think you will find something inside, if you unloosen the knot." He gives me a knowing smile.

Slowly I unfold the little package. There, resting within the bright square, a pendant of two bees sharing a honeycomb gleams in hammered gold.

"This is"—my hand goes to my heart—"fit for Minos' queen!"

"It was made by a young goldsmith at the Hall of the Double Axe. The style is much-requested by the ladies of the court. And when I remembered the bees at the rock, I knew I must have one for you."

He slips the neckpiece onto a golden neck-ring that he fastens around my neck. Then I remember my gift for him, which I bring from its hiding place in my wheeled weaving basket and unfold to drape around his shoulders.

"I must return to the harbor now, to give the men their payment," he says as he embraces me, "but I have several days yet before my next voyage. Say you will see me tomorrow."

. . .

From that moment we spend as much time as possible with one another. One early morning just days after his visit, he comes to the villa bearing a bow, a quiver of tooled hide, and a sling of twisted wool. He shows me how to hold safely to him, one arm on the rail and the other around his body, as we fly up the road from the farm in his pretty new horse chariot of fig wood and horn, Euphemia's light-footed dogs racing and baying behind. At day's end we return from the wild lands with sheaves of pungent herbs and a boar shoat for the fire.

More days on the graceful *Pheidas* follow, and as we circle the island rings, Theion tells me even more stories of the places he has been and the people he has met; of strange-customed men living within walled cities in the desert lands east of the sea; of an imperishable beast called the gamal, which stores its water in a hump on its back and dwells in the sun-beaten wasteland east of the river Nile; and of an enormous painted sandstone sculpture near Giza with the face of King Cheops and the body of a lion under whose massive paws, it is said, scrolls holding all the knowledge of the world are hidden.

. . .

Soon comes the Festival of the Bull God, and the rites of thanksgiving for the harvest, at the Bull Court. On that day the waters of Kalliste are so thick with flatboats that a man might with little daring step from ring to ring across their decks. It is the island's most amazing spectacle: women in bright flounces, hair crimped and crowned with glittering headpieces; men in golden skirts inwoven with purple; figures so brazen in ornament they rival Talos the Circular, bronze child of Daedalos' invention.

The Exalted Priestess of the Goddess invokes the Holy Ones in prayers of thanks, her boy votary sounds the triton, and King Gadirus, face hidden behind a bull mask encrusted with gems, signals the start of the games.

The boxing boys come first, followed by the wrestlers, the spear-men, then the speed-runners in their costumes of feather and hide. But the assembly saves its biggest voice for the bull-leapers as they are called forward. Most are young. All are small and quick-limbed. They work in teams of four, two to distract the beast, one to perform a vault and one to catch the vaulted. Each acrobat performs a series of leaps. And it is by the cheering of the crowd at the end of the competition that the winners are chosen.

One team after another excels. And just before darkness, after the victors have been proclaimed and awarded with gifts of gold, grain, and costly oils, and torches set ablaze around the great arena, the courageous

First Bull, trussed by the Bull Masters in garlands of flowers, is sacrificed by the male acolytes to the priestess with the double axe. Up comes a mighty cheer from the crowd as his dear blood, caught in the stone bull's head rhyton, is poured forth onto the earth: our gift to the god of land, sea, and sky, who holds our lives in his hands.

With the changing of the seasons, the heavens grow lustrous and the days as cool as the nights. One such evening, in the gilded light of the low-hanging moon, Theion arrives at the villa carrying a wineskin and a two-handled skyphos cup forged with lovebirds. We sit together on the rooftop garden next to the little pool where the lotus still bloom. Cicadas sing their last songs in the shadows and the fire bowl flames up at the touch of the new northern breeze. Theion takes my hands into his, then turns them upward to kiss first one, then the other. "Acasia, I am fortunate. We are fortunate. Because if our lives had not been moved by such like events as the loss of our parents, I might not be so favored to ask you this now."

He kneels before me in supplication, his left arm encircling my calves, right hand placed gently upon my cheek to speak the marriage invitation. "My beloved, hear my plea: I wish you to be my wife. I can dream no greater honor for myself." He pauses, then adds his own words: "Say you will be mine alone forever, my dear Acasia. I know the goddess brought you to me. And I will love no other than you, even beyond this life, if it be granted."

Tears fall down my tunic to touch his hair as his head rests upon my knees. Lying my head down against his, I reply, "My life began again the day we met. And I would not have it end without you."

. . .

My brothers convinced, in part by Euphemia, that I should marry for love, at last agree to the match.

"Whatever did you say to them?" I ask my aunt two afternoons later.

"Well, my dear," she says, putting aside the pistachios she is shelling, "it was Chrysos, you know, who was the problem. Leski was thrilled for you. So I said to Chrysos, 'She is old enough for children. Do you not want more men in the family?' 'Men who will probably become sailors,' he said. And I said, 'So what if they become sailors? Sailors are traders and traders make deals. Wouldn't you like to save yourself the money spent on negotiators? Look what Duekalion's made off you over the years!' He walked away, shaking his head, but he must have"—the old lady paused to laugh and slap her leg—"reconsidered, because the next morning he came over and said, 'You know, Euphemia, for an old lady you're very smart. Theion just might be an excellent brother-in-law for Leksi and me.' 'How wise you are, nephew!' I cried, and hugged him. And that, my sweet niece, was the end of it."

I clap my hands, run to her and sit on her lap, where she rocks me as she did as a child and we laugh and laugh together.

At daybreak the next day my brothers make sacrifice for me; a long-haired goat of pure white, who submits to its fate quietly—a sign of good luck—at the Altar of the Dove Goddess in the woodland shrine.

Two days later, Euphemia helps me dress for my marriage: my most colorful flounces, my mother's bridal tunic, of sheerest linen edged in sea blue, and my corset of red, white, and black wool made by Euphemia when I was young especially for this day. My hair we crimp and tie high on my head with a knot of many-colored yarns, then finish with a head-dress of bright feathers strung with copper disks.

My family accompanies me to the harbor where my bridegroom awaits in a magnificent ceremonial kilt. Around his neck, a golden torque with, at its center, a perfectly round cabochon of the Anatolian stone, turkoise, the very color of his eyes.

Around the rings we travel in the little wedding caïque, itself splendid in raiments of flowers and vines, to the pier that leads to the Temple of the Goddess. A hanging garden shows the way along a white stone path that follows a watercourse meandering up and under trees so broad they touch the leaves of their neighbors to form a canopy above. We emerge into the sunlight at the steps of the temple, an open loggia of six columns incised with brightly painted codes of love, harmony, and marriage.

We are met by Vestals of the Priestess, young virgins who take me by the hands and lead me into a secluded bower not far away. There, they prepare me for the rites, removing my sandals, pulling my tunic away from my breasts in the custom of married women, and tying the sacral knot, symbol of my new standing, at the nape of my neck. Now, I enter the second stage of my life, in which I will serve the Goddess, the Great Mother of us all, as an adult woman who will give love to my husband and children to the world. Brazier bright before her, the Priestess of the Goddess appears inside the temple, her arms coiled with snakes of gold, reaching forth to us in invitation, tiered skirt covered by an apron bordered with gold, her head of dark curls crowned with a headdress of yet more gold on which sits a small rock-crystal dove that blazes like a second sun.

Theion salutes her by placing his right fist to his forehead as I, in the woman's way, place my hands to my heart, palms outward. Then, facing one another, arm upon arm, we declare for each other as the gods and votaries bear witness. And when our vows are spoken, and the marriage tablet marked with our sealstones, the Priestess blesses our union, scatters barley upon the tuff under our feet, and offers up the rhyton of bull's blood mixed with honey and wine which he, then I, drink. As we return down the path, a warm zephyr lifts flower petals from the vines overhead and showers them upon us, a blessing from Poseidon Helios above.

It is a merry celebration at our farm this evening and we dance, laugh, and drink far into the night until, spent with mirth, the two of us are led by torchlight on the backs of donkeys home to my bridegroom's, now our, villa above the harbor, just as the lamp of Phosphorus shines its last light above the horizon before the brightening dawn.

. . .

How can I tell of our first days together as one? Our hearts seek union in waking and in sleep. I learn the map of his body; his beautiful feet, legs, the muscles of his stomach, squared chest, and shoulders, his perfect manhood. In turn, he explores my body as if a newfound land, his mouth and hands seeking to discover everything about me. We are like two wild animals who, having suffered a lean year, cannot now get enough of that which sustains them.

As if blessed by the hand of the goddess, our home becomes the fertile land of our love. I hang Theion's beautiful Anatolian torque over our bed as a reminder of the color that drew me to him, and as a talisman that our love may endure. I fresco the walls of the central hall with the rare creatures of the Theran Plain. In our sleeping alcove, I paint a mural of my husband's ship tended by a court of dolphins and flying fish. I plant a garden on the rooftop: jasmine on fig trellises, mint and rosemary and thyme, papyrus in the central pool. The steward of the Temple Icons places Horns of Consecration on our roof facing the harbor, and a small double-axe above the lintel of our door. We hope for sons and daily I offer prayers and clay idols for such blessing.

. . .

"So, not only have I taken the most beautiful woman on Kalliste to wife, I have also gotten its best farmer!"

My husband greets me on the rooftop where I am tending the garden. He has been away for many days ferrying grain and oil to Krete, for the largest of the Kyklades has suffered great crop losses this year.

"Old Deukalion got the better of Akil again at the Knossos' market. The trade wars between those two! One always suspecting the other holds the dagger!" He kisses me, then starts toward the bathing alcove. Then he stops, and comes back. "Acasia, have you heard the old people tell a story about a time when the seas around Kalliste turned strange colors?"

"Yes, I think Euphemia might have said something like that at one time. An old myth, wasn't it?"

"Well, the strangest thing, as we rowed into Therasia, the water in some places was white, like goat's milk. At first I did think it goat's milk, until I saw, running through it, streaks of pink."

"Perhaps a land creature died somewhere near the water?"

"No, and not one man on the ship had ever seen such a thing before, either."

"Oh, Theion," I call after him, "the water is so hot today. I have put a jar of cold near the stone tub should you need it."

Just as I am nearly finished scooping millet from the tall jar in the storeroom below, it hits, first a low moan, then a rumble, as if a herd of monstrous beasts was charging directly for the house. Closer the din grows and still closer until the rafters above me start to squeal. In an eye blink the gypsum floor tilts under my feet as plaster flies across the room. Tossed rolling under the big work table, I cover my head against the clash of heaving stone and wood as the little room rocks from side to side, over and over, cleaving the walls at their corners, upending shelves, tossing baskets and amphorae around the room like toys.

Then, as suddenly as it began, the earth violence stops. Dust-fog swirls around me, and my lamp, which somehow still burns where it landed, reveals foodstuffs floating across the floor on a growing pool of wine. I touch my limbs to feel for breaks and, though there are none, I sense the warmth of blood trickling from my head. Worse, all I hear is silence above. Theion!

Holding the hem of my tunic over my nose and mouth against the choking dust, I crawl over broken pots to reach the light-well. Theion is there, unhurt, though he is covered, as am I, with a coat of white. He sits me down, binding the gash on my forehead with strips of clean cloth and putting my head against his shoulder, stroking my arm, and kissing my cheek gently until we are both calmed.

Within several days it becomes apparent that nearly every structure in the village has been damaged in some way. The family villa, where Euphemia now lives, seems to have taken the worst blow this time, though she still refuses the safety of the farm, saying to Theion, "I'd rather be buried under plaster and murals than under goat fur!"

My mural in his villa, Deukalion laments, was lost when the earthquake shook the plaster from the brick. Chrysos and Leksi tell me they must rebuild both the stone shed and goat shelter but that, fortunately, the farmhouse is sound. The goats, Leksi relates in disbelief, had, several days before the upheaval, quit grazing entirely and bayed endlessly.

But the wounds to Pyrgos Island seem worse than that to Thera and its harbor. Looking across the rings of water the day following the big quake, I see the gigantic horns atop the Temple of the Bull God half-fallen, lowering ominously toward us. One of the columns at the Temple of the Goddess has toppled completely. But, most curious of all, is a cloud that looks like smoke rising from the green shoulders of Mt. Pyrgos. Since the sky is perfectly blue, I can only guess it is escaping from somewhere inside the mountain itself.

I ask Theion, who is busy setting stone back in the garden, "What is that? It is like mist from hot water on a cold day, yet the air is warm."

"It cannot be fire, for there are no flames." He squints over the rooftops to Pyrgos, shading his eyes with his hand. "But something is not right there."

"Do you think it is an ill omen from the gods?"

"Perhaps the workmen at the harbor know what is going on." He takes me by the shoulders, walking me toward our sleeping alcove. "You, my dear, must rest today. Worrying about such things will only slow your healing."

He places me on our couch, where I finally fall into a half-sleep on the fleece, a comfort against the clusters of quakes that have followed.

The sun is lower on the garden when I sense Theion leaning over me. "And how are you feeling now?" he asks, his hand upon my arm.

"A bit rested. How is the harbor?"

"The *Pheidas* is fit, but the agora and storehouse bore the strain badly. All free and indentured men are working to clean and shore up the buildings." He sighs, runs his hands through his hair, and looks in the direction of the harbor. "It is a big job. And our trading schedule is sure to be disrupted."

The palace, he says, stands strongly enough, but the baths have suffered greatly and are no longer usable because the water for them, which comes down from the side of the mountain, now carries with it a peculiar odor and is so overheated it blisters the skin. Nikodemos the prophet, who has the ear of King Gadirus on such matters, has said that the smoke on the mountainside is not smoke at all, but water so hot it is turning to cloud.

The disturbances continue for days. On Pyrgos the white cloud rising from the flank of the big mountain grows larger. And one morning, Theion and I awaken to yet another wisp similar to the first, this one emerging from the opposite slope.

That same afternoon I make my way down the hillside of the village past what once was the fountain at Kyklos Square, where Theion and I met for our first day together. The pretty landmark is now broken, its water lost. Most villagers have performed what repairs they can, but with so much to be mended, workmen are scarce, and those villagers without help seem to have abandoned any efforts.

Therasia's agora and storehouse, first priorities for trade, are being reconstructed, many of the timbers on both having snapped clean, leaving their flat roofs in danger of collapsing in the center. Few merchants or fishermen are present, even fewer food baskets or wine jars. I find Theion, standing on the stone quay, speaking with the harbormaster. He presses his seal to the record disk, bids the master farewell and walks toward me, his smile a comfort itself.

"Ah, my lovely wife!"

"Have the last of the traders sailed? My brothers tell me the fleece left at the farm is contracted for on Naxos and I wondered." As I speak, an odd sheen on the water catches my eye; an ugly tongue of yellow liquid oozing toward the mooring stones. Mingled with crimson, it has the effect of making the water appear to be on fire. And it seems to be coming from the inner ring.

Theion looks over. "Yes, that is what Mnesos and I were just watching." His jaw is hard set, his brows knit. "They say a substance like molten bronze is flowing down the side of Mount Pyrgos where heated clouds were seen before. Gadirus has just called all members of the Council of Augurs, the Priestesses, the Guardians of the Sea, and all Kalliste's mariners to a meeting at the palace tomorrow to decide what course to take."

"Course?"

He eases a strand of hair away from my healing wound. "There is talk, just rumor, that we may have to leave. I think it best for you to go back to the villa and choose what household goods we might need to take with us. If we must go, it will probably be soon."

"Leave? But where are we to go?"

"I do not know. It is yet but talk. But we must be ready. I will be home before sunset, but I must tend to the ship now."

Abandon Kalliste? The place that gave birth to our love? The place that has been my family's home since before time began? As I climb Therasia's winding streets the story of early Kalliste comes back to me from Deukalion's party. Perhaps the quakes are nothing but a demand from Poseidon that we renew our hecatombs as tribute to him. Surely, sacrifice will be made by the priestesses. The Earth-Shaker will be appeased. It has always been so.

. . .

The following morning the wind blows acrid and sour with the same odor that meets the nose when a broken bird's egg has gone bad from the heat. The terrible stench is everywhere and I stay indoors to try to avoid it. At the one household shrine we have repaired, I pray and make offerings for our safety.

Theion returns in the middle of the day. His once-golden face now pale, he asks me to draw a bath to cleanse the smell in the air from his skin. I tell him I will fill the stone tub for him, but that the water seems now to have the same vile smell as the air. He coughs and sits down so heavily he nearly falls.

I hurry to bring him a cup of wine from the last unbroken amphora in the storeroom. As we share the pretty citrus wood bench overlooking the harbor, he takes me into his arms. We hold to each other without words for a long while.

Then he tells me. The king's oracle had read the organs of the sheep and found the portents highly unfavorable. The king, island council, and holy seers agreed unanimously that every mariner, sea trader, fisherman, anyone possessing a sea-worthy vessel, was to gather together family and neighbors, as many as he could. It was decided to first travel to Malia, then by land to Knossos, where their king was kindly disposed toward us and we could lay plans for a new community. Beyond this, the portents were clouded, and the convention could not say. Many on the rings had already abandoned their homes for Krete.

We work side-by-side late into the darkness, packing wicker trunks, jars of food, wine, rugs, clothing. We dismantle my loom and bind its sections together with rope. Tomorrow we will sail for Krete with Euphemia, her hounds, Maia and her father, my brothers and Galea, who will join us in the morning with the donkey cart.

All night the earth shivers in terror of the god as we cling to one another, entreating our world to be still. Yet when we open our shutters the next morning, we hardly recognize the island as ours. A thick plume of smoke boils from the summit of Mt. Pyrgos as vapor rises from her flanks. A rivulet of orange liquid slithers down her south slope through the valley near the Temple of the Bull God and into the first ring of water, raising a hot fog which blankets the waterways of the first and second rings. The choppy waters of Therasia Harbor glow an insane swirl of clashing colors, green to copper.

Theion is the first to speak. "Quickly, Acasia! Find Euphemia and Maia. Your brothers should be here soon with the wagon."

Dressing in yesterday's tunic, I hurry downstairs to discover I must fight my way up the lane mobbed wall-to-wall with villagers clutching pots, baskets, goats, and sacks of wool, dragging along crying children and over-laden donkeys—a flood of life mad with fright rushing toward the salvation of the ships.

But all is silent at the family villa. Only one of the hounds barks and the other nudges his nose against my leg, begging for food. Entering to the side, I step over plaster chips, bits of pottery.

"Euphemia!" Hearing no answer, I call again, louder. "Euphemia!"

I stop, hear a soft mewl and run up the stairs, over smashed idols, plaster, splintered wood, to find my aunt trapped, her shoulder caught and pinned under a fallen joist.

"Acasia!" She reaches a hand out to me. "You are from the goddess! The quakes last night—"

"Where is Maia?"

"She left." The old woman cries again from pain. "In the middle of the night."

Sliding a roll of shearling under her head and covering her with a goatskin rug, I promise to return with a doctor.

Now I run to our villa, to hear Theion call as I enter, "Your aunt?"

"A brace has fallen on her and she cannot move!"

A crackle breaks through the air; the earth lurches. I reach for a post.

"In the name of—!" Theion turns to the open window facing the sea. There, on Pyrgos, the mountain is now throwing not only ashy spume but red flames into the sky and ever more burning liquid down her flanks. Though only midday, the northern heavens grow dark. Theion hurries out, calling behind, "Go to your aunt; I will find help!"

The sun is far past its zenith and falling to the west when Theion finally arrives with the only surgeon still remaining in the village. Working together, the two men manage to lift the timber without injuring Euphemia further. I cradle her head while Theion straightens her shoulder and the surgeon sets it back and binds it. The three of us help her onto her bed and Theion gives the good man a pledge of gold for his services.

The doctor shakes his head. "I'll take that measure in Malia, friend, if we get there alive! Gods preserve us!"

Quickly I gather what I can for Euphemia, make her as comfortable as I can in the bit of space left in the donkey cart, which waits below. Leksi leads the cart, followed by the dogs, down the deserted street, now an obstacle course of fallen masonry, lost sandals, jewelry, pottery, broken amphorae, rotting food, and rivers of spilled wine. To keep the smoke from suffocating us, we must cover our noses and mouths with wine-soaked rags as we load the boat, but, just before the red sun falls into the sea, we are sailing south on a following wind and current that seems to issue from Kalliste herself.

The seared moon floats upward, orange and blistered in the smoke-filled sky. We run by dead-reckoning for a distance until, at last, the smoke clears enough to navigate by the stars. I am glad now that my husband taught me the steering oar, for Chrysos and I are able to take it in turn to allow Theion to study his chart by the light of the hand lamp and adjust our course. The little ship rocks and sways, perhaps from the force of the quaking on Kalliste. Oddly, at this moment, I am overcome by memories of the first day I sailed with Theion, how happy I was. How long ago it now seems.

And now he holds me close, lifts my face to his as he did that first afternoon on the rock, and kisses me as if in memory of that happier time. Our tunics are torn and filthy, soot lies in the creases of our skin, our bodies near exhaustion. Yet through the night we are always at one another's side, not wanting to be any place else. And then, with the welcome light of morning, we see a dark landmass silhouetted on the horizon: Krete.

We moor at Malia Harbor just as the sun peeks over its great temple. Here, in the capital of our world, the order of the gods still reigns. Chrysos and Leksi winch the ship onto the beach and then set out for help, for my old aunt can travel no farther and we must hire a cart and porter to carry our possessions to Knossos.

Many Kallisteans are in the harbor helping others, and within a short time, all our clan are offered shelter at the villa of an envoy who has long been a friend to my husband. Wearily, Theion and I climb the steps from the harbor, past the slanted sea wall and up to the court that leads to the temple but a short distance away. Perhaps a message from our king is there.

At the top of the steps we look out over a broad black-and-white-checkered terrace to see men, women and children standing motionless, like living pieces on a gaming board. All face north, their faces dumb with horror. Theion and I stop, look to each other, then ourselves turn to see what holds their attention.

There, where Kalliste would be, a solid mass of black smoke billows upward then spreads out sideways in the shape of a sky-filling cypress tree. Beneath this awful sight, lightning streaks flash between masses of tangled, writhing clouds.

Suddenly a boom splits the sky. Behind us where the temple complex begins comes a sickening crescendo of rent wood and stone crashing to earth, then the desperate shrieks of humans and animals.

Another blast hits, even louder, and we are torn from each other and thrown to the terrace just as others fall themselves. The sky to the north is now blacker than a starless night. A third blast slams us and with it the din of more destruction at the temple. Before us the mole, rent by the shock, is now breached by the driven sea.

My body is numbed by the fall, my ears roaring, yet I can see Theion near me, hear him shout, as if from a great distance, "Take my hand! We must get away from the sea wall!"

It is then, as I stand, I see the ocean recoiling from the fury of the earth away from its own shore. Where water had been great creatures of the deep convulse helplessly on naked sand and rock, their world stolen. A scream gags me and I fall hard to my knees, palms pressed to my eyes.

Now the very air around us shakes with dread. And another sound builds, an angry sky-driven thunder, coming fast. I look up. The sky overhead grows dark, then darker still. Yet not with smoke or ash. With a wave, a wave of water so high it is drowning the light as it rises over us with all the seas of the world captured in its awful maw.

"Acasia!" Theion screams.

The darkness from above falls over his face. With my last bit of strength I try to reach for his hand…but the wave…

FOUR

Emily

August-September, 2003

Of all things, I was least prepared for the desolation that set in after Nick's funeral. Three weeks later, when everyone around me had returned to their daily lives, I was sleeping late, waking sluggish from the sedative, crawling back into bed by early afternoon, if I got out of bed at all. My morning jog on the San Vicente median was a thing of the past and I was grateful when one of my neighbors, an older woman named Mimi-Ann Thibault, volunteered to take Fizzy, who missed her runs, on her stroll every afternoon.

On top of this, or perhaps because of it, the work on the tapes became confusing and frustrating. After I found the thread of the first and typed it, I lost momentum. The stories now seemed a twisted web of places and people, converging and parting only to crop up somewhere else. At times it seemed I had been asked to compute Pi to the last digit or, like Hercules, shovel out the Augean Stables. On one occasion I burst into hysterical laughter, threw hard copies of my work across the room, then downed two Diazepam and fell asleep on my desk.

So far, I had found neither further clues as to why Nick had left the tapes, nor any evidence of Clare's life in Southern California. Having no surname for her made such a hunt all but futile from the start. All I could hope for was to glean more identifying information about her dropped casually on tape. I wondered if Nick had purposefully erased any reference to her residence or address in order to shield his patient's privacy after he'd obtained her permission to publish the results of her work with him. Perhaps he would have given me her name, had he still been alive.

Maybe I was rationalizing, but what could Clare have told me that had not already been recorded by Nick anyway? Besides, I knew the highly private nature of her work with Nick. What if she didn't want to talk to anyone about the tapes now? Nick had told me once that many patients, once healed, seemed almost to go into amnesia about their therapy, frequently claiming not to remember what had transpired during the sessions, as if closing a book and placing it on a shelf. And the copies of the lawyer's documents, from which her last name had been removed, did not make any mention of Clare approving any further contact with Nick or his heirs. To insert myself into her life now might jeopardize my work. I would have to continue on my own, if I could.

One afternoon as I was struggling to work loose the details of one story, I accidentally answered my cell. It was my friend, Margo, who lived on Channel Road, just a few blocks down from me in the canyon.

Her voice was unusually subdued. "Sweetie, I've been trying to reach you for two days. I wanted to bring a few wrapped dinners up. I even made my apple bundt cake for you."

The last time I'd seen her was at the funeral. I wanted company, but I wanted to be alone. I mumbled something about being so tired, or lazy.

"You're never lazy. You just need to get out. Come over. Have a margarita with me downstairs at least. Please? Just to give me a break from worrying about you?"

I hung up and looked at myself in the mirror. The dinners Mom had put away for me were still in the freezer; I just didn't feel like eating. No wonder my skin was so pale, my eyes sunken in my head. Like a sleepwalker, I abandoned the clothes I'd been wearing for three days, showered, climbed into fresh jeans and T-shirt, hooked Fizzy to her leash and started down the long flight of steps to Channel Road.

Margo's loft was right above The Beach Boy, our favorite hangout, a gay bar-and-grill where we knew most of the patrons as friends. She and her husband Jeff were great aficionados of the South Pacific and their sunny home above the restaurant was bright with wall hangings and other souvenirs of the tropical places they loved. A well-known local photographer, she had recently begun experimenting by fusing elements from her huge collection of photographs into large-scale works.

I found her sitting in front of her monitor putting together her latest project, a view from her window of Pt. Dume. She'd stuffed her hair up under a cotton bandanna-turned-turban and was wearing one of Jeff's old shirts over her jeans.

"Girlfriend." She tossed her bifocals down and threw her arms around me. Please don't try to cheer me up, I thought.

Years ago, Margo and Jeff had lost a baby at eighteen months, an irreparable heart defect, and she had never been able to conceive again, so she, of anyone, would know what kind of hell I was in right now. She was almost twenty years older than I. We'd known each other so long, we were more like sisters to each other.

"What do you think?" She pointed at the screen.

I looked at her work, then out across the street. Seeing the sun-and-shadow angles on the chunky white building at the corner of Coast Highway and Channel, I was suddenly reminded of Clare's "Theion" and "Acasia" in Santorini. What would those characters have made of this sprawling seaside village 3,600 years beyond their "Ocean Stream"? Out of the corner of my eye I glimpsed two boys on skateboards careening down the sidewalk below, a girl in a pink-flowered bikini leaning into a shop doorway, and

Jeff, folding up his phone as he came in from the terrace.

"Hey, kid." He squeezed me next to him, kissed my cheek.

"Hi, Jeff." My own voice sounded so small, so dead. Why had I come down here? My legs were tired. My head was tired. I had nothing to say to anyone anymore.

Margo, washing up in the kitchen, called to Jeff, "We'll be downstairs, okay? Give us an hour, then we'll all have dinner. Okay, Em?" She took my arm and guided me down the narrow staircase to the entrance to the restaurant.

The bar was empty except for a couple chatting with the bartender, and we chose a table in a quiet corner on the restaurant side. Margo ordered a pitcher, then went on about her life. Gallerie Azul had liked her latest portfolio, *PCH 24/7*, and might include several images in their next show. Her sister Stacy, a financial analyst, loved her new job. Jeff was going fishing next week in British Columbia.

"So, are you working at all, or taking some time to rest? You are resting, aren't you?" she asked.

I wanted to tell her about the tapes, about the pieces I was trying to put together. But I couldn't talk about Clare. And I wouldn't talk about Nick. Instead, I said, "Oh, I finished the article for *Flex*. But other than that, no."

She stared right through me for a moment. "Take care now. Look, it's none of my business. What am I saying? I love you and it *is* my business. Be kind to yourself now."

I poured myself a second margarita. I knew I wasn't supposed to drink as long as I was taking the sedative, but who cared? They tasted good. And their chill quelled the constantly rising pain in my chest. "I will," I said, then saw her leaning her head down to look up at me. "Really."

At dinner, I picked at my tostada salad while Jeff and Margo went on about the details of their lives, but instead of cheering me up, which I knew they were trying to do, their presence as a happy couple only intensified my alienation. Margo loaded me down with dinners and the cake, and Jeff drove me and Fizzy home. Then I stared at something on TV for a half an hour before returning to my rumpled, now-gray bed.

. . .

Valerie came by the next day. I had to move all my notes on the tapes to the other end of the sofa so she could sit down.

"Dad came to town the other day."

"Oh. How are they doing?" I asked.

"Oh, Dad, I don't know. He's the strong, silent type. Mom, she's been spending more time with her church group." She paused. "They're going to sell Nick's house."

"What?"

"As soon as they can, I guess." The distress must have shown on my face because she added, "Why?"

"It's just, it's hard to think of it, of his things not being nearby." Just in case this was a nightmare, I wanted Nick's life to be preserved for him. For me.

"I'm sure if there's anything you wanted—"

"No, no. It's not that I wanted anything." If everything stayed the same as it was when Nick was alive it would be like he was still here. I could visit it sometimes, like going over when he was away to water the plants and take in the mail.

Valerie's gaze fell on one of my prescription bottles empty next to the phone where I'd called for a refill. She looked at me. "I don't know if I told you, but there's a bereavement group starting over on Fourteenth, next Wednesday night."

I hung my head, fiddled with my keychain. The idea of sitting in a room of grief-stricken people made my stomach twist. I didn't want to hear anybody else's story of death. My own was enough.

"It's at seven. I could pick you up, if . . .?"

"I don't know," I said.

And I really didn't. Because in the days right after the funeral I had called Nick's home number just to hear his recorded message. The last time I'd called, I'd heard myself screaming, "Pick up, Nick, goddamnit, Nick! Pick up the fucking phone!" then dropping the handset and falling into my chair, banging my hands on the chair arms and talking to myself incoherently.

I knew I needed help and, after another call from Valerie about the bereavement group a few days later, I did try it. The ten people there were mostly senior citizens who'd lost a spouse after many years of marriage, or children mourning the loss of an elderly parent. For each one, the transition had been slow: the discovery of illness, a long course of treatments, the coming-to-terms with impending death, the death itself, frequently merciful for all the suffering the deceased and their loved ones had endured. The incomprehension in their eyes when I told my story only made me feel freakish. It was not that they were uncaring. They cared very much. It was that my situation was so *different*, one they could comprehend even less well than I could. I left the group after three meetings.

Is there really any point in going on without Nick? I thought in the middle of the night five weeks after the funeral. My future had been ripped out from under me. All I could see ahead for myself was years of loneliness. I had applied myself well at school, then work. I had, I thought, led a decent enough life. What had I done to deserve such a fate? Maybe I just didn't belong on this earth. Besides, there would never be another Nick. And he was the only one I'd ever really wanted.

I tried to concentrate on the tapes, tried to stay with my original plan, which I'd based on the methods I'd seen archaeologists use at research excavations I'd volunteered on with Earthwatch a few years before: mark where each shard was found, photograph it *in situ*, brush it off and clean it, label it, then fit it in with the other pieces of its kind.

But now unable to organize my thoughts clearly, unable to sleep properly, I seemed to be existing in a world of half-light, stranded on a barren sphere in the void of space; a place where I could observe life on earth, but not return to it. Many days I sank into my chintz armchair moments after getting out of bed, only to stare out the window for hour after hour, watching the sun move across the sky, the mountains etched against the dusk, the planes taking off from LAX. Curled up into a ball, I'd rise only to visit the bathroom or take another sedative before going back to the safety of my chair, wrapping my blanket around me and waiting hopelessly for a rescue from the truth.

Such inertia would never have overtaken me in the past. My friends had always known me to be outgoing, energetic, optimistic; an inventive self-starter. That "me" was slowly unraveling.

* * *

Family and friends did call to check up on me, encourage me to join them outside. Usually I begged off. When I did go out it was to try to show them nothing was wrong with me. Which was about as far from the truth as my life could get.

One evening Margo arrived unannounced and insisted I come with her to see an Italian comedy, but with the theater just blocks from Glenwood Gardens all I could think of was the memorial service. I left the laughing audience halfway through and hid inside a bathroom stall.

After several minutes, the outer door squeaked open and Margo called, "Emily, are you here?"

I slunk out from the stall.

"Oh, Em, I seem to be doing the wrong things by you lately."

"I...it's just me. I should be sorry." She was trying so hard, but the force of the grief that gripped me had tightened its hold on me so that I found myself now barely able to communicate at all. With anyone.

Well, maybe Margo was right; maybe humor was the answer. The next day I drove over to Cinemanic and collected a half-dozen comedies and fed the DVDs one-by-one into the machine. But even the antics of Harold Lloyd, Nick's favorite, couldn't make me smile. Instead, I fell into a stupor of alcohol and Diazepam, then dropped into something like sleep on the den sofa.

. . .

I must have left my alarm on because its beeping from the bedroom awakened me. The DVD player was flashing. The TV clock read 7:00 AM and the drumbeat of pain in my forehead was nearly blinding. I stumbled into the kitchen for some aspirin and milk.

Fizzy suddenly went wild with barking at the front door. I put on the caftan I'd left on the floor, opened the door a crack, and squinted out at the morning. It was Mimi-Ann.

I mumbled a hazy "Hullo" while holding my head. "Isht time for old Fizzy's walk, huh?"

My neighbor stared. "My dear, you're pale as a ghost."

"I think it's… maybe it's the sleeping pills."

"Let me bring over some of my medicine. I never get a hangover from it."

"Oh, thanks, Mimi-Ann, that's okay."

"That way you won't have wasted any money if you don't like it."

"You can keep Fizzy today, if you like," I said, as I watched my dog stretch her leash down the stairway.

"Are you sure?" She made a face at Fizzy. "You're such a funny girl, aren't you Fizz?" Fizzy yelped and pulled on the leash with her teeth. The old woman waved her cane at me and followed her.

Mimi-Ann had been so kind to me in her Southern belle way, especially in the days right after the funeral, bringing a casserole, just-baked cookies, even an extra-large box of aloe vera infused tissue. ("When my Herbie died,

I cried until my nose was red and raw," she'd said, an old sadness clouding her eyes.) Seeing her having such fun with Fizzy relieved me.

But Mimi-Ann was right about the sleeping pills. I had never taken pills before except vitamins and the occasional over-the-counter for headaches, and on the rare occasions when I did need something stronger, I'd usually end up taking at most one or two of whatever was prescribed.

I called my GP to see about a different sedative. He had a cancellation that afternoon.

Meanwhile, Liv called. Her next-door neighbors suddenly had to be out of town and had given her two tickets for the inaugural performances at the new Disney Concert Hall in October.

"Please come. We can dress up!" she said.

Downtown L.A. seemed so far away. I thought of the traffic.

"It's Stravinsky, some modern composers, soloists, opera selections," she continued.

Film hadn't worked out too well for me. Perhaps I could handle music, especially a classical program. I'd grown up hearing Mother play Chopin, Czerny, and Brahms on the old Steinway baby grand in Carpinteria. Since those days, it had always had a positive, calming effect on me.

"October twenty-fourth. It's a Friday. Okay?" she asked.

"Oh, I'm not so sure I'm good at . . going out."

"Oh, Em, you don't have to, I just thought, knowing something about music, you'd enjoy it."

"Really, it's okay. I'll be okay. I'll have to figure out what to wear."

"Want to go to Beverly Center?"

"Oh. No, no, it's all right." My closet was a mess, clothes moldering where I dropped them in heaps on the floor. Half the time I didn't even bother to change out of my robe and pajamas. The other half I only wore jeans and T-shirts. Liv was right: just the act of fixing myself up might do me some good. I told her yes, then wrote on October 24 on the calendar, *Liv, concerts, downtown, 7.*

. . .

Later that afternoon, Dr. McGee listened to me without taking notes, then said something that surprised me. "Even though they take a bit of time to work, I think you might benefit from one of the SSRIs."

"I did research on them for an article last year."

The doctor went on as if not hearing me, "The side effects are minimal, really."

I remembered Nick talking about the side effects of these twenty-first century panacea medicines: nightmares, chills, memory problems, seizures, infections, and worse. He'd even shown me a circular from one of the companies: nearly a foot square in a font so tiny I needed my big magnifying glass to read it. "I never prescribe them," he'd said, and I'd thought: *I'll never take them.*

Dr. McGee was still talking as I stared straight ahead, not really hearing. I watched as he wrote a prescription out, then handed it to me: Fluoxetine.

"I'd like to see you back here in two weeks," he said.

I stuffed the slip into my bag and drove home. Was this what things had come to for me? An expensive and risky medication versus a half-life in complete darkness? Nick wouldn't approve. But Nick wasn't here.

I closed the shutters in the living room, sat down on the sofa, and stared off into the dim light.

Well, maybe I'd take one. Maybe I'd take more than one. Finally I drove myself over to the pharmacy on Montana Avenue.

They were very busy and the assistant said it would be at least twenty minutes before the prescription could be filled. I was wandering around the aisles staring at bubble baths, fragrances, eye makeup, when I noticed my poor chapped hands; little wonder, this time of year, with humidity in the single digits and water feeling dry just coming out of the tap. I turned the corner into the infant care section for some Advanced Care, the only product that worked for me, when I saw a figure who looked so familiar, the slender build, the wild hair, the easy stance, that for a moment, my heart and breath gave way.

He looked just like Nick.

I spotted the lotion I wanted, just in front of him, and nervously excused myself to reach past him for it.

A voice above my head asked brightly, "Is that good stuff?"

I jumped, and looked up. He was smiling.

"It seems to work for me," I said, standing back.

"Yeah, man, this air. Not used to it yet, I guess." Then, "I just moved here. From Ohio. Well, via New York, that is."

"I've heard there's a bit more humidity there."

"'Heard there's humidity.'" He laughed. "You must be one of the friendly natives."

"Southern California, not L.A."

"Oh." He stared at me, appraising me. Almost as if he'd been thinking the same thing I had when we saw each other. "What part?"

"Just south of Santa Barbara. A little citrus and avocado ranch."

"Cool." He shifted forward on his left foot. "Hey, I'm Curt."

"Emily." I smiled and shook his hand. A ray of heat shot down the front of my body.

"So," he said, "you got a few minutes? Maybe for some coffee?" He nodded in the direction of Javaland across the street. "I need somebody to explain this place to me."

I couldn't think of a reason not to, especially in broad daylight. Besides, the staff at Javaland knew me well and wouldn't let anything happen there. So, after making our purchases—I could pick up the medicine later—we sat down for late-afternoon coffee.

As it turned out, he was an actor with a few commercials and a couple of soaps to his credit, who had been persuaded by his acting teacher in New York to audition for a few roles out here. He was just settling into a flat at 21st and Montana. After an hour or so of chatting, he asked for my number, and I handed him my business card with my cell number on it.

My world seemed a little brighter that night. And considerably brighter two days later when Curt called and asked me to see *Endgame* at Santa Monica Playhouse the next night. As it happened, I'd always wanted to see that particular work in performance.

I dressed carefully in my embroidered jeans, a pale blue silk blouse, sandals.

"Wow!" was all Curt said when I opened the door. "Do I need glasses or are you taller than I took you for?"

I lifted my three-inch heels.

"Nice," he said, and held his arm out to me.

He didn't drive an old Land Cruiser like Nick, but a shiny new BMW 3. Still, it seemed perfectly natural to be sitting next to him. I relaxed into the evening far more easily than I thought I could. Curt suggested a club after.

"Well," I said.

"Hey, better idea," he said.

We ate fries in the car at McDonald's on Santa Monica Boulevard. I told him about the best places for a late-night snack, the best car-washes and gyms for meeting filmmakers, which casting directors I had heard lived in Santa Monica and the Palisades. When he complained about the amount of time commuting between auditions, I shared a couple of my secret surface ways of getting around the Westside.

"You should write a guidebook," he said when I paused for a fry. "Was I lucky to run into you, or what?"

Me, too, I thought.

He brought me home and I think he wanted to come in, but I was tired. We stood at my door. "You know, I've been wanting to kiss you all evening," he said shyly.

My cheeks grew hot, but I didn't turn away.

He pulled me to him, and gave me a sweet, not-too-serious kiss. Then he stood back from me, and smiled. "I'll call you." He pointed his finger toward me and winked as he walked backward down the stairs.

It was almost as if fate had given me a reprieve. I didn't think I could tell any of my family or friends about him; it might seem inappropriate, I suppose, dating someone so soon after Nick's death. But however strange it might look to others, to me it was wondrous.

Curt didn't call over the weekend, which seemed strange after such a pleasant date, but he finally rang Tuesday to explain. "Hey, I missed you."

"Me, too. What did you do this weekend?"

"Oh, you don't want to hear about it. My dad was in the hospital again, his heart, and Mom needed me. I took the red-eye Friday and got back just last night."

"You must be exhausted."

"Oh, a good night's sleep and I'm back with the world." Then, "Listen, I have to go into Westwood tomorrow, just to drop off some headshots. Think you could play hooky and come with me to the movies?"

"I think I could do that," I replied, smiling to myself.

"I'll pick you up at noon. We'll have lunch, too."

* * *

I did better at the movies this time: *Pirates of the Caribbean.* Perhaps it was the topic, or that Curt said he knew a couple of the CGI staff. He held my hand all during the film and when we put our heads together to whisper questions, he kissed me and I felt his tongue on my earlobe. I squeezed his hand and put my head on his shoulder.

As we walked out of the theatre, I took his arm. He patted my hand, pulled me closer. We strolled down Glendon, stopping to look in shops, watching the students. Curt was admiring a silver hip flask in the window of a men's store when I felt a pair of eyes on me and I turned my head and recognized, behind her baseball cap and sunglasses, Liv, stopped at a light a block down. The light changed. Her car did not move. I heard horns behind her, then saw her white VW slowly turning right.

This time when Curt brought me home, I invited him in, and offered him some of Margo's cake from the freezer.

"You don't by chance have any milk, do you?" he said, as he made himself comfortable on the sofa.

"Well, no," I said, pulling a screw top bottle of chardonnay out of the refrigerator, "just this."

"Always have it with cake," he said, forking in a mouthful of the cake.

I poured us each a glass and he toasted me, then pulled me down toward him. We kissed, gently, then deeply. His hand slipped, warm, under my T-shirt. Then he slid me down on the sofa under him. I wrapped my legs around him, felt his lean body against mine, played with the lock of hair on his collar.

He smiled. "Lady, you got me going," he whispered.

"Really."

"Yeah." He bit my neck. "To Romania."

I laughed, kissed him again. "Do you know any websites with deals on rooms in bat-filled castles?"

He sat up. "Hey, no, I mean it. Would you like get out of here together for a few days? You know, where there are no interruptions."

I sat up, too. "I thought you were kidding."

"Of course not," he said, pulling on my ear. "Well, about Romania."

"But, where?"

"I don't know. Up the coast?"

"Well—" I said.

"Or, how about down the coast? To Cabo?"

"Oh, yeah. I've never been down there." Although I still hadn't mentioned my trauma, getting away, really getting away, sounded appealing.

Especially with him. "When were you thinking of?"

"Maybe in a couple of weeks? Let me look at my calendar when I get home."

"There aren't any bats, are there?"

"No gloomy old castles, either!" He made a horrific face.

"Well done!" I said, applauding.

"I learned it in acting class."

At that point Fizzy, who'd been working up a growl from her bed in the corner, ran toward us, barking her staccato go-away bark. But Curt laughed.

"Okay, okay, gal! Chill!" He checked his watch. "Actually, I've got a reading this afternoon. To be continued?" He slid me a look.

"Maybe."

"Oh man, you're as bad as that dog."

He kissed me quickly. Tied up his shoes.

Fizzy bared her teeth and snarled.

"Fizzy!" I scolded.

"My cue," Curt said. "Catch you later."

The phone rang just as Curt's sneakers hit the last tread of the stairs.

"Em, was that you?" I could hear the traffic in the background, orders for coffee and panini. Liv.

"You mean, in Westwood? Just a while ago?"

"Was that some . . .? Who was that guy you were with?"

Liv and Nick had always been on great terms with each other "Oh, just someone I met at the pharmacy a couple of weeks ago," I said as casually as I could.

"Oh," she said, as the call broke up, ". . . know what you've been through?"

"Well, not yet."

The call dropped.

Later that afternoon, she called back.

"I didn't hang up on you," I said.

"I know. Everyone was on the phone in that place. So," she asked, "who is he?"

"An actor. I met him at Montana Pharmacy."

"Is this, like, a romance thing?"

"Hmmm, sort of."

"I don't mean to sound bossy, Em, but is this, well, is this something you want now?"

"It's really nice to be with someone again. Don't you think he kind of looks like Nick?"

"Nick? Well he was kind of tall, I guess."

"Really, Liv. He's a doll." I tried to sound reassuring. "Just what the doctor ordered."

"Have you checked him out on the Internet? "

"Liv, I don't think he's a serial killer."

"Well, okay, I just, you know, I just don't want to see you hurt again."

"Hey, just being with someone who cares about me is making me feel better. I think Nick would approve." I heard a click.

"Just a second," she said, "I'm waiting for the word on some work." She was back in a couple of minutes. "They need the orchestra piece finished by next Thursday for that film score I told you about. I've got to be over in Burbank in an hour."

"See you."

"Just be careful with this Curt guy, okay?"

*   *   *

Though I didn't see him that weekend ("Auditions," he said. "You know this business, everybody working twenty-four-seven.") but he did come by the following Tuesday, and every day the following week. Maybe Liv was right: maybe the timing was odd for a relationship, but who was to say life couldn't continue nearly as it had before? And Curt and I were going to take a little holiday together, a major step toward a relationship. How quickly life could turn around!

I hadn't paid much attention to the details of daily life in the weeks since the funeral, and I wasn't entirely surprised when the bank sent a notice that I was in overdraft. I needed to get back to work at the job that paid me money. *Marathoner* magazine sent me an e-mail about a query I had sent them in July. Yes, they were interested in my idea for an article on health rituals of runners at the ancient Olympics. Buoyed by my new sense of some future returning for myself, I e-mailed back my promise that I'd have it to them within two weeks.

Some of the research I needed to do even dovetailed with the Minoan era described in Clare's stories. Hard training, unguents, sacrifices, oracles, all were factors in the cultivation of early Greek athleticism. And the volume of research done on Minoan, Mycenaean, and Greek athletics was so enormous and readily available online that I became, coincident with writing the article, even more convinced of Clare's stories as fantasies based on prior knowledge, conscious or unconscious. At any rate, I got through the article and salvaged my bank balance without having to dig too deeply into my savings.

I cooked dinner for Curt that Wednesday—Sicilian chicken with polenta. Nick had loved my cooking and Curt said he was thrilled to be eating real food again, instead of the "garbage," his word, he usually grabbed between acting classes and auditions. We watched the sun set over Point Dume, then drank half a bottle of wine as we cozied up on the sofa together, necking, laughing, playing in front of the TV. We talked a little more about our trip, what days he thought he could be gone.

He didn't leave until after eleven that night and gave me a long, full-body hug at my door. Then he lifted my chin up to him. "You realize, of course, I'm falling in love with you."

I just smiled, then reached up to kiss him. As I settled in to sleep, I thought: So quickly, and so perfectly, it had become love for both of us.

.   .   .

The next morning at my desk, I studied what work I'd done on Clare's case, which had not received as much of my attention with so much of my attention focused on Curt. From what I had unearthed so far, Clare's next story seemed to unfold over a period of just five days; five momentous days that altered the face of a city, even as they brought Clare's lovers together again.

FIVE

Clare/Elena

532 A.D.
Byzantium

"Glory to the Father and the Son and the Holy Spirit, now and forever, and to the ages of ages," the priest intones as my hands move reflexively in the sign of the cross. The acolyte swings the censer again and I follow as the smoke curls high, above statues of saints and prophets, and upward past windows of mullioned marble, to disappear into the glittering mosaic dome of the Church of the Holy Wisdom.

And son of God, redeemer of human souls, please keep our city safe from further harm, I say in silent prayer. The street factions were out again, and with the chariot races coming to the Hippodrome again in five days' time, no one knew what might happen.

Just two weeks ago the city had suffered its worst riots yet, and with them, death, fire, and property damage. In the eyes of many, this continual strife stemmed directly from the policies of Emperor Justinian, who had come to the throne with an ambitious plan to build a new Rome in the East, founded in Christianity and with a supremacy beyond the Rome of the Caesars.

But Justinian's plan had instead brought famine and civil unrest to Byzantium. For one thing, its implementers were three of the most ruthless strongmen in the empire: Prefect Eudaemon, who had set up a torture chamber in the bowels of the city Prefecture; the corrupt judge Tribonian, an expert at taking bribes and fixing trials; and tax collector John the Cappadocian, whose policies had led to near-starvation conditions throughout the empire.

I had been an indirect victim of the Cappadocian's policies, whose money-saving ideas had included strict limits on farmers' use of public carts and barges for carrying their harvests to market. My father was one of those farmers, and had died under the weight of his own grain harvest as he tried to carry it to market himself. At sixteen I was orphaned and destitute.

To survive I danced for food in a tavern near Ephesos until, one night, a drunken patron left a leather money-pouch lying on the earthen floor. I retrieved it and looped it over my belt, hoping for a tip when he came back for it. Only after two weeks had passed without his return did I untie its greasy knot and empty its contents out onto the planks of my tiny attic room. There in the light of the oil lamp flickered twenty folles, the coin of the empire. Though not a fortune, this small cache meant freedom and I quickly bought myself passage on a ship bound for Constantine's city.

Within a short time I found work in another tavern in the city's bawdy Hippodrome Quarter, performing the belly dance a Beiruti freedwoman had taught me. This exotic dance had gotten me enough tips and food to stay alive despite the grain shortages that plagued Byzantium. It had brought me the attentions of many men, too; in particular, those of a lean, sun-bronzed man of about my age, who came to the tavern several nights each week. Each night he moved closer and closer to me as I danced. And one night, ignoring all the tips thrown my way from other men, I stepped down from the low stage to dance just for him. He stood quietly, eyes following me as I circled around him, cymbals ringing in my palms, hips swinging and jangling the tiny discs of my hip scarf until they nearly touched his arms while the men in the audience hooted and shouted.

"Who is that man?" I'd asked Talike, the other dancer, later that night.

"I don't know. Someone said he came from Alexandria, I think," she said as she folded her pashmina. "Is he a good tipper?"

Also watching me that night, as he had for weeks, was Licinius Nestoros, a high-ranking soldier in the city prefect's guard. His attentions, and intentions, were hard to ignore; his mere presence oozed power.

As a newcomer to such a large city, I was flattered by the interest of a uniformed officer and when he offered me the safety and security of marriage, I accepted with gratitude, and quit the city's seedy burlesque neighborhood forever.

But Licinius' ruthless side showed itself soon after our vows last year. Now, where I once saw strength I see instead a volcanic temper. And where I once saw a handsome physique I see only wild eyes, a bullish body, and a scarred face, marks of a brutal nature. Licinius is ambitious; somehow, he hopes to wrest power away from his commander, the highly unpopular Eudaemon. To this end, he is frequently absent from our apartments.

Not long ago his militia was granted an audience with Empress Theodora. Having also gotten her start as a dancer, albeit one whose dance had included a segment in which live geese plucked grain from her exposed pudenda, she took an interest in meeting me and, being Licinius' wife, I could not refuse her request to report to her, as one of a network of women, the machinations of the demes, or government-sanctioned street patrollers, who watch out for their neighborhoods under the Blue, Green, Red, or White banners.

Favored by the emperor and empress are the Blues, wealthy and orthodox. But equally as powerful, if only in number, are the Greens, mostly working men. Everyone takes sides. But it is the extremist element in each deme which usually starts trouble. And most of that trouble begins in the Hippodrome, where Blue and Green fans cheer the teams who drive for their colors, celebrating with ardor when they win, weeping on their comrades' shoulders when they lose, and fighting each other in the narrow, coiling streets outside the Hippodrome when the races are over.

More unrest was coming, I reported to the empress, particularly from the Green demes whose ranks had swelled with hungry, desperate men. And this civil discontent that now bubbled up to the point of boiling over again—this, I omitted from my message—was in fact fostered by the emperor and empress themselves, who refused to hear any pleas for reform that might bring more food and goods into the city, and peace to our streets.

* * *

My worries are broken by the sound of the communicants around me who rise, almost as one, to leave the basilica. Tradesmen, shopkeepers, fishermen, high government officials, the living mosaic that is this city moves like a slow wave out into the morning light, blinding us all with its white halo of mist now lifting over a sea of pink tile roofs. Eager to plunder the waste at the Harbor of Phosphorum, ever-present gulls and kites scream overhead. Donkeys bray and dogs bark in reply.

After finding my way through the crowded Augusteum, I begin my walk home down the grand central boulevard. But just before I reach the Arch of Constantine, I turn back toward the Hippodrome Quarter, unaccountably drawn to my past there. Citizens who aspire to maintain their respectability, especially women, cannot afford to be seen in this part of town. I pull my cloak closer; yet still, I walk.

Soon, I am upon it. As I remembered, the shadowy backstreets enclosing the arena are a fracas of noise, stink, and color where the demi-monde of the city makes its home. I pass an Egyptian wrestler leading a gilded crocodile on a tether, prostitutes perched high on painted clogs in sooty doorways, a pair of Goth midgets practicing a dual-fellatio act.

A bony hand strikes out from the shadows and grabs my arm. "And what might a perfumed lady be doing here, eh?"

A blind crone, shrouded in layers of threadbare brocade, cackles, blares her offer in my direction. "One follis for your future!"

Bewildered, I take a coin from the purse at my waist. Her white eyes stare up, her free hand reaches toward the sound, claws the coin from my hand, then clutches at my tunic and pulls me close.

"The one who loves you is near. He seeks you, yet he will only know he does when he sees you. But the one you call husband is no husband to you. Look to the streets. There is danger coming."

My flesh withdraws and I wrench my hand away from her. A stitch pricks my heart and with it a light the color of the sea rises before my eyes. I back into a juggler, who winks and grins too close as he madly tosses balls into the air. Near panic now from the crush of the close walls and the stale air, I flee down the dark alley and, before I am aware, am inside the Hippodrome itself.

The great circus is empty, its open space a relief from the jumbled confusion outside its walls. I climb the stone steps and slip into the stands unobserved, then look around to get my bearings. Along the spina at the center of the track, a ridge of copper icons crowd each other for position around a larger-than-life statue of the seated Herakles. Placed at intervals to his left and right are no less than five statues of the great charioteer Porphyrius Calliopas, hero to both Blues and Greens. At the center of the spina, the Serpent Column soars high above all.

Just above the stables at the north end of the arena break the famous quadriga of gilded bronze horses, each striving to flee the bondage of the pediment to join the competition on the track. On the eastern side of the arena sits the emperor's box, the ceiling of which is said to be embellished with a great mosaic of the racing factions.

The morning air thaws as the sun burns the last mist from the sky. I hear shouts and horses on the opposite side of the spina and see charioteers practicing for the races on Tuesday as their captains and coaches observe from the sidelines.

As I watch, one of the drivers stills his reins and halts deftly before two of the trainers below. I shade my eyes before the brightening sky to watch. The charioteer is as lean and muscular as the statues behind him. Despite the fact that he is helmeted, I can tell he has broken into laughter at something the coaches at the rail have said, for he throws his head back, as do the two men he has paused to talk with.

Suddenly a gust of wind bursts off the Bosphorus, pushing my hood back from my cloak, loosening my hair to the sun. The movement must catch the charioteer's eye because he looks up toward me. Embarrassed by my own staring, I cast my eyes down into my lap then, feeling his gaze still upon me, I look down to the track again. As he slaps the reins on the horses and drives forward, he is still watching me.

He is clearly expert, even to untrained eyes like mine, for he balances the four horses swiftly and at even pace. I stand and my eyes follow him around the track. He returns, slowing, then stopping the handsome sea-green car below me. He looks up as if transfixed. Then, in one graceful movement, his right hand touches his heart, then reaches out to salute me.

For a moment I am paralyzed by the same strange feeling of disorientation I had felt moments before outside the arena. Then, overcome by his action, I stand and extend my hands out to him in supplication. His horses nod their heads, huff, and scrape the dirt. He stares up at me for an instant more as his team pulls forward on the reins. Then, still watching me, he spanks the reins on the horses' rumps and starts back down the track.

Carefully descending the steep stone steps to the track, I approach two oddsmakers observing the practices.

"Excuse me, could you be kind enough to tell me the name of the driver who passed here, the man in the sea-green car?"

The squat, simian man on the left looks me over with a lascivious, sidelong sneer. His companion slides a glance at me, then returns his attentions to the matter at hand: handicapping the field. "Well, Miss Golden Hair," he says, "that happens to be an odds-on favorite for Tuesday, Dakis Amianus. I'd put my money on him, if I were you."

I smile politely. "Thank you. Oh, and please"—he barely takes his eyes off the Armenian charioteer now circling the Spina, as I ask, remembering the blue-green of the car—"does he drive for the Blues or the Greens?"

"The Greens," is his dismissive answer, as he watches the field.

. . .

For once the noise and busyness of the grand boulevard seem remote as I travel within my own thoughts back to our apartments. Who was that man? Why did he seem so familiar, even under cover of a helmet?

Tonight, several friends will be visiting for supper, Licinius' friends, who will drink heavily and talk late into the night. They arrive just as Serena and Octavian finish lighting the lamps.

The evening air is unusually mild for January and the men, many of them minor city officials, become gossipy after several cups of wine. From my room, I am able to hear much of their conversation, and much of it is about the upcoming races.

"Atticus! Oh, he'll never make one lap around the track! And that outside chestnut, still nearly lame from that last shipwreck of chariots two weeks back."

"My money's on Patricius. He's the man to go with."

The sound of wine being poured.

"Say, what of the fellow the odds-makers are talking about now? Dakis-something?"

I tiptoe from my couch to the heavy curtain separating the gallery from the atrium.

Leo, the deputy city treasurer, is talking and another guest picks up the thread.

"Dakis Amianus, the name is, just arrived back last month. A real hero in North Africa, I hear." A pause, and the sound of more wine pouring from the jar. "Originally a stevedore from the docks, willed the horses by his uncle, they say. Old Marcus spent a bundle to polish him for the Hippo. Guess we'll see what the Greens can do."

"Aw, screw the Greens," another voice growls, and they all laugh.

. . .

Licinius stumbles into bed in the middle of the night. Once again he is drunk and reeks of stale sweat and soured wine. I turn my head away. He pulls me toward him to kiss me and I recoil. He pulls me back and slaps me. After several minutes of brutal fumbling, he simply passes out and starts snoring so violently the couch shakes. I escape to an adjoining room.

By the hour I awaken, Licinius is already gone. I have slept little because one question has consumed my mind all night: Who was the man in the Hippodrome, the man they called Dakis? After dressing quickly, I start down the grand boulevard toward the big arena just as the central market of the Augusteum begins its day.

The walk is neither long nor taxing, but today takes more time than it did yesterday since I make frequent detours along every side street as a precaution against being recognized.

The arena complex is colossal, a warren of passageways leading to the baths, administrative offices, barracks. As I pass one hallway and another, I continue to take special care to avoid contact with anyone, especially guardsmen here who might know Licinius, for I have no way to explain my presence within the forbidden Hippodrome complex. Not only that, for the wife of a Blue city official to be found in the stables of the Green, especially now, might cause Licinius trouble all the way to the palace, which would lead to terrible trouble for me at home.

Following the sound of horses and calls of grooms at the north end of the track, I come at last to the stables. Pulling the hood of my cloak down so my face is in shadows, I approach a lone blacksmith shoeing a glossy white Arabian.

"Farrier, I am a messenger sent to Dakis Amianus. Could you tell me where I might find him?" The smith, a bearded fellow in the mold of Vulcan himself, looks up from the mare's hoof, shoeing nails clenched between his teeth, and points with his file to the far end of the hallway.

I follow in the direction he points, down a long hallway of small rooms, each filled with horse tack and what looks like charioteers' uniforms. But all the rooms are empty. "Sir," I ask the farrier again, "might he be in another part of the arena complex?"

He lets go of the horse's leg, scratches his head. "Last time I saw him, miss, he was putting away his helmet and greaves."

I thank him and return to the main hall. Here are rows of doors, so many closed, doors I dare not open and those open seeming to lead to even more closed doors behind which may sit a man, any man, who knows my husband. I see horses being walked toward the stables, and officials dressed in the tunics of the Hippodrome Corporation chatting with each other. Eyes watch me in passing. I think I hear murmuring and wonder if someone has recognized me.

Somehow, I manage to find my way back to the track entrance. Several cars are out practicing and I wait and watch as they pass, each leaving a cloud of dust and churned earth as they round this end of the arena. None of them is Dakis' sea-green car.

A cloud passes over the sun. I return to the labyrinth of the Hippodrome's interior, now lighted at intervals only by glassed lanterns flickering amber light on the stone walls. Shadows appear and fade. A man with the slender, sinewy body of a charioteer appears in front of me some distance ahead.

I rush toward him calling, "Dakis!"

He turns around. "Sorry, ma'am, that's not me," he says.

I beg his pardon and back away into yet another corridor leading into even more lamp-lit recesses. Voices call to each other and their echoes fade along the deep arcades and passageways.

Finally, at a loss as to where to turn to find the man called Dakis, I retrace my steps out of the stables and trudge home, mind ringing in a blur of cold, swirling grit from the street, and sellers' last calls. The tension on the streets seems higher than ever, risk in every shadow, at every corner.

Constantinople feels like a city on the brink of calamity.

* * *

To my surprise, Licinius is waiting for me in the atrium. He does not think to ask where I have been but simply grunts a greeting of sorts as he looks up from a message scroll. "Old Eudaemon screwed up good this time!"

"What, husband?"

"He's got the ringleaders of the Hippodrome riots two weeks ago. Four are to lose their heads, three to keep their heads as they're hanged." He leans back in his big chair and laughs. "And then the rioting in the streets will do Eudaemon in by his own hand!"

The worst punishment meted out by the city courts, and usually to hardened criminals only, is exile to a monastery, or blinding. "What?" I asked.

"Tomorrow, at the Blachernae. Blues and Greens together. That'll be a first. And when Eudaemon goes down in flames, I make my move!" he answers with a snort.

He is still laughing as I enter my rooms off the gallery. After a short prayer for safety, to steady myself, I hurry out to the Augusteum to the candle stall of my friend and confidante Castalia.

The afternoon wind off the Golden Horn is up. My friend is wrapped in a heavy black shawl, preparing to close her shop for the day.

"Castalia!" I call as I see her pulling the shutters down. "I must talk with you!"

"Elena!" She sees me, comes out front, then brings me to the back of the little shop where a small urn of tea is brewing. She pours me a silver-and-glass cup and sits down with me while I catch my breath. "Are you all right? Is it Licinius again? It must be Licinius. You really should leave him, you know." She puts her hand on mine. "As I suspected, cold as frost."

"Have you heard about the hangings?" I ask.

"Hangings?"

"Tomorrow at the Blachernae. Some rioters of a fortnight ago. Blue and Green together!"

"Executions?"

"That is what Licinius has just told me."

"Holy Saint Sophia. Trouble on top of trouble! That will bring the rioters out of the woodwork! What is Tribonian thinking?"

"I do not know, Castalia, but there is something else, a message I must get to a man I saw at the Hippodrome yesterday."

Castalia simply stares at me. As if I could bring any worse news.

"I saw him on the track. He stopped his car the moment he saw me in the stands, then saluted me, hand to heart. His name is Dakis. And he drives for the Greens." My words tumble out and I nearly drop the glass.

"You went to the Hippodrome and now you want to meet with some charioteer who drives for the Greens?" Her dark eyes bore into me as if she is looking at a madwoman. "Never mind Tribonian. What are *you* thinking?"

"I cannot explain it. Only that I must talk with him, and soon. With the city's blood up, I dare not go back to the arena now. If I could explain, I would, but I can't, only that I must at least get a message to him."

"Well, anyone but Licinius," she says, shaking her head. After rummaging around in a jeweled box on the table behind her, she pulls from it a square of paper, a pen, and a bottle of ink. "Write your note. I know an urchin who knows every pathway in the city. If your man is here, he will get it delivered. I trust you will tell me what this is all about later."

I pick up the pen and dip it into the ink. But just as I am about to begin, I realize: with the number of spies about, anything on paper might be traced back to me, with disastrous results for Castalia. I lay the pen on the table. "No, just tell him to tell the charioteer Dakis at the stable of the Greens that Elena, the woman he saluted on the track yesterday morning, will meet him wherever he pleases, but that our meeting must be a secret from everyone."

Castalia looks doubtful. "All right. But be careful, sister. There is no use creating trouble for yourself when trouble is already looking for us right here."

We embrace, and I hurry home. Licinius, however, is gone and indeed, does not come back all night. Perhaps, as so often in the past, he is at a tavern.

. . .

Dawn comes late and cold in a pall of fog and dust. I have missed Mass, but decide to visit the basilica anyway, for now, more than ever, I need the comfort of Sophia.

Her candles burn brightly and, safe behind the walls of her church, I pray fervently for peace, and for a meeting with the mysterious charioteer. Little do I know, as I beseech the saint for guidance, that a terrible incident is happening just three miles away at the north end of the city. I hear the first stories in the street in front of the church.

"They beheaded the first four all right, but the other three, well, the executioner botched the job and killed only one in the noose."

"And the other two?"

"Two tries. That's when the crowd, Blues and Greens together, took the poor fellow, fallen twice from the gallows ropes, mind you, to Saint

Conon, where the monks got them over to the Church of Saint Laurentius on the other side of the water."

"Blue and Green street demes together? Almighty God! And today a Sunday."

"Well, we'll see what old Eudaemon will do. Won't be any good for the likes of us regular folks, you can bet on it."

Already the street around me is dissolving into chaos. Extreme partisans of both demes materialize out of nowhere in their Hunnish costume: long, matted hair, wide-sleeved tunics, knives unsheathed and ready on their belts. I dare not go to the Hippodrome or Castalia's today.

It is Octavian, back at the apartments, who finishes the day's story for me, his words nearly tumbling over one another. "And lady, Eudaemon's soldiers have surrounded the church and won't let a soul in or out. The monks say the men were spared on Sunday by the hand of God and must be released. Lord God have mercy on our city!"

The poor man's hands are shaking so badly the wine sloshes in the jar he is holding. I place my hands over his to calm him. Now the tension fueled by the City Prefect and his guard, my husband among them, has edged into our own home. The gentle Octavian looks to me for reassurance.

"All will be well with us," I say with a calm I do not feel. "There is no need for worry."

If only I could believe my own words.

· · ·

Monday morning dawns grim and frozen in the thin midwinter light. Licinius is still, apparently, with the guard holding the prisoners and monks hostage. The streets are quiet, but in the distance I hear the shouts of the demes, their calls for an honor guard around the doomed men whose lives now hang in limbo at the Church of Saint Laurentius. It is the only sound breaking the dark silence gripping the city. No decrees have issued from the palace, voiceless in the face of the expanding emergency. Tomorrow, the Ides of January, is race day.

Did my message reach Dakis? I borrow Octavian's dun-colored cloak for disguise and steal out the side door of the building.

Castalia's shop is locked. The streets, so full of swaggering, shouting partisans yesterday now stand deserted. But within a few blocks of my home I know why. A throbbing din rises from the direction of the big arena, the sound of chanting, angry men. The closer I get to the arena, the louder the sound becomes until, at the western gate, it is deafening.

As the throng crosses over to the north end of the Hippodrome, I slip into the nearest open door at the Dihippon, behind the stables, and back into the maze of the great structure. I search the stables quietly, calling "Dakis!" through the western arcade, now resonating nonstop with the echo of the demes screaming slogan after slogan against each other, the emperor, and his guard.

I work my way east until I see flags marking Green territory over a stone archway. Finally, near the end of the line of stables, I recognize the car. His trainers, like the others, are inspecting the fit of the tack on his horses. One of the men looks up at me.

"Sir, I have a message for Dakis. Could you tell me where he might be?" I ask.

For some reason, the man finds this request funny. When he stops laughing he says, "Right inside, miss, just around the corner." He is still chuckling as he turns to say to one of his cohorts, "Another crazed fan! Well, at least this one's not like yesterday's, checking the horse shit to make sure they've been fed grain."

"Dakis! Dakis!" I call in a loud whisper as I look into each of the stalls.

Then, from the last stall, a man steps out. He sees me, stops dead.

The downy hairs on my neck, back and arms stand upright.

It is the man I danced for at the tavern.

"Elena, wife of Licinius," he says my name slowly, deliberately.

My head goes light, my mouth dry. A bead of sweat trickles between my breasts, down my stomach.

"You are the Alexandrian," I say, my throat rough. "You came to the tavern."

He stands watching me, then finally says, "I did not mean to disturb you."

Though I had never heard him speak, even his voice seems as familiar as that of an old friend.

"Nor I, you," I say.

For a moment, everything is completely still, as if the sky has ceased to move around us; as if the heavens are listening in.

"You are a Blue." His tone is formal. He is staring at me hard and I know: He would not salute me hand-to-heart now.

"My husband is a Blue sympathizer, yes."

"And you?"

"I—I only wish the violence to stop."

He shakes his head. "A Blue, the wife of the law?"

"You misjudge me."

He comes closer. Heat pours off his body. He smells of fruit and wild herbs. His skin is smooth and flawless. My tongue touches the inside of my lower lip.

"Then do this, Elena, wife of Licinius the Blue," he says, staring down at me, "tell your husband to tell his friend Justinian to stop persecuting the Greens and clean out his administration. They are the ones responsible for the disaster brewing out there." He puts the halter up on a rack, then brushes past me, down the aisle to the entrance to the stables.

I take a deep breath. "Wouldn't you rather I told Theodora that directly?" I call out, just as he turns to enter the last stall.

He stops, looks back, walks back to me. "Who?"

"I am one of her city watchers."

"The Empress"—his eyes widen—"Theodora?"

"I report to her on the activities of the street demes."

"You have her trust on such matters?"

"As much as she can trust anyone she has drafted."

He stares through me for a long moment. Finally his expression softens. "Come this way." He motions to me to follow him down the arcade and into a low, arched recess. The great stone hall is as silent as a tomb here, its damp stillness insulating us from the hot noise of the mob above.

"You are serious?" he asks.

"I swear it."

"Because if you can meet with Theodora, many innocent lives may be saved. Are you truly prepared to become involved? It could mean danger to you, if your husband—"

"What do you wish me to tell the empress?"

He watches me for a moment longer, then says, "This: that although the extremist street demes threaten violence for the sake of violence, a number of us charioteers are standing with a new group, Blues and Greens united. We call ourselves The Humane Blues and Greens and we plan to petition the emperor peacefully tomorrow between races for the removal of the Cappadocian, Tribonian, and Eudaemon. They, more than anything, are the cause of the civic disorder we have suffered. If, somehow, the empress can influence Justinian to make the changes we seek, the streets may well be spared. If not . . ."

"I will do my best." As I turn to leave, I feel Dakis' hand on my wrist and my arm tingles. I stop.

"Elena," he says, "be careful."

. . .

The great palace occupies the eastern side of the Hippodrome complex but with crowds wall-to-wall in the adjacent streets, reaching the palace takes me some time. When finally I arrive, I see the huge bronze doors of the palace locked against the mob, the only sign of life on that side of the high fence a sullen guard, one of the elite Scholae who, oddly, seems completely oblivious to the foaming crowd on the other side of the gates.

"Please, Guard!" I shout as loud as I can over the din. "The Empress Theodora expects a message from me!"

He saunters up to the gate. "And you are?"

"Please, she knows me, Elena, wife of Eudaemon's man, Licinius."

The guard gives me a snide smile. "Of course you are."

"It is a matter of utmost importance. She is expecting me. Please!"

"I don't know nothing about it, lady."

But before I can renew my plea I am crushed onto the iron fence by the demonstrators, Green partisans shouting, "Burn, Blues, burn in hell/Greens rule everywhere!" Even the women, rough types I remember from my time near the Hippodrome, join in with the jeering and insults. Someone heaves a rotten persimmon at the palace walls and it hits hard, leaving a blood-red clot on the stone.

The guard reaches through the fence, grabs the man with the fruit and pulls him up against the iron. "We'll have no more of that or you'll have some of this." He pulls a sword out and lays it across the man's chest. The crowd screams as one and for the moment, falls back.

Throughout the afternoon more guards appear as the crowd increases in size and noise. Now the group bellows to free the prisoners, then screams threats if they are not released. My voice cannot even be heard over the din. Thirsty and near exhaustion from calling to the guards, I squeeze out of the angry pack and reel down the nearly deserted central avenue to reach home before Licinius, if he returns at all.

I arrive home to find he has returned, along with some of his men, who lay sprawled in the atrium garden. Octavian and Serena rush about with pitchers of wine and bowls of olives, bread, and fruit.

I slip into my weaving room, but not before Licinius snarls his greeting. "Wife! Where in the name of the saints have you been?"

"At the market, husband, trying to find some meat for supper!" My throat is so raw from calling to the palace guards I can scarcely speak.

"A waste of time, silly woman. There will be no fresh food until this sorry mess is over."

He returns to his comrades, who laugh and chat as if nothing was going wrong. I wonder if they even realize what a terrible danger they are fueling, for us and for the city they are sworn to protect.

. . .

All night there is shouting, now in the streets, later from the rooftops. Then at daybreak, an uneasy peace, like the dead silence before a great summer storm off the Bosphorus, falls over the city. Justinian's men must be out now. I steal through the back alleys, picking my way among broken roof tiles and small fires set by smashed oil lamps. Byzantium has not slept, nor did it ever intend to: Today is race day.

Perhaps there is still time. Perhaps the crowds at the palace have dispersed. Wrapped up against the gray and cold, I nearly run down the Mese to the Augusteum. The streets are strewn with broken glass, oil, and bricks; graffiti jumps out everywhere. "Slut Queen of the Blues" one proclaims next to a drawing of the naked Theodora on her back. "Send the Greens back to hell!" another. Still another demands, "Shipwreck Justinian!" Small shops have been vandalized, cobbles torn from the street and used as projectiles; in this quarter, only the charming Church of Saint Irene has escaped damage.

The closer I get to the Augusteum, the thicker the crowds become. I fall in with their step and am soon embedded in the mass. Most seem to be heading to the stadium and by the time I reach the palace square, I am virtually alone. A guard sits half-asleep at the gate. I rouse him, tell him I have a message for Theodora.

The man scratches his beard, appraises me. "Now why would Theodora want to hear from you?"

"Because I am one of her city watchers, enlisted to give her news on the demes. Elena, wife of Eudaemon's top man, Licinius."

"You got an appointment?"

"Sir, this is of utmost importance to Theodora and the city. Please, let me in to do the job the empress asked me to do."

"All right." He grimaces. "Wait here while I check on it."

He disappears behind the great bronze doors of the palace courtyard. I wait for some time but he never returns.

I turn back toward the Hippodrome. All I can do now is tell Dakis I tried. As I run I feel tears on my face, for my failure and for our city-under-siege.

Once inside the stables of the Greens, I hurry around corners, nearly colliding with corporation officials dressed in velvets and jewels, and busy young grooms, rushing to finish polishing tack.

Finally I see Dakis dressed in the uniform of the Chariot Greens: pale green tunic, greaves, and rib bracings of hide. The moment he sees me, he takes my arm, pulls me into a stall.

"What of Theodora?" he whispers.

Great tears course down my cheeks as I tell him the futility of my efforts, and the inevitable chaos to come. "The guards, they thought me an assassin; I could not get past them." I weep and try to talk in great gulps.

He takes a deep breath. "We will handle it," he says.

"But—" I choke.

"Elena." He smiles to me. "The Hippo is about the contest, on the track and in the stands."

A trumpet sounds. He looks toward the direction of the track. "We charioteers know how to handle things. If we ask for silence, there will be silence. If we petition the emperor, he will listen. That is the call for the Pompa. There is still space near the wall of the stables for you to sit and watch the races, if you wish, but I must go now." He starts down the arcade.

I hear a voice, my voice, crying out, "I am afraid I will never see you again!"

He stops mid-pace, turns and walks back to me. For a moment that seems like forever we stand motionless, staring at each other's faces. Then, he pulls me to him. His lips touch mine and our kiss becomes strong and real as his hands hold me against the wall. His sinews, bones and flesh press against me, enveloping me in warmth. I hold to him, never wanting to let go. A second trumpet sounds. He stands back, stares down at me, touches his fingers to my lips. Then, he reaches for his helmet and walks toward the track.

As I watch him walk into the light patch swelling through a doorway followed by the stable boy, I see his charioteer's knife, the one instrument that might cut him free from a shipwreck of chariots and perhaps save his life—the knife he had put down when he brought me inside, now forgotten on a small table nearby. I pick it up, run after him, calling "Dakis!" but I am too late: He is already out on the track, easing his car toward the starting line. I back into the darkness of the stables. Then I hurry out to the entrance to the stands and squeeze myself onto the stone bench in the shade against the southeast wall where I hope I will not be noticed, for women are banned from viewing the sport.

The stadium, overflowing with men from all corners of the world, is an extraordinary sight. Every spot that can serve as a seat is taken, benches, parapets, even plinths. The pre-race Pompa, that had opened with a parade of exotic animals, pantomimes, acrobats, dancers, and musicians, now comes to a close with the processional of demarchoi, notarii, factionarii, judges, and finally, the charioteers themselves, waving to their hysterical fans from their cars of blue, green, red, and white, led by proud, elegant teams of horses as idolized as the drivers.

Finally, I see Dakis cross into the circus to the adoring calls of a large contingent of Alexandrian fans near me. As I watch him take his team of white Arabians around the course I say a silent prayer: *Dear God, keep him safe from harm that we may meet again.*

The trumpet sounds the monarch's standard, Justinian enters the kathisma and greets his subjects with the sign of the cross, the first charioteers draw lots from the big bronze hopper and take their places in the traps. The steward of the race, standing forward in the kathisma, pauses. The stadium goes still as death. The white square flutters down from the emperor's hand.

The teams explode out of the traps and the Hippodrome goes mad. Pigeons on the spina fly up in a frenzy. Every man in the arena jumps to his feet, stamping, shouting, cursing, screaming. The clamor of the crowd and the roiling of the horses' hooves as they round the ends of the spina, spurred on by their drivers, reins wrapped around their waists, whips in hand, is bone-shattering. The track dissolves into a storm of dust from which emerge the leaders pushing their left lead horses as close as possible around the ends of the spina so as to graze it with their hooves.

Again and again the teams round the spina, chariot wheels just far enough apart to avert a shipwreck, drivers shouting to their teams, coaches on the sidelines urging them on, yelling warnings above the pandemonium in the stands.

Seven laps without an accident, and a victory for the Greens, who erupt in glee.

The track is watered, the crowd settles somewhat and the second race is called. But before the drivers can take their places, a demarch, a Green, rises from his seat on the southwestern end of the great stadium to address the emperor.

"Thrice August Emperor Justinian," be begins, "with the greatest respect due your eminence, and honoring your position as God's vice-regent on earth, we humbly beg you to free the two men now held at the Church of Saint Laurentius, two men whom God Himself has seen fit to release from the fate of death. May your compassionate wisdom continue to lead our great empire and worthy citizens." The demarch bows. But the emperor, as if having heard nothing, simply turns to speak to one of his advisors, then looks straight ahead, awaiting the next race.

The demarch bows again and returns to his seat. The second race is run, won by a Bithynian driving for the Blues who, in turn, explode with hysterics. When the din fades, a Blue supporter, standing on his seat, addresses the emperor on behalf of the Blues, renewing the plea of the first demarch. Again the emperor is unmoved, mute, as if unaware even of the petitioner's presence.

Nineteen more races are run, none with serious injury to horse or driver, and in all either a charioteer or citizen spectator implores the emperor to release the prisoners. As the afternoon wears on, the pleas begin to include requests for the emperor to remove from office John of Cappadocia, Tribonian, and Eudaemon. The emperor remains silent.

And at each silence, the crowd grows more livid.

Finally the twenty-second race is called, and the sea-green chariot emerges from the stables: Dakis. As each team for the race is introduced, the drivers push their horses forward.

"Dakis Amianus, winner of over two hundred races in his native city of Alexandria, a driver in the tradition of the great Porphyrius Calliopas!" At the mention of the most famed charioteer in the empire, and seeing Dakis' splendid team, the Green fans erupt again, stamping their feet in unison and yelling across to the Blues.

Dakis bows gracefully in acknowledgement. But instead of returning to his position at the starting line, he draws his team forward until he is standing before the kathisma on the opposite side of the track.

The stadium settles so completely I can hear the rasp of a man coughing in the U-shaped Sphendome at the other end of the track. Dakis removes his helmet, looks up toward the emperor's box and speaks:

"Thrice August Emperor, whom we know to be God's vice-regent on earth and patron of this, the most holy city of the Roman Empire, as one, we, the Humane Blues and Greens, who seek peace with one another and peace for our great city, humbly petition you to release the two prisoners now held hostage at the Church of Saint Laurentius, men we believe to be innocent of crimes, as evidence by our Lord's deliverance of them from death at the hands of their human executioner. We also, great Justinian, petition for the removal of the men who, we believe, have been the cause of this extreme condemnation, and of the hunger and turmoil we suffer in the streets: City Prefect Eudaemon, Counsel Tribonian, and John the Cappadocian. Great Justinian, we wish you a long and glorious reign, with victory over the enemies of the empire and continued compassion for its citizens herein."

Now the only sound that can be heard in the Hippodrome is that of Dakis' team, slowly returning to the starting mark. But just as he reaches the place where I am seated, he slows the quadriga and comes to a halt. Holding the ends of the reins with one hand, he looks up. Then, just as he did that first day we saw one another, he once again touches his hand to his heart, then reaches it out to me.

I can feel all the eyes in the arena turn from the kathisma to my direction here in the shadows of the stables. Tears fill my heart as I bow my head. Dakis' team, smelling the race, pulls on its harness and stamps in the dirt. I start to stand, to acknowledge Dakis' salute.

But before I am off my seat, a voice, a single voice, rises from the southern end of the stadium. All eyes shift that direction. A bearded man in a gray wool tunic, a Green, stands and shouts "Long Live the Humane Blues and Greens!"

The words of the declaration ricochet off the stone. I see Dakis trying to hold his team steady as he searches for the origin of the cry. His horses back up, ears flattening in fear.

For a single long moment, the stadium is completely still. Then another voice shouts the same as the first, then another, and another, until the crowd becomes one booming, rolling voice, shouting louder and louder, vibrating the stone supports under our feet.

"Long Live the Humane Blues and Greens!"

"Long Live the Humane Blues and Greens!"

"Long Live the Humane Blues and Greens!"

Men all around me stand. Some stab their fists into the air, others scream in fury and the screaming becomes a war cry:

"Nika! Nika! Nika!" *Win! Win! Win!*

In an instant, a desperate citizenry transmutes into an angry horde. As if by instinct, I crouch for protection against the human swarm cascading down the benches above me, spilling over the parapet, bursting onto the track below.

I look up to see Dakis hoisted reluctantly onto the shoulders of two Hunnish demes bolting for the western gate. Then I see his team, un-hitched by someone, racing for the safety of the stables. A guard appears, tugs my sleeve, urging me away from the chaos. But I pull my arm away and, frantic now, run down onto the track, against the wave of Byzantines surging toward the gate and out onto the streets of the city.

"Dakis!" I scream as I see him held over the frenzy, his tunic being torn by a Blue. He reaches a hand out to me. I try to reach him, but am pitched back to the wall by the force of the mob. My head hits the stone. Everything goes dark.

It is not long before I regain consciousness, but by now, the arena has almost emptied. I feel smoke burning in my nostrils, hear more shouts outside the Hippodrome. When my vision clears enough, I find my way onto the track. A piece of green wool catches my eye, Dakis' tunic. But he is nowhere to be seen.

. . .

The riots boil over, ignited by the Hunnish demes, fed by the emperor's indifference to the calls of the common citizenry for mercy, civic order, and bread. Justinian, hoping to distract the population from their anger, wished to renew the races the following day, January 14. But the crowd's blood was up; they had no further interest in the races and, in fact, used the Hippodrome as their citizen platform for several days, demanding the palace surrender and crowning their own "new emperor," a relative of the emperor drafted reluctantly by the group and later executed by Justinian.

At last, on the fifth day after the races the emperor and empress, prisoners in their own palace, agree to the citizen's demands and release the two prisoners, then remove the hated Eudaemon, John of Cappadocia, and Tribonian temporarily from their respective offices.

By then, it is too late for our city. Gone are the Senate House, the Baths at Zeuxippus. Gone are the Church of the Holy Peace, the Church of Saint Theodore Sphoracius, the Church of Saint Elena, the hospitals of Eubulus and Samson, and the irreplaceable Baths of Alexander. All broken, burned or destroyed in the name of justice. Gone even are the cherished relics of our faith, which preaches peace and forbearance, taken from the hands of the monks of the Church of the Holy Wisdom and smashed to bits by Justinian's commandant Belisarius and his northern Goths. The magnificent basilica had burned from the inside out, then collapsed in on itself from all four sides.

Gone, too, are 30,000 souls, many of them Humane Blues and Greens, who returned to the Hippodrome to rally for the freedom of the two prisoners, and for the liberation of this splendid city from the tyranny of the few, slaughtered by the hand of Belisarius and his henchman Mundas and his tribe of mercenaries, between the western gate and the Nekra gate, the last path of mortally wounded charioteers. I know these things because I am a witness, having searched in vain the field of dead and dying fellow Byzantines, the blackened streets, and the churches on both sides of the Golden Horn for Dakis Amianus, the charioteer.

. . .

Three days after the races a ragged, half-starved boy comes to my door. Fearing the rampage in the streets he had taken cover in a basement since the Sunday night of the botched hangings. He stutters out a message, "D-D-Dakis, he says to m-m-meet you in the stables of the Green on the palace side of the Hippodrome the day before the races."

And without ever having received Dakis' message, that is what I had done. The day before the races; the day before Dakis was carried away by the mob.

I feed the poor little waif and give him a blanket and a warm place to rest in a quiet corner at the back of the house. But when I return to check on him before the evening meal, he is gone.

. . .

I live alone now. Soon after the Nika Revolt, as it is now known, Theodora seized greater power and with that, enacted reforms, many to women's benefit. My marriage to Licinius declared null on grounds of un-Christian cruelty, I cherish the quiet of my small rooms in the Pittakia district. I have become expert at dyeing and weaving silks, especially the story-telling brocades so sought-after by patricians these days.

The much-loved chariot races are now a thing of the past. Justinian cancelled any further racing after those terrible days of fire and bloodshed, and the contests have never been held again. Byzantium is a safer place now, and the great arena is, but for government spectacles, quiet.

Many evenings after I have finished at my workshop, I return home and, lighting the lamp at my table, take my favorite piece of fabric from the cedar box where I keep it always hidden, away from the eyes of the world. It is just a shred, a frayed bit of tear-stained, sea-green wool. My most precious possession, treasured emblem of my beautiful moments with Dakis, the Charioteer, whose soul I pray for every night.

SIX

Emily

October 1-25, 2003

By early October, Curt and I were seeing each other at least three days a week and talking daily on the phone, or at least e-mailing. It wasn't just the physical attraction, it was that he seemed to like so many of the things I did: Radiohead, historical mysteries, biography, '50s Westerns, art house indie films, tennis, baseball. And now I had no doubt about my feeling for him: I knew for sure it was love.

We made our reservations for Baja, a vacation now extended to five days, with a side trip over to Mazatlan, for the end of the month. I'd already started assembling a few resort clothes at one end of the closet, located my passport, and pulled my suitcase from the hall closet.

One morning he called and suggested we play tennis, since we both enjoyed it so much. The weather was lovely and the courts on the bluffs empty, but we had to give up after less than an hour, laughing ourselves silly after we came to the mutual conclusion that the disparity in our heights made it almost impossible to put a rally together.

As we were packing up to leave the courts, I thought of something that had been bothering me and asked, "I was just wondering, when are you going to invite me over to your place?"

I thought I saw shock in his face. Then he said, "I know. It's just that, my place, it's not really too put together yet and, well, it's such a mess most of the time. I'd be embarrassed to have you see it. I know; I should get a cleaning service." He hung his head and looked guilty.

Having a brother, and knowing a bit about bachelors, I shook my head and teased, "Well, maybe I can help you do something about that sometime."

"For now," he said, "I need a smoothie. You shorties move so fast you wear me out!"

I nudged him in the ribs, he made an exaggerated grimace of pain and we walked off the court holding hands.

We had lunch together at my place, then lay around on the sofa; him tickling me, and me teasing him back. Just like Nick and I used to do.

"Cabo will be romantic." I kissed his nose and his mouth.

"Very . . ." he whispered back, kissing my cheek. His lips were so soft on my skin.

. . .

Not until late the next morning did I discover that he'd left his cell on my kitchen counter, where he'd taken a call while I fixed lunch. I thought to call him about it when I remembered the only number I'd ever had for him was his cell. I opened it and scrolled to the addresses. There it was, right up top: "Home/Hardline." Oddly, it looked like a Brentwood prefix. I hit the number, expecting a message.

"Hello?" a woman answered.

"Hi," I said. "Is this Curt's home number?"

"It is," the professional-sounding voice responded.

"My name is Emily. I'm a friend of Curt's. Are you by chance with the cleaning service?"

"The what? This is his girlfriend, Diane."

The blood in my head plunged like an avalanche into my stomach.

"Hello?" she said.

"I'm…sorry," I said. The kitchen was spinning. I braced myself against the counter. "I've been, uh, dating Curt for a month and a half."

From the other end of the line, silence. Then, after a tired sigh, "Curt. Oh, no."

"I think he'll be wanting his phone, " I heard my voice say.

"Where are you?" she asked, then gave me her address and said she'd wait for me there.

I stumbled into the bathroom, threw up what was left of my breakfast and stood for long minutes with my head against the cool glass of the shower door. Then, somehow, I managed to get myself cleaned up, found the car keys, and pulled myself together enough to drive.

· · ·

Curt, it turned out, did not live in a messy flat in Santa Monica, but in a classic twenties bungalow with a pretty gated entrance and well-tended garden in Brentwood.

A woman who looked to be in her late thirties, perhaps six or seven years older than Curt, answered the door. She was tall and elegant, dressed in an expensive wool suit. She extended a manicured hand to me, smiled a wan but gracious smile and said in a modulated tone, "I'm Diane. You must be Emily?"

We talked for about half an hour. She was an attorney with a big downtown L.A. law firm and had stopped by home today, of all days, after taking a deposition in Santa Monica. She had met Curt at a party three years ago, right after he had arrived from the Midwest. Yes, he was an actor. She supported him while he took classes and read for parts. This was her house. They'd been living together for a little over two-and-a-half years, and were planning to marry early next year. His parents, as far as she knew, were perfectly healthy and living in Tucson. Almost everything he had told me about his life had been a complete lie.

"I'm terribly sorry about this mix-up," she said as I stood to leave.

Mix-up. Somehow I managed to hold the tears back as I answered, "Me, too."

I drove home blurry-eyed, climbed back into my bed and rocked back and forth in a daze.

What had I done to deserve to have my happiness with Nick taken from me at the eve of its celebration? Then, when I most needed understanding, to be lied to, and by someone as callow as Curt? What did the world want? Need? To punish me? To destroy me? I walked into the kitchen, poured myself a drink, took a couple of pills and curled up in bed until late afternoon.

. . .

For weeks I'd barely maintained phone contact with any of my friends. But Margo had left two messages in the last three days and late the next morning I tried her number.

"Honey, quit trying to be so goddamned independent now, will you?" she scolded.

Backed into a corner, I told her about Curt, how he seemed like another Nick, how I'd let myself be used.

"Oh, my God, Emily. Oh, my God. Why didn't you tell me before?"

"Why do you think? Because I've been such an ass, that's why!" I slammed the phone into the cradle, washed down a Diazepam with another drink, then fell to my knees against the sofa pleading, "Help me. Oh Nick, please help me."

Margo was at my door in fifteen minutes. "Emily." She put her arms around me. "I've never heard of such a bastard. Even around here."

"Oh, I'll be all right," I said, disengaging myself, determined not to dump on her. "It was just … It was just stupid."

She followed me into the kitchen, where a half-gallon of cheap vodka sat on the counter next to a glass. She looked at it and the bottle of pills next to it, then led me out of the kitchen to my armchair in the living room and sat down on the coffee table facing me, folding my hands in hers.

"Emily, I think you need help. Not just from friends, from a professional."

I told her about the bereavement group. That I'd tried.

"It's just that … Well, obviously you wanted another Nick, naturally. And look what happened. You've got to work through your grief with someone who's expert at it. Let me find a counselor for you."

I told her I'd try to find help, that she didn't need to worry.

"What the hell do you mean, 'don't worry'? How can you say that to me after all our time together? Let me find someone for you to talk to. Agreed?"

All I could do was nod at my knees.

That evening Margo left the number of a therapist who had an office in Santa Monica canyon. But, too drunk and stoned to operate my phone correctly, I accidentally hit Erase instead of Replay. Then I fell into bed.

· · ·

My brother Michael came over the morning of the 12th on his way to work in Torrance. "If you don't start answering your e-mail or cell, I'm calling 911 on you," he joked.

I could hear the concern in his voice, see the frustration on his face. I hadn't talked to him for more than a week, since the last time he dropped by to check up on me. I told him that I'd been working, which was true.

What I didn't tell him was that the whole world seemed to be vaporizing around me as I watched. I also didn't tell him how much I drank, how many pills I consumed. Fortunately, the evidence was hidden away in the kitchen cabinet; I'd cleaned my place up after Margo had come over.

He and my sister-in-law Mindy were going home Friday and wanted me to come along. Our younger sister Sylvia would be down from Napa. I suddenly remembered Mom asking me to come up, and me forgetting.

"Mom's been so worried about you. How about it?"

It had been nearly ten weeks since Nick's funeral. I apologized, tried to explain that I'd felt no need for human company.

He stood there, not moving, letting all my excuses slide by.

"All right," I said, trying to smile.

"See?" He gave me his trademark bear hug. "Was that so tough? Five on Friday. I'll drive."

. . .

Michael and Mindy had a new car and Michael had fun weaving around SUVs on the curves of Pacific Coast Highway. Mindy scowled at him. He laughed, made a face, pinched her cheek and slowed down. But I knew my brother: He was putting on the act to cheer me up. He opened the sunroof and the aroma of our world blew in; salt air, chaparral, sticky-sweet exhaust. Sammie's Fabulous Fish was already jammed. Precious parking spaces at Spyglass Bistro were going fast. Late surfers at Surf Rider Beach were throwing hoodies on over their board shorts, packing up their Jeeps, laughing and talking in knots by the side of the road.

Traffic cleared. We flew past the sedate Getty, the Bel-Air Bay Club, Malibu Colony. Brown pelicans skimmed above the waves single-file, gliding northward. I watched the tide going out, leaving the sands to reflect the layered colors of the evening sky. The end of the world, where Nick and I had tried to join our love as one. Where our relationship had been smashed, like waves flinging shells to fragments on the beach below.

As the sky turned teal, Michael flicked on the headlight, the control panel, and a jazz station. Hadn't Nick once said he liked "Stella by Starlight"? I tried to remember a time or a place we'd heard it together. Then I dozed, wishing for sleep, and a dream of him.

"Port Why-neemee!" Michael called out. I sat up, rubbed my eyes, dug into my bag for a mirror and comb. I hoped Mother would not be as distressed at the way I looked as I think Michael and Mindy were. On top of my misery and alienation, for the first time in years, my skin had broken out, as if my sins had caught up with me, as if I'd turned into my own Dorian Gray. And I'd lost weight, ten pounds since the funeral. Nick would be upset. "Women are supposed to be soft!" he'd always said, usually after standing in line behind an overly tanned gym specimen at the deli.

Padaro Lane. And then the scent of avocado and orange trees as we wound our way up Toro Canyon. Past the Miller's and Ulysses-the-dog, a shepherd/St. Bernard mix barking and running so hard from his doghouse tie-out he threatened to pull the house down their driveway behind him. Then up our gravel drive past the funny wooden cutout in the shape of a sheep, on which Michael had painted, when he'd had a 4-H project as a child, "Ewe's here!"

The old white ranch house stood in the middle of what was left of grandfather's original property, just thirty-five acres now, since Dad had sold the original hundred off in parcels to contractors. "As long as it's not tract homes, let them build," he'd said. I could see those new custom homes up the hill now, stucco and plaster, fireproof roofs, solar lighting meandering up their estate drives.

"Is that Mom's fabulous beef stew I smell?" Michael called out.

The three of us humped up the steps with our duffels and into the living room. Sylvia popped her head around the kitchen corner. "Hey, you!"

"Hey, kid!" Michael lifted her up and whirled her around him.

A slender, dark-haired fellow wearing thick-rimmed black glasses and a neatly trimmed goatee emerged quietly from the kitchen behind Sylvia. She introduced him as Adam.

So Sylvia had someone special. Adam put his arm casually around her shoulders and she looked up at him adoringly. I tried my best to smile.

Mom, arms outstretched to us, came running down the hallway. "Oh, oh, oh! At last!" Mother hugged and kissed me, then planted kisses on Michael and Mindy's cheeks. "All my chicks back in the nest!"

Dad was already over in the pantry bar. "I've got some of that Rolling Hills Chardonnay you liked, Em."

"That's okay, Dad." I picked a highball glass off the shelf, dropped two small cubes into it, filled it three-quarters with gin and pitched a cocktail onion on top.

My parents exchanged a shocked look. They had, to my knowledge, never seen me drink hard liquor.

"My doctor says martinis are actually good for us." Dad smiled at me kindly as he poured wine into the other glasses.

"Before I leave, Dad, could I get your doc's number?" Michael asked from the other side of the room.

It was too obvious. The family had decided to be as cheerful as they could for me. I wondered if they'd had a confab about it, the way we'd done when the doctors had found the lump in one of Mom's lymph nodes and we waited for the biopsy report, each one of us determined to show an optimistic face for her no matter what the diagnosis.

Now I sat folded up in the Stickley armchair off to the side of the living room while everyone else talked. Nearly two-and-a-half months ago they had been ready for a wedding and instead we had all gone to a funeral. I guessed they wanted to ask me how I was doing, wanted to talk as a family about what I—we—had all lost, but the invisible shell around me had closed shut. And if I, of all people, couldn't talk about my loss, they couldn't talk for me.

Mom rescued the moment. "Em, could you help me with the table?" she asked, rising from her armchair.

An extra place had to be found to make the odd seven. I pulled the little kitchen Windsor from Mom's worktable and put it at the end for me. Then I counted the mats and silverware out, and filled the big Fiestaware pitcher with water, two tasks, fortunately, I had done for so many years at this house that I could perform them without thinking.

I picked at my dinner, even at the strawberry-rhubarb pie, known to be one of my favorites, while everyone else talked about wine country, farm prices, cars, and neighborhood gossip here and on the Westside.

"You're looking pretty thin," Mother said later as we were loading the dishwasher.

"I know."

"Can you stay up here for a few days?"

"No, I've got to work, Mom."

"Is it money? Because we have money if you need it, dear," she said, then added, "and at a time like this you can't be expected—"

"Everything's fine Mom, really," I said.

. . .

The next day we took Adam up into the hills to see the inside of Painted Cave. Under the play of our flashlights, constellations of anthropomorphs, splayed hands and fire wheels careened across the rock sky like our own primitive "Starry Night." But the place smelled of bats, and reminded me of shallow caves in Australia where aborigines secreted the wrapped mummies of their loved ones. The heat on the ledge was searing, but I shivered.

By mid-afternoon the wind, mild all morning, was blasting down the canyons toward the ocean with such wrath that we all took refuge in the house to drink lemonade; mine spiked surreptitiously with vodka. At these temperatures, even the beach would be unbearable, because of the crowds, if nothing else. I disappeared into my old bedroom and fell asleep instantly on top of the bedspread.

I woke to the sound of low voices in the hallway outside. Mother, saying, "I don't know what to do."

Then Michael. "Always wants to be strong . . ."

Mother. "A counselor?"

Then Father. "We can't force her. She just needs time to heal."

Footsteps echoed on the floor as the three retreated to the living room.

I dragged myself out of bed at 5:30 to find everyone getting ready for dinner out. It had gotten too windy to barbeque and we now had a reservation at La Paloma. I found my skirt and blouse at the bottom of my duffel, stepped into my cowboy boots, washed my face and ran a comb through my hair. Mother was right: My arms were getting bony, my formerly round cheeks skeletal, and my dimples, Nick's delight, long lost.

I forced myself to eat dinner, even tried to join in the conversation in my own detached way. But with the hot winds screaming through my brain, complete thoughts eluded me.

When we returned home, I was the first to turn in, and the last person to wake on Sunday morning.

Michael had a meeting on Monday to prepare for, so we left just before noon. Mother asked me to please check my e-mail more often, or answer my phone messages, and I promised I'd try. Either way, she said, she'd be down to see me soon.

Coast traffic was horrendous and it took us an extra hour just to reach Topanga Canyon Boulevard. The shoulder of the highway was littered with parked cars as the inland population fled the tandoori heat of the city. Radio reports estimated nearly one million beachgoers. The surf was dead flat. The horizon yellow as bile. It was weather like this that had sent the Chumash and Gabrielino of ancient times hurling themselves from the cliffs into the sea.

· · ·

Back home, I looked over the work I'd done on the tapes. Somehow I'd managed to transcribe two of the stories. But what did they mean? The only thing they seemed to have in common with each other was a man, a woman, and the color turquoise. It seemed I was at a dead end; my so-called "dig" had yielded nothing of any particular weight or meaning.

And so, having failed to uncover any message from the envelope's contents, even why it had my name on it, I yearned even more, if that were possible, for Nick, the real flesh-and-blood Nick, not the canned voice of the tapes. What did I have to live for now? My whole life was on a pyre.

I remembered the Fluoxetine I'd gotten weeks before in mid-September and began taking it in hopes it would improve my mood. Within several days I recovered a semblance of my former, normal sleep pattern. My dark mood lifted, too, and in its wake a passive calm descended over me. Soon after, however, I became lightheaded and disoriented. I kept taking the pills, anyway—at least they numbed the pain. Then, darkness closed in on me again, worse than ever, and with it, the lure to self-destruction.

For the next few days I survived mainly on a diet of vodka and Fluoxetine by day and downers by night. A few days later, I looked up a Web site that had info on suicide. Then, after the one, several. I was just researching, I told myself. I'd write an article on it.

How many ways were there to die? Suicide by hanging, drug cocktail, shotgun, even one story of a man who committed suicide by leaving his car engine idling in his sealed garage while writing in his journal. The last entry: "Breathing becoming difficult…"

Carbon monoxide poisoning, I learned, was immediately recognizable by the plethora of black bruises it left just under the skin. This was an exit method favored more by men. Women chose methods that would leave their bodies more or less untouched, as if they had simply fallen asleep. Like drugs.

I checked in the bathroom cabinet, wondering what I had left. Thirty Diazepam and, behind some Milk of Magnesia, an old vial of Oxycodone left over from my wisdom tooth extraction last year. I counted them out on the tile. Twelve, with an expiration date of 2005.

The phone on my desk went off like an alarm. Michael.

I cleared my throat and tried to speak up. "Oh, hello!"

"You sound better. How's it going?"

"I'm sleeping a bit. That helps. How about you guys?"

"Man, this heat's wicked. We're both working here today, so how's about you come over this afternoon and keep us company?"

I looked out my front window. Ten o'clock Thursday morning and the already-overcrowded beach at the mouth of the canyon looked like a nest of fire ants. A pool sounded good.

"Should I bring anything?"

I heard him cupping his hand over the phone as he yelled to Mindy.

He came back with, "Just you, sweetie!"

.   .   .

A couple of hours later I was diving into Michael's big freeform pool, swimming underwater, a figure in a post-modern collage, my body flickering square by torn square through the flashing deep.

Michael and Mindy looked amazed as I downed burger, chips, and juice with an appetite they had not seen the week before with the family.

We made small talk during lunch, but afterward Michael excused himself to the lounge chair by the jacuzzi and Mindy leaned forward and put her hand over mine. "How are you doing, really?"

I couldn't make eye contact. What was the best way out of this? "Oh, better, I guess."

"Because," she paused for a moment, "if you ever need someone to talk to . . ."

"Oh, thanks," I mumbled, "thanks, really. I'm okay."

"Just, you know, if you ever want to talk, I'm here."

The truth was, planning my own end had released me from my pain in a way nothing else had. Now it was as if I had shed an annoyingly heavy and useless backpack off to the side of a dusty trail hiking up a mountainside on a July afternoon. Especially now, I didn't want to, or need to, talk to anybody.

Mindy went to the kitchen and came back with more bottles of water.

"Two big fires down by Claremont," she said as she handed Michael and me each a bottle.

Although Michael cleared the brush around the property, the hills above his house were so dry they looked as if they'd explode into flames any minute just from the heat of the wind. Only a few years earlier, the Malibu fire had burned from the mountains to the sea, just north of here, incinerating everything in its path.

"We'll be okay," Michael said, readjusting his sunglasses, and himself, into the chair.

"Won't we, babe?" He reached his left hand down to scratch Lulu the Lab's ears.

"The Santa Anas make people do strange things," Mindy said. "Isn't that what they say here, Em?"

Mindy was from Oregon.

"People change. That's what Nick said," I replied.

· · ·

Back at home later that afternoon, I pulled out my little cache of pills and emptied them out onto the bathroom counter to inventory them again. Then I went back to the Internet.

Killing oneself, especially with drugs, was apparently more difficult than I'd first thought. Take too few, and you simply slept. Take too many at once, and your stomach summarily rejected them. Take the wrong ones, like acetaminophen, and you wound up existing on a dialysis machine, with ruined kidneys. If I were going to do this thing correctly, I needed a more reliable source than the Internet in order not to botch the job. I climbed into my car and headed over to the library.

I thought the librarian eyed me suspiciously as he ran the wand across the code strips of several books on the subject.

"Research," I said, putting on my sunglasses to hide my bloodshot eyes.

"Yeah." He smiled. "You don't look like the type."

What type did I look like? The jilted girlfriend? The failed actress channeling spirit entities? No. I was alone in my category: young woman whose life partner was killed days before their wedding.

I spent the night reading the books I'd checked out, reading more intensely than at any time since Nick's death. I couldn't sleep anyway, thinking about what I needed to do, and I didn't want to waste any of the pills. About three AM, I knew how I'd use them.

Naturally, everyone would know why I left. I just didn't want anyone who couldn't say good-bye to feel guilty, as if they hadn't done enough to recognize "the signs" in me. I wasn't angry at any of them.

The thing was, my life was already over. With Nick gone I had nothing to look forward to, no real reason to stay here now. And if I felt anything at all, it was anger at the so-called God who would take Nick from me at the zenith of my happiness. Well, okay. He'd get his Big God wish. I'd be gone. Off the earth. If my life didn't matter to such a ruthless god, it didn't matter to me, either.

Liv e-mailed the next morning. "Don't forget Friday!"

I had forgotten. I shoved the clothes on my closet rack over to one side and went over what little was clean. Black silk trousers and gray ruffled blouse. High-heeled mules. I wouldn't need a jacket. The weather being what it was, we might as well be trapped inside a chemist's glass retort.

. . .

By Thursday afternoon even more of Southern California was burning. New fires had broken out in Los Padres National Forest to the east and in Val Verde near the Santa Clarita oil fields in the north. The humidity was eight percent and falling. Dad called to say he could see the smoke from the Ventura County fires blowing out to sea. He asked how I was doing, told me half-jokingly that Mother was coming up to see me in a few days, whether I wanted her to visit or not.

By Friday, the world seemed actually to be ending around us. The winds moaned and wailed as they ripped around the corners of the building. New fires had broken out in Ventura County, the Baldy Fire had spread and the smoke from both seemed to be heading in our direction. To the south, Fallbrook was burning. And the heat storm showed no sign of abating.

Weather was turning to apocalypse.

At 5:30 PM I picked Liv up on 16th Street. I'd never told her about what happened with Curt and when she asked about him, I just said simply, "It didn't work out." At this point, there was nothing more to say, really. Besides, even if there had been, it was too hot to get into serious conversation about anything.

Normally, traffic going downtown from the Westside would have been light. But this evening, perhaps because of the concert and other events downtown, it was anything but. We inched the car along the melting asphalt for over an hour, and finally parked with just fifteen minutes to spare before the beginning of the program.

The new concert hall was a tribute to the city's dream of its future: matte steel panels several stories high, leaning, swooping, rising, and falling, simultaneously witty and graceful. Inside, the pipes of its fabulous organ grew upward organically, like living reeds on a lake shore.

I knew Liv was excited, and I tried to share in her excitement, but with the conditions outside, "Le Sacre du Printemps" seemed incongruous, discordant. However, when the orchestra slipped into the first bars of the new "Dharma at Big Sur" I found myself transported away from this ring of fire and into the misted cool of the northern forests. The eerie notes of the electric violin seemed to underscore the otherworldly moment.

I glanced at Liv; she caught my eye, and flashed one of her megawatt smiles back. For a time the music was lost to me as I considered my friend. No, I couldn't do it tonight, couldn't make her the last one to see me, leave her with even a hint of guilt that she had said or done anything to precipitate my action.

We went out after, to a little bistro downtown on 3rd Street, where I ordered not one dessert, but two, Tiramisu and crème caramel.

"You need those," Liv commented over her tea.

Back home, I shredded files, letters, and other documents. I wouldn't want anyone, like the coroner's office, to see, all except the tapes, notes, and transcriptions of Clare's stories. It was two AM before I climbed into my bed. I would have to remember to put fresh sheets on it tomorrow.

. . .

Saturday morning the whole world seemed in flames. The air outside singed the throat and eyes. Smoke plumes seemed to be drifting in from all directions. And if it was bad at the beach, it would be even worse inland. All the local channels had nonstop coverage, and it was all horribly familiar: homeowners standing on their roofs with garden hoses, traffic jams as others tried to escape down one-lane mountain roads, teenage girls pulling on terrified horses silhouetted against the flames as the conflagration raged behind them.

I found all this oddly validating for me in my last hours on earth. That the final days really were upon us. That I had heard the message. That I was doing the right thing.

Mimi-Ann was away with her daughter in Pasadena until late evening, so it was up to me to walk Fizzy. At sunset we followed the jogging path down the median of San Vicente under the big coral trees where I used to run, a place I had not been since before Nick's death.

Fizzy got not only her regular meal but half my steak that evening. I pulled her canister of kibble forward on the kitchen counter and wrote on it, "For Fizzy," filled two big mixing bowls with water, shook out her bed and put it in her favorite corner next to the sofa, then checked under and around the furniture for all her toys, which I placed inside her toy basket.

Fizzy sat in the middle of the living room floor, not going for a single toy, staring at me.

"Good girl, Fizzy."

She continued to stare.

"It's okay, Fizz. You like Mimi-Ann!"

I scratched her ears. Then I made sure the front door was unlocked. Fizzy lay down, put her head between her paws and, not taking her eyes from me, refused to move.

At eight PM I changed the sheets on the bed from the white cotton to the cream-colored linen. For the last time in my life, I showered and washed my hair. For the last time in my life, I brushed down that stubborn cowlick on my crown. I smoothed some moisturizer onto my face, brushed and flossed my teeth. I took Nick's chambray shirt out of the garment bag where I'd kept it, and buttoned it on, then slipped on a fresh pair of panties underneath. Then I wrote my note:

October 25, 2003

Please forgive me. It isn't about any of you, whether you gave me enough love or not, whether you listened. It's me, and the awful

emptiness of life without Nick. I count myself blessed to have had such
wonderful family and dear friends.

    Mimi-Ann, I know you will take good care of Fizzy. Her leash is
on the key rack in the kitchen.

Love, Emily

    · · ·

I had one more thing to see to. The tapes were in a shoebox in the corner.
The notes, hard copies of the stories, or what I thought were the stories,
sat in a jumble on top of the desk. I found a cardboard box full of travel
paraphernalia in the closet, emptied it out there, placed all the work,
notes, tapes, and Nick's notes, inside, folded the flaps down and taped
a message to the top: "Confidential/Medical Records." Maybe someone
else could make sense of Clare's strange stories.

    Back in the kitchen, vials of Diazepam, Oxycodone, and a sleep-in-
ducing anti-histamine sat on the counter. I picked Fizzy up, remembering the day I brought her home from the shelter, and held her close to
me. She cried like a puppy and polished my cheek with her soft little
tongue. I hugged her and her tail wagged under my arm. Then I kissed
her good-bye and set her down in her bed. She turned around three
times and settled in.

    At five-past-ten I poured a tumbler of vodka, toasted a slice of bread
and ate it in small bites as I began slowly sipping the alcohol. Then I
started with the pills. First a Diazepam, then an Oxycodone. Toast…
anti-histamine. A bit more of the alcohol, another bite of toast, another
Diazepam. And on. Within the half hour I started to feel sleepy so I stood
and put all the drug vials in my robe pocket, picked up the drink, and
went into the bedroom.

    The pills and vodka I placed on my nightstand. I took off my robe,
climbed into bed, then took two more pills, two more sips of vodka. I

picked up the framed photo of Nick I always kept on the nightstand, traced the lines of his face, his nose, his mouth. Then, holding the photo to my heart, I sank back into the pillows.

SEVEN

Clare/Omida

c. 970 A.D.
Kyoto, Japan

Now is the eighth day of the Ninth Lunar Month. Puffs of fog rise above the lake to mingle with the trees climbing the hillsides to the east. Cranes wing south in pairs and a maple leaf drifts silently to my feet. Soon winter will hide our garden with snow, and we ladies of the Nijo Shinden will wrap ourselves in quilted jackets and roll snowballs into great orbs where, in the fourth month, we had composed poems to honor the blossoming cherry.

"Did you see the princess this morning as her carriage passed by?" Myobisi gazes across the lake. "Her robes were most exquisite and worn in the perfect combination of colors, did you not think?"

I smile. She is so young, barely fifteen, so it is quite natural for her to be awed by the princess and life so near the Imperial Palace. How close her story is to mine: Lord Nichimaga of the powerful Sujiwara clan visiting her father, in this case, the provincial governor, requesting they send her with him as consort; her parents, flattered, knowing well what such a connection could mean to her family's future prestige. Watching her now as she sends fallen leaves across the water with her delicate fingers, I wonder how long it will be before she, too, will learn of court intrigue and betrayal in this pretty world that can keep no secrets.

"Yes, the princess was lovely this morning," I reply, "and I understand from her ladies that her robes for the festival banquet will be even more exquisite than last year." Rumor has it that Nichimaga no longer visits the princess' apartments; the princess, now age thirty-five and having already born Nichimaga two daughters and a son, lost much of her youthful appeal to him. Gossip within the ward hints that she now spends many long hours alone in her quarters playing melancholy chords on her koto.

As if reading my thoughts, Myobisi asks, "Has our master visited your cottage recently?"

"The visits of Lord Nichimaga are as unpredictable as the colors of the autumn leaves, but always welcome and memorable," I respond.

In truth, Nichimaga has not visited my apartments in over a fortnight. Tamura, Lady Rokujo's attendant, told my attendant, Mitsu, that he is in Settsu province on family business. The "family business" of late seems to add to the family's power over the emperor, who is now dangerously close to becoming a figurehead manipulated by the many-armed Sujiwaras. What next action by the family to show the emperor who is really holding the reins?

But perhaps Nichimaga is losing interest in me, too. I am lonely, having been removed from my family farm to Heian-Kyo, but in truth, during these long periods of terrible loneliness for even Nichimaga's presence, I have been imagining how different my life might have been had my parents not sent me with his retinue in Nara. Many days as I sit with only my thoughts for company, visions of an intriguing stranger, one who seems to have been with me all my life—as if I had dreamed him while yet in my mother's womb—well up from somewhere deep inside me.

Yet my blood grows cold at entertaining even the thought of another man. For I had never forgotten the hard set of Nichimaga's face as he left me at the shinden that first day, his palm resting casually on the curved sword, a weapon whose blade is so sharp it could neatly behead a man in the blink of an eye, as he explained what was expected of me.

"Madame?" Such distressing memories are dispelled by the gentle voice of my attendant Shosho. "A letter has just come for you from Lady Matsuko's messenger."

She hands me a knotted paper of pale green attached to the stem of a fir. It is a reminder of our outing this afternoon to the lower Kamo Shrine at the Hour of the Horse to present our offerings in honor of the upcoming Chrysanthemum Festival.

I excuse myself from Myobisi, herself spending the afternoon in robe-fitting, and return to my apartments to dress. The afternoon outing is sure to be a stylish pastime, with aristocrats from all the northeastern wards of the city parading in their most beautiful carriages.

To honor the flower the festival celebrates, I select a singlet of pale yellow and over it, two robes, the first in willow-green silk lined with cream, the second in orange and yellow silk brocade lined with burnt orange. Taking care that my sleeves are layered and extended correctly, I open my fan, itself a garden of chrysanthemums painted on silk, and present myself before my ladies for approval and adjustments.

Once my costume is complete, Shosho brushes my hair, lovingly tended for all my nineteen years, until it falls into a shining pool of its own waves beyond the hems of the robes. I know both attendants wish I would follow custom and shave my eyebrows away and blacken my teeth with walnut juice as other ladies do, but I have yet to succumb to extremes of fashion preferring, instead, to keep my face and body as natural-looking as I can.

• • •

When I arrive at Lady Matsuko's quarters in the Nine-Fold Enclosure, I hear her and Lady Hoshi laughing exuberantly behind the kicho in what sounds like a game of Rango, first one player, then the other, balancing Gō stones on her first finger until the stack topples and bounces across the planks like pieces of a broken vase. The ladies-in-waiting scurry about, giggling merrily as they retrieve the playing pieces.

I enter as noiselessly as possible for as second guest my position is to be that of detached calm.

"Omida! You look especially beautiful today!" calls Lady Matsuko with her usual cheer.

> *Like the most delicate maple leaf of autumn*
> *She floats weightlessly on palace waters*
> *To arrive at our welcoming shore,*

—says Hoshi, who is renowned for her poetry, which has won the day in many poetry competitions and earned her much praise at court.

Bowing deeply, I respond:

> *The winds of the season do in their grace*
> *Give me the extreme fortune of such pleasant harbor*
> *And most elegant companions.*

"Ahh, bravo!" says Hoshi, and they both laugh.

Soon we are seated on our rush mats behind the blinds in Lady Matsuko's brocaded palm leaf carriage drawn by a white ox so outsized he looks like some beast brought to life from a child's fairytale. Lady Matsuko, perhaps feeling playful, dangles a good length of her ten sleeves, layered each so her arm appears as a many-colored banner rippling from the window as the cart rocks forward and sways out onto the broad expanse of Suzaku-Oji.

We quickly find ourselves embedded in a jam of oxen and carts many, like ours, filled with happy parties of aristocratic ladies also displaying rainbows of silk sleeves from behind their carriage shutters. As Lady Matsuko and Lady Hoshi laugh over a cat-and-mouse story circulating around the palace, I take in every aspect of the grand spectacle before me.

The famous willows that line either side of the great avenue glow like gold in the afternoon sun. The oxen bellow to one another as the passengers, recognizing one another's carriages, wave fans in hello from behind their bamboo screens. On the walkways, merchants from the seventh ward, hurrying about with their wares, pause to bow greetings to one another. A small group of women in very bright robes and garish makeup laugh together in a doorway. I abandon myself to the delightful afternoon, and to the cooling breeze falling down the mountain slopes toward the city.

Lulled by the peace of the moment, I lean back against the carriage, only to be yanked back to reality: Someone ahead of the cart is shouting, and an argument begins. Apparently our driver, in attempting to maneuver our cart into a better position for viewing the goings-on of the street, has caused our ox to butt heads with another ox and the two drivers are now deep into a "carriage quarrel," a potentially embarrassing situation that happens occasionally here, especially when Suzaku-Oji is as crowded as it is today.

Lady Matsuko, the smile now faded from her pretty round face, peers out the screen, perturbed and with good reason: Neither of the two drivers show any intention of backing down. Nor, apparently, do the oxen, who now look, from my vantage point nearer the front of the carriage, to be digging in against each other.

The clamor of the driver's disagreement is attracting attention all over the street, and my two companions hide behind their fans uncertain as to what, if anything, to do. It is at that exact instant that I notice a gentleman about my age striding confidently from the corner of Shino no Oji toward our cart.

What an astonishing figure he is! Taller than most, and dressed in the vermillion robes that suggest a high position in the government. It is all I can do not to tear aside the blinds to peer out the window for, as the sunlight breaks through the arriving clouds I am struck dumb, because this stranger bears an amazing resemblance to the man who has floated up in my dreams since childhood.

I watch as he puts his hand on our driver's shoulder, then the other's. A few words, some help with the beasts, and the argument is settled. Our cart continues on its way as I strain to see which direction he is going.

My companions eyes turn to me. In a world of subtle gestures such as ours, they have been quick, despite the distraction of the quarrel, to notice my agitation and attempt themselves to see what has captured my attention.

"Omida, I think you are enchanted!" Lady Hoshi says, laughing as she attempts to peer out my side of the carriage.

"Was it that young man? Oh, she is blushing!" Lady Matsuko cries in delight.

For a moment I think to tell them my thoughts of the gentleman, then think better. Gossip races through the First Ward like fire and, once started, any rumor, however innocent, is difficult to stop. Sometimes it even grows dangerous.

"It is the two oxen, so amusing despite the little tiff!"

As my two friends return to their conversation about the festival banquet, who would be wearing what, who would be seated in the most prestigious positions, I ponder the possibility that the young man I have just seen might be employed in service to the emperor. After all, his manner of dress would indicate Fifth Rank or above.

I am still reflecting on him when, after a time, the carriage comes to an abrupt halt, sending the three of us laughing and crashing into each other in a heap of silks and fallen combs. As we reassemble one another, the driver and attendants jump to the front of the cart to unhook the ox from the reins and open the front of the carriage to help us down.

How perfect the shrine seems this afternoon with its red columns standing out against the white sand where lie translucent maple leaves of many colors, radiant from the night's rains. The Lower Shrine has many visitors today, mostly men, though I notice several women in small groups sequestered behind large fans and shielded by escorts.

Having brought an offering of chrysanthemums from the shinden garden, I bow in prayer for the harvest, and for happiness in love despite the saying that the Month of Long Nights is said to be an inauspicious time for romance. Lady Matsuko ties a prayer wish onto the sakaki tree and as I tie my own wish, I notice nearby a note that looks familiar. I separate its damp folds gingerly and laugh when I read it: It is one of my own notes wetted from the night's rain, a wish for love tied to the same branch of the same tree at the Festival of the Weaver Star but two months earlier.

Laughing at my own superstition, I turn to leave but instead freeze like a startled hare in the winter grass for there, to my utter astonishment, is the gentleman who resolved our carriage quarrel earlier, standing next to one of the pillars at the shrine. He too is placing an offering of chrysanthemum blossoms, his of lavender and yellow. Since my companions and our attendants now stand with their backs to me, I am able to observe the stranger from my distance and to relish every extraordinary detail of his figure, from his amber skin, so different from other men who cultivate a whitish pallor, to his shimmering brocade robe, so exquisitely cut and dyed.

He rises to stand and our eyes meet over the top of my fan. Had I not known better, I would have thought I saw a glimmer of cool green, green like a pond reflecting the summer sky, in his eyes; eyes that now seem to dance with happiness, as if in recognition of me, though he could not have seen me before. As if by instinct, my hands lower my fan, revealing my full countenance to him. It is an outrageously impudent thing to do but he reciprocates by coming toward me.

Quaking from fear he will speak to me, I attempt to back away. But as I do so, my foot slips from my clog. I lose my balance completely, my fan flies, and I tumble to the ground, entangled in my voluminous robes.

Now the mysterious man hurries quickly to me. Without taking his eyes from mine, he bends down and helps me to stand. His incense is delicious, a warm and spicy scent not unlike those just discovered in the mysterious West. His touch brands my arms with heat. As I stand petrified, he reaches down for the lost fan. Brushing the sand from its pleats and closing it with care, he caresses its delicate ribs lovingly then, opening my hand with his hardened fingers, he places the fan into my palm and wraps my fingers around it. Then, bowing deeply, he departs.

Before I know exactly what has happened, one of our attendants appears at my side to escort me back to the carriage. I worry he might have noticed the untoward exchange between the mysterious gentleman and me, but his composure reveals nothing. Before returning to the carriage, I regain enough composure to remember to pluck a small cedar seedling from the ground, a tradition at the shrine for luck in one's prayers. But as I do so I see Tonaga, of the Sachio clan, a shadowy figure in the Sujiwara's ever-vigilant clique, following my movements from behind a tall lantern nearby—the same man who watched me on the palace grounds when I visited several days ago. A spy for Nichimaga? His brothers keep a number of watchers in their employ.

· · ·

Evening at my cottage seems more beautiful than I ever remember, with just enough of summer's warmth still in the air to make lounging on my veranda exceptionally pleasant. As I meditate on the events of the day, the melancholy cry of the hart seeking after her mate drifts across the garden. The harvest moon rises, filling up the dark sky and bathing the world in ivory light. Somehow the encounter at the shrine, however brief, has lightened my spirit. I call Shosho to bring me my inkstone and brush and, after a bit of thought, I write

Like a fir in the mists of a dream
My heart stays evergreen through all the seasons
To weather love's storms in every life.

His fragrance, those eyes, the touch of his hand as he enclosed the fan in mine…I stare at my own hand and imagine it reaching up to caress his cheek, then touch it as if his, to my own. Then, looking over the edge of the veranda to see the little seedling I had brought back from the Kamo Shrine, I say a little prayer to myself that I may be able to see the mysterious gentleman again.

A cloud pauses before the face of the moon. A wave of cold overtakes me. Sighing, I move inside to the chodai, where Mitsu lights my brazier against the night chill. Before retiring, I turn my robe inside out for luck in love. But my heart is restless, and I cannot sleep until much later, well into the Hour of the Rat.

I awaken late to the sounds of my attendants bustling about the apartments. Shosho peers behind the kicho. "Lady, we are preparing your robes for the Viewing of the Chrysanthemums at the palace. Would you prefer the gold brocade jacket or the mulberry beaten silk?" Mitsu brings me a bowl of rice with octopus. "As the Bureau of Divination predicted, the weather is perfect today, Lady Omida."

Robing for an occasion such as this, one of the year's most popular festivals, takes a particularly long time, for all elements must blend in the utmost harmony. Today, I will wear two singlets in different shades of yellow, a green-and-white trouser skirt, another unlined singlet of white, a robe in dark red over a robe of crimson and the mulberry brocade Chinese jacket. Mitsu brushes my hair until it reflects the sky. I choose a fan of gold silk bursting with layer upon layer of autumn flowers.

. . .

The gardens of the palace are indeed a dramatic sight today, especially in complement to the lively silks of the guests. I follow after Lady Matsuko and her maidservant, along with Myobisi, her serving girl, and my lady, Mitsu. The Imperial palanquin is a study in elegance, topped with a gilded phoenix, born aloft by costumed bearers and surrounded by no less than thirty men in matching court dress.

Nichimaga, having returned from what I am now told was on a pilgrimage to Hase Temple, strolls with several of the emperor's courtiers, again without the princess. As I catch his eye I bow a little bow, but he only glances in my direction and returns to his conversation. I retreat in humiliation behind my fan and the gaggle of ladies' attendants surrounding me, but my spirits are lifted almost immediately at the sight of the flowers. In the morning sunlight, the entire chrysanthemum garden radiates color, as if the scene on my fan had come to life.

As I discover only a short time later, the great hall of the palace, too, has surpassed the grandeur of last year's event. Painted silk panels hang from every wall, brocade cushions have been placed at proscribed intervals on the polished planking, each before its own table, for palace dignitaries, and low, silk-encased screens set off to one side form a gallery behind which invited ladies may view the ceremonies. A string of braziers burn here and there about the center of the hall, giving the cavernous room surprising cheer. The scent of the finest incense perfumes the air.

Late into the Hour of the Monkey the imperial party enters and, with a great rustling of robes, is seated behind the oversized screen on the dais. Then, in order of standing, invited guests and dignitaries of the Fifth Rank and higher file in. As each name is announced the courtier or official bows in the direction of the emperor, his son, and the royal household. One after the other chancellors, imperial advisors, administrators, and aristocrats take their places.

Sequestered as we are behind our low screen, we ladies are able to enjoy the spectacle without concern for appearances, and take every opportunity to comment to each other on the guests and any gossip pertaining to them. The Captain of the Inner Palace Guards is in attendance, as is his Excellency the Chancellor, a fine man of excellent repute, aristocrats of the Sachio, Shosirakawa, Nakiwara, Kiyowara, and Oye clans and, seated somewhat near the emperor's dais, Lord Nichimaga. Myobisi's eyes meet mine in a wordless exchange, as Lady Hoshi smiles and puts her fan to her lips. The grand procession continues in silence until all the guests are in their appointed positions.

The Assistant Minister of the Bureau of Books and Instruments stands to announce the start of the Gagaku and in moments the music begins; music that seems to come from another sphere, so ethereal are its harmonies. Then the dancers appear: the Tagyuraku, who enter from the left as if borne on the autumn winds, then the Hannari, the dancers of the right, richly attired in the colors of the forest and the sea.

The gracious notes of the pipes and kotos transport me into a state of light meditation. I remember my prayers at the shrine, the translucent beauty of the maple leaves on the luminous sands—and the intriguing gentleman who held me in his hands.

Just then, breaking through my reveries, the sound of a single flute reaches my ears. So beguiling are its notes, as if floating on the gossamer air like the lightest of autumn leaves, that I find myself leaning forward to discover which musician is performing the solo.

As fortune would have it, a stray thread on the sleeve of my robe catches the frame of the screen, moving it slightly forward, and revealing, for an instant, my countenance to the royal musicians. I am certain the sound of my sigh is heard by my attendants, indeed the entire retinue of ladies seated behind the screens, for there, in the midst of the musicians, playing the refrain from "The Singing Cicadas" is the appealing court gentleman I had seen twice before.

It is too late for me to try to hide and his head turns slightly toward my movement. For a brief moment he draws a breath, as if feigning an actual pause in the selection. Then, he continues to play. Is it my imagination or is one of his hands quivering slightly? I raise my fan over my face as Mitsu succeeds in pulling the screen back into its original position. I touch Lady Matsuko's sleeve.

"Lady, who is that gentleman? The flautist in the Imperial Consortium?"

"Why, my darling Omida," she whispers, holding her fan aside, "that is Yukio, the new Junior Assistant Director of the Imperial Stables who is also in the emperor's musicians ensemble." She slips me a furtive grin, one I return. "From Settsu, they say. The eldest son in a fine family. A singular man, do you not agree?"

Too soon, the music slows, fades, and the banquet is served: white trout and chrysanthemum wine for good luck and long life. Since any attempt to look past the screen would draw only more unwanted attention to me, I can only guess whether Yukio is still within. But from my vantage point I can see Nichimaga absorbed in conversation with one of the Kiyowara elders.

Although we are forbidden ever to look upon the emperor, his shadow behind the great screen signals to his attendants the beginning of the revelry, a night of drinking and carousing for the men, and a warning to the ladies of the gallery to take their leave. As we are led out, I make a discreet attempt to see if Yukio is still present but, in that all-too-brief moment, I sense another man nearby and turn to see Tonaga again, silently observing my movements.

Bonfires light our way across the palace grounds back to our carriages. The golden moon reflected in the lake, the heady fragrance of the burning pine resin, the strange and wonderful sense of the evening's ending as its beginning, and the song of the cicada fresh in my ears, all seem the ingredients of some magic potion brewed especially for my delight.

Later, after sitting in meditation in my room, I write

Like the brilliant leaves of autumn all are made to scatter
Who could dream beyond this world
We would live by love forever?

I lie awake for some time, thinking on the events of the evening. Somewhere near the Hour of the Ox the setting moon slides one last, low band of pale light under my screens just as the brazier, its embers crumbling, sends a final plume of silvered smoke up into the dark. I sigh and turn over.

Then, a sound. Not a sound from the hills, nor from an animal foraging in my garden, nor even from a sudden breeze. It is the song of a flute. It is "The Singing Cicadas." Nearer and nearer it comes. Then, it pauses, as if awaiting an answer.

I reach for my koto and begin the first notes of "The Lady in Hiding":

She stays alone in her darkened room
Quietly waiting the moon
Which gilds the willows that weep in the pond
As the fox slips away to his den

As I play the very last note, the flute responds with a favorite song at court, "The Joyful Crane":

The joyful crane delights
In love that comes again
And his cries float softly
Across the face of the moon

And then, utter silence, as if I had heard the music in a fleeting dream.

*   *   *

It is morning, and Mitsu is calling to me through the screens around the chodai. A letter has come, a most curious missive. Would I care to receive it?

Moments later she returns to present the "letter" to me. Her eyes are sparkling and, as I brush sleep away, I hear her and Shosho giggling on the other side of the screen. The "letter" is indeed unusual: a flute, tied with a page of fine, blue-green paper. Although I have heard of "gifts" I have never before received one, and I tear the knot open to read

> *Like cool raindrops on smoking autumn leaves*
> *Only the joys of love remembered and shared*
> *Can quench the flames of a burning heart*

I stroke the smooth bamboo of the flute, think of its music from Yukio's lips. Then I bury my face in the delicious fragrance of the paper. What shall I reply? Perhaps something simple, yet charming, a message he would reply to, but not one so strongly worded that he might be tempted to come to the shinden by the dark of night, as had happened with some consorts I heard rumors of in the past. I had Nichimaga's possessiveness to consider.

My response, in my best hand on a single sheet of my finest Michi-noku paper strikes the note I strive for

> *The fire that burns without a flame*
> *In darkness tells of deeper love within the heart*
> *Whose inner secrets must be so forever*

I tie the paper carefully and instruct Shosho to deliver it to Yukio at the palace. But as I watch her step down into the garden I see the pretty "aoi" heartvine, whose name means blue-green, just like the paper Yukio sent, blooming just below the veranda. I call to her to pluck a stalk and attach it to the note, my reply in kind to the beautifully presented gift of the flute.

How difficult it is to remain calm today while I await his response! Mitsu and Shosho, perhaps sensing my restlessness, suggest a game of Infutagi and we pass the rest of the afternoon trying to guess the missing Chinese characters from our favorite poems. But I am distracted, and today miss many guesses, giving Shosho the advantage and the win.

The Hour of the Monkey comes and goes without an answer to my letter. The sky clouds over and the gray turns to darkness. A terrible sadness envelopes me. Perhaps I have been mistaken about Yukio. Perhaps I have been foolish.

"Shosho," I ask, "are you certain you delivered my note into the hands of Yukio's man?"

"Yes, mistress."

"And did his man say anything about Yukio being away from the palace?"

"No, mistress. I asked exactly that question."

Mitsu lights my brazier and we dine on rice, seaweed, and gobi fish, one of my favorite meals. Later, the evening is mild enough for me to make myself comfortable behind the lattice shutters of my veranda. The preternatural stillness of my garden, its gold-tinged rushes, wild wisteria, and weeping willows; even the camphor tree, whose tangled branches are said to symbolize the intrigues of love, bring to mind *mono no aware*, the eternal sadness of beauty's passing and return. I remember Yukio, his strong hands, his incense of warm spice, and wonder if we will ever meet again. A gust of wind sends willow leaves floating into the pond.

Mitsu emerges from behind the inner screen. "Lady, would you care for your quilted rose coat? The wind brings with it many omens of sickness this time of year."

"Yes, Mitsu, please bring my coat." I am never ill, but my servant is right. In the Month of Long Nights, one cannot be too careful. I have ignored, carelessly, the priest's admonitions about my direction. South is a particularly unfortunate direction for me this month and I have been sitting facing south on my very own veranda.

The air grows heavy and still with its own weight, as if before a storm. I yawn and prepare for my sleep, then unroll the padded mat Shosho designed for me. In the beginning it had seemed strange not to sleep on a single grass mat as others customarily do, fully dressed in clothing. Within several nights, however, I had grown so comfortable with it that she designed another to place over my body. It is like the cocoon of a butterfly, yes, but also eliminates the need to retire in one's robes, which I now find confining. Tonight I remove all but one white silk singlet and slip into my unusual, but inviting, padded bed.

. . .

Flakes of silver moonlight spangle my room from the other side of the sky when I am awakened by the *shush* of the exterior lattice of the veranda sliding open, then the interior blinds. Past the kicho I see the moon, bright between the clouds, illuminate the silhouette of a man entering from the terrace. He kneels beside me.

A hand lightly covers my mouth as his fingers weave into my hair. Lips touch my cheek with the silken feel of the first spring blossom. The fragrance of sweet spices surrounds me and warm breath excites my ear with words meant only for me, "In the Month of Long Nights, this night will not be long enough."

"But," I whisper, "Yukio, if Nichimaga—"

"He is outside the city."

The reassurance in his words fuel the fever already spreading throughout my limbs. Now he turns me tenderly onto my back, his lips press to mine, and the taste of spiced plum touches my tongue. His hand slides slowly under the arm of my singlet onto my breast. My whole body seems poised between the earth and the moon as more kisses melt into my skin and smooth fingers explore my secret places. I run my hands through his hair, caught with an ornament at the nape of his neck, then push his robes back from his shoulders.

His head moves down, his lips touching my belly, my thighs, the backs of my knees, my feet, then return, to linger where my flower blooms. More than once I feel my wild senses rising beyond the stars, releasing, falling until I can speak, can move no more.

"Forever." My whisper escapes my lips like a vapor.

In answer, more kisses from his sweet lips, kisses everywhere, now urgent. And at the exact moment when our love can wait no more—

"Stand away!" a voice shouts outside the shutters. There is a violent crashing, followed by other angry voices and a pleading one, Henjo's, I think, as the outer screen slaps open and Nichimaga explodes into the room.

Yukio dives for his robe. I pull the coverlet over me. But before Yukio can even stand the bed-screen comes clattering down and Nichimaga charges at me, screaming, "You filthy whore!"

Three words cross my mind: *Tonaga, the spy.*

Mitsu and Shosho cower in the corner. Shosho starts to whimper.

Nichimaga, face powdered ghostly white, hair pulled sharply up like ox horns on his head, grabs my hair, pulls me to his face. His eyes, now dark slits under angry brows, burn black and red. Yukio rushes him, but Nichimaga's men, two of them, dart out from the shadows and catch Yukio between them.

Nichimaga tightens his grip on my hair, nearly pulling me off the floor completely. He slings me around by the arm and I scream as my ankle hits the brazier, sending sparks flying about the room. From the corner of my eye I catch Mitsu crawling quickly over, extinguishing with her robes the embers scattered on the planks.

Now clenching me by both arms, he shakes me. "I should have known better than to take a provincial like you into my fold! What did I tell you about other men?! What?!" With that, like a child angered by a toy, he cuffs me to the floor and spits on me.

"And you." He advances toward Yukio, staring hard at him as he is held in the henchmen's grips until he and Yukio are nose-to-nose. "Do you know who I am?"

"Yes, you are Nichimaga, the emperor's first minister."

Nichimaga takes his short sword from its scabbard, studies its blade and swaggers away. "The emperor." He whirls back to face Yukio again. "The emperor is a puppet." He pauses, sneers, "And Yukio, the stable boy, what do you think happens to the fool who beds my mistress in the night, hmmm?"

Yukio stands perfectly still as Nichimaga presses the tip of the blade to his neck. One of my attendants is sobbing. "What a man of power wishes I cannot change. That this lady not see it happen, that I beg."

"A last wish?" Nichimaga howls and his henchmen grin. "Take her out," he yells to them over his shoulder.

"No, no!" I scream. "Oh, master, I will do anything if—no!" I fight as the two men drag me out. "Nichimaga! Oh, please, please!"

One awful, silent moment. Then a hard scream from Yukio followed by a shriek from Mitsu. And Nichimaga's voice, instructing, "Throw his body into the Kamo River like the common thief he is."

The door slides open and Nichimaga bends down, pulling me up. "Look at your lover now, whore!" he says with a voice of stone, pushing his sword back into its scabbard at his sash as he storms out.

Back in my chamber Yukio, blood streaming from his throat and chest, lies dying.

I stumble to him and cradle his head in my arms as his blood slips down onto my hands, my robe, my arms. "No, no! Yukio! No, no!"

Nichimaga's men push me away onto the planks, then pick up Yukio's body and carry it out, but not before one of them slices off Yukio's ears and, laughing, tosses them into the bag at his waist.

I fall to the floor, face down, sobbing. Mitsu and Shosho come to me.

"Mistress," urges Shosho, "come away from here. Please, mistress."

"Oh," I cry out, "gods forgive me!"

"Mistress," Mitsu pleads.

I manage to stand, try to run. Mitsu stops me.

"Yukio! I must go to him!"

Shosho takes my other arm. "Mistress, listen! To encounter the lord's men again would mean death for you, too. Please, come to your senses!"

"No! No!" I hear my own voice, shrieking, delirious, as if a mad woman had taken possession of my soul. "I must go to him!" I fall to the floor again and they cover me with a shawl, then finally persuade me to come to the bath.

Once there, they gently wash the blood from my skin and hair, dress me in a fresh robe. When all is completed and I am a little comforted, I am able to ask, "Help me to the shrine, please."

"Mistress, please, lie down," Mitsu begs, "so we may give you a quieting massage."

"Please, I wish to sit at the shrine," I insist.

There, I kneel, touch my head to the floor and sit for meditation, a position I hold the entire night as my attendants sit quietly behind me. And then, with the first gray light of dawn, I turn to Mitsu and make my request.

Mitsu and Shosho exchange a terrified look. "Oh, no," Shosho cries, "please do not do this. We beg—"

"Do not worry. It is not what you think," I promise. "Please bring me the water basin, the dipping cup, and the dagger."

Within moments Shosho returns, bows, and places the water and scoop before me then, hesitantly, gives me the dagger. Both ladies return to their seated positions behind me.

I take the dipper and basin, wash my right hand, my left hand, rinse my mouth, and bow in supplication before the shrine gods. Taking up the dagger with both hands, I present it to the gods for blessing. Then, with one swift movement of the wrist, like that my father used when dressing game, I slice my hair away like a nun's. There is a sharp intake of breath from my ladies as the mass of hair drops to the planks. The dagger plummets from my hands, stabbing into the mat.

"Please send Henjo to the priests." I sob. "Yukio's body must be rescued from the Hungry Ghosts!"

Mitsu and Shosho help me up, wrap me in my quilts, lay me down to rest, and close the shinden.

I awaken much later to the rain on the veranda deck, remember my moments with Yukio, then fall into delirium again, crying in sorrow even from closed eyes. My skin is covered with bruises, my sleeves are wet with tears and the screen of state is spattered with Yukio's blood.

· · ·

Word of the tragedy travels quickly throughout the First Ward. Though Nichimaga is feared, Yukio, it becomes quickly apparent, was greatly loved and respected by everyone in the palace ranks for his fine character and many accomplishments. Late in the day, Lady Matsuko and Lady Hoshi are by my side, comforting me the best they can and sharing what they know.

Lady Matsuko is first to speak. "Word is that you were a victim of a plot."

I look up to them. "A plot?"

Lady Matsuko continues, "Yes, a way for Nichimaga to test his power to control the imperial throne. He set a spy on you, and when you exchanged letters with Yukio, he saw the perfect opportunity to rid himself of love competition and to humiliate the emperor by killing one of his most respected courtiers."

"So it was Tonaga," I say, staring out the veranda.

"Yes. Tonaga, that was the name they mentioned," Lady Hoshi says. "Oh, Omida, what cruelty you have suffered!"

"If only we had never seen each other!" I say.

"But, my dear—" Lady Matsuko starts to say.

"He played the flute outside my window. The next day he sent me the flute, tied to a sheet of blue-green Michinoku paper. I wrote back to him, kindly but without any invitation, and attached a stem of the aoi heart-vine, knowing its meaning to be blue-green, just as his letter. But he came to me and once my body spoke, my voice could not refuse him." A tear falls onto my jacket.

Hoshi puts her hand on my arm. "Did you not say you were from Nara province?"

I look up to her. "Yes."

She takes a breath and puts her hand over her mouth. "And so you did not know because your language is somewhat different: In Heian-Kyo, the *aoi* stands for more than just heart-vine and blue-green. It also means 'day for meeting.'"

. . .

By sunset, my ladies and I have completed preparations for a retreat to Ishiyama Temple. My carriage is already well-outfitted with blinds and we are able to leave in secrecy before sunrise. Mitsu and Shosho accompany me and, traveling those same streets where, days before, my heart leaped with joy at the discovery of the handsome gentleman who had seemed such a familiar vision, I wonder if I actually have been living inside a dream. Or perhaps life and the dream are one.

Late in the day we arrive at the temple, perched beside a cascade of rushing water where sinuous pines and rocks in fantastical shapes cling precariously to the hillside. Here there is no birdsong, only the occasional bawl of the wild deer in the ravine below. I welcome the austere meal of rice and radish the monks serve to us and later, after the evening service, as candles flicker among offerings of fruit and flowers, I pray to the Buddha for the soul of Yukio, that he may find rest and peace.

Before retiring, I meditate on the veranda overlooking Lake Biwa, then watch the cormorant fishermen light their fire baskets and send the birds out on leashes to snare fish in their bills. At last I sleep, comforted under my padded bed, imbued with Yukio's incense mingled with mine, a reminder that, somehow, the tender bud of love we were allowed could not be destroyed by the force of man.

We start home at daybreak. Snow had fallen during the night, and the road back to Heian-Kyo is now covered in its first layer of crystalline white, as are the trees and plants all around. I find my senses soothed by the beauty of this stark landscape, as if its cold purity could cleanse my soul for the next world, the white path to the Pure Land, where Amida Buddha reigns, where Yukio and I might again meet, and dwell in peace.

Upon our arrival, Henjo approaches Mitsu. Then she comes to me. "When Henjo told the monks at the palace what had happened, they came late in the darkness and retrieved Yukio's body from the river to give it proper rites, which have now been performed, as you wished." She bows.

. . .

At the shinden early the next afternoon, a note arrives from Nichimaga. Serenely and without fear now, I unknot it to read the bitter words:

> The ungrateful ones who betray the trust
> Of those who have taken them in
> Must suffer the weight of their sins in solitude

Am I now to be removed from my home? In resignation to my fate, whatever it may be, I hand the note back to Shosho.

On the tenth day after my temple pilgrimage, Lady Matsuko's man calls to Henjo. Her carriage is outside and she wishes to see me. Slipping into fresh robes, I prepare to meet her behind the kicho. She enters a few moments later, her brows furrowed with sorrow, and takes my hands into hers.

"Omida! We have cried for you, and made supplications at the Upper and Lower Shrine. I believe our prayers have been answered. You will at least be permitted to remain at the shinden. But you are never to be allowed to leave Heian-Kyo again!"

Sadness troubles her beautiful countenance. I see a tear on her cheek. But my eyes are dry. It is I who have caused Yukio's death. And it is I, as Nichimaga said, who must suffer the weight of my sins in solitude.

. . .

As I watch the snow fall the next afternoon, I see a new tree planted next to the pond.

"What is that tree?" I ask Shosho.

"Mistress, do you not remember? It is the cedar you brought with you from the Kamo Shrine. Umako the gardener says it should do well where he has planted it. In fact, it may, in time, become the greatest tree in the entire garden."

EIGHT

Emily

October 26 -late December, 2003

Something was pushing on my face. Sharp, scratching. Hurting.

One of my eyes opened. My body lay facedown on the floor, my cheek in a pool of cold vomit.

It was Fizzy, now clawing at my elbow, jumping away, crying, coming back at me.

There was a pounding sound outside, a voice. Fizzy barking, far away, then close. The room was spinning around me.

Then, sunlight.

I lay inert. Alive.

I heard the door latch, a voice calling "Emily?"

Mimi-Ann.

Fizzy ran in, barking. I watched the old lady's stooped figure following her, heard Mimi-Ann cry, as if from far away, "Oh, Lord! Emily!"

Consciousness fled.

. . .

The next I knew, Mimi-Ann was holding my hand in both of hers, trying to keep pace with the paramedics beside the stretcher as they bundled me into the ambulance. I saw the long row of palms on Fourth Street rushing by above as we raced to the hospital. Then the glare of the emergency room, the clanking of steel, cuffs, the prick of needles. People moving around me at a speed my mind could not follow. Tubes inserted down my throat for gastric lavage, charcoal. Finally, warm, practiced hands gently removing the dirty chambray shirt, exchanging it for a hospital gown.

Then I was being wheeled down a hallway, lifted by two Latino orderlies into a bed. A nurse moved around the bed, entering data into an electronic chart, checking the IV with a speed I could not follow.

"If Dr. Nafe hadn't been on duty…You're very lucky to be alive," the nurse said. She examined more readouts, double-checked my pulse by hand, said evenly, "Your brother's been called." She moved her hand to mine, squeezed it, finally smiled, and said, "You're going to be fine."

I heard footsteps in the hall, then saw Michael and Mindy talking with the nurse in the doorway. The two of them walked in. Michael's freckles stood out against his drained skin. But all he could say was "Emily!" before gathering me up in his arms in the middle of all the tubes, catheters, and monitors.

I buried my face against his shirt pocket.

"Mom worried something like this—" He stopped himself.

I held onto him more closely. His arms tightened, too. "Em, why?" he asked.

Mindy came around the other side of the bed, touched my arm as it lay on his shoulder, smiled down to me and said quietly, "Hey, sis, what's the idea?"

. . .

Mother and Father were at my bedside early in the afternoon. Father was quiet, from anger or shock I didn't know. Mother had a brave face on, but her eyes were red, her makeup streaked from crying. They would be staying with Michael. I was not to leave the hospital. The hospital had their number. Mother had already been to my apartment and had all my keys.

A different nurse came in the afternoon and introduced herself as Ellen Routh. She had known Nick from UCLA, had followed his work. She had lost a daughter to cancer the year before and knew how difficult it was to overcome such a trauma. She told me they would be sending a social worker over later but that the best thing would be to rest and make the best of the therapy they would offer. For now, I would probably be required to spend at least two weeks at Care4, a convalescent and rehab facility adjacent to the hospital for patients who needed additional treatment or counseling before returning home.

A rehab center. For me, a health writer. How badly had I screwed things up?

"Well, not a rehab center in the classic sense," Ellen was saying, "more an extended care unit with a broader reach. Your parents have already agreed to it."

So I don't do this again.

"I spoke with your dad a while ago," she said. Then, in a more somber tone, "Emily, your family loves you very much."

Shame engulfed me. I picked at the starched hospital sheet. Nick would have thought me a fool for what I had done. That was the most shaming of all.

. . .

Then, despite the pain in my stomach and the action of the cleansing charcoal, I slept, waking hours later, after dark, to the sound of crying next to me. Someone was holding my right hand in theirs. I turned my head.

The chair from the corner was pulled up next to the bed and a head of dark curls was resting next to my hand, itself wetted with tears.

"Liv," I managed to grate out through my chafed throat.

She sat up, staring at me, as if I'd returned from the dead. I'd never seen an expression like that on her, or anyone's, face; a mixture of anguish and hurt that made me feel even smaller than I already did.

"Thank God," was all she could say. "Your mom called me from here. I didn't get the message until . . ." She wiped her eyes with a hanky. I tried to speak but my voice was gone. I squeezed her hand.

"Water?" she reached over to the bedside table, poured a cup, and helped me drink, then reached inside her bag and brought out a portable CD player and set it on the table. "Music. What else can I do?"

"Just sit with me, Liv," I whispered. "Please."

• • •

I was kept in St. John's for three days while they did EEGs to test my brain waves, tested my reflexes, memory, and ran multiple EKGs to assess the condition of my heart. I had only been able to ingest a few of the pills. After three months of drugs and alcohol my stomach had rebelled, saving my life.

On the morning of the third day they released me to Care4. My room, which I shared with Cherry, a young meth addict, looked out over busy Santa Monica Boulevard.

The first thing the doctors at Care4 did was replace the Diazepam with an herbal sleep substitute and start me on a de-tox program to get the remaining drugs out of my system. I was still tired, and I slept most of that day in the darkened room while Cherry was at group session.

On my second day there, an attendant showed me into the office of their resident therapist, a psychologist specializing in the cure of trauma in young people. Her name was Jane Shaeffer.

I was so flustered at the prospect of having to talk about myself that I accidentally sat down on the tissue box left on the patient's chair. We both laughed until my laughter nearly turned to tears and I needed a tissue to hold them back.

Dr. Shaeffer said, "I hear you've had a pretty rough time of it."

"I feel so foolish," I said, watching my hands tearing at the tissue in my lap.

"That can happen when we get overwhelmed," she said. Then she began explaining her method of therapy. Unlike talking therapy, the approach developed by Care4 combined cognitive behavior therapy, in which the patient was given the tools to change behavior patterns based on negative emotions, with discussion and life-coaching. It was a treatment plan designed to get otherwise "normal" people back on their feet as quickly as possible from physically, mentally, or psychologically destructive behaviors.

Though I suffered neither chronic drug addiction nor an eating disorder, as did a majority of the patients here, I would, if I stayed, be required to attend a private session with her four days a week, along with daily group therapy. I could spend as much time as I liked in the meditation garden, an outdoor room in the atrium of the hospital. Although I could sign myself out at any time, I was to understand that my best chance of help was now, and if I agreed to stay for a month I would be taking the first step toward a permanent recovery.

At twenty-nine I could be mistaken for an old woman, technically, almost a widow: one failed suicide attempt, my body malnourished, pale and slack. Dr. Shaeffer smiled kindly and I tried to smile back. My coordination was still slow; my right arm shook as I signed the paper.

. . .

Within my first two sessions with Dr. Shaeffer, I began to understand what a selfish act suicide was. Afraid to express and deal with my own hurt I had not only come close to destroying myself, but had unwittingly compounded the hurt of my family and friends, many who had known Nick and missed him, too. They had wanted to help, but I hadn't let them. They'd been stonewalled, shunted aside, confused that I hadn't, but for the funeral, confided my pain to them so they might, in turn, confide in me. I had, in essence, refused their loving kindness, excluding them from a healing process at which I was the center. Then my suicide attempt, the ultimate betrayal.

"Did you think suicide was a way out?" Dr. Shaeffer asked.

"Out, out, I guess, of the pain."

"And yet others were willing to help you. To listen."

"But they hadn't lost Nick," I choked out.

"But Emily, they had, in a sense, because his life was entwined with yours; he was a part of you, and then they lost you, too."

"Are you saying I'm responsible for healing their grief?"

"No, Emily, just your own."

.   .   .

In the days that followed, Dr. Shaeffer also helped me see how important self-forgiveness was, and reminded me that, as a writer on the healing arts, I had much to contribute, perhaps with information that would save a life. I had, she said, been confronted with a choice in life: Would I expand my thinking and go on as happily as I could under the circumstances, or would I let Nick's untimely death destroy the life I had on earth? On considering her challenge late one night just before sleep, I began to realize that perhaps the world did need me; that maybe there was a place for me here.

During the coming days, with self-forgiveness and self-understanding,

I approached the grief I had tried to bury inside me, the same way Nick's ashes had been buried at the cemetery.

Some sessions, I hardly spoke at all, only sat staring with a few small tears trickling down my face as the doctor sat next to me, her hand on mine. At other times, I tried to analyze my own motives.

"I guess I thought I could be strong enough."

"Strong enough for what, Emily?"

"To, I don't know, to reason my way through my situation."

"It doesn't sound like a very 'reasonable' situation to me, Emily. You've been carrying around the burden of grief for the loss of a life partner, on the eve of your marriage to him. I honestly don't believe I've ever heard of something like this happening to anyone."

* * *

"It wasn't just Nick," I said to her the next afternoon, "I thought I'd found his replacement."

"His replacement?"

"There was someone else," I said, "who hurt me recently."

Dr. Shaeffer looked puzzled.

I told her about Curt, how I'd thought he was another Nick, how I believed his stories. How I'd been humiliated by his act. How could I have been drawn in by such a charlatan?

"I don't know of a single therapist who has met a single client who did not need love more than anything," she said.

"But why me, now?" I asked.

"Actors mine human emotion," she said. "It's their business."

"I don't understand."

"Well, they seem to have an almost sixth sense about where to find it, or create it, with or without strings attached. And you've been swimming in a bath of them," she said.

"But why lie about your whole life!"

"Emily, from the way you've described him, his betrayal of the woman who pays his bills, his lies to you, he sounds like more of a sociopath than a professional actor."

"A sociopath?"

"Well, we used to call them psychopaths."

"And—you don't have to explain this part: I projected Nick onto him."

Dr. Shaeffer watched me.

"I better go over those stories again," I muttered into my lap.

"I'm sorry, what?"

It was then that I told her, the only person I thought Clare would approve of me speaking to about the stories, of the notes and tapes I'd found in Nick's desk.

"How lucky for you."

"Lucky? Nick died!"

"Yes, but—"

I couldn't keep the bitterness out of my voice, "Do the stories really matter, now that he's gone?"

She took off her glasses, leaned forward. "I think what you do with these tapes mattered a great deal to him, because he knew you were the one person he could entrust them to. That as a science journalist and a humanist, you would know how to translate them for the world clearly and honestly, if that is what is called for, in a way everyone could understand."

Suddenly thrown back on my old self, I said, "But isn't that an argument for keeping my irrational emotions out of the process?"

"Well, then you must ask yourself," she paused, watching me intently, and said slowly, " 'Why is it I am pursuing this work?' "

And, nearly two weeks after nearly killing myself with painkillers, the lump in my throat, swallowed down for months until it could hold no more, burst wide open. Now the tears rose up like a well overflowing its source. I leaned forward, palms pressed against my forehead, knowing only that, this moment, I still breathed.

"In…memory of," I sobbed, scarcely able to form words, "our…love?"

The doctor's voice was now kind, but resolute. "And is love, as you say, 'rational'?"

A bolt like lightning struck, first my brain, then my heart. My body seemed suspended in space for a moment as my mind and core united again, and the layers of insulation I had carefully constructed between me and the outside world began to fall away like the layers of an onion.

Dr. Shaeffer came over, sat on the arm of the chair, put her arm across my shoulders. "You okay?" she asked softly.

I swallowed hard, nodded, and finally managed to say, "So you think… I can…redeem my life…by discovering why he left them?"

"By finding whatever message he had for you," she said.

"A message about…what?" I cried out in the midst of my broken sobs.

Dr. Shaeffer smiled down like the Cheshire Cat. "That," she said, "is between you and Nick."

That is between you and Nick. Those words echoed over and over in my mind all that night. Because in way I did not yet understand fully, they validated what I felt inside, gave me hope that others might still honor what Nick and I had. I rubbed my palm against my swollen, aching chest and my eyes filled yet again. Nick might be gone but Nick-and-Emily lived within me. Dr. Shaeffer had helped me see that. And that shared knowledge alone sowed the seeds for the beginning of my healing.

. . .

On the thirteenth evening of my residence at Care4 the heat broke and the air outside settled into an ethereal calm. At that same time, my lungs became filled once again with what the ancients called *pneuma*, the life breath, and my eyes opened to see not only the light at the end of the tunnel, but the whole world awaiting me beyond it.

The next day our cool, misty mornings and mild afternoons returned. With the normal onshore flow restored, the fires were brought under control and mop-up crews spread out from San Diego to Ventura to douse them completely. Traffic returned to its old rhythm on the street below.

That my life had been spared from my own hand sobered me as nothing since Nick's death. With that understanding came a curious but not unpleasant mix of guilt and elation, the same contradictory aftereffects the survivors of mass tragedy are said to experience. I had nearly slid off the edge of the world, and I had returned. But to what purpose?

. . .

After two weeks at the center I was allowed visitors and when Margo came over she asked if there was anything I wanted from home. My leather notebook, I said, and my Waterman fountain pen.

The next day she returned with the journal and pen, and something unexpected: the file storage box I'd left sitting next to my desk, plus my laptop. and the old cassette recorder.

"I think you forgot something," she said, holding up the recorder. "They still make these?"

"It's for…something Nick left me. Tapes."

"So that's what's kicking around in the box." She looked at me as only Margo could, with that come-clean expression she was so good at. "I thought it was your medical records."

"They are someone else's." I touched my hand to my heart and smiled. "A case Nick left for me to write up."

"A patient's records. Isn't giving them out, um, illegal? Not to mention kinda, well, kinky?" she asked, looking suspiciously over at the file box.

"Not if the patient approves."

"How? Oh, well." She looked bewildered and reached over for the box. "Maybe you shouldn't be listening to these now."

"Margo," I said, putting my hands over hers on the box, "it's okay, really. Please do leave it. Dr. Shaeffer's working miracles with me. Really."

"Good. For Jeff and me, well, it's water under the bridge. We just want this place to work out for you." She sat down on the green vinyl armchair in the corner. I watched her, thinking about her history.

"Margo? I was just wondering . . ."

"What, honey? Anything."

"Do you believe in reincarnation, past lives?"

She burst out laughing. "Sometimes I'm hard-pressed to believe the present one!" Then, after a few seconds, "Yeah, I guess I do. And?"

"I, it's something to do with this"—I pointed to the box—"project. Do you think Christians would ever buy the reincarnation concept?"

"Well, it's been a long time since my Bible-belt childhood." She looked at me strangely, then said, "Hmm, well, probably not. Actually, now that you mention it, I was having lunch with another photographer last week and she was telling me about a book she was reading on Gnostic Christianity. According to her, anyway, they believe there was lots of stuff taken out of the Bible, especially about reincarnation, by Emperor Justinian way-back-when, so it may have been an early tenet, before the politicians and popes got ahold of the Bible."

"Really? That's actually very helpful," I said.

"Glad I could help. If I did," she said.

"You always do, Margo."

Visiting hours were almost up. She stood up and I did too. "Well, I don't know what this is all about, but you look a ton better and when they spring you from the big house here, call me and we'll do something really esoteric-y like go shopping. The last time I did a show I looked like a homeless drunk who'd wandered in for the appetizers."

. . .

I continued with rest and therapy and, in between, studied my notes and Nick's on Clare's curious case. As my head cleared, I considered the men who had appeared in Clare's stories. Were they all supposed to be "Theion"? My own recent experience with Curt had proved to me that even if it walked like a duck and quacked like a duck it might not actually be a duck. Clare might be as guilty of projection as any of us, even in a hypnagogic state.

But more importantly as I looked over the work I had done, my heart and mind began to reconnect again. Just working on the stories seemed to take on, beyond their content themselves, another deeper meaning for me personally, one of salvation through concentration. And slowly, with real sleep, my dreams returned, a rush of them, night after night. I even dreamed, amusingly enough, of a golden hand opening mine to give me a blue-green stone.

Valerie, who had been there my first afternoon at St. John's, sent flowers, then came by.

She was still with the bereavement group and found it helpful, though she understood why it might have been different for me. She and Dwight were taking care of the sale of Nick's house. Anything I wanted from the house or garage, she said, was mine. His office lease, as it turned out, did not expire until February. His patients' records had been gathered together and sent to an associate who had in the past filled in for Nick on vacations.

Within another week, I was released from Care4 and Mother brought me back home. The apartment had been cleaned of weeks of grime I'd never noticed. In honor of my homecoming, Mother had taken Fizzy to the groomer and, smelling of pet shampoo and wearing a bright red bow on her collar, she leaped into my lap, kissed me until my face was wet from ear to ear, then raced from room to room barking with furious dog joy.

I went into the bedroom to drop my bag. As I was walking out, a photo sitting on top of the bureau caught my eye: me, with Curt, on the sofa.

"We found it under a pillow," Mother said, walking in behind me. "We didn't know him."

I stared at the photo. Curt's hair was streaked blond; he had green eyes, not brown, and not a touch of windburn in his cheeks. Except for the height, he didn't look a thing like Nick.

"Neither did I," I said, and tossed the photo into the bathroom wastebasket.

Mother stayed with me for the next week. We talked a lot. I asked her to please forgive me for clamming up after the funeral, then the stupid pills and booze. She simply put her arms around me and said, "Emmy, you don't even need to ask."

Margo came by and we did some shopping on Montana Avenue. Mother and I had dinner out with Mindy and Michael. I even found myself laughing at Michael's never-ending repertoire of groaners. My sister Sylvia called. Her new employer, a French winemaker just setting up in Napa, was sending her as part of her training to France to understand methods of production there. Would I like to join her?

"We'll leave next Thursday and be back before Christmas. All you need is a ticket."

"She asked if she should ask you," Mother said after I hung up.

"I don't even know how much a ticket would cost. It's pretty late on," I said.

"I've already got your ticket," she said, holding up a small packet with the Air France logo.

*   *   *

The following days were a constant stream of activity. Dr. Shaeffer agreed that, if I felt well enough, a change of scenery would be excellent therapy, but that I was to call her if things seemed to be getting ahead of me. The internist at Care4 also thought the trip a good idea but cautioned me to continue to avoid alcohol while my liver and kidneys recovered. I was so happy to have something to look forward to that I promised to follow their orders exactly.

Forty-eight hours later, Syl and I stepped half-asleep from the plane at Charles de Gaulle. We stayed in a cozy hotel on the Left Bank for two days while Sylvia attended classes at the American school. While she studied I walked as much as I could, to the Tuilleries and the Louvre, around the Right Bank, stopping at street-side cafes to people watch, strolling on the Rue St. Honoré to window-shop, reveling in the comforting fragrance of roasting chestnuts and baking bread.

Sylvia's class work completed, we took the train to Dijon. While Syl talked with an expat American vintner there, I wandered from café to bistro in the crisp sunshine, eating better food and feeling more alive than I had in months.

We spent our last full day in Paris at the Musee de L'Homme and the Eiffel Tower. It was dusk when we arrived back at the Metro stop by the Arc de Triomphe and just as we stepped up to street level, the beech trees lining the length of the Champs-Élysées from the Arc to Cleopatra's Needle burst into sparkling light as miles and miles of mini globes winding through their branches were illuminated. At that moment I knew that all the synapses in my body, so crushed with pain and numbed by drugs, could reconnect. That I could once again be whole.

We arrived back in L.A. the next afternoon and the first thing I did after a good night's sleep was to sit down at my desk to go over the work on Clare's stories. What a strange coincidence that her very next story should transport me back to France, west from Paris, to the resting place of King Henry II, and Eleanor of Aquitaine.

NINE

Clare/Renée

c. 1265-75 A.D.
Anjou, France

Yes, that is the old rooster crowing in the coeur below. Gradually, I awaken, to soft woolen blankets, sweet linen perfume.

I step down from my bed's platform. The sun is just rising over the fields below, where the tenants in their rough tunics, heads covered closely in stirruped skullcaps, tread behind their plows. Their women follow after, scattering oats and beans from cloth bags slung across their bodies. The last shards of ice have long since melted into the Thouet, and where the sun's rays touch its waters, drifts of clouds form over it, only to disappear in an instant. Candlemas, February 2, is nearly a fortnight past and soon we will throw off our cloaks of camlet and fur to welcome spring.

I was born in this very room sixteen years ago. Over the many decades my family has owned Rochemont, it has grown and now encloses stables, mews, cellars, orchard, flower gardens, and houses for its many resident workers. I, along with Aunt Felise, visiting cousin Marie, and younger sister, Caterine, live in the Chambres des Dames in the gynaeceum of the west tower, where we dine together at our own table, sing as we weave and embroider for the household, and play backgammon and chess.

Friar Denis says daily Mass at our chapel and, on special occasions, we are granted a visit from a charming minstrel named Jollivet and his companion, a dwarf with amusing tricks and stories. Each day we are allowed to visit the garden, but heaven help us if we are ever found to be in the coeur or worse, the orchard, rumored to be a hideaway for lover's trysts. The tower, Father says, is a haven from the rough world for gentlewomen like us, although sometimes it seems more like a prison, especially on the cusp of spring.

Of course, I should have been married and governing my own house long ago and if Father had had his wishes, I would have been, to Rogier of Picardie. It would have been an alliance which would have enriched both families with land, coin, and, I suppose, children. But it was a betrothal I resisted, for my brothers had told me of Rogier's ill health and bad temper. Even so, before the matter could be settled, Rogier, much in years upon me, was afflicted with the winter ague and died just before Christmastide last year.

So very many of our men have heeded King Louis' call to battle against the Mohammedans, or have been killed in strife between the provinces, that both my parents now despair of contracting a husband for me at all. Add to this that Father's coffers, seriously depleted by his own funding of knights traveling to save the holy lands, now do not permit him to offer a dowry large enough to attract the landed nobleman I was expected to marry. They now speak of committing me to Fontevraud Abbaye with an endowment, to live my life as a lay sister, a possibility which chills my soul.

A tap at my door. Onfroi, the steward, calls, "Mademoiselle Renée!"

Quickly, as I catch the fragrances wafting up from the kitchens, I perform my toilette, setting my hair with pomade then pulling on my favorite côte, the one in wine-red velvet. I observe myself in the big looking glass: straight and slender arms and legs, flaxen hair and lashes, small breasts, tapered hands and feet. It is a picture that pleases me for its modesty.

Breakfast this morning is light, just blanc mange on a hard bread plate, with the gravy-soaked plates going to the poor for their dinner. Mother joins us at the table today to discuss our current project, a tapestry of the hunt, which we hope to finish before Lent.

"Daughter," she says, turning to me, "are you near completing your section?"

"Yes, Mother. It will be finished within just a few days." In my corner of the tapestry, a young falconer will sit his horse, peregrine standing proudly on his gauntlet.

"Good," she says. "Caterine, perhaps you could assist Marie. Her forest scene will certainly take the longest amount of time to complete."

The halls of the little chateau are filled with tapestries and hangings, nearly all woven by the ladies of Rochemont. As we weave, we sing our favorite *chansons de toiles*, today to honor the coming of spring.

The shuttle flies across the loom and before late afternoon the warper's design comes up before my eyes. A young woman approaches the falconer on Mother's section, perhaps to take the falcon from him. When Mother's is completed, hers and mine will be joined by a thread of yarn, and the tapestry will be completed with Aunt Felise, Marie, and Caterine's quadrants, open fields surrounded by low, forested hills, exactly the scene we enjoy from our windows each day.

"And do not forget. You ladies are going hawking in the morning," Mother reminds us as we all kiss each other goodnight.

How could I have forgotten? Tomorrow will be our last falconry expedition for several months since Lent begins in early March this year, at which time the birds will be enmewed for their molts until August.

Birds have always fascinated me, even since early childhood and I had, on several occasions, brought adult birds, even injured fledglings fallen from their nest in the garden, back to the tower, where I tried in vain to save them. Father, perhaps tired of my many months of begging, has finally agreed to let me visit the mews, starting the day after tomorrow, for instruction in bird care with Didier, his oldest and most trusted falconer.

It is just past sunrise as Caterine greets me at the entrance to the chapel. Already Friar Denis arranges the candles before the altar. He looks up as we enter and it is all we can do not to giggle, for our kindly confessor has recently found a way to remedy his poor eyesight by wearing a new invention brought from Genoa; roundels of thick glass, one in front of each eye, connected by a wire across the bridge of his nose, giving him the look of a toad peering out from the ivy.

Mass is abbreviated today for the preparations for our outing must be completed within the hour. We breakfast in haste, while Felise's little white dog, Bobo, yips and begs for morsels. I slip him a bit of chicken from the plate Caterine and I share, as Marie recalls our last hawking.

"Oh, remember Didier that morning? The merlin that wouldn't come back? I never thought to see her again!" she says, herself giving Bobo a nibble of meat.

Caterine giggles. "And the lure that got caught in the tree as we tried to call her back!"

"Your mother tells me your father has hired another falconer, a Breton well-educated in bird medicine," Aunt Felise says. "I do hope he is able to save the peregrines from thrush this year."

The addition of another man would bring our birding staff to three, a good number, though some houses employ many more, for hawking is such an important social activity that all the birds must be closely watched for health problems that might be passed to other houses' birds, and be trained to return to the hand that calls them. Many different birds reside in our mews now and last August Father's head falconer, Bayard, traveled with father to Valkenswaard to buy more young branchers for training. Two of Father's gyrfalcons were even used by him in payment of a debt. Little wonder the mews needed another expert.

By mid-morning we are on our mounts, riding out beyond the walls of the great house down past the weir and into the open fields, as yet unplowed and so perfect for the hunt. With the horses in their colorful coats and polished tack and the ladies in their equally bright cloaks lined in marten, we seem as if in a tapestry ourselves. I look back: Didier follows along with Remy, the young cadge, who carries the three merlins in a box on his shoulders.

We stop at a sloping glade away from tall trees where the birds will have plenty of sky. Already flocks of blackbirds preen and chip on the grass. Didier takes one of the falcons from Remy and, removing her hood with his fingers and teeth, transfers her expertly to Marie's gauntlet. The little bird adjusts herself on the glove, takes her bearings and, as Marie lifts her hand up, is off, climbing higher and higher into the blue. Seeing her wheeling above, the blackbirds take flight. The merlin hits.

Didier retrieves her, gathers her catch into a small basket to reward her with later and Marie sends her out again and again, until she has captured a half-dozen of her prey.

Next is Aunt Felise's turn and she has her own bird, Alette, lifted from the cage. Costumed in a suede hood with a topknot of chicken feathers and pearls, the merlin stands patiently on her gauntlet until my aunt removes its blinder. The bird shakes her belled foot, smoothes her breast feathers and looks around. And then she is off the fist and into the light, to snatch one blackbird, then many more within the next hour as we move along the open fields and meadows.

Just as Didier is returning with Alette and her prizes, I hear someone approaching on horseback behind us. I turn to see a young man dressed in the uniform of the falconer, tunic, close-fit shirt, tall boots and linen cap, pull his mount to, and stop to watch Didier. Bobo suddenly becomes animated, races to the visitor's horse, paws the air, and looks back to me. The falconer laughs, bows his head slightly to me and dismounts.

He is of middling height, calm, and deliberate in movement, as a good falconer must be.

His face is ruddy from outdoor work and his nose, perhaps once straight and strong, appears at one time to have been broken, yet these flaws seem only to add to his refinement, as do the few stray curls of auburn hair escaping from the back of his cap. But it is his eyes, the blue-green of the Thouet on a summer day, that hold mine.

My mouth falls open and I must shake my head to clear my vision. If I had not known better…No, it is as if the falconer on my tapestry has come to life before me.

Didier is calling as he returns with Alette on his glove. "Ladies, Gabriel Coumance, our new resident expert on training and medicine."

"Good morning, Master," we respond, almost in unison.

Didier addresses me. "Renée. Renée." I have been so busy looking at the falconer that I have not heard. It is now my turn and the merlin sits on Didier's glove, waiting. I reach inside my cloak to retrieve my own gauntlet but find to my dismay that I have either lost or forgotten it.

Didier holds the merlin by her jesses. Having heard the other birds hunt, she is anxious to be off and her ankle bells shake and ring. I see from the corner of my eye Gabriel the falconer walking toward me. Wordlessly, he removes the gauntlet from his right hand and opens it out to me.

I reach my hand toward the glove and slip my hand inside. It is a bit large and the warmth there mingles with mine. Didier transfers the merlin to my hand and I pull her hood forward with my teeth and the other hand. She takes her bearing then is off my fist, tracing up the sky.

Minutes pass and she does not return. Nor do any blackbirds. Didier picks up the lure, strides to the middle of the glade, swings the lure high around his head and calls, "*Ooh-la, oiseau, ooh-la. Viens, oiseau, viens!*" I jump as she appears from out of the far reaches of the sky, striking the bait and bringing it down. Didier returns with her on his glove.

"Poor Renée! I am afraid we have done our job too well this morning!" Felise says as I extend my hand back to Gabriel and he removes his gauntlet. As we follow Didier home, I cannot resist the urge to glance back at the new falconer. He smiles back to me.

We continue with the tapestry the following morning, hurrying, for Lent is soon and our days will be for contemplation in that time. It is a sunny day, good for close work and we labor busily until the bells for midday prayers.

Normally, we take time to rest our eyes after dinner, but this afternoon I am not the least bit tired and decide, instead, to pass the hour as I spin new wool, enjoying the view of the Thouet and its sun-splashed weir from the large workroom window. The big wheel turns rhythmically and the yarn falls silently into the basket below. Just as I am about to gather it together, a thud sounds against the glass next to my head.

I jump back and look out to find the cause of the noise. Then I see it: A bird, thinking the window an open space, has tried to fly through the room. It is a kestrel, a young falcon. Other than appearing a bit stunned, she seems uninjured until I notice her left leg jutting out at an unnatural angle.

Slowly, so as not to startle her, I unlatch the window and grasp her light body firmly yet gently, taking care to keep her talons from piercing my hand. Since she is without jesses or bells she must be wild. I remove a linen pillow covering from the corner and, placing her inside, I knot it closed with a length of wool.

My first thought is to ring for a retainer to convey the bird to the mews for care. Then I think better: This being an injured wild bird, fully grown and unsuitable for training, she would elicit little sympathy from the household staff, who might well let her go with her hurt.

I throw on my surcotte and steal from the workroom with the sack, down the curving staircase to the ground floor. The guard, who has been known to take too much cider at dinner, lies snoring in the corner at the foot of the steps. Knowing I only have permission to go to the mews for one day, and next week at that, I sneak past him on tiptoe and unlatch the door.

Rochemont, like many great houses, was built for security, with a number of secret escape passageways, one in each of the towers. Ours is just a few steps away from the base of the spiral stone stairway and leads out across a corner of the orchard through a low, arched passageway, then through a small gate and into the coeur.

The coeur appears to be deserted save for a few stable boys. The mews is on the inner perimeter of the castle grounds, a low stone tower capped with a fleur de lys. Raucous chitchat from the congregation of peregrines, lanners, merlins, and goshawks echoes through its high window slits.

I enter through the narrow double doorway and call, "*Personne! Personne!*" Hearing no response, I back out into the courtyard. Perhaps the falconers are all away on expeditions today, or still having their dinner. Finally I see Gabriel tending a sealed merlin on a weathering block.

"Good day, Master." My heart is racing.

He continues with the bird, his back to me, making no response. I try again.

"Master?"

He turns in my direction and starts as if surprised. Then he nods his head, removes his cap for a moment and smiles. His upper lip turns up a bit, most charmingly, like a pouting child. He looks down at the linen sack, now threatening to become completely uncontrollable in my hand. I set it down at my feet.

"It is a falcon, I believe," I say as he unknots the yarn at the top. "Mistaking the window for clear air she hit hard against the glass. I fear her leg is broken."

He lifts her out to examine her, then says slowly, and with some difficulty, "Come."

I follow him inside the mews and am soon within a sort of medicinal cabinet for birds, where small phials of tinctures, salves, and powders stand neatly organized on shelves next to various-sized mortars and pestles, and a clean, well-oiled table holds dressings, string, and knives.

The falconer soothes his wounded patient and lays her with care upon the table. I reach for a hood, but he shakes his head. Instead, he takes my wrists and shows me where to place my hands on her so she stays quieted. He affixes a short splint and, with great delicacy, wraps the leg with a length of light cotton. He then lifts her and places her inside a cage large enough for her to stand in without re-injuring the leg. I am amazed at the speed of the whole process and at the kestrel, which seems to have been calmed merely by Gabriel's expert handling.

"Thank you. I was worried the staff would send her off with her hurt. Is bird medicine your specialty?"

He watches me intently, frowns and shakes his head. Then, he touches both of his ears, and his mouth.

Just then the outer, then the inner mews door swings open and Didier walks in. "Child! Your lessons do not begin until tomorrow!"

"A bird hit the glass in the tower and her leg"—I point to the cage— "needed mending. I helped Gabriel, but he will not speak to me."

"Ah, yes. Well, he doesn't talk to any of us. He is deaf." He slaps Gabriel heartily on the back. "But you can talk the birds' language, can't you, friend?"

Gabriel watches Didier's mouth closely, then nods his head as he smiles.

"At what hour might I expect you tomorrow?" Didier asks.

"After dinner, in the early afternoon," I say. Gabriel is looking over at me. Those extraordinary eyes: a detail I have yet to weave into the tapestry.

* * *

What strange dreams walk the paths of my mind the night after I visit the mews! In one, Gabriel and I escape to a strange land of glittering mosaics. In another we inhabit a decorous world of exquisite gardens and great ceremony.

Although I am anxious for my falconry lesson, I must stay longer with the tapestry work than anticipated. Midday prayers cannot come and go quickly enough and the moment we are finished and, the other ladies resting in their rooms, I rush downstairs. In contrast to yesterday's calm, the heart of the castle is busy this afternoon, with knights joking and playing knucklebones, and grooms and farriers tending horses. As I approach the mews I see Didier in front, cooling a young peregrine with a spray of water from his mouth. "It has the effect of calming them," he says. "Come inside the mews. We have a very interesting first lesson for you."

For a moment I am blinded by the darkness. Then I see Gabriel, standing in the corner studying the back of a merlin. A godbeam of sunlight streams across the room from one of the small, horizontal windows above to touch his hair, which is shot through with strands of gold I had not seen before.

"Lady Felise's merlin," Didier informs me, "has broken a tail feather."

As he points, Gabriel bobs his head slightly at me then turns the bird so I can see the broken feather.

"Is something to be done?" I ask.

"Watch while I hold her," Didier says. "Perhaps you have heard me speak of it before. It is called 'imping.'"

Already Gabriel has laid open a suede roll containing several feathers of different lengths. He selects one, then, using a short knife, neatens up the tear on the broken feather, and cuts the new feather in the correct shape to match the old. This completed, he dips a small, triangular needle into a jar of brine and joins the two feathers together with it.

"And what does this do?" I ask.

"Well, Renée," Didier says, "the feathers are the mind of the bird. Without all its feathers, a bird cannot fly safe and true. He needs this one as much as he needs all the others."

Gabriel continues with the work as I stand next to him. Except for a horizontal birthmark resembling a slash across his lower neck, his skin is smooth and carries on it the dusty, downy scent of birds. He lifts little

Alette back to her perch.

"And what happens to the needle?" I ask.

"It stays where it is; rusting will keep the old feather joined to the new," Didier explains.

And thus my education in the arts of falconry begins.

. . .

In the next week the weather turns fair and warm. The buds of the apple and pear peek out from their green sheaths, then burst forth en masse. How fares my kestrel? And Gabriel. I cannot stop thinking and dreaming of him. Despite Father's warnings about leaving the tower without permission, I creep down the staircase after dinner, past the sleeping guard, and into the mews, where I find Gabriel, sweeping up the floor.

"I came…to…I wished to know how the kestrel …" I stutter. Then, just "Kestrel."

He studies my lips, points to the cage where she stands, then nods. He is smiling at me. Waiting for me to speak.

"Didier?" I say the name as neatly as I can.

He puts his hand to his head, as if hot. "Ill," he says.

The winter fever was still about. It is not, at this time of year, life-threatening, but Didier would be confined to his room for several days.

"May I come to learn more tomorrow?" I speak as slowly as I can, so he can understand.

His smile is my answer.

. . .

Though Mother once expressed concern for the competence of the drunken guard, I myself am now grateful for him because, as I soon discover, the cider keeps him asleep nearly all afternoon every day, so there is no one to stop me from visiting the mews.

Gabriel and I soon work out a simple sign language with our hands and eyes. He places the tips of my fingers on the voice box of his warm, smooth throat to show how one should hum softly while one works with a hooded merlin that she may gain trust of the human hand and voice. Taking my fingers in his and running them gently across the breast of a bird, he shows me how to feel the vertical bone there to correctly judge the bird's weight. We take turns walking a young peregrine on our gloves, then passing her from his hand to mine and back again to teach her to be calm in the field.

By the day before Dies Cinerum, we understand each other well, but with the coming noon hours marked as a time of prayer, I know I cannot be gone from the tower. I show Gabriel by placing my hands in the attitude of prayer, then touching my thumb to my forehead. He nods "yes" to show me he understands.

Before I leave, I go to the injured kestrel, as I have done every day. Her leg seems, if I understand what Gabriel has taught me of bird medicine, to be healing well. Gabriel, standing beside me, looks at her and points beyond the windows.

"Fly?" I ask, pointing up above me.

Gabriel nods his head enthusiastically.

"Free her?" I point past the windows.

He watches carefully, nods and makes a funny flapping movement with his arms. I laugh, then he laughs, too. Then he takes my hand, bows, and kisses it. How soft his lips are! How gentle his hand! I back slowly toward the door. Our eyes do not look away from each other as I leave the mews. How soon, I wonder, as Friar Denis marks my forehead with the ashes of palm the next morning, will my kestrel be freed? For the next weeks, much of our time will be spent in prayer and meditation inside the gynaeceum. Hawking season is now finished until the end of summer. My only chance to see Gabriel again for many months would be for the release of the bird.

But the very next morning a message comes from Didier. The kestrel is to be returned to the wild in exactly one week in the orchard. Without having told Father how the kestrel came to be in the mews, Father has told Didier I may be present when the bird is released.

. . .

When that day finally comes, I hurry down the staircase and through the garden, where now roses, violets, daffodils, and iris mingle in scent and color, then past its gate into the orchard with its blooming quinces, apples, medlars, peaches, pears, all in their ordered rows. I follow the deliciously fragrant path of fennel and mint and as I approach the old laurel tree, a roe deer crosses my path, her belly round with fawn.

Gabriel is there at the very end of the lane of trees, standing in front of the stone wall verdant with arabesques of ivy. On a stump next to him sits a small cage with the little bird inside, moving her head left, then right, taking the measure of her surroundings, sensing her freedom near.

He hands me a pair of gloves to put on, opens the cage door and extracts the bird, then places her gently in my hands. I close my eyes for a moment of silent prayer for her safety, smile to Gabriel, and open my hands out above me.

She takes to the air with much flapping, then lands neatly on the highest branch of a nearby pear tree to observe her surroundings. Her beautiful head dips low, watching, then she springs from her perch and flies up and over the orchard wall.

I turn to Gabriel, my face warm with excitement. I have saved the bird and the two of us together have healed her. Gabriel reaches over and, as I hold out my hands like a child with mittens, he removes both the gloves. He watches me for a long time, then runs the soft backs of them down the side of my cheek. I hold his hand where he holds the gloves. And then, we lean to each other, and kiss. His mouth is as smooth as his skin and I am enveloped, once again, in the delicious perfume of the mews.

Feeling the heat on my cheeks, I back away from him, try to collect myself. "I must return to the tower," I say. "Prayers are soon." Then I turn and run down the path, looking behind me only once to see Gabriel, a troubled expression on his face, holding the empty cage, watching me.

How difficult during afternoon prayers to concentrate and be calm! Because I could not lie to myself: That single kiss had fed the flame in my heart, a flame not to be extinguished by thoughts nor prayers. In the long hours of evening, I kneel before my little statue of Saint Praxedes, praying for guidance as I try to ignore the pulsing of my heart and loins. Finally, Michel the concierge enters the room to lay a fire in the fireplace, and I dress for sleep in my blue velvet gown.

The moon rises full and fair, reflecting gauzy light off the slate cone of the north tower and sending filtered rays of red and gold down from the stained glass above onto the silk of the coverlet and onto the stone floor. An owl's song floats across the coeur. The night watchman passes by below calling "*Huit heures!*" The fire has warmed the room so that I go to the window and open it to let in the cooler air.

And there, standing below, is Gabriel, holding a small torch and staring up at my window. I run to my bedside, pick up the candle stand, set it on the ledge and lean forward. My hair falls forward out the window, catching the light from his torch. He smiles, puts his hand to his heart and extends it out to me—a gesture that, coming from him, somehow seems familiar. The torch flares and dances in a sudden gust of air. Without thinking, I run to my bed, throw on my surcotte and steal down the staircase.

The tower guard sleeps soundly at his post. Silently I hurry past him, out through the garden and into the coeur.

As if by magic, Gabriel appears at my side. Standing on my toes, and laying my palm against his cheek, I reach up and touch my lips to his. Then, taking the torch from his hand and placing it in the standard on the stone wall, I urge him to the covered entrance to the orchard where we will be hidden.

Now his arms, arms so gentle they hold an injured bird tenderly, come around me with a strength I did not know he had. For an infinitely strange moment my mind is engulfed by a sense of déjà vu. Then I return his embrace and his mouth comes to mine. His whole body pushes against me, leaning me into the stone and I feel a new strength about him, desiring, resolute.

Gently I push him away. He seems surprised. But driven by some strange force, I take his hand and pull him with me, down the lane of fruit trees to the very end of the orchard where, only yesterday we released the kestrel to her freedom.

There, behind the grizzled pear tree, I lay my robe upon the earth, kneel down upon it, and motion for him to follow. For a moment he only watches me, then, quickly, he falls to his knees, pulls me to him and kisses me until my body melts into his touch and everything in me reaches toward him.

He lays me back, kisses my throat, my arms. His hands slide under my linens to my flanks, my legs. I hold him to me as I feel him reach down to loosen his leggings. For a moment he draws back as if to take all my presence in. I feel his whole body urgent against mine, asking. In answer, I press myself gently to him. His body bears down upon mine and the cool, turned earth comes up to meet me with the scent of crushed muguet, leaves, castings, and the musk of fox. The pain of first love passes quickly and soon we move to the rhythm of two hearts made one, two peregrines, flying upward higher and higher, their enraptured wings beating in concert with one another's. He gasps and shudders, thrusts a few more times against me and still united we fall panting, like forest animals, onto earth.

A lone nightingale sings on a branch above. I reach over to caress Gabriel's face, his neck. He captures my fingers in a kiss, rolls over to me, follows the line of my nose, my mouth, my chin, then kisses me again. We are like that a long time, clinging to each other with wonder.

Then, I hear the night watchman calling "*Neuf Heures!*" from the coeur. I realize my gown is damp and wet; my robe caked with dirt. I arrange my clothing as best I can as Gabriel takes me into his arms again and kisses me. I place his hand on my lips so he can feel my answer, and know.

"Tomorrow," I say.

. . .

The ladies and I pray throughout the next morning, then later settle in with our embroidery until early afternoon. Felise reads from one of our favorites, *The Consolation of Philosophy*, but all I can think of is Gabriel, over me, Gabriel joined to me. In the middle of the afternoon, Mother arrives and, smiling sweetly, motions me to sit with her at the bench near the window.

"My dear daughter," she says, "your father will be here shortly. He is returned from Valois today to discuss your future with you."

My future? I search her face and, finding no answer in her expression, reply simply, "Yes, Mother," and, as I return to my embroidery I cannot help but watch the mews. Gabriel is there. What is to become of me?

I do not have long to wait to find out. Footsteps echo on the stone stairs and in a moment Father appears at the door with several of his retainers. All the ladies rise and curtsey. Father is a large, dark man of imposing presence, especially today in his velvet-and-ermine pelice and jeweled amulets of gold. He kisses my bowed head and as if by magic the ladies of the gynaeceum, all save Mother, disappear. Even little Bobo scurries out. As she departs, Marie glances back at me with worry in her eyes, her lips pressed tightly together.

Father takes the large armchair, the one at the hearth reserved just for him, and Mother and I sit next to him on footstools at either side. For a moment, the room is completely silent.

Then Father, laying a hand on my shoulder, speaks. "Daughter, you know that, with the death of Rogier, we have had some difficulty contracting another husband for you. However," he continues, "the Holy Virgin has heard our petitions, and we are most fortunate in being able to secure for you a marriage with a young man of fine family. His name is Esdelot, the eldest son of the Hardouin family of Tours. Having served nobly in the great crusade, he is returning from Jerusalem. His father expects him home within four months, at which time you will be married."

His smile is one of satisfaction, but I must look down at the floor to hide the shock on my face.

I turn a desperate, questioning look to my mother. Her hands are clasped together tightly in the folds of her camlet gown, her eyes cast down as well. "He is a good man," she says. "Dame Fortune has smiled well upon you."

Fortunate? To have to leave Gabriel's side? To be the wife of a man I do not love? Though Father's hand rests lightly on my head, his pronouncement weighs like a stone in my heart. And when he speaks, his voice seems to come from across the room.

"Esdelot's father has presented me with this cameo of his son that you would know his fair face before the marriage," he says, withdrawing the little memento from his pelice.

I take it from him and look down to see a decent enough young man, though not nearly as handsome as Gabriel. Before they can see the tears falling on my dress, I lower my head and drop to my knees. "Thank you for your wisdom, Father. I ask your blessing on the alliance you have graciously arranged for me."

. . .

I excuse myself from supper early, pleading tiredness and the need for private prayer. As I watch the dance of the firelight in my room, my mind is full of Gabriel. Why is it that joy and sadness are so often enjoined? I have found my true love, yet I am now told I must marry another!

I pray at my little bench until I hear the watchman's call, then throw my already-muddied robe over my gown and sidle down the staircase, candle in hand. Tonight the guard is missing altogether. So anxious am I to meet Gabriel I can scarcely keep my feet under control as I scurry through the garden and into the reaches of the orchard.

He is there, behind the pear tree, arms open. I run into them, my body convulsed with sobs. Gabriel takes me into his arms, holding me, stroking my hair as I weep. Then, he takes my hands in his and reaches down into a leather pouch at his waist from which he withdraws a silver ring; at its center is a bruited stone of turquoise. He takes my left hand and places it on the third finger and holds it there.

I am still crying. He holds me away from him, searches my face. I try to tell him, but he does not seem to understand. I point over the orchard wall, then show him the cameo of Esdelot. Finally, the expression of disbelief on his face tells me he understands.

"Oh, my Gabriel, I do want to be your wife. But I am bound by Father's wishes by custom as well as by law!" I know he cannot understand what I am saying, but I go on, "What can I do? What?"

But suddenly there is a voice. "There! In the orchard!" And there are flames of torches held high, coming our direction. I start to run, but Gabriel does not understand until it is too late.

A low grunt sounds nearby, then a voice in a harsh tongue I have never before heard shouts a command at the same instant a crooked shadow springs from between the cleft trunk of the pear tree. I am blinded by the glint of a dagger against the moonlight as Gabriel's hand is violently wrenched from mine. As I fall to the ground I hear a voice, my voice, screaming *"Arrêt!"* and I crawl to my feet to see Gabriel being held by two strange men.

"Arrêt!" I scream again. One of the men must speak my language for

they relax their hold on Gabriel. Within moments the orchard is filled with torches held aloft by knights and guards. Behind them all Father, in his nightcoat, is striding forward in anger.

The armed men move aside to let him pass. He looks to me, then Gabriel and asks, "What is this, daughter?"

One of the two men holding Gabriel speaks first. "We caught him seducing your daughter here in the darkness."

Father turns to me, a dark anger in his voice, "Daughter?"

I try to keep my voice calm. "We are in love with each other. The meeting was my wish."

"What?"

Now I see Gabriel, desperately trying to shout "No!" as the two men pull him roughly back.

"Take him to the great hall. And call Didier forth. We'll find the truth in this," Father says to the men.

"Oh Father, no! Please do not harm him. Oh god, please do not harm him!" I cry as two more men drag me, sobbing and fighting, back to the tower.

The next moment I am in Mother's chair upstairs. My aunt is attempting to persuade me to take a draught of wine. I do not want the wine, and I repeatedly push the goblet away but Felise, as if coaxing a reluctant child, takes one sip herself then persuades me to follow.

Later, I realize I have been taken to my own bed. The turquoise ring placed on my finger by moonlight this evening is gone.

* * *

I remain locked in my room for two days, taking neither food nor drink and speaking to no one. On the third day, forced out by thirst, I find Friar Denis kneeling in prayer at my door. His beads drop from his fingers to his robes.

"Sweet sister," he begs, "I have persuaded them not to disturb you for fear you were in prayer. But you must make peace with your family, please, at least for your health's sake. The kitchen has prepared soups, pies—" His arm is around my shoulders.

I pass my hand across my forehead. "What of Gabriel? Have they sent him away? Where is he?"

"Child," he repeats, "please come with me. You must—"

"But, Gabriel!" I cry again.

"All right. Here it is: To remove temptation from you both, your father, in his infinite wisdom, has sent Gabriel to your Uncle Joachim's house in Brittany. He knows Gabriel will have difficulty finding any other civilized employment with his…condition…and he knows that your uncle will watch over him as he tends the birds in their mews. But," the expression on his face tells me there is even worse news, "you are never to be allowed to see him again."

My sight is so blinded with tears that Friar Denis must hold me against his arm to get me downstairs. Father, seeing me enter the dining hall, says nothing, just looks relieved and nods his head. Mother smiles and asks me to please sit with her. I can only drink a bit of broth, though I do finish an entire goblet of wine, and return to my room to sleep.

. . .

The incident is not spoken of to me or before me at any time during the next few weeks, leading me to believe that no one knows about our first meeting in the orchard. Closer and closer my marriage draws to Esdelot and now, all I feel is fear, for I know the relationship between the two of us will never be anything like that which Gabriel and I had, even for one brief moment. To compound my troubles, my body seems to have turned against me. I am losing weight, feel too ill to eat whether I wish to or not, tire easily, and sleep much.

Mother calls Dr. Martot to look at me. The doctor thinks I am suffering from a dark humor and recommends bleeding. The bleeding only makes me feel more tired. After several more days Mother, at her wits' end, calls the healer Audine from the village.

Some call Audine a witch, but she is also known to cure bad sickness with her powerful mixtures of plant and flower essences. After examining me, she recommends several tinctures for my dilemma. But just before she leaves, she turns back and asks me one more question, something the doctor did not ask, "My dear, are your menses regular?"

"I have not had them for two months," I say, "though they were regular before."

She sits on the bed next to me, studies my eyes, takes my pulse again. "May I look at your stomach?"

I push the bedding back and open out my sleep robe to reveal my abdomen. She runs her hand over it, touches it in several places, then leans her head down and lays her ear against me. "Renée, my dear, could you be with child?"

I search her face. If I tell her, she may tell my parents, or people in the village will somehow hear and not only will my reputation be ruined, but my family's.

Audine smiles. "The answer is yes, is it not, Renée?"

"Please, do not tell my parents. I am to be married to Esdelot soon."

"Our talks, as with all those who consult me, are in confidence. My diagnosis is a broken heart, that is all they will hear. But I will tell them that to marry you to Esdelot may destroy you. Are you prepared for the consequences if you are not married?"

I think I know what they may be. And if I cannot be with Gabriel... "Yes," I answer.

"Good. I think it is for the best." She takes a small phial from her bag. "Mix this with warm water and drink it twice a day. It will help you recover, and help the baby grow strong."

Two days later, having confessed my pregnancy to Mother, I am riding in the big cart with my brother Robert and the driver, along the rutted and muddy road to Fontevraud Abbaye, where I am to live out my life as a lay sister at La Madeleine, the priory for "lost" women.

· · ·

Just over eight months to the day from our only moment of love in the orchard, my pains begin.

My fellow sisters help me and within only a few hours, the first, insistent squalls of a tiny boy are heard. It is bliss to cradle him in my arms. His eyes look like his father's, his hair is a fluff of auburn curls. The sisters take delight in the coming of new life and love to share in his care. It is then that I write the note I have waited for months to write:

Husband of my heart,

Please do not be angry, nor feel betrayed. You see, you have a son now, born just two days ago. He is a handsome boy, with auburn hair and straight, strong limbs. I have named him Clovis. He came into the world with a healthy squall and takes milk well.

Already he smiles at me. Oh, if I could send you those smiles! Please, though seeing your son is your birthright, do not come here, at least until the ban is lifted or my father forgives us. For I would rather Clovis had a father he could find living in Brittany, instead of one who lies dead in Anjou.

I miss you every moment and I long for your touch. I cry that you cannot see the fruit of our love. But we, both of us, must be patient, because someday he will stand before you, and you will be proud.

My sweet Gabriel, though we must be apart for the sake of our son, I shall love you forever and I know that, if there is a just and merciful God, he will join us together again, in a place where no man can confound our union.

Your loving Renée

I send the letter care of Audine, asking her to somehow get it to Gabriel. But I do not know if it ever reached him, or a reply was intercepted by one of the monks, or Father's men.

And only three mornings later I awake to find my beautiful Clovis dead in his cradle. As she comforts me while I weep, the nurse tells me these things happen, especially when babies are born before their time. For some reason God must have wanted him home. We bathe his little body in warm rosewater, wrap him in soft linen. A service is held for his little soul in the chapel of La Madeleine. Then we bury him in the town graveyard.

· · ·

Word has come from Brittany that the plague has returned and that the number of dead is mounting. Now, I pray for both Clovis and his father every morning at Mass and every evening at Vespers. Perhaps they are together in God's Paradise. Neither is ever absent from my heart.

As at Rochemont, I frequently spend my afternoons in the upper floors working by the light of a big window overlooking the river. One afternoon, as I am weaving, a kestrel lands on the ledge next to the casement. I can see she is wild, not a kept hunting bird, and when I look more closely at her, I notice that one of her legs, though properly mended has, at one time, been broken. She stares in for a moment, inclines her comely head toward me as if in recognition then, the next instant, opens out her wings and leaps from the ledge, sailing up on a summer updraft and wheeling away along the course of the river to the west, where she is free.

TEN

Emily
January, 2004

To live beyond death. To breathe in light. I found myself in a new world, one of possibilities that stretched before me endlessly; one of joy experienced by moments that, linked, made every day, however trembling in its delivery, seem a miracle.

This bud of optimism had to do with the message, as Dr. Shaeffer had suggested, that I might find on the tapes. Now that I was off the drugs and alcohol and my mind had cleared, I began investigating what might be fact and what was fantasy in the stories I had assembled.

In Clare's tale of Minoan Santorini for example, I discovered that an excavation conducted many years earlier on Crete had yielded a golden bee pendant like the one Clare described the young woman, Acasia, receiving. That Clare could have heard of such a find was not in itself remarkable, especially considering her education. That the gold pendant had been unearthed at a burial site in Malia where her character Acasia had died in the tidal wave, perhaps was.

In Roman Byzantium, two urban factions called *Prasenoi* and *Venetoi*,

Blues and Greens, did riot in January of 532 AD. This civil insurrection became known as the Nika Revolt and had altered Western history by cementing the powers of Justinian and Theodora over the eastern Mediterranean, Italy, and North Africa. But such information was easily available; in fact, I found it in only a few minutes of Internet research.

Of Heian Japan, much information correlated, such as the name of the famous clan of strongmen, Fujiwara, so close to Clare's "Sujiwaras," or that is the name I thought I heard her speaking. Not surprisingly, despite hours of research online and in the library I found no record of any concubine named Omida. Yet the detail of that story fit so neatly with historical descriptions of the distinctive world of early Kyoto I could not dismiss the possibility that Clare might be tapping into information or scenes she had absorbed at one time and, in her creative unconscious, woven into her own tragic tale.

I was also surprised to find that, among ancient Kyoto's upper classes, it was not at all uncommon for a woman to be visited for sexual favors in the dark of night by a man she did not know and might not recognize by daylight. But again, the fact that I found this information also meant Clare could have found it and stored it away mentally, only to retrieve it later in the mind-opening experience of hypnosis.

To me, all three stories argued for the hidden-memory theory. But could they perhaps be evidence of a more serious diagnosis, like dissociative identity disorder, that had surfaced during the hypnagogic state?

. . .

My next priority was still to find "Clare," if that was her name and if she existed at all. Nick's patients' medical records were now long gone, and it would have been unethical in the extreme for me to have gone rummaging through them anyway. Why hadn't I thought before to go to Marks, Janowski and Miller, the lawyers who had drawn up the original document releasing the records to Nick? Knowing that the removal of property from Nick's house, even with consent of Nick's family, could constitute a gray area of the law, I called and asked to speak with Jerome Rosedall, the attorney who had signed the document. Unfortunately, Mr. Rosedall was not available; would I like to speak with his paralegal, Barbara Hughes?

A week later I sat in Ms. Hughes' office high above Century Park East. She was polite, friendly, and understood my situation, but she was sorry, she could not help me. Legal consultations, like medical ones, were confidential, and she could provide me with no further information; even the name, or pseudonym, of the client had to remain private. However, if I could prove that the information had been willed to me specifically as part of Nick's estate, then the information they had might become available to me. As it was, the only hint that I had been designated an "assign" was that my name was on the front of the envelope. What they needed was a will confirming the deceased's wish that this information be passed to me.

"Nick didn't have a will. Nothing."

"I'm so sorry. I wish we could help. But without a will or directive from the deceased or the court, our hands are tied."

"I understand," I said as I picked up my tote to leave.

She walked me to the doorway. But just before I walked down the hall, she asked, "Does his executor by chance have access to his financial records?"

"You mean checks, that sort of thing?"

"Perhaps if a client paid by check . . .?"

"I think his father has his personal records now."

"Well, you might contact him to see if any of the records can be released. Though I doubt it, I have to tell you." She paused for a moment. "Wait. Wouldn't Dr. Turner have had an accounting firm doing his taxes? At least for his business."

Nick's accountants. I think Valerie had said they were out in the Valley.

As I drove out of the underground garage I thought of the sheer size of the Southern California Basin. Five hundred square miles, plus. Chances were, somewhere out there off the maze of freeways, in the hills, near the ocean or even somewhere on the Westside, lived the woman I knew only as Clare. The only person who could unlock the secrets of the tapes. And no way for me, short of a miracle, to find her.

I called Valerie on the way home to find out the details of the estate, just in case I hadn't heard correctly in my brain-fog at the hospital. Yes, she said, their father had been named executor by the court. All Nick's records were now with Burney and Myers, Nick's longtime accountants in Van Nuys. We talked a little more about the disposition of Nick's household items, and made a date for lunch the following week.

By nine the next morning, I was on the phone to the accountants' office. My conversation with Susan Burney followed almost verbatim the one I'd had in the lawyer's office. It was tricky, she said, but if I could prove a financial reason I needed to see the account records, perhaps. Meaning that to get the records, I'd either have to prove financial need, monies owed or withheld, for instance, or I'd need a solid legal reason to present to the court.

"Then there's the medical confidentiality issue," she said. "I just don't know how you'd get around that, unless you had a legal document from the client, releasing her records."

"In which case I'd already know," I said.

Stumped by my conundrum, we were both silent for a moment. Then she said, "You've tried the Internet, of course."

"I think I've officially reached the end of it."

"Hmmm. How about a good, old fashioned detective agency?"

"A PI?" It had never occurred to me. "I just assumed the Internet had put them out of business."

"Actually, I know one; he's doing just fine. Insurance fraud, employment histories, that sort of thing. I'll get his number. Let me put you on hold." She was back in a few seconds. "His name is Dan Pierce. He's out your way, actually. Westwood."

. . .

Four days later, I stood in the high-gloss lobby of a Westwood high rise, double-checking the directory for Mr. Pierce's suite number. I arrived on the twentieth floor to a modern office with "Investigative Associates" decaled in gold lettering on its smoked-glass door. A young woman in a navy-and-white silk blouse and navy miniskirt came forward from behind her desk and strutted toward me, sharp heels clicking across the terrazzo.

"Emily Reidell for Mr. Pierce, three-thirty," I said, smiling.

"Of course, Miss Reidell. This way," she said, trailing a light floral fragrance behind her.

I followed her down a long, glass-enclosed hallway to what appeared to be the largest space in the suite. Evan Pierce's office faced southwest, looking out at Century City to one side and Santa Monica and the ocean on the other. The view must have been spectacular on a clear day. But today, in the West L.A. soup of bright murk, I couldn't even see past Sepulveda Boulevard just a few blocks west.

A middle-aged man, heavyset and balding, but fashionably dressed, stood up to greet me.

"Emily Reidell." I offered my hand.

"Dan Pierce." He motioned to an armchair facing his desk. "I understand you're looking for a doctor's client."

I related the whole story, including what work I'd already done.

"No surname for this woman. No place of employment, spouse?"

I folded my hands on top of my lap. My shoulders sank under my shirt as I sighed. "None," I said.

"No arrests mentioned. No delinquent speeding tickets, unpaid taxes."

"Not that she mentioned."

"Did your fiancé ever talk about her case to any other medical professional?" he asked.

"Possibly, but I assume they're bound by the same ethical code Nick was."

"Mmm, boy." He put his palms together in an attitude of prayer under his chin and stared past me for a moment. "You know, a Guatemalan woman came to me once wanting to find her birth parents. All she had was the name of the village she thought her mother came from. That, and a few pressed flowers that had been put with her in the basket at the steps of the rectory where she'd been left as a newborn. And we found her mother. The key was the plant; it was specific to that area of the country. It took us a while, and her some money, but we did it. But this, I'd have no place to even start."

"That's my problem."

"I'd love to help you. It does sound like an interesting challenge."

"But . . .?"

"I'd just need more information. But if you came upon anything, would you like me to have my administrative assistant give you a fee schedule just in case?"

"Sure," I said, standing to shake his hand, "and thanks for your time."

. . .

As I stood in the shower that night with the hot water pounding on my back and neck, I wondered where to turn next. And then it came to me. Yet another casualty of my months of confusion. I'd forgotten all about Nick's library, if it was still there. And the telephone. Perhaps there'd been a message left on his answering machine.

I phoned Valerie again the next morning.

"Me, again. I didn't want to trouble you about this before, but I'm still researching those papers I found at Nick's house. Did you by chance get any messages from his office answering machine?"

"Actually, just one. Someone wanting to make an appointment. We gave his name to the same doctor who took all the other files."

"No other communications from the day he was killed?"

"No, but maybe he'd checked his messages before lunch that day. He was always pretty good about returning his calls."

"Well, would you mind if I went over to see if there are any books in his library that might help me?"

"No problem, but I've got to go to Palos Verdes and won't be back until later in the afternoon. I'll leave the key inside the fake rock in the fern at my front door, okay?"

"Thanks a million."

"Good luck," she said.

. . .

I was up early, and over to Valerie's by ten. Back at home, a call came in about one of my previously written articles, suddenly squeezed down to fewer columns, and I spent a couple of hours midday revising it. While downing a quick lunch of yogurt and fruit I realized Dr. Willis, the dentist whose office was next door to Nick's, might know something about Nick's clients' comings and goings. He'd sent flowers to the funeral, condolences to the family. I knew he and Nick had talked occasionally. I got into the car and drove up to his Palisades office.

Except for one teenage boy reading *Road & Track* and tapping his foot with nerves, the standard-issue dental waiting room was empty. Three woman sat behind the front console, a receptionist and two assistants, all in candy-pastel surgical uniforms.

"May we help you?" asked the receptionist, a plump-cheeked girl with hair drawn back into a ponytail. "Heather" her name tag read.

The whine of a dental drill penetrated the waiting room from the back of the office.

"I don't have an appointment," I said.

Heather smiled. "No problem."

"Actually, I was a friend of Dr. Turner's, next door," I said.

Both assistants glanced up at me.

"We were so sorry about that," Heather said.

"He used to come by sometimes to talk to Dr. Willis," said one of the assistants, an older woman with short blond hair.

"Well, that's actually why I'm here," I said. "I'm a science writer, a friend of his, and was wondering if you might be able to help me with something. It's a case of Dr. Turner's that he asked me to write up. It's about a young woman, one of his patients. The lawyers had cleared him to leave me the information about the case, but I have some questions and all I have is her first name, Clare."

The three looked at each other.

"Gee," Heather said, "we hardly ever saw anyone come or go from his office. It was so private there."

I pulled out my folder, checked my notes. "She was here between September, nineteen ninety-eight and January, 'ninety-nine. Do you by chance happen to remember anyone coming once a week during that time frame? A young woman?"

"That was before I worked here," the short blond-haired assistant said.

"Sorry, me too," Heather said.

"I was here," volunteered the other assistant in back. She stood up and came to the desk.

Ginny. "If I was in the back in the lab, I could see people sometimes coming and going."

"Do you remember . . .?" I asked.

"Hmm. Wow. Honestly, I'd be terrible with a police lineup. Let's see... Fall, 'ninety-eight. MJ—my daughter—started at Pali High." She stopped for a moment, then looked up at me. "You know, I do remember one person from that time, only because she looked so much like I thought my daughter might look in a few years."

I opened my notebook.

"Medium height, as I recall. Blond hair, real blond, not bleached, except, you know"—she touched her own head—"by the sun. Curly. Actually, she was dressed sort of like MJ does now." She looked for help to the other two. "Bohemian, wouldn't you say?"

"Well I'd call her style interesting, a mix," Heather said.

"Not," Ginny said, "sporty. Like you."

"Did she drive here? Walk?" I asked.

"I think I did see her getting into a car once. A Toyota. A smaller one. Blue."

Probably the most popular make in Southern California.

"Anything else? Anything at all?" I asked.

Ginny shook her head. "I don't know if I've helped or confused you. But, Dr. Willis might know something. Shall I have him call you?"

"Sure, that would be great." I pulled a card from my wallet.

．　．　．

When I finally stepped into Nick's old office later in the day, I remembered that it was such an afternoon that I first saw this place, the first time Nick kissed me. I shifted the blinds open and streaks of dusty amber sunlight drifted through the darkness and settled on his oak roll-top desk. I ran my fingers across its golden patina, remembering the first time I'd touched it. He'd been standing at the long console opposite, putting the kettle to brew for my tea.

The desk looked like an antique. "Is this . . .?" I'd asked.

"Yeah. It's the real thing. My grandfather's."

He'd brought the tea over in an earthenware mug with dark stripes across it. As he'd handed me the mug, our fingers had met. "Careful, it's hot," he'd said.

I looked down at my hands. Nick's collection of mugs, always lined up neatly in the left corner of the console when the day began, and scattered about the right when the day was over, was gone.

Now, though, the once-verdant ficus was bent from lack of water, a ring of yellow leaves around it on the floor. His library, at least three hundred books, I guessed, not counting journals, sat on the bookshelves. I filled the teapot left on the console with water, tended the poor tree, found a towel in the bathroom and brushed away the cobwebs that had started to form book-to-book.

Knowing the private and highly sensitive nature of Nick's work, I had decided, after our relationship expanded beyond that first interview in his office, never to pry into what he called "my other life." He had seldom mentioned any specifics of his days and told me he appreciated my discretion. Making the whole topic of doctor-patient interaction off-limits had made life so much easier for us as a couple. As such, I'd only visited his office a few times after our first meeting there and we'd rarely discussed, even in general terms, his daily work. But I knew he had made most of his library available to his patients. Now I was a patient with a problem to solve.

What must have been the complete works of Jung, twenty volumes anyway, occupied the top shelf. Next to them, fortunately, were books explaining Jung's theories. I pulled one and continued down the shelf. More books on analytical psychology and several by Jung's famous amanuensis Marie-Louise von Franz, including a paperback titled *Alchemy* with a curious cover illustration of a diademed snake in a circle, devouring its own tail. I pulled it out and continued along the same shelf, to what seemed to be mostly abstracts and post-Jungian periodicals. After leafing through a few, I returned to the set of volumes until I found the Swiss doctor's famous essay "On Synchronicity."

The next shelf appeared to be devoted to general psychiatric topics, and to reference works such as the 2003 PDR and the DSM-IV, though interspersed with these I also found several books on the use of hypnosis in therapy. I chose a couple of those, then scanned the rest of the shelf, with its books on various schools of therapeutic method, from Freud to Rogers.

But the most interesting shelf of the entire wall was the bottom one. There sat the eclectic assortment of paperbacks I'd commented on the first time I'd visited. Some explored Eastern philosophies, others investigated the structure of world mythology. Several related true-life stories of individuals who claimed they had been reincarnated. But the most curious group of books, considering that Nick's specialty had been psychiatry, were several paperbacks on speculative physics and the physics of the human brain.

I picked the one with the simplest title, Evan Jacobs' *Physics of Mind*. Hadn't I seen this book somewhere before? Was it at the bookstore? No. I sat on the floor, thumbing through its pages. There was something familiar about it, and then I remembered: It was the same book that had been on Nick's desk at home the morning I went there with Valerie.

I went through the little stack I'd put together. I sighed, shoved them into my tote, picked up the key and locked the office up. Maybe something in one of the books would give me a clue as to Clare's state of mind.

· · ·

Mark Willis called me that evening.

"Thanks for calling," I said. "I guess you heard the story."

"How are you doing?" he asked.

"Oh, fine. It's kind of a slow process, some days better than others. Work helps."

"That's good to hear. I remember meeting up with Nick the Monday after you two met. We went around the corner for a cup of coffee and he couldn't stop talking about you."

Reminiscence still came hard to me. "Oh, that's nice to know," was all I could say.

"Sorry," he apologized.

"It's okay, really." I cleared my throat. "I just thought you might possibly have seen the woman your assistant mentioned. She sounds like a possibility."

"You know, I just don't think I ever did. And he never, well, you know, we can't discuss our patients."

"Yeah, ironically Nick's line of work is working against me here."

"Other than the 'everybody's-in-a-bad-mood-today' sort of thing. Usually it was 'guy stuff,' his motorcycles, my boat." He paused. "You've tried the Internet, of course."

"Extensively."

"How about a private investigator?"

"That, too."

"What are they doing about his office?"

"I don't actually know what's going on with that now."

"Well, if I can help with that at least, in any way, just let me know."

"Sure, and thanks," I said.

I made myself a cup of hot chocolate and plopped myself down on the sofa. Fizzy jumped up into my lap and I stroked her ears. I flicked the TV on, scrolled up and down and back again. Seventy-five channels and nothing to watch. I took another sip of chocolate and my eyes wandered over to my desk, where the books from Nick's library and my work on Clare's case were piled high, like materials at a building site. I had no idea in the world how I was ever going to make sense of Clare's stories, know for sure their origin or meaning. But Dr. Sheaffer had articulated my challenge quite clearly: Was I going to sort out Nick's last message to me, or was I going to let the loss of Nick defeat me? Nick himself had left me the answer to that one. And there it was, calling to me from my desk.

ELEVEN

Clare/Maggie

1774-75 A.D.
Virginia Piedmont

I re-tie the apron over my old linsey-woolsey dress and bend down to pick up another load of wood for the kitchen fire. The sun has been up near two hours now and we've long since served breakfast for the master and his visitors. If I'm lucky now I can get some pone for myself because I'm so hungry the slop I gave the pigs looks like a feast.

Though I'm now eighteen years, the only home I've ever known is the Beeches. I was born in a shed here and been owned by the Pritchard family since that August day. My mother come to the plantation pregnant from her last owner, who made a deal with Ebenezer Pritchard to take her off his hands so he didn't get in a fix with his wife, 'cause there'd have been hell-to-pay for sure if his wife saw a mulatto baby on the farm looking anything like her husband. I never knew my mother: Right after I was born, old Pritchard sold her to yet another planter outside the county. I was raised up by old Zillo, my "aunt," who does the cooking here. Now I'm a house slave, worked from sunup to sundown, just like all the other slaves on the farm.

Some of us try to escape, but most don't make it, and the ones who are hunted down and sent back to their masters suffer terrible, like Jake, a runaway we all knew about. When Littleton's overseer caught him, he beat Jake until his back was a crust of blood, then shut him inside a cage hanging from a tree where, we all heard, the crows pecked his eyes out before he died. He was three days dying.

Then there was a time when a visitor's dog set on me; a big hound dog, the same kind used to hunt runaways and tear them up. He went for my ankle, cutting my heel string. Some masters cut their field slaves' heel strings so they can't run. Mine was cut by a dog's teeth, while the visitor laughed. That's why I limp now.

Every year I do more of the tasks Zillo used to do herself. At first, when I was young, I helped her cook and serve, but ever since Zillo's joints swelled up sorely on her, I've been hauling water and butts of pork, too. Zillo sews, and she has taught me. She tells me I am now very good with the needle and thread. I began by mending for the house servants, but a while back the workers on the farm asked me to dress up with stitchery the old shirts and breeches they had from other houses to wear for church, or when they get together to dance and sing songs of the old country on free Saturdays.

*   *   *

Just as I'm about to pick up a griddle cake for myself, Samson Terrent shows up in the doorway. Samson is the overseer now, the white overseer having quit for lack of wages. Usually Samson stays away from the hot, smoky kitchen except to steal wine from the cellar nearby so he must be up to no good.

He lifts the cake off the fire. "Say, Miz Maggie," he says, leering sideways at me with those nasty stained teeth. He runs his hand across my bottom as I try to duck away. "Say, Miz Maggie," he starts again, "how'd you like to take a little trip?" He takes a bite out of the cake.

I glare at him. "What kinda trip?" I mutter as I drop another on the griddle, wishing the cake was his hand.

He leans against the doorjamb, tosses the half-eaten cake outside. "Git your sewing bag. I'm gonna make some money off you."

Zillo's eyes meet mine. She turns to the oven, shaking her head. Fear rises burning up my throat.

"Git your bag, girl," Terrent repeats, grin fading on him. "And git your shoes. Charlie and Joe are taking you in the market wagon." It is then that my eyes rest on the worn-out whip sticking out of the top of his grimy boot. "I said, GIT READY!"

I find my boots and pick up my cowhide "housewife" bag with its paper-o'-pins, thimble, chalk, needles, buttons, and threads. Samson grabs my arm and drags me behind him. The gravel on the kitchen path cuts my feet and with my gimp I can barely stay upright. He dumps me into a covered cart next to a load of chickens, flapping and pecking at their crates. I push my cut feet down into my boots. The laces on the right one are broke halfway, but I tie them anyway, then the other shoe because I don't know where I'm going and who knows if there'll be more rocks?

Samson picks up the chain attached to the sideboards of the cart, presses my ankle down and locks the chain to itself around my leg. Then he hands the key to Joe. Charlie undoes the brake, puts the reins to the horses' backs, and the cart rolls forward.

I push one of the crates aside with my foot so I can turn 'round, and pull the cover aside. "Charlie! Where'm I going?"

"Rutledge Hall."

"Where?"

"Rutledge Hall, Miss Maggie. You're being hired out."

Oh, I'd heard of that place. Hell's House, they call it. A slave was beat to death there, a relation of Zillo's, for stealing something, some bacon is what I heard. A chill travels through my bones, top to toe. Maybe

Rutledge's is worse than the Beeches.

The cart grumbles along the long avenue of beech trees at the start of the property until we reach the main road, with the Occoquan River off to the left. I crawl to the rear of the wagon, as far as the footlock Samson has put on my leg will let me, to look out. The air is thick with new-blossom smell, and a single white cloud floats across the morning sky, on its way to some beautiful faraway place, probably.

So much has changed on the plantation in the last two years, none for the good. The bad times started with Master Henry's new horse. Going against Master Ebenezer's wishes, Henry took the horse, just greenbroke, out across the fields. The horse, being so unsettled, threw Henry. Henry's boot stayed stuck in the iron, though, and the horse, crazed to be loose, threw Henry off. The field slaves carried him in and lay his broke-up body on the big velvet settee on the veranda. Master Henry never came to, and died before the sun came up the next day.

There was no comforting Miss Abigail, Master Ebenezer's wife, nor Henry's sister Rebecca. But worse was coming. The winter after, an epidemic of the winter fever come to the Tidewater counties. No plantation was spared, and planter was like as slave to catch it. I myself had it mild two years before. But in the year 1772, it was real bad, and Rebecca died before Christmas.

Master Pritchard took to drink then, and Miss Abigail went mad as a spring hare, Henry and Rebecca being their only two children. She shut herself up in her room, and we could hear her screaming half the night sometimes. The master mostly kept to his study, we think. Of course, the only way we knew was by the empty Madeira bottles outside the door. Finally, Miss Abigail must have just decided to go away from her sorrows because a big carriage came one day to take her, we heard, to stay with her sister in Charleston, and we haven't seen naught of her since.

That was last spring. Now the plantation is run almost entirely by Terrent. He is the worst black man I've ever known, wasting his precious freedom on evil, stealing money from the plantation accounts, or keeping the money from the crops himself. And now the field slaves hardly never get their full weekly ration of meat and corn, since Terrent keeps some of that to sell, too. He takes advantage of me whenever he feels like it but I don't cry any more 'cause there is no one to rescue me. It's a miracle I haven't got his bastard child in me now.

The wagon bumps along and up a bit, it seems like for hours, until, finally, it clanks and stops. Charlie calls back to me, "Maggie, we got a bucket of dinner here, if you want some food."

It's only ham scraps and sweet potato, but nothing ever tasted better, especially washed down with the cold water from the creek we're sitting by, and it's fine indeed to be resting without the chain on my leg under the big dogwood tree, filled with yellow and black birds singing their love to each other from its blossoming branches.

After eating, the men chew and spit out tobacco without talking much until Charlie finally says, "Well, best be on our way. Don't want to be around these parts after dark."

Back in the rear of the wagon with the chickens I get bumped around even more, for what had been a road now seems mostly rocks and holes. Charlie halts the team. I hear Joe and him discussing something. The chickens quit clucking and flapping like they're listening in. All I hear is the sound of the wind high up in the trees and a woodpecker, tapping like crazy on some tree far away. I peek out from under the cover. Charlie and Joe jump down from the wagon. Now they are fighting.

"I tole you, we shoulda turned at Randolph Farm!"

"Naw, that road only goes t' the tallow works this direction."

"Let's go look over the rise. Maybe we can see Rutledge from there."

Joe relieves himself against a tree, then follows Charlie. I am alone in the wagon now. Me and my sewing bag. It is then that I see: Charlie forgot to lock the iron on my leg.

I don't know what's running through my head exactly, maybe my awful life at the Beeches, maybe just the idea of freedom, like the birds in the trees or the cloud sailing through the sky. If they were free, why not me? One thing is for sure: Anything would be better than the prison of my life. And if I'm going to Hell's House I'm like to die anyway.

I've heard of slaves escaping to the frontier and we seem to be quite a stretch inland from the Beeches now. Surely there are wild Indians here. But I'd take my chances with a wild Indian over the wild men of the Tidewater.

Birds hardly ever fly away from me, and I unhook the chain and move the chicken coops ever so quietly none of the birds squawks and calls the men back to the cart. I slip out and, crouching down real low like a tomcat, peer out from behind the rear wheel. Charlie and Joe are standing some ways away at the rim of a clearing, looking out over the valley in the opposite direction. They are too far away for me to hear what they are saying but I see one, then the other, pointing off into the distance. And Charlie taking his straw hat off to scratch his head.

Near sick with terror, I crawl on all fours into a thicket of creepers behind a big tree a ways up the incline from the wagon and tell my shaking body to keep itself still. Pretty soon the two return. They climb up onto the bench and Charlie turns around to the back to say something to me. Lucky for me he doesn't wait for an answer before slapping the reins on the rumps of the team and the wagon, chickens complaining, rolls over the low hill and away.

We seem to have come to the frontier far away from the Beeches. There are bushes blooming pink and white just about everywhere. I hear the sound of water close, maybe the big river, but I don't know.

Hugging my little bag close to my chest, I pick my way through the tangle of vines and branches slowly as they say the red men do. The forest is very dark and I hear weird sounds, animal-like sounds I never heard before. The air is heavy with a green heat that makes me sticky and thirsty. After some time, I get away from the fingers of the undergrowth into a little clearing.

I've come west I think, not knowing directions really, but with the sun going down now, I will need to find some shelter before nightfall. When I look ahead I see I have been traveling on some kind of animal path, maybe one that will lead me to water, for now that is all I can think of. After a time I do hear a trickle and, just as the sun drops behind the hill, I come to a little creek. The water livens me somewhat, but when I stand I hear a pop and look down to see that the last of my shoelace has broke off. I sit down and tear a strip from my shimmy to pull the beat-up boot back together.

It is then, looking up and ahead, that I see something I didn't notice before: a cabin, or what is surely going to be a cabin. A raised floor is ready, a few cut logs stacked off to one side and a few more set in place. Maybe it might be a shelter for the night. Maybe there's food or a blanket there. Tying my boot best I can, I drag myself up the hill to it.

Except for a bucket with a ladle and what looks like a deerskin hide on a branch nearby, it doesn't look like humans are here. Maybe the builder has been ambushed by red men and killed. Anyway, I can no longer walk, what with my lame foot and broke-down boots, plus darkness coming down, so I pull the buckskin from the tree and wrap it around me and lean up against the built side of the cabin. I guess I fall asleep, because the next thing I know the dark of night is all around and I hear the leaves dancing and singing in the trees above me. I draw the hide closer to me and look up, beyond the treetops and to the stars. I never knew the sky was so full of color. And that it moved over my head.

· · ·

Someone is talking, far away—no, close. My eyes fly open. It's morning. I hear men's voices, coming nearer.

"Is that some bossloper hiding under that old skin?" one says.

I rub my eyes clear, then peek around the top of my cover. Two frontiersmen are walking toward the cabin with a sturdy-looking little horse. Oh, Lordy Jesus, slave-hunters! And they've seen me now.

The horse man ties the horse to a tree and both come toward me. Horseman is dark of eye and hair. Until I can shade my eyes with my hand, the other one is just a tall shadow with the sun perched on his shoulder.

Then he moves so the sun's on him. His face looks weather-roughed, but gentlemanly. His hair is reddish, like wet earth at the plantation, and tied in a queue with a strip of leather. His skin is darkened with freckles, like white folks get if they're out in the sun all the time. To tell truth, he seems darker than I am. Just when I'm thinking how beautiful he is, I remember Zillo's warning: A flowering face does often hide an evil heart.

He unshoulders his rifle, rests it against a tree. "How did you come here, young woman? What is your name?"

I begin to speak, open my mouth, then close it again.

"You may speak freely. We will not harm you," Horse-man assures me.

I get up slowly to my feet. "I…I got lost in the forest."

"And you have escaped," says the freckled one.

Then I remember: *Jake and the crows.*

Quick as I can, I throw off the deerskin and take off into a run as fast as my gimp will let me. It seems I'm getting away. But someone is running hard behind me, the freckled one. I try to run faster, but he gains on me and pulls me down before the little creek I crossed last night.

My face hits the leaves and twigs on the forest floor and the fall knocks the wind out of me. He grabs my arm and holds it so tight I nearly cry. I begin fighting, slapping at him with my other arm, kicking out at him like a frantic half-drowned cat, trying to bite his hand. But he is stronger, and gets a grip on my other arm.

"Let me go!" I scream, fighting his clutches as he pulls me up. "Let me go!"

He is shaking me, yelling at me. All I hear is, "Girl, girl!"

I put the boot to his shins. He howls like a kicked dog, then slaps me hard against the face.

Before I can kick again, he presses me against a tree, holding his knee against mine to still me.

"Girl! Good God! Stand quiet for a moment and let me speak!"

I'm caught for sure. There's nothing I can do now but try to stare him down.

"Girl—who won't tell me her name—first, we are not slave-hunters, I swear. We can, will, help you, if you will just calm yourself. But you must let us get you out of this forest."

"Let me GO!"

"The red men here take scalps for their belts. Have you seen a man scalped? Not a pretty sight."

I'd heard such, but thought they were just stories to scare us from escaping to freedom. "You just say that so I won't run." I squirm again.

"You are absolutely correct. Do you want to test the truth for yourself?" He drops his hands from my arms.

"No sir, I guess I don't."

"All right. Shall we start again, as civilized people do? My name is Elijah, Elijah Burke, and my friend is George Winsett. May I not know your name and from where you hail?"

I look at him, then the other who has joined him, both waiting for me to explain myself. "My name is Agatha, but they call me Maggie. I come from the Beeches, the plantation." I look down at my feet and croak like a frog grabbed up in the swamp, "I ran away."

"If you will come with us, we will take you to a place where they will not find you. All right?" Elijah asks.

I look at the man George, then back at Elijah. "I guess so," I mutter, not looking them in their eyes. It is either them or getting killed in the forest by some wild Indian or eaten up by some nasty animal.

I try to walk, but with one foot near useless and other in a broke boot,

I am near crippled completely, especially after trying to run so.

"Here, Eli, we'll put her on Sixpence," George says.

Scowling as he sees my dragging foot, Elijah lifts me up onto the little farm horse. "I suppose your masters cut your heel?"

"It was a hound dog tore me."

He moves his fingers forward like to soothe the place where my scar would be then, catching himself, he pulls his hand back. He clears his throat, "Is your seat secure?"

"I guess so," I reply, because I've never been on a horse.

George leads the mare as Elijah walks alongside and after a while, we stop at a cabin in a place that is cleared, but only slightly so, with many tall trees still making shade and decoration, not all cut down, like around the Beeches. The house is only whitewashed board with two windows in front and a brick chimney at one end but seems more of a home than the Beeches ever was to anybody.

A pretty woman in a white cap is standing outside the door holding a baby in her arms, smiling. I hear the pounding of ax to wood, then a man who looks like the Elijah man, only with darker hair, cleaning his hands on a rag and coming out from back of the cabin toward us. George helps me down from the horse.

"George! How good to see you again!" He holds his hand out to the man who is obviously a friend, then looks at me. "And who is this?"

I balance myself on one foot, leaning against the horse and hoping no one will really see me here, until the baby gurgles out a mouthful of bubbles, and I can't help but smile some.

"Daniel, this is Maggie, who became lost in the forest," Elijah says. "Maggie, this is my brother Daniel and my sister-in-law, Mary. Oh, and baby Rachel."

Mary holds her hand out to me real polite, like greeting a white person. "Please, Maggie, come in. You must have suffered a very trying time in the woods."

Inside, the little house is very roomy and bright. Mary and the baby sit down next to me at the table as I eat the bowl of porridge Mary gives me. I sure never heard of free setting down to eat with slave and wonder how far from the Beeches I must be now. From outside I hear conversation passing between Elijah and Daniel and I think they are talking about me. It is a violation of Virginia law—and I think I must still be in Virginia—to take in a runaway. Mary and Rachel are likely breaking the law just setting here beside me.

I hear Mary asking how I came to be lost in the forest. At first I don't want to talk, for fear of telling her where my owner lives, but my fate is in the Good Lord's hands now. So I begin to tell her a little about the Beeches, and Samson, and the ride I was supposed to be taking to Rutledge Hall, how I jumped off the wagon, not thinking of anything but freedom, and that I know I am a runaway and in danger, the colonists that hide me, too.

"Maggie," she says, "you are in the company of friends here. Neither my husband, nor Elijah, nor any friend who passes through our door countenances slavery. And none of us will reveal your whereabouts."

Suddenly, a sound like a person's voice comes from behind a closed door next to the main room. I look up; so does Mary. Then she says, "Elizabeth must be needing help. Excuse me for a moment."

I hear a bit of conversation, and just as I am trying to peer around the half-closed door, Mary comes out.

"Come, Maggie, and meet Elizabeth." She motions for me.

It's a small room, with only a bed and washstand to it, plus a plain chair off to the side. A woman is sitting up in the bed, covered with a quilt, her head propped up against some pillows. She looks just like a normal white woman, except for her hands, all bent up like the claws of a dead bird.

"Elizabeth," Mary says, smiling, "this is Maggie. Maggie, Elizabeth."

I curtsey and Elizabeth nods and smiles, but does not move as she says, "Welcome to Orchid Hollow. I must have been sleeping when you came in."

"Yes, ma'am, though I tried to be quiet."

She laughs. "Oh, it's lovely to have a visitor."

"Maggie is just having some food. We'll return in a while," Mary says.

I sat back down to finish my porridge. "Is Elizabeth a relative, ma'am?" I ask Mary.

"My sister-in-law. She is Elijah's wife."

Elijah has a wife. "She's taken ill?"

Mary shakes her head, looks down. "No, she is a cripple."

"How?" I ask, wondering why Elijah would marry a cripple.

"An accident, not long after they were married. The creek was high and she slipped and fell in. She was near death when we found her downstream. The doctor guessed she hit her head against a rock and broke her back. Her arms and legs . . ." Mary shakes her head and wipes tears from her eyes with the corner of her apron.

"How long ago, ma'am?"

"Nearly two years, now. Poor Elizabeth. And poor Elijah. He loves her dearly."

The door opens and the three men come in, still talking about politics.

"We must find a way to hide Maggie," Mary says to Daniel. "Perhaps the little attic above the loft?"

"That, or the cellar," he answers. Then, turning to me, he says, "Until we can find a way to get you to freedom and safety."

"Which we may all enjoy, God willing, soon enough!" George says, laughing, and the other two laugh, too.

Elijah goes into Elizabeth's room and I see him leaning over and kissing her. Mary leads me up a narrow ladder, above the loft and into a tiny attic, just a small space snug between the ceiling and the rooftop, not high enough for a body to stand up in but, she says, the perfect hiding place for that very reason.

At supper, there is talk of the "rebellion" they say is coming. It must be related to the Tea Party in Boston around Christmas last year. At the Beeches, we native-born Negroes shared more gossip than the white men knew, like about the Stamp Act, and what trouble it caused everybody, having to pay more tax to the English, and I think the Tea Party had something to do with this, but I do not know more than the gossip, and I don't speak.

"Do they talk about the rebellion at the Beeches, Maggie?" Elijah asks, who has been keeping an eye on me from his side of the table.

"You mean a slave rebellion?"

"Maggie, I think the men are talking of the rebellion against the English crown, for our freedom," Mary explains.

"Oh," I say. "I don't know a thing about rebellion against the English."

"When we are freed from the English government," Daniel says, "we will have the chance to make our own laws, free of King George and his parliament, and free of slavery. That's the way we see it here on the frontier, anyway."

As I climb into my little attic bed later, I think how strange it is that after running away, I am holed up in a place that must be near as tiny as the slave-holds the new Negroes tell of inside the big ships from Africa. My guts tell me the Burkes are good people, especially Elijah, taking such kindly care of his poor, crippled wife. But they all are, firstly, white men. I better find a way to make myself useful here so they don't turn me in for the bounty-hunter's price, which they may need, being so poor. Not until I can think of one does sleep come over me.

· · ·

For the first time I can remember in my life the sun is up before I am. I hear Mary working in the kitchen below. She tells me the men left before daylight.

"Will they come back?" I ask.

Mary laughs. "It's Elijah. He's working away from the homestead today."

"Ma'am, I'd like to work, too. I can do any sewing you want. I can cut a pattern for shirts or breeches. I can mend, too, and have lots of buttons." I open my "housewife" bag and lay its contents out on the table.

Mary puts her fingers on first the spools and then the buttons. "What beautiful sewing materials! I know the men's clothes could stand repair, especially Eli's." She pauses, thinking. "I do have some plain linen. Perhaps a shirt each for the men?"

She brings out a fair length of fabric from a big old trunk in the corner. Soon, I am busy cutting pieces for the tunic the men wear for their outdoor work and by early afternoon, I am sitting on the settle by the window, needle and thread flying like a bee.

At the end of the day, I hear birds call the coming of someone down the road. Mary looks out, then lights the candle at the table. Daniel and Elijah, both burnt by labor in the sun, enter.

Elijah, seeing what I'm doing for him, thanks me with a smile. Then he takes up a bowl of the deer meat stew we're having to eat and goes to Elizabeth's room. I see him, through a crack in the door. He kisses her on the cheek, then sets down beside to feed her.

Mary and the two men talk late, way past dark. I hear them, as I lie on my bed, discussing about an important meeting in the town of Williamsburg, where another frontiersman has made a speech about the colonies. I hear the words "tea party," "port closed," "quartering act," then talk of a man named "Mr. Henry" and his resolution for a day of fasting and prayer to end King George's meanness to everyone.

"Well, London can keep its tea for as long as it likes. I'll be happy with blackberry leaf, until the Crown gives our government to us," Daniel says. "And the first Redcoat who tries to quarter in this house will be greeted with a musket ball!"

Ports closed? British soldiers taking the house? Oh, Lord, is there no safe place for me in this world? Only long after the men have said farewell and the house gone quiet do I finally get some sleep.

The next morning my greatest fear comes to pass. I am helping Mary with Rachel while the men chop wood and mend the pig fence when the door swings wide and Elijah calls, "Maggie! Two men—a Negro and a white man!"

I hear horses, then Daniel greeting the men outside nicely. I just get up the ladder and pull it up after me when I hear the men entering with Daniel and Elijah, below. I hold my breath and listen, too afraid to even peek through the notch in the floor. My heart turns over when I hear Samson's awful voice.

"...and Abel van Houten here, he tracks runaways and that's exactly what this girl is, according to the law. Charlie the driver said she may have escaped somewhere around here when they stopped the wagon."

Daniel sighs as if he's gone bored. "Mr. Samson, excuse me, Mr. Terrent, the only visitors we have seen in the last three days are two friends from the other side of the hill. And frankly, I find your story hard to believe. What young woman would risk her life in this wilderness? Why, only a fortnight ago I came upon a bad-tempered black bear with cubs, not to mention a diamond-backed viper, not far from this cabin."

He stops talking for a minute, and I imagine Samson's eyes widening big as a catfish for he, I now remember, is scared out of his wits of wild animals of any kind, even small ones. "So even if your slave girl did escape, as you say, no unarmed person could survive long here. My guess is that the runaway you describe is probably closer to Baltimore seeking passage north in a hogshead barrel."

"What's there behind that door?" Samson asks, and I hear footsteps moving in that corner of the house, then the sound of Elizabeth's door opening, Elijah's boots on the planks, and the door closing firmly.

"My wife," Elijah says, cold and angry like I never heard him before.

"Now that your curiosity is satisfied, Mr. Terrent, will you please leave."

"Well," Samson says, with his voice shrinking, "Master Pritchard posted 'Runaway' notices from the Beeches to Fredericksburg. And he says if she's hidden by anybody he'll have King George prosecute that man for harboring a runaway and for stealing property, too, so you best tell your neighbors 'n case she shows up here."

"As I said before, Mr. Terrent, we have few visitors here in the wilderness, and all white, but if I should see the girl you describe we shall certainly notify Mr. Pritchard," Daniel replies.

Samson must be persuaded enough, because the next sounds I hear are of the two bounty-hunters leaving, then the click of the door latch.

After things have been still for a time, I hear Elijah's voice calling up in a loud whisper, "Maggie!"

I climb down from my hiding place, still frightened to my guts by Terrent and van Houten hunting me down. But at least I now know one thing for sure: These people won't turn me in.

The day goes back to normal after the scare, for the Burkes work near as hard as the plantation workers. Mary asks if I would mind helping with Elizabeth, since Elijah wouldn't be home until later tonight.

I didn't have an idea in the world how much work it was, dealing with the wants of a cripple. Feeding was the easy part. Changing her out of one nightshirt and into the other took both us together to make sure we got her dressed all right. And when the poor lady needed the chamber pot, it took Mary and me both to lift her out of the bed. I ask Mary how she could go about doing this all alone.

"Oh," she replies, "well, as you've probably seen, Elijah usually comes home at the dinner hour to help, then again later. But if you could help me, just until he finishes his daily work . . ."

"Yes, ma'am, I'll try to be of help to you any way I can." Besides, Elizabeth was a truly nice lady, that way to everybody, Mary said, visitors, too, and one never minds helping a person kind and grateful as she is.

. . .

That evening the men set themselves down by the fire, drawing on their old clay pipes and talking with two guests, James Wheeler and William Dempsey. From my hiding place in the attic, I peer down through a crack in the floor.

Tonight, the men are reading from a book and turning its words into English, then talking all about it. I'd heard that language before, from a balcony at the Church of England services we were sent to attend at the church near the Beeches. Mostly the services were all about what sinners we were, but the part that I always loved was the singing, sounding mostly like what I'm hearing Daniel slowly read now.

Horatius Cocles then advanced to the first entrance of the bridge, and being easily distinguished among those who showed their backs in retreating from the fight, facing about to engage the foe hand to hand, by his surprising bravery he terrified the enemy.

"Ah, if only, when the time comes, we find such a brave man among our own!" Dempsey cut in.

Daniel puts the book aside. "But if only we do not have to, William."

"The Crown shows no signs of letting up. As I see it, what choice to we have?" Wheeler asks, and conversation turns again to the troubles of the colonists.

Elijah leans forward. "If only they would read Otis! Why is it that parliament refuses to even entertain our ideas?"

"Because they are simply making too much money from the Tidewater elite, who might as well be sleeping in King George's bed with him, that's why!" Wheeler exclaims. "Why should they listen to us frontiersmen, build us the roads we beg for, and give us the protection we need, when, in the Crown's sight, we are lower than dogs?"

At the plantation, whites, from what I heard, always said there was one sure thing: Anyone living on the frontier must be poor or stupid. I see the two muskets and the rifle over the fireplace, and the real smart men under them, talking about important books and laws and it seems like I have really just left the unimportant place and come to the grand one.

Elijah looks up at the attic, as if he is seeing me watching him, and says, "Well, gentlemen, I must retire, for my work calls me early. I can only add, as regards our future versus that of King George: *detur digniori.*"

The next morning before he leaves, Elijah asks, "Maggie, has anyone ever taught you any letters? Have you had any schooling at all?"

"Yes, a little. From Mistress Abigail. She wanted me to learn to read so I could read the Bible to her before her sleep. I heard it was illegal for a slave to read, but I guess the white men wouldn't come after a lady. Before she took ill in the head, she taught me the alphabet and some of the easy passages from the Good Book, with her helping me. I didn't get further than that."

"Well," he said, staring at me hard, "that is a good start. If you are to be a free woman, and you *will* be, you must learn your letters, and that includes the language you heard us quoting last night, Latin. Would you be willing to sit with me for a time each evening to advance your knowledge and learn to read other books?"

I try to sound calm. "Oh yes, if Mary can spare me."

"I will talk to her," he replies, putting his hand on my shoulder.

We begin the following evening, after supper is cleared and a pine-knot lighted, with a children's storybook, one that belonged to Elijah during his childhood near Germantown. In just a very few weeks I can read the book by myself. By the time the summer sun is high up and the light good into the evening, I can read one of the long readers on my own.

Elijah pats my arm. "Well done, Maggie."

I hear him, but mostly feel the warmth in my skin where his hand touched me.

One August morning, without saying a word of good-bye, Elijah disappears on his new horse Flyer, and my lessons are cancelled. When I ask where Elijah has gone, Mary smiles, and says, "Actions speak louder than words."

"Oh, I never heard that. But Elijah likes words!"

"Well, what it means, really, is that one may determine a man's character by the things he does rather than what he talks about doing. And talk must be followed by action."

"Like standing up for the free colonists?"

"Yes, like that, and doing for others to show caring, rather than simply talking about it."

"Oh. But where did he go?"

"You'll know that tomorrow," she says, smiling at me, as she spoons some more porridge into Rachel's mouth.

When Elijah does return late the next afternoon, he walks in carrying an armful of the most beautiful books I ever have seen, all made of gilt and leather on their outsides and all shiny with wear, like they had each been read over and over.

As Elijah places each on the table, Mary touches one and smiles at him. "Lord Fairfax is most kind."

I stare at Elijah. After all this talk against the Crown, they are friends with an English Lord?

Elijah laughs, seeing the puzzlement on my face, then explains that they come from the library of Lord Fairfax of Greenway Court, who is a sympathizer with the free colonists and lends them books when they want. These, Elijah explains, are very dear, and all brought from England. They are for me to read.

He hands me a volume and I look at the spine, "Par-a... Par-a-d-i..." I try.

"Paradise, yes," Elijah urges.

"Paradise L-O-S-T. *Paradise Lost*." I look at Elijah, who smiles back when he hears me reading it right.

"By John Milton, a very famous writer." He proceeds to read off the titles of the rest, "*Essay on Man*, by Alexander Pope; he is very popular right now. *Henry V*, by William Shakespeare. *The Republic*, by Plato. *The Odyssey* by Homer. And here is the one I chose especially for you: *Gulliver's Travels*, by Jonathan Swift."

"Were they English?" I ask, wondering why he reads books written by the English, when the English cause so much trouble.

"Some of them, yes, but . . ." He looks at me seriously. "These are good men who believe, or believed, all people should have the right to speak and act for themselves, not as a king or tyrant would make them do. Maggie," he says, turning me toward him, "the first step to freedom is knowledge. If you are to be free, and stay free, you must be able to understand the works of great thinkers, and to express yourself clearly. That is what reading these writings can teach you."

After supper that evening, we open the book called *Gulliver's Travels*. It is full of pictures and is the story of a man's trip around the whole world, where he meets giants and small people, even horses that talk and are smarter than men. When we reach a page with a picture of the man Gulliver tied down by the little people, a blue-green satin ribbon, hidden between the pages, falls down to the floor. Some lady must have left it as a mark, but Elijah picks it up and, before I know what, he has tied it in a bow around my neck just like I'd seen fine ladies at the plantation do.

I'd be lying like a sleeping dog if I didn't confess that being so close to Elijah now made it hard for my mind to work sometimes. He wasn't just beautiful. What with saving me in the forest and teaching me to read, he was near my savior on earth.

Many times, I feel him watching me, too, as if he can't take his eyes from me. At those times, he looks away quickly, as if he feels bad for staring, but can't help it. I want to ask him why, or if he will walk with me outside, if he has something to get off his chest, but don't, fearing he will tell me he won't teach me anymore.

．．．

By the end of the summer I can copy parts of the Swift book, also speeches from plays by a man named Ben Jonson. I love the evenings when Elijah reads from Pope, especially his favorite passage that I memorized, just because he loved it:

> So man, who here seems principal alone,
> Perhaps acts second to some sphere unknown,
> Touches some wheel, or verges to some goal;
> 'Tis but a part we see, and not the whole.

Elijah also teaches me mathematics, multiplication and division, which is much more difficult than reading for me but which, he says, everyone must know when selling crops and buying up supplies. The local gazette tells of an important meeting of colonists, who decide to make a petition to the king for "redress of grievances" and it makes me proud that I can, like the white men, read the little article myself. Elijah watches me while I read, looking softly at me, then says, "You are a very hard worker, Maggie, and very brave."

"Thank you, Eli."

He is still staring at me. Then does something it feels like he's done before: He moves a plait of hair away from my face.

．．．

Winter comes early this year. Needles of iced wind bore through even tiny cracks in the attic and Mary gives me rags to stuff the holes. On Christmas Day, Daniel reads from the family Bible and we all pray together for the English to grant us freedom instead of war. On the eve of 1775, we toast each other with the drink called wass-ale made from the Hollow's apples.

I study during the brief times I can be spared all winter long, for it is in the cold months especially that all hands are needed to keep wood at the hearth and animals tended to. Elizabeth asks me to read to her, Bible passages she likes, mostly, but also from the borrowed books. When I can't get a word, I hold the book in front of her and she says it for me, then I repeat it as I look at the letters.

Often as not, I spend more time with her than with Mary; Mary being busy with Rachel, who's learning to walk and getting into mischief like little ones do when they get their legs under them.

Then, with spring coming on there is even more outdoor work. We have new chicks and I gather them into my apron, palm-sized balls of yellow fuzz, to be kept warm in cages near the fire. The fields are turned with Daniel's new ox pulling the plow, the corn shoots up, and the sow is going to have a passel of piglets. And Elijah teaches me. It's the first time I've ever known what happiness is.

The men who come to the Burke table these evenings talk about resisting the Crown and the words "Redcoats," "Militia," and "Loyalists" are in near every supper conversation. I still run up to my little attic for safety when visitors come calling, even though it is awful tiny. But, from my hiding place I can watch them all through the crack in the floor, and hear all their news.

Talk of rebellion is now everywhere in the Piedmont, Elijah says, and the men may have to leave to fight. They all think a civil war is coming between Loyalist and colonist, the Piedmont against the Tidewater. And they're afraid the British army will steal their property and hang resisters for the evil deed called treason. So I am not surprised when, one morning with the magnolias and gooseberries full in bloom and the sun warm, William Dempsey gallops up on a big bay, lathered up something terrible. He starts shouting out his story even before he's off the horse.

"It's happened! The Redcoats attacked the patriots near Boston! The papers in the North say it's war!"

Mary rushes out from the cabin and Daniel and Elijah, mending a fence, drop their axes and hammers. I hurry up the ladder.

"Come in, William, and take some refreshment," Mary says, trying to keep everyone calm, and the whole family gathers around as Dempsey tells the whole story.

Some silversmith had, just days before, ridden up the Charles River to a little village called Lexington, warning of the coming of the British army. The Redcoats threw him into the stocks but not before he told the story of the army's coming to a man named Prescott. Prescott rode down the back roads to a place called Concord, yelling the news to everybody, telling them to get ready. The British had lots of foot soldiers there, but word got back to Lexington of the Redcoats' march back down the banks of the river.

Up the river, a little army of their Minute Men had met the enemy in a field called Lexington Commons. The militia leader, a Captain Parker, commanded the Patriots to stand their ground, but if they had to, to start the war just like the British wanted. Then the Redcoats' nasty commander ordered the rebels to disperse. The king's soldiers started the firing and Captain Parker shot his rifle off right back at them. Then near every farmer in every village from the frontier to Boston took up arms and attacked the Redcoats' line as it marched down the Charles River.

The battlefield was miles long, they said, from the Lexington all the way to the big town of Boston, but when the smoke finally cleared out, the Patriots had beaten those Tories all the way back down the river.

Daniel is the first to respond. "Then it *is* war King George wants. Damn him!"

"And what does Mr. Washington say?" Elijah asks.

"I am told that, though he is distressed by this turn of events, having relatives himself in England and, living on the Potomac where so many Loyalists reside, he believes the king has given us no choice but to take arms against the British government for our freedom," Dempsey replies. "There is to be a meeting down in Richmond in ten days to determine the course we are to take. Josiah Markwell and I plan to go there. Might one of you join us?"

"I must stay with the spring work," Daniel says, "but perhaps my brother will represent our family."

"I will be ready when you are, William," Elijah says.

"Meet me at Lee's Corner at sunrise. I'll bring the greenbroke mare for you. Long miles will do her good. We should be able, fair weather, to reach Richmond within the week."

I watch in the evening as Elijah oils his boots and packs his bedroll by the light of the fire. He is up even before cock crow and just as the first light falls on the Hollow, he bids us all farewell. But as he steps out the door, he asks me to come outside behind the big chestnut tree below the house. He puts his hands on my shoulders and says in a low voice, "Elizabeth is very worried by all this, being so helpless. But you are strong. Please, I know you will, be strong for her. And please stay with your studies. You are a fine scholar, Maggie, and becoming more so every week. Can I depend on you?"

"Of course, Elijah," I say, and before I know it, he is gone.

. . .

The next weeks are especially full of work, for we all know how important it is to lay up stores now. Although I try to keep any fears of Elijah being injured or killed in war away from my mind, still they press on me so hard. Some nights I cry quiet tears in my straw bed, remembering the moment the Good Lord brought him to save me, scared I may never see him again.

Finally, one warm afternoon as I am sewing a bonnet for Rachel, I am surprised by the prattle of birds below at the far end of the property. Then I hear a shout, and I hurry to the window to see Elijah, musket over one shoulder, bedroll over the other, striding up to the cabin in the sunlight. His skin is darker from being out in the sun even more than normal and he's lost some weight but my heart is grateful to see him looking as well as ever.

"Ho, how good to be back!" he says as he comes into the cabin.

Elizabeth calls, "Eli!" from her room, and Elijah goes in there straightaway to put his arms around her.

Over cider and biscuits he tells his story, and we listen close, just like with Dempsey weeks before.

"Mr. Henry spoke—oh, what a glorious orator he is!—the great Cicero himself was not so well spoken!" He opens out a square of paper. "Here, let me read you this: 'Why stand we here idle? What is it that gentlemen wish? What would they have? Is life so dear, or peace so sweet as to be purchased at the price of chains or slavery? Forbid it, almighty God! I know not what course others may take; but as for me, give me liberty, or give me death!' "

Elijah's voice grows strong at the last words. I see Daniel's hand clench suddenly at his side.

Elijah refolds the paper slowly as he speaks. "At the meeting, the men of our area joined with those from Culpeper and Orange Counties and decided to form a joint militia. All fit men over the age of eighteen years are to muster for drill, and our battalions are to be modeled after the Minute Men of Boston. Franklin Dobbs has volunteered a fallow field at his farm, and we are to join them there next Monday morning."

I can feel Elijah's eyes on me, but I look down so as not to allow him to see my distress. As if speaking only for my sake, he continues in a quiet but determined way. "All those at the meeting agreed there is no other course for us now."

I hear the hard set to Daniel's voice. "Mary, it will be up to you, and Maggie, if you will stay, to keep the farm working. And we will certainly need supplies, especially if the Crown enacts a blockade."

The family agrees this evening by the fire that a musket will be left at Orchid Hollow for protection if the British come here. Elijah will take the other musket, which can be fit with a bayonet and which loads up to four times as fast as the rifle, and Daniel the long rifle, which can hit straight on the knot of a tree at 200 paces.

At dawn the following Monday, Daniel and Elijah shoulder their weapons for the hike to Dobb's field. The volunteers, calling themselves the "Culpeper Minute Men," will practice drilling three times weekly until they hear something else new from Williamsburg. The whole Virginia frontier, they tell us, after their first day's muster, is up in arms and war talk is near everywhere.

One evening, however, they return with other news, news that brings relief to my bones, weak with worry over slave hunters: Ebenezer Pritchard has died, the Beeches has been bankrupted and put into what they call "receivership" by agents of the Crown. The slaves from the plantation have been taken into military duty by Lord Governor Dunsmore and His Majesty's government. For now, I am safe. Elijah's eyes shine as he tells this news over supper, and these kind people, my salvation, bow their heads in a prayer of thanksgiving for my deliverance.

. . .

Mary and I set to work making the men's clothes ready for the field. After setting a large cauldron to boil outside, we collect leaves, bark, and moss, all kind of growing things from the forest, and put them in the water. After a while, when the water's real dark, I throw in the homespun shirts and breeches to dye. It takes a good while, but by the end of the day, we have two shirts and two pair of breeches in a greenish-brown that blends with the color of the woods.

"Perfect!" Mary says. "And they won't show any dirt!"

Although the clothes are perfect for the forest, the color has come off all over my hands, which now look greenish, like I'm sick with something bad. My feet, too, having got hit with some of the stuff as I was stirring the pot.

I walk downstream along the creek to bathe the color off. It's a hot day, so I remove my chemise and dress, too. The water is delicious, running across my bare skin so cool and fresh. There is a sound nearby just as I am getting out to dry off and fetch my clothes from the tree limb where they're hanging. And suddenly, there's Elijah: him, with his tunic off and his breeches halfway down.

"Maggie! I had no—I didn't know . . ." He hangs on to the tops of his breeches, fumbles for his tunic.

I tell him, after taking cover behind a big tree, "I'm nearly all the way done, Elijah. Just let me get my shimmy and dress here." In a moment, I got my clothes back on. Of all the time we spent together we've never seen each other without clothes.

What can I do beside make polite conversation with him, like I always do? "Did you say you had a saying, some words you wanted on the shirts?"

He still looks embarrassed, but he says, "Liberty or Death. Mr. Henry's words."

* * *

When they see how nice the embroidery turns out on the shirts, Elijah and Daniel also ask me to sew a flag. It's made out of bright yellow cotton given by Dobb's wife Martha and I appliqué it with a large coiled serpent and the motto "Don't Tread on Me" in black letters below, just like one the *Gazette* showed being carried near Philadelphia.

I suppose the cotton was meant for a lady's summer dress, but when I am finished with it, I consider it more beautiful than any dress I ever made. Daniel says it's going to be the standard for the Culpeper Minute Men.

As summer days get warmer and longer, we work from sunup to sundown grinding corn, smoking deer meat, laying squash and carrots in the cellar. Rachel is walking now and she is a happy child, loved right, and held close every night at supper by her father. Elijah helps me, when we can make the time, with my education: I am now able to copy, though he's got to translate many of the words, from Virgil and Pope. We do not talk of ending my lessons, though we both know in our hearts that day will come soon.

That day comes sooner than any of us expected. Daniel and Elijah, who near-always return to Orchid Hollow after noon each day, instead return to the house late one morning with their orders. Patrick Henry has called the Culpeper militia to Norfolk to stand against the forces of Lord Dunsmore there.

"So it is us against the Crown and the Tidewater loyalists!" Daniel states.

Talk at the dinner table is all about the future. Mary thinks we will be fine for as long as six months, through the worst of winter, anyway, on our own. There will be an extra blanket each for the men and they'll be building their own shelters. Mary will send as much cornmeal as they can carry, plus some coffee, saved up in the cellar just for them. I put their clothes in order, from linen shirts to their buckskin waistcoats. And of course the flag, which I watch Elijah fold up neat and tidy that afternoon.

When he is finished, he turns to me. "Maggie, will you come with me up the road? You may ride Flyer to save your ankle, if you like."

He leads the horse and as we follow the first steps we took together, the ones that brought me to the Hollow, he says, "I have something for you, something I wish to know is safe with you before I leave."

We continue in silence, only the steady thump of Flyer's hooves on the damp ground. And then we are in the place where we first met, now a simple cabin in the noonday sun of the clearing I came to so long ago.

What once was just a few boards that sheltered me from the wilderness that spring night, is now three big rooms, a cooking area, a living space and a sleeping loft, filled with benches and table, a big chair on curved runners that, Elijah shows me, rocks back and forth and, even—because this is Elijah Burke, who says knowledge leads to freedom—a small bookcase. He throws open the shutters and the sunlight comes in, blinding us.

"Well, do you like it?" he asks, smiling.

"It is a wonderful home, Elijah. Is this what you've been working on this all last autumn?"

"It is. Do you think you could ever live here?"

"Why, of course, Elijah."

"Come with me, here." We sit side-by-side on the long wooden bench at the table.

"I may be gone a long time, Maggie. The truth is, I may never return. This is why I've asked you to come here. " He looks at me with great seriousness. "You are, in this place, a free woman. But Virginia law states that for a slave to be declared legally free, even if freed by his owner, that slave must have possession of at least twenty-five acres of land and a house. This cabin and its land surrounding should, by law now, be enough to confirm your freedom."

"You want me to . . .?" And I understand. All those days gone from sunrise to sunset. All those days, he was finishing the cabin.

"After Elizabeth's accident, I didn't care. But when I saw you here"—he smiles, puts both hands on my shoulders—"it seemed this was really yours."

"You built this for me?"

"Finished it for you, yes." He looks down shyly, then says, "But there is something else. If I die in the war, there is something I want you to have."

He strides across the floor and presses the toe of his boot on one of the floorboards. One end lifts and he slips his hand into the recess and takes out a small leather pouch. Returning to the table, he opens it and empties it all out. I hear the chink of metal, and see some silver coins glittering in the pool of sunlight. Without warning my mind suddenly doubles on itself, as if I had seen such a pouch with coins before. But surely I hadn't; in fact, I do not remember ever having seen any money at all.

"It is not enough to buy your freedom here, I'm afraid, but if they do not recognize this land as yours, take these Reales—lawful money—and find your way north, Philadelphia if you can, where I believe you will be safe. I wish I could do more for you but for now this must suffice."

I touch one of the silver pieces. My heart is stuck in my throat and I can contain myself no longer. I throw my arms around him to pull him near, so near I can hear the beating of his heart. "Oh, Elijah. You have saved me and I have loved you for so long . . ."

His arms come around me, tight, warm. I had forgotten how strong he was. "Maggie—"

"I mean, I love you the way a woman loves a man," I say against his shirt.

"What?" He pushes me away from him and looks at me.

"I don't mean to speak wrong, but I've loved you since that first day," I say.

Lord, he sounds stricken when he says, "Dear Maggie, my God."

"I'm sorry, Elijah. I don't mean to go saying what's wrong by the Good Book, but I—"

He puts his hand against my lips. I look up at him, feel a tear coursing down my cheek.

"Oh, my dear Maggie, I love my wife."

"Eli, I don't mean saying anything against her. I just thought you might like some comfort before going off to war, and you've been so kind to me, besides the fact that I love you."

He sits on the bench, head in his hands, then runs his hands through his hair and I sit next to him. We are both quiet for a while. Then I slowly unlace my dress. I take his hand, pull it toward me, slide it under my shimmy. He looks at me and his eyes are filling with tears. Then he turns his head toward me, I look up at him, and we kiss.

And then our bodies do the speaking for us. His calloused hands travel over my breasts, my stomach, my neck. I push his tunic away and as I do so, he stands.

His voice is thick. "Come," he says, and leads me up the ladder.

I follow him into the aerie, fragrant with new-cut wood, thinking of all the times I dreamed of him coming up to be with me in the little loft at Orchid Hollow. He sets me down on the straw-filled muslin mattress, removes my boots, then his own. I push the braces from his shoulders, then help him with his shirt, the same one I made for him so long ago.

Now his hands slide under my chemise, down the sides of my body, my legs, and up again, and he whispers, "Maggie, oh, Maggie," kissing me and kissing me until I press myself against him, begging, "Oh, please!" Then, he is lying between my breasts and I feel the essence of him meeting the heart inside me.

. . .

Later, we lie side by side, beyond words, only listening to the barely-heard sound of our hands gliding across each other's bodies, for remembrance. At one moment he turns me over onto my stomach. I feel the tip of his finger following the scar-veins on my back. And then, drops like rain. I turn around to face him.

"Damn them to hell." He runs his hand over his eyes, and I hold him close.

We sleep, but again and again, wake to kiss and love each other more. But finally, as the late sun touches the tops of the trees, he must speak the words I've dreaded to hear, "I must prepare for the journey tomorrow."

I touch his cheek. "Yes, I know, Eli."

We wash each other's bodies in the late amber sunlight with buckets of water from the well. He braids my hair. I buckle his boots. In hours, he will be gone.

"Thank you, Eli," I say.

"Thank you?"

"Now you've taught me what love is."

He looks at me, puzzled.

"Your folk taught me what kindness was. You taught me what words were. Now"—I hold his hand against my cheek—"I know what the love between a man and a woman is; that it's not rough, but sweet and gentle."

"Yes, sweet," he says, and smiles down at me, pushing a curl of my hair away from my face just as he'd done before.

"'…it is a part we see, and not the whole…'"

"Alexander Pope. You are a good student, Maggie: I told you that, too."

"It's like," I can't believe I'm hearing myself say what I do, "I'm something more than just being a house slave now."

"You are no one's slave. Remember that." He takes my hands in his, kisses each of them right in the center of the palm, which is still green. "But you might be a forest elf."

We both laugh. He links my arm through his and we start to walk slowly back through the forest, pulling Flyer behind, I not noticing even my weak leg, as if something we said between us healed it, or being with him took all the weakness away. Could I have ever asked the Good Lord for more than that the day I jumped out of that cart?

I wake the next morning to the grating of equipment as it is organized, low voices, the aroma of corncakes on the griddle. I pull my dress on and hurry down the ladder. Daniel is just finishing breakfast. Elijah is sitting with Elizabeth, holding her hands in both of his. The atmosphere is as solemn as a burial. Mary has been crying. Only Rachel breaks the mood as she bangs her spoon on her bowl and sings.

The men sling their leather traveling sacks across their shoulders. Daniel picks up the rifle and Elijah the musket. We walk together out into the warm autumn sun.

Daniel and I embrace, as do Elijah, Mary, and Rachel. Mary circles her arms around her husband and he holds her. Elijah holds me near, and whispers, "Your love will be with me always, no matter where I am."

Pulling out the folded note I have carefully copied for him, I slip it into the pocket of his buckskin waistcoat and say, even though I'm crying a river of tears, "For luck, Eli. When you read it, think of me."

He looks into my eyes and smiles, this man who has taught me to read, shown me what love between a man and a woman really is, and now goes to fight for the most important thing in life: freedom.

"Ready?" Daniel asks.

"Ready," Elijah says.

They clap one another on the shoulders and begin down the little horse path and over the hill. Just before they disappear over its brow, Elijah turns and waves to me. As I wave back, I repeat the words I have written to him, the words of wise Solomon I now keep close to my heart like a prayer, for his return:

Make haste, my beloved, and be thou like to a roe
or to a young hart upon the mountains of spices . . .

TWELVE

Emily

January-February 2004

As I thumbed through *Alchemy* the next day, I came across a bookmark left there. On its back were words translating a passage from the *Bhagavad Gita*:

> *Even imperfect, the work of one's own heart is more worthy*
> *Than that performed in blind obedience to another's will.*

I stared at it for a few moments then, for the first time in many months, I truly laughed deep inside. Had Nick left it there? Or was it a souvenir left by a reader? I pinned it at the top of my bulletin board next to my desk as a reminder to continue with my work no matter what obstacles popped up.

I only saw Dr. Shaeffer once weekly now and her role seemed more that of a twelve-step sponsor than therapist. As she saw it, my deepest depression was a natural response to Nick's death but the acute depression that had led to my suicide attempt had, most likely, been caused by the combination of drugs and alcohol. Absent chemical crutches, depression or sadness would, if allowed to take their course, eventually yield to my normal optimism, she said, and she warned me against any methods, chemical or otherwise, that would deny me access to my own grieving process. I had both her office and cell number, and was to call her any time I felt overwhelmed. The challenge for me now was to stay in touch with my feelings.

That is exactly what I was doing. Except that my biggest emotional problem at the moment was actually simple frustration. I had no way to find Clare. All I could do now was to try to understand the matrix from which her fantasy stories had emerged.

I remembered a colleague Nick had mentioned a few times in the context of his work, a psychologist named Raoul Sewell, and I finally located him in Sherman Oaks. Yes, Dr. Sewell said, he did at times use regression hypnosis in his practice though usually, like Nick, for stubborn cases as a way of freeing up the patient's voice for talking therapy. He'd be glad to meet with me, even regress me if I wanted to find out what the experience was like.

One week later I sat in Dr. Sewell's rather cloistered office, recounting my own story and that of finding the tapes. He was not surprised that some of the information had correlated with historical facts Clare had claimed no knowledge of prior to her hypnosis.

"Well, what do you think causes such a thing?" I asked.

"Honestly," he said, sitting forward, "we just don't know. It could be a message from the collective unconscious, facts or stories unremembered except in the hypnotic state."

"I remember Nick saying that they were a 'phenomenon' that could be observed but not measured, but that they effected healing, and that was their value," I said. Then I told him I was surprised at the truths contained within Clare's fantastical stories, coincidental or not. Where had they come from?

"Well, the fact of the matter is, most of these very charming stories turn out to be healing fictions and nothing else."

"Or an elaborate deception?"

"Another possibility. Have you read the story of Bridey Murphy?" he asked.

Nick and I had discussed it once. In the early 1950s, a Chicago woman had supposedly been regressed back into nineteenth century Ireland where she claimed her name had been Bridey Murphy. Under hypnosis she spoke with a Gaelic accent, even remembered family members, specific names later found engraved on headstones, and events no one else could have known about. The subject was later found to have had, as a young child, a good deal of contact with a garrulous neighbor fond of reminiscing about her early life and family in Ireland, a woman named Bridget "Bridey" Murphy. Some now thought it long forgotten childhood knowledge recovered, others a misleading practical joke.

"Still," the doctor said, "it's surprising what can be uncovered and released under hypnosis."

"Like?"

"Here's another one, a local story. It happened in Lake Elsinore." He lifted a book from the bookcase beside him, opened it and handed it to me. "More than thirty-five people there, on separate occasions of hypnosis, mind you, told stories of their lives in a specific small town, Millboro, Virginia, around the time of the Civil War."

I looked down at the daguerreotype of Millboro. "Proven?"

"The town of Millboro was, and the details matched up with the recorded history of that area, even the people who had lived there."

"Any explanation?"

"None that made any sense to me. But you'd have to be talking an awfully big conspiracy, for no particular reason whatsoever, to make a point."

"Do you think," I asked, "there will ever be an explanation?"

"Well, if you can find one, I know a hell of a lot of people who'd like to hear it!" Sewell laughed and checked at his watch. "You know, I've got a client next hour. Perhaps we could get started if you still want to give the process a try."

As I lay back in the reclining chair, Dr. Sewell spoke to me in quiet tones, repeating key phrases, such as "total relaxation," "safe," "nothing to fear," until I seemed to be floating in a warm cloud, weightless, alert, secure.

"Now," the doctor intoned, "you are walking down a stairway, slowly, one step at a time. As you descend this stairway, each step you take moves you further and further back in time."

I found my way slowly and cautiously down my dimly lit stairway. It was constructed of stone and the walls on either side were covered with moss and ivy. It seemed I had come to a place beyond even sleep, yet fully aware of all around me: a different reality from any I had ever experienced, including drug overdose.

Suddenly an image swam before my eyes: a high plateau atop steep, forested hillsides. My voice came out, higher, different; me yet not me.

"What do you wish to say, Emily?"

I described what appeared to be an equatorial place, a warm, humid mesa with clouds boiling up from below.

All I heard from the doctor's direction was silence. I waited, still watching the scene around me.

Finally, he asked, "Are you Emily?"

"No," my voice answered.

"Are you a man or a woman?"

I heard myself giggling, something I was not known for doing. And in a voice of higher pitch than mine, said, "Oh, a woman!"

"What kind of clothes are you wearing?"

There was a light fabric touching my skin, a soft belt around my waist, short, boot-type covering over my feet, and I related this to him.

"Look around you. Can you describe more of this place for us?"

I did look around, as if looking at a wide screen on the inside of my head. "Tall, peaked buildings, stone close-fitted to stone, roofs made of thatch."

"On a hill, did you say?"

"They took the top of the hill off."

"Who did, Emily?"

"The king and his architects."

"What king, Emily?"

"I don't know. He does research."

"What research does he do?"

I giggled again. "Potatoes." I looked around me. Potatoes were everywhere. "Many kinds of potatoes."

"Why are you laughing?" I heard him ask in an amused voice.

"We have created so many potatoes!"

"Who is 'we,' Emily?"

"Ichuan and me."

"What is your name here?"

"Miqana."

"Ichuan, is he a farmer?"

"No, he works for the king."

"Making food?" The doctor sounded confused.

"Yes."

We continued for a few minutes more, but I could offer no visions beyond my first impressions. After he brought me fully back to consciousness, he admitted he had not expected such detailed images to appear for me so quickly, and theorized that perhaps my recent trauma and rehabilitation had opened my mind to go deeper.

What had happened? If I hadn't known better I might have sworn I had been describing Machu Picchu in the Peruvian Andes. But wherever the place was, the fragment of story I had told to Dr. Sewell seemed to me to be as close to the heart of my own truth as my life at this exact moment:

driving home on the Ventura Freeway, slowing for an accident clean-up, tuning in KFI in the slow-and-go traffic over Mulholland Pass.

Perhaps I had happened on such a vision so quickly because my mind had been opened in the therapeutic process. Or perhaps I had a better imagination than I had given myself credit for and, as with many people, hypnosis had relaxed my mind sufficiently that my natural creative energy had expressed itself in story form. After all, many creative people described the sense of "flow" in their work, emerging from a state that was deeply meditative, removed from the world around them. My own hypnotic experience had helped me at least empathize with Clare, and several days later, I remembered having done a school project on Peru, where most of that little story seemed to fit. But could "Ichuan" have been Nick? Or just a fantasy conveniently connected by my mind using information it already had?

One thing was certain: If I were truly to make sense of the tapes, I had some catching up to do on several topics relating to Nick's work. So I began where I thought Nick would have: with information I had on the psychology of the patient.

I had taken as part of a psychology class in school, the same personality test Clare had been given, and I finally found it in a box of old essays and term papers and set it down on the desk next to hers to compare the two. Whereas Clare was an extroverted type, leaning toward intuition, I was an introverted type, leaning toward thinking. So Clare might understand a topic without ever cracking a book on it, while I might spend time in quiet research, exactly as I was now, to grasp a subject or situation. We might reach the same conclusions; our *modus operandi* were just different. And Clare would trust in the real existence of the unseen, while I'd need some intellectual proof.

Was it possible that, being so intuitive, Clare had been more predisposed to fantasy or suggestion? Some books suggested that might be the case. Then again, the more likely effect of Clare's highly intuitive approach might be her ability to cull historical facts from the collective unconscious.

And if it were externally received knowledge coming to consciousness in the form of autobiography? Perhaps that was what that particular diagnosis was about, after all: the intuitive "uncovering" of hidden information previously obtained by way of the five senses, information that was then stashed away deep in the hard-drive of the brain where it lay dormant, only to come out under the hypnotist's de-frag program as a personally experienced truth.

And then there was the altered state called sleep, and the dreams that came with it. Clare had come to Nick haunted by a dream of a turquoise stone given to her by a human hand. I knew from the small bit of work I had done years before with the Australian aborigines that, in their construct of parallel consciousness, dreams were simply another reality; that if you dreamed you walked across the canyon to visit your brother, your spirit self actually did walk across the canyon to visit your brother.

Well, Clare had taken her dream seriously, and I knew from Nick that a dream was frequently where therapy began and ended. Dreams were laden with symbols and symbols were the key to understanding.

So, as I sat noodling on my laptop that evening, I looked for any information I could about Clare's dream symbol, turquoise. Mined since approximately 6,000 BC, it was sometimes called "the stone of everyman" because it could be found worldwide in jewelry and artifacts stretching back to the third century BC, where it decorated relics in tombs. In the 8,000 years since man had discovered it, it had been mined on almost every continent.

Its name came from the French word meaning "Turkish stone." In English, it was known as turquoise, turkois, turkoise, turcois, or turkis; in Spanish, turquesa. In Japanese, turkodama. The ancient Persians believed it cured eye infections, insured its wearer victory in battle, protected him from injury on horseback as well as from drowning, snakebite, or lightning. It was said that anyone who looked directly at the stone on the first day following the new moon would attain vast wealth. The Navajo believed that the very heart of the earth was made of turquoise. In Tibet, the essence of turquoise maintained balance in the wearer's life. In prayers of the ancient Egyptians, the words "turquoise" and "water" were interchangeable. And, in the ancient Near East, it had been said to reconcile the love of a man and a woman. One modern dream analyst likened the color turquoise as an inspiration to the mind to reach beyond the boundaries of its self-imposed limitations, and into universal consciousness.

.   .   .

By the following week, I had read all but one of the psychology-related books I'd brought from Nick's office and had scoured the Internet for descriptions of the regression experience by doctors and testimonials by their patients. As Nick had said, the opinions of the mental health community on regression therapy ranged from dismissive to believing. For most legitimately educated mental health experts, the method was seen simply as a means to an end: getting to the heart of the patient's trouble and alleviating their distress.

But very few were willing to go out on a limb to defend the client's stories as authentic. One of the few exceptions was Evan Jacobs, a psychiatrist practicing in London and an outspoken advocate for the healing properties of regression hypnosis. Dr. Jacobs, who claimed to have regressed more than four hundred patients in his practice, believed in a far more mysterious explanation for these regression journeys: inner physics, that is, the quantum mechanics of the brain. And his book, *Physics of Mind,* was sitting next to me, waiting to be read.

Although I was intrigued enough by this last book to want to settle in for an evening of study, Dr. Shaeffer had warned me not to shut out the outside world, so I called and invited Margo, herself alone for the week while Jeff worked in Sacramento, over to dinner. She helped me cook, and for once, everything came out at the same time perfectly done. After dinner, we spent the rest of the evening lounging on the sofa, consuming chocolate sundaes and bad TV.

It wasn't until she got up to leave at eleven that she asked the question I'd been expecting from one of my friends, "Emily, tell me the truth. You haven't had any thoughts like, well, doing what you did before? You haven't, have you?"

Yes, this was another facet of the healing process the doctor had warned me about: the constant watchfulness of friends and family afraid I'd "try it again." After what I'd put them through I could hardly blame them.

I looked her in the eye, and hugged her. As my best friend, she deserved the truth. "Oh, there are days when I feel a bit down. I'll always miss him. But see?" I pointed at Clare's case work on my desk. "He's left me a job to do." I smiled at her.

"You're the most persistent woman I've ever known," she said, laughing through tears. She hugged me again, and whispered, "Keep rollin', kid."

. . .

Realizing how much work I still had ahead of me, and how little information on Clare I had been able to find, I tossed all night merely out of aggravation. After finally getting to sleep at three, I woke at six. It was a bright, cool Friday, and after jogging with Fizzy I poured myself another cup of coffee and sat down with my notebook and the *Physics of Mind*.

According to Dr. Jacobs, time had not existed as a point of scientific inquiry until the seventeenth century, when Galileo, watching a hanging lamp above him in church swing back and forth to the beat of his own heart, decided that time could be quantified. Novelist HG Wells took the time construct further when he created a clock/travel vehicle for his character on which to travel forward into the future.

Now, modern physics saw our best chance of time travel in black holes. Not only that, science had discovered that black holes, technically speaking, existed not only in deep space, but inside each and every electron inside our own bodies. Considering that these tiny black holes were comprised of the same matter as those larger black holes, the ones in space, there would be no reason why traveling via these small ones might not have the same result as the larger ones. Might it have somehow been possible for Clare, under deep hypnosis, to actually enter the black holes of her own electrons to travel back into her own experiences?

Even stranger, scientists were now theorizing that larger black holes actually existed within the face of the earth, in the Bermuda Triangle, for one. I thought back to Clare's tale of multi-ringed Santorini. Born of a clod of earth tossed into the sea. Destroyed by the volcano at its center, whose eruption had opened its crater to suck in all the seawater and everything else around it, creating a second response eruption, and a series of tidal waves. Presuming Clare's fantastic stories were somehow true, could that catastrophe have created, if only for moments, an earthly black hole which had pulled the lovers through it, and forward in time?

Presuming the lovers existed in the first place.

I dreamed that night that I was looking at a large blackboard in a college classroom. Though I couldn't read the complex equation written all over it, I somehow understood that the lesson I was to take from it was that time was simply an invention created by the human race to keep everything from happening at once for man, in reality, lived only in the "now." Looked at from that angle, time might to be nothing more than an illusion we carried around with us like a baby's blanket.

I suddenly remembered a college roommate, an Eastern philosophy major with whom I'd had numerous discussions and disagreements about science versus religion. I looked up at the Sanskrit quote above my bulletin board, checked a Web site, and called Liv. She had been working late the night before to finish recording a piece, and sounded exhausted.

"Uh-oh. I woke you up."

"No. No. I couldn't sleep. The sound engineer was completely nuts."

I burst into laughter.

"You think I'm kidding? Oh, my head!"

"Come with me to Lake Shrine tomorrow," I said.

"You want to go to church? Well, sure. What time?"

"Nine. Or eleven, whichever works for you."

"Hmm, how about eleven? What's the topic?" Liv had attended Sunday services there off-and-on for a couple of years.

"I don't know. I just thought it might be worth a visit."

• • •

The talk, highlighting the similarities between Christian and Asian philosophies was positive and comforting. After the service we strolled around the lake, with its monuments to the religions of the world and its storybook swans tearing across the water for visitors' treats. After making a date with Liv to visit Bottle Village in Simi Valley the following week, we hugged good-bye.

As I walked in the door, Fizzy made a beeline for the stairs so before she could escape again, I grabbed her up, leashed her and took her down the San Vicente median for a walk. When we returned, the first thing that confronted me was the stack of books I'd already gone through, now sitting next to my chair. Maybe there were more that might help me back in Nick's office.

• • •

I unlocked the door to Nick's office a little over an hour later. Most of the furniture was gone—the Eames chair and cloudlike sofa, the desk, even the ficus. But all the books remained.

I began the process of filing the ones I'd borrowed back on the shelves where I'd found them. When I finally got to the bottom shelf, I was back in the eclectic section, Indian and Buddhist philosophy, reincarnation, case histories of "past life" phenomena, and one I'd missed before, *The Search for Omm Sety,* the biography of a respected researcher who claimed to have lived a former life in pharaohnic Egypt.

Said to be "A True Story of Eternal Love," the book recounted the story of an Englishwoman named Dorothy Eady who, after surviving a serious concussion as a young child in 1907, insisted that, not only had she lived in Egypt centuries before, but that she had, in fact, been the teenage companion of the great pharaoh, Seti the First in Egypt's Middle Kingdom more than 3,000 years ago.

Ms. Eady had believed so seriously in her previous life that she moved to Egypt, changed her name to Omm Sety and took a position with the Egyptian Antiquities Department as archivist and research associate at Abydos, seat of Seti the First's temple. Over the years, her instinctive knowledge of undiscovered archaeological sites and ancient ritual earned the respect of Egyptologists around the world, who frequently came to her for information and included her monographs in their journals.

Interestingly, the one aspect of her "past life" that she kept a close secret was her claim that Seti the First still visited her in the deep of night, sharing stories and caresses. Only after her death did her closest friend disclose her repeated claims that the great pharaoh himself had made nightly visits to her in the mud hut where she lived and worked for over forty years.

A childhood concussion, a fascination with Egypt, a secret lover from the past. It all sounded highly romantic and quite implausible, except that the information she had provided archaeologists excavating ruins turned out to be eerily correct most of the time.

The epilogue of the book contained much information on the history of thought on the subject of reincarnation, including portions of the transcript of an interview with a Cambridge biochemist, who guessed that, beyond a collective unconscious that can be tapped into by all humans, lie a similar field of memories that we could pick up, much like a radio picking up radio waves through time and space.

This point of view made some sense in light of my investigation. The question was, would these be our memories, or someone else's? Underneath *Omm Sety*, I found another, older book, *Twenty Cases Suggestive of Reincarnation*.

This work contained clinical studies of "past life" recollections of people around the world. Although the book was too dense to skim, I gathered from reviews on the cover that its author, a child psychiatrist, had produced the most respected treatise on the subject based on forty years of research, a collection of studies so scientifically airtight it had received accolades from no less than the American Medical Association.

Rubbing my eyes and wondering how much more reading I could do with regard to Clare's case, I added these two books to the stack. Between these and the several books on Hindu and Buddhist philosophy on the topic of reincarnation, it looked like I needed to do quite a bit more indeed.

I got up to leave, but as I stood up, I knocked the books at one end of the bottom shelf askew, and they tumbled to the floor in a heap. When I bent down to pick them up, I noticed that a postcard and an envelope had fallen out with them. As I reached to pick up the card, a name caught my eye: *Clare*.

THIRTEEN

Clare/Arcadia

c. 1838 A.D.
Alta California

Papa died four days ago. Father Platon, who will leave in days to minister to the Indians of the inland, said funeral Mass, his last at the mission church.

The party that came back to the rancho with the casket was enormous, friends and officials from Monterey, the adobe's vaqueros. Uncle Luis presided over the burial and wake. Now the only people left at the adobe are Benita, the cook; Maria, our caretaker; my uncle, Luis; and my older brother, Ignacio. The last two who will leave tomorrow to supervise the matanza, the round-up and slaughter of the rancho's cattle. My eldest brother, Estevan, is still in school in the Sandwich Islands.

My father was not a Spaniard by birth, but a fair-haired Yanqui, who stepped from a Boston whaling ship onto the playa at Monterey in the spring of 1818 and decided to stay. Within two months he had traded his American citizenship for that of Spain, converted to the faith of the fathers at Mission San Juan Bautista and married my late mother, Maria Constanza de la Guerra. Soon after, Papa had been granted a league of land south of the mission pueblo, a holding how increased to five leagues, where our adobe now stands.

By law it is now Estevan's; but Estevan, never interested in ranch matters, has often written to me of his plans to go to Boston to become a banker and, in fact, he swore to Papa before he left that he would never keep cattle as a living. The managing of the rancho is now in the hands of Uncle Luis, Mother's brother, whom none of us has ever trusted because of his lies, and Ignacio, who seems concerned only with the amount of silver tack he can accumulate for his stallion.

But I am too worn to think about all this now, and as night's stars fade, I feel sleep overtaking me. Just as I am between waking and sleep I hear what sounds like a gunshot. Perhaps the vaquero Joaquin scaring away a puma, for they have been harassing the horses lately.

· · ·

A voice is calling me through my sleep. The sun is low in the sky and the house is wrapped in silence so I cannot have been asleep long. But a voice called, I am certain. The wine I drank last night must have clouded my head. Perhaps fresh air would clear it. Rising noiselessly, I step into my riding clothes and steal out through the kitchen's outside entrance.

Our corral, enlarged just last week to hold all the extra horses needed for the matanza, is today shoulder-to-shoulder with caballos. I look them over and choose the first young mare who noses at my arm. I have ridden all my life, ever since the day Papa sat me, a giggling baby, on a dead-broke gelding. The vaqueros now declare I am expert enough to ride with them. Of all Father's children, I am the most independent.

"Ah, that is because you think like a caballo," Jose, our head vaquero, had once said.

The air is cool and dry. Blond grasses glitter with fiery dew, glades and hollows echo with the arias of the meadowlark and dove and the pungent scent of sun-dried amaranth and mustard rises to meet me.

The mare's ears prick up. She stops, still, watching. A puma? She takes off and I stay with her as she gallops across the little valley and over the low hill to the south. Then, she halts short.

"Good girl," I stroke her neck, whisper into her ear. "What is it, beauty?"

A red-tailed buteo circles overhead, calling "kee-arhh, kee-arhh!" then vanishes over the western hills. The mare huffs again, scans the horizon, head high, ears swiveling, and starts toward the creek.

Thirsty from the dry air, I dismount for a drink of water. But just as we lean together toward the creek, she lifts her head again. I hear it now, too; a voice, labored, crying from the direction of a great boulder some ways up the creek bed.

We walk, following the sound, until we arrive at a boulder just above a small pool. I peek around the granite to see an Indian lying on the wet sand next to the water.

He sees us and struggles to raise himself up on his left elbow, then falls back. "Oh, Señorita," he gasps, "good angel, I beg your help."

Hoping he is not a member of the fearsome Tulares tribes that have burned ranchos secluded in the hills, I approach cautiously. It is then I see the ugly wound to his right thigh and blood soaking through his leather pants, staining the sand.

"I was shot from my horse," he says in perfect Spanish, "before sun-up…could not go on." Seized by pain, his head falls back on the sand.

I kneel at his side. I have never been so close to an Indian, but I say as calmly as I can, "Our adobe is not far and I will bring help. Here." I remove my serape and place it under his head, then wrap its excess around his shoulders and chest which are shivering under his thin shirt. As I do so a charm on a lanyard, a turquesa joined with a crescent of black glass, falls aside on his chest. Untying my kerchief, I lay it against his wound, then attach the kerchief with the lanyard from my hair. "I will be back with help quickly, I promise."

By the time I arrive back at the rancho, the mare is lathered from chest to tail. I call to José, who is checking the horses' hooves before the cowboys set out. "Quickly! I need your help. There is a man, injured by the creek. Shot!"

José simply stares. "Señorita?"

"A man lies injured by gunshot at the creek!"

"Oh, Señorita Arcadia," he goes back to cleaning the horse's hoof, "Joaquin says he shot at a man this morning, an Indian. Probably a Tulareño. You know what they do to ranchos!"

"Yes, José, but he is no Tulareño. He is a blue-eye, and speaks Spanish!"

To my knowledge, José has never taken orders from a woman, but something in my tone must convince him, because within minutes we have two horses hitched to the carreta and are bumping quickly up the valley and across to the creek where we see the wounded man motioning weakly to us from the bank. Although he is rather tall we manage to lift him, arms across our shoulders, and place him in the bed of the carreta. I hold him there as still as possible, his head resting in my lap, my arm circling him as the wagon bounces roughly over the rocks. Only twice, in crossing hard ruts, do I feel his body wince. He clutches my hand tightly then and I do not let go.

The vaqueros are tacking up as we arrive and José calls for Carlos to help us. Benita watches suspiciously as I wrap a blanket around the man on the bed in Estevan's room. Uncle Luis and Ignacio, Carlos says, have already gone. The injured man will be safe here, if only we can save him.

"Benita, please." I stand and take her hands in mine. "Please, we cannot let this man die. We need the tea for fever, also the plaster of ashes and egg whites to stop the bleeding. And a poultice of yerba mansa, and linen to bandage with, too."

The cook backs up and gathers her shawl around her, but hurries in the direction of the kitchen. She returns in minutes with a Chumash basket full of wet yerba mansa leaves, a gourd of egg whites and ash, and a butane filled with her decoction of herbs, a Costeño recipe for fevers and ague. After cutting the blood-soaked leather pants away from the wound with a knife, I gently probe it for bits of lead. Now semi-conscious, the poor man jumps only once. Finding no evidence of shot, we spread a layer of the egg-and-ash mixture over the wound to staunch the bleeding, then cover it with the leaves and wrap it in the linens.

"His fever, it must be broken. Please, Benita, we need more blankets, the ones from my bed will do."

I look down at the Indian whose black hair, now dripping with fever sweat, sticks in shiny plaits to his forehead and neck. His skin is pale and the entire length of his body is shivering. Benita and I wrap him in blankets. He groans, then falls back into delirium. I sit down on a steer head stool, basket of leaves in my hands, next to the bed. It is now late morning and the vaqueros long gone.

I must fall asleep where I sit, because I wake some time later as the basket hits my feet. The sun, having arced across the sky, now burns white-gold ingots into the floor from the windows at the west. The Indian stirs, turns his head toward me.

His voice comes as a whisper. "Gracias, Señorita. You are…very kind. Your name is?" He reaches his hand out for mine. Even in his weakened state, his grip is sure, a good sign.

"I am Arcadia. Can you drink some tea? It will help break the fever." I lean toward him and offer the butane.

He reaches up blindly. I lift his head from the pillow to hold him while he sips a bit from the hollowed-out longhorn. When he is finished, he asks, "Where…am…I?"

"Rancho La Cuesta de los Robles." I lean forward so he does not have to strain to listen.

"Tuketu." He tries to touch his chest with his hand.

"Tuketu," I repeat.

"Mission San Juan Bautista." His voice gives way, and trails off as his eyes close again.

I tuck his blankets in around him. Of course. The reason his Spanish is so excellent. But the mission was closed several years ago. What is he doing here? With the abandonment of the missions by the government in Baja California, most Indians had returned to their tribes, especially those of the Valle Grande. And he does not look like the type to linger sickly and impoverished at the mission pueblo, waiting for a handout.

Maria, our caretaker, is at the doorway. "Evening is here, Señorita. You must have something to eat. And you have missed afternoon prayers." The worry in her voice makes me realize just how worn I must look.

"I will be fine. But could you ask Benita to fill the bowl with fresh leaves? And more tea for the butane." I look at Tuketu the Indian who has returned to sleep, peacefully now, with fewer chills. "I will eat here this evening. Could you bring me some stew, some wine and a candle, and any blankets I might use for the night?"

Maria, fascinated, leans forward to look over the mysterious visitor whose long body stretches beyond the end of the bed.

"His name is Tuketu. From San Juan Bautista," I say. "That is all I know."

Maria bites her lip. "If he attacks you, just scream. Ignacio unlocked your father's gun cabinet last night, you know."

I do know, and I suspect it is one of our guns that caused Tuketu's wound. "I doubt he could hurt anyone in his condition," I reply, as I watch him pale and helpless on the narrow cot.

I sit with him until evening, taking a spell only at the hour of eight for prayers with Benita and Maria. When I return to Tuketu, I kneel at his bedside and add prayers for him to my rosary. Finally, having missed sleep for two nights, I am overcome, and wrap myself in a blanket on a small cot in the corner, waking only once when I hear my patient stirring to check on his wound.

As I offer him more tea, he whispers, "You pray for me. No Californio woman has ever prayed for me." His sunken eyes are soft with gratitude and he tries to smile. "Thank you, angel Arcadia."

"Shhh." I caress his hair back with the damp rag. "You must sleep now, Tuketu." When sleep overtakes him and his breathing becomes regular, I return to my cot.

My eyes flutter open with the rooster's crow, my heart pounding, my head full of a dream of a beautiful ring of islands, one inside the other, shaped like a ship's bull's-eye of glass, or the water rippled by a stone's throw. Tuketu and I are in a ceremony of some kind there. It is such a beautiful fantasy I do not want it to retreat into the storeroom of memory, as dreams often do with the dawn. My patient, who has turned onto his left side facing me, sleeps quietly.

Rising as noiselessly as I can, I walk through the courtyard. My riding clothes of yesterday are stuck to my skin, my hair crumpled into knots. Maria and Benita have breakfast made and insist I sit down.

"Oh, Señorita Arcadia," Benita chides me, "look at you. Your mother"— she crosses herself—"would be so upset. I will boil water for your bath. But you must eat."

As I sit at the long wooden table under the arcade of the courtyard, I realize just how famished I am, as I devour without tasting the corn bread, sugared squash and beef. Even the burned-wheat coffee—the ships must not have arrived yet from the south lands—seems palatable today.

After my bath, I return to Tuketu's bedside and, perched on the steer skull stool near the window, take up my embroidery. Stitching has always had a calming effect on me, but I have difficulty keeping my eyes on the hoop, for I am drawn again to watch with wonder the man lying on the vaquero's bunk. Even clothed in a simple muslin camisa, as Maria had done for him last evening after she had bathed him; even bruised and wrapped in a frayed blanket, he has the bearing of a nobleman. And after the dream, it seems almost as if I had always known him. As I attempt to turn my concentration back to my needlework, I hear the squeak of the rawhide lattice.

"You have been here all morning?" he asks.

"I believe your fever is gone. Would you like midday meal? I will stay, if you like."

"Only if you promise to tell me about La Cuesta de los Robles. And you."

My head still full of my dream, I blush. He sees it, but his eyes do not leave me.

Tucking my kerchief more closely into my camisa, I hurry to the kitchen. I return with dinner for both of us and, adjusting the pillows under his head, set the wooden bowl of steaming beef and onions with flatbread onto his lap. Only after I am comfortable with my own bowl does he begin to eat, spooning the stew with the gusto of the newly recovered into the tortillas and eating hungrily. He reaches for the tea, and smiles apologetically.

"I do not mean to be rude, Arcadia."

"I will have Maria bring more?"

"No, it is well," he assures me. "Arcadia. It is a beautiful name. You are not pure Spanish though, not with your green eyes and gold-threaded hair."

I set my bowl aside. "My father was a Yanqui, from the 'United States of Boston' as some call it. My mother was Spanish."

"And I, like you, am half-Yanqui."

"Your father too?" I ask in amazement.

"His name was Joseph Reade, a whaler on a ship from New Bedford."

"Your mother, she was Ohlohne?"

"No, she was Mi-wuk. Her name was Paht-ki-yu. She worked at the mission."

I must look baffled, for I have not heard of these Indians.

"They live in the great lands to the east. She was from the Valley of the Awahnee."

"How did she come to be at San Juan Bautista?"

He looks across the room, as if seeing something far away. "One autumn, she joined her father on an annual trading expedition from her home to the Valle Grande, for my mother's people traded their very fine bows and arrows for animal skins with the Mi-wuk clans of the lowlands.

"At the village of the Siso-chi Mi-wuk her father met a man named He-le-jah, Mountain Lion. He-le-jah fell in love with my mother the moment he saw her, and offered my grandfather a beautiful rock of glittering yellow for her. I think"—he pauses and smiles—"I think she very much liked He-le-jah as well. When he left her, my grandfather gave her this turquesa pendant from the south, joined with the black glass bear claw, from the Washo, the people on the other side of the Sierra where, they say, the mountains made these stones out of fire."

"A bear claw?" I stare at the crescent-shaped pendant he holds out toward me.

"It is the stone used by the Mi-wuk in Uzumati, the grizzly bear ceremony. My grandfather had worn it since he was a child. Everyone knew him by it."

"And, Tuketu. What does your name mean?"

Now it is his turn to be embarrassed. "My real name is Joshua Reade, but my mother gave me the name Tuketu one day as she watched me play in front of the mission. It means 'Bear Making Dust.' "

I clamp my hand over my mouth, trying not to laugh.

He begins to laugh but winces from pain. After a deep breath, he continues, "My mother was happy with the Siso-chi, but one day a raiding party came inland while my mother and He-le-jah and their family were fishing at the great inland lake, the Lake of the Tulares. They hid in the reeds, but the soldiers saw them and took them to the mission. He-le-jah died of a fever there that summer. Mother met my father, Joseph, in October. My father wanted to marry her, but before he could join the church and become a citizen of Spain, he was lost at sea, just outside the waters of Bahia Monterey. The fathers at the mission gave me my education. I learned Latin and Spanish and my mother taught me some of her language."

"And why," I ask, leaning forward, "were you leaving the village?"

"When the missions were given to the government we, my mother and I, were entitled to grants of lands from the church holdings. After my mother died, Father Antonio Anzar, he was a good man, helped me submit a diseño to the government. They gave me the land. I had sheep. My fleece was good, and I got a good price from the traders.

"But bad men came into the pueblo. New men, Yanquis and Mexicans, who did not care about land rights, especially for an Indian. They killed my sheep, scattered others, so it would look as if I was not working the land, as required by the grant. Then they broke into my cabin and threatened me with guns. When I wouldn't give in, they went to Monterey to accuse me of cheating the government with an illegal diseño.

"Arcadia," he says, his face serious, "you know what disorder is in the government now? First the governor is in Alta, then Baja. We have had nine governors in ten years! How am I to know where my diseño went? And does it matter anyway, with the new men coming to take any land they choose?"

He stops, folds the blankets over himself. He sighs heavily and his shoulders fall. "Four days ago, the same men came to my cabin with guns again. They were drunk and threatened to kill me. I could not fight them off alone. I know I cannot expect help from the alcalde; he is crooked as a rattlesnake. And I am just a mission Indian, a bastard Indian in the bargain. I have seen what they do to Indians they do not want around. We have no protection now, with the fathers gone."

Silence hangs like a lead weight over the room. "What are you going to do?" I ask, afraid of the answer.

"I am going to the only people I can trust: my mother's people, the Awahnee Mi-wuk. Perhaps they will remember my grandfather and Paht-ki-yu. There perhaps I can live in peace."

As I listen, I am reminded of other stories I have heard of Indians who "died" just before their mock trials could be held at the alcalde's office;

of Indians jailed, then released to the ranchos where they became, once again, indentured servants.

He looks at me and tries to smile. "But that is enough of my troubles. What I wish is to know more about you, Arcadia."

I tell him of my mother, who died of the typhoid fever two years ago, of my education, rare for a Californio girl, by a mission tutor, just as he had. And finally, that my beloved father had died just a week earlier. Then I tell him about the changes in the rancho, and about my uncle.

He listens closely, but not wishing to be pitied for something I can do nothing about, I attempt to collect myself by changing the subject. "It might be good for you to see if you can walk a little now. If you lean on my shoulder, perhaps you could."

"All right, Arcadia, I will try."

He pulls himself up by grasping my hand and then places his arm across my shoulder. I hold his hand and we take a few tentative steps together. He limps only a little; the leg seems to be healing well. After a few more steps, we turn. As we do, my breast touches the side of his chest and my whole body is suddenly ignited. I back up. He stops and looks down at me. I can scarcely breathe or move. A sole mockingbird sings a wild medley at the window as a wind stirs the leaves of the young oak there. A burro brays in the corral.

I pull back. "Tuketu, I . . ."

"Arcadia?"

The bell for prayers and supper sounds in the courtyard.

"I must help you back to bed and attend prayers, but I will have your meal sent and return after," I say with a quietness I do not feel.

I hurry through supper, now unable to think of anything but his touch. When I return he tells me, by the light of the little candle on the wine barrel, more of his early life at the mission, of the boys' choir there, of learning to read music by color and of the frescoes, which I always admired as a child and which, he tells me, were painted by a shipmate of his father's.

. . .

I am at his side early the next morning, and he is eager to talk about the place he says he is going.

"The Valle Grande is so beautiful, more beautiful than Eden, some say. In spring, it is as if it has been painted with every color you could imagine, all flowers. You cannot take your horse across it without stepping on these flowers. There are herds of elk, more than one can imagine in one's grandest dreams, and beautiful wild mesteños, and so many birds, dancing cranes, geese, duck, that they cover the sky. And the rivers and lakes, it takes several men to haul one net in from their waters, they are so filled with fish."

"And the Valle of the Awahnee?" I ask.

"Mother always said that once you saw the Valle of the Awahnee you never forgot it, for it was a place where the rocks grazed the sky side by side, as if a giant had played with the earth. She said in winter came the thing called snow, which is made from raindrops so cold they turn white and blanket the world in silence, but that in the spring, when the sun once again became strong, one could not hear speech among the men in the Valle for the great music of the snow returning to water and falling down the rock faces from the sky. My mother, she said the Valle of the Awahnee proved God saved His most beautiful creation for last."

"I cannot imagine such a place."

"It is real, Arcadia." He touches my arm and watches me. "I wish you could see it."

But now all I can think of is the heat of his touch.

. . .

The following morning I find him walking up and down, aided with only the cane.

"Good morning, good angel," he greets me cheerfully. "You have made me well. My leg—I can walk again without too much help. I will be able to ride now."

Suddenly I hear voices, then the heavy tread of boots in the courtyard. Uncle Luis.

"That must be the one the alcalde's officers were talking about, the Indian shepherd with the false diseño," he says. "The mission ones never were good for anything, and now they're busy squatting on land that isn't theirs. Well, if he wants to stay, he's got a choice: field hand or jail."

As quickly as I can, I help Tuketu back into bed, then straighten my skirts and kerchief and hurry out, where I run directly into Ignacio and Uncle Luis.

At first my uncle is obliging. Then, his nostrils flare like a mad bull, and he explodes. What do I think I am doing, bringing a wild Indian into the rancho? Spending time with him, alone! He is a wanted man, they say, and you know what trouble they have had in the pueblos with those drunkards, those animals! He threatens me with hell's wrath, tells me if I were his daughter he would take the switch to me and force me to say rosaries from sunup to sundown in penance. With each threat, rather than becoming more concerned for myself, I become more concerned for Tuketu.

"But uncle, he—"

"Maria will see to your patient now. Do you understand?"

He storms away, slapping the horse bat against his leg as if for practice. I back into Estevan's room and walk directly into Tuketu.

"I heard it, Arcadia, I heard it. Oh, forgive me, my angel, forgive me!" Tuketu whispers, my hands in his. "You must not come here again. And I must leave as soon as I am able."

"No!"

"Arcadia, what kind of man would I be to submit to the slavery of a rancho Indian or the certain death of a pueblo jail? Even death by wild animal is preferable to imprisonment, especially for an innocent man." His jaw is set. "If you could get me a caballo, even a burro . . ."

"But," my words surprise me even as I speak them, "please do not leave me!"

He looks shocked. Then, slowly, he smiles. His hand touches the side of my face as he says softly, "Then come with me."

Come with him. To an alien world, a place I had never seen and where I had no family, never to return. "Oh, Tuketu!" I begin shaking with tears. "How could I live in the Mi-wuk world? I am not an Indian!"

His hand drops. He turns away, hobbles to the chair. "No, you are not," he says bitterly as he traces an invisible pattern on the planks with the cane. "And I am."

* * *

I spend the evening praying the rosary, then take Maria aside in the kitchen. Although she is at first reluctant, I eventually persuade her, through my tears, to tell Tuketu that I will leave a horse, charqui, and butane behind the bunkhouse for him, that I will pray God be with him on his journey.

The coyotes' wails begin as soon as the sky darkens. But they have no need to hunt tonight, only to scavenge the offal of the slaughtered cattle all around. At daylight, it will be the condorés, immense winged beasts who descend on the carrion like great flapping shadows until the rancho, picked clean of cattle entrails, resembles the Golgotha of the Hebrew Bible, strewn with white bones everywhere one walks or rides. A world of death.

At midnight I sneak into the corral where I choose a young, strong stallion that seems to have a sturdy build. I have no way to get to the tack now without waking the vaqueros, so I slip him into a halter and tie him to a post on the opposite side of the corrals, along with a butane and a leather knapsack filled with charqui and flatbread. Returning to my room, I cry myself to sleep. When I waken, the sun is already peeking over the eastern hills. I dress quickly and rush to Estevan's room.

Tuketu is gone.

I try after breakfast to concentrate through my tears on my needle-point until afternoon prayers. Evening table is strained again and my uncle cannot resist commenting, "I see the Indian took off. Good-for-nothing mongrel. At least you will be able to sleep now, Arcadia. No more nurse-maiding a savage."

Yes, I think, *a savage*. Whose hands are so gentle they feel like a kiss upon the skin. Who speaks three languages. Whose absence is tearing my heart in two.

Exhausted by the events of the last days, I go to my bedroom. Picking up my pillow to exchange its linen, still damp from my tears, something hidden beneath it catches my eye: a folded piece of parchment. I am barely able to control the shaking of my hands as I open it.

Arcadia

Forgive me for asking such a question of you. I know my words were a surprise and I did not mean to scare you. But nothing has ever felt so dear as my closeness to you. I know I am just an Indian and you a Californio, but I must ask again, one last time, for you to come with me. Your father gave up his country and his religion to come to a new place; my father left his home, too. It is in our blood, you and me, to be free and to live as we choose. When you found me I found what I had longed for all my life. But I would be only half a man, and no man to you, if I allowed myself to be indentured or imprisoned here.

My sweet Arcadia, I leave with you a map I have made using my memories of the maps I have seen of Father Montoya's travels to El Arroyo de los Baños, as well as the memories of my mother's stories. Should you ever need to depart, or want to come, I will be waiting at the Valley of the Awahnee for you, and no other.

> *Say my name and point east, to the Sierra. The Mi-wuk are friendly people, and will help you find your way.*

> *God be with you always, my angel, my savior,*

Tuketu

At the bottom of the page is a map showing a route east, which follows the Rio de los Tulares, then a river called the Rio de Nuestra Señora de la Merced. He is somewhere on that map now, perhaps already crossing the Valle Grande, two days away from me. Cold pain spreads through my bones when I realize that with each hour's passing we grow farther apart. Forever.

I lay awake all night, longing for his touch, wondering what to do. Then, suddenly, I know who might help me. Before breakfast I am dressed and mounted on the mare I used a few days ago, and by noon I am at the mission.

Father Platon, busy counting stores in the kitchen, greets me cheerfully. When he sees my tears, he leads me into a corner of the chapel. "My dear Arcadia! "

"Father," I cry, and my story of my uncle and the precarious position of the rancho, and then of Tuketu and my feeling for him pours forth with my tears.

"Come, sit down." He motions to one of the long benches facing the choir. I look up, see the figure of the Redeemer above the altar with his court of angels and flowers.

"A fine young man, Tuketu," Father Platon says. Then, after a moment, "And do you love him?"

"As if I had always," I say, hiccoughing with tailing sobs, "but he is an Indian!"

"If you truly love him, why does such a thing matter?"

I look up to him. Then to Jesus and his angels. Perhaps it was not that

Tuketu was an Indian, but that I was afraid of his world, a world so different from mine. "Allow me this night in prayer, as you should as well, and return tomorrow," Father Platon says kindly. "With God leading, we will find an answer to your dilemma."

· · ·

By early the next morning I am back at the mission. Father Platon comes at the entrance to the courtyard, arms opened to me, smiling. He leads me into the chapel and motions me to kneel beside him. We pray together, for some time.

"Arcadia," he says, when we are finished, "it is God who knows the hearts of all men and women, and God who made each man's skin different from every other. And it is God who brought Tuketu to you. Yes, he is half-Indian, but he is also half-Yanqui, as are you. I am leaving for the inland the day after tomorrow before dawn to preach God's word to the tribes there. Search your heart, Arcadia, and if he is the one meant for you, we will journey together."

I remain in prayer at the rancho the remainder of the day, and much of the night. And then, I know what I must do, the only thing I can do to be true to myself, and to God.

After silent preparations, I slip out of the adobe in the early hours of the following night and into the full moonlight. The household, still tired from the matanza, seems as if in opiate sleep. Only the coyotes, now retreated into the surrounding hills, keep the night awake with their otherworldly cries. I begin my escape at a walk then, when I am accustomed to the pale light, a canter, through the valley down and to the mission. I have left a note for my uncle and bring another for the church fathers to mail to Estevan. With luck, by the time the rancho thinks to ask at the mission about me, I will have put many leagues of ground between us.

. . .

As the sun rises on the following day, Father Platon and I are beyond any place I have ever ridden, yet we are still in the Costeño mountains, at a high point, the same, Father Platon tells me, that Father de la Cuesta traveled, as shown on Tuketu's map. Tomorrow we should descend into the Valle Grande.

We travel easily on this new terrain until late in the afternoon. The mare is tired, I know, but I push her around one more low hill. As we come around its brow, we are brought to a halt by an astonishing sight.

Stretched out before us like a vision of another world stands a grand plain of immeasurable distance, traversed by mercurial ribbons of water, dotted with enormous spreading oak trees, thick with grass nearly as high as the trees. Along the banks of a river running to a north/south aspect, directly below, an incalculable herd of elk, more than I have ever seen together in one place, graze silently. Beyond, rising behind this boundless Eden like a painted backdrop from an opera, the indigo spires of the Sierra seem to pierce the sky. It is that Sierra that Tuketu must be riding toward, just days ahead of us.

"Yes, this is the way," Father Platon says, smiling as he touches the rosary on his robes.

It is then that we see a smoke rising, a campfire, near the river to the north. My last thought before I fall asleep under the moon-shadow of the broad oak is of meeting Tuketu at the Valley of the Awahnee. When I awaken, the sun is just rising over the jagged spine of the Sierra.

We skirt the low hills, where our view is unobstructed for the better part of two days until, on the third afternoon, when we must again turn east to follow the campfire we had spotted days earlier, still sending smoke into the sky. Nearer the valley floor we emerge from the curtain of grass at what seems to be the confluence of two rivers, El Rio de los Tulares, and another river running east to west, probably El Rio de Nuestra Señora de la Merced. Rio de los Tulares seems to be shallow enough but very broad, and we see no easy way to cross at any point.

I am washing the dust from my face at the river as the first sunlight touches the water when I have my answer about the Indians. Sensing eyes observing my movements, I look up to see, on the opposite bank north of the Rio de la Merced, two men crouching, peering at me from between the reeds. I stand, as do they, and we regard one another's presence warily.

Father Platon comes up behind me. He holds his crucifix before him as a sign of peace.

The Indians exchange a glance, then look back in our direction. We walk closer to the water, motioning to them that we would like to come over to their side. They seem to be talking to each other by both word and gesture. Then, from behind the rushes, one of the men pulls forward a large, flat-bottomed boat constructed of reeds and grasses. He lays this punt down on the water, crawls on and, balancing on his knees, poles his way across. We put the mare between us and look out from behind her rump as I keep my hand on Father's French cavalry pistol.

The Indian climbs from the little boat and stands knee-deep in the reeds. His face is tattooed with a design of dark lines, giving him a cat-like appearance. His only clothing is a breechcloth made of hide.

"*Wu-meh*?" he asks, as he points all around. "*Wu-meh*?" Where are you from?

Father Platon says "*Olowitoko*" as he motions south and west, then: "Tuketu?"

"Tuketu!" The Indian laughs and slaps his leg, then points along the river, east, then to the sun, and holds up three fingers. Tuketu was here three days ago. "Awahnee Mi-wuk. Uzumati!"

Smiling, he motions us to come and I wade into the shallows and nervously board the craft on all fours, while one of the Indians takes the mare's reins. At first she hesitates, but the Indian seems to have a way with her and before I know it, we are poling evenly across the sleepy river, me hanging onto the reed gunwales with the mare walking, then swimming, behind us. The Indians repeat the process with Father Platon and the burro.

As we lead the animals into the village, men stand up and put their conversations aside. One of the fellows we first encountered at the river speaks to a man who appears to be the mayordomo of the village.

This important-looking man looks me over and strides forward. He gestures to the blue mountains behind him. "Tuketu."

"Yes. Our friend," Father Platon says.

That night the mayordomo's wife insists we stay inside their little hut, which is surprisingly cool and comfortable. Throughout the night I see visions of Tuketu and me together, of the two of us on an island in a far-away sea, in a stable full of beautiful horses, in a castle garden—places I have never been, yet seem to have called up from memory.

We resume our journey at dawn, our saddlebags and panniers now laden with supplies of dried fish, squirrel, and venison. Late afternoon we see another line of smoke rising ahead and by nightfall we arrive at a second village. Yes, Tuketu was here, four days before.

I sleep an irregular sleep, anxious as I am to be on my way, yet fearful of the dangers in the hills to the east. Six more villages offer us food and a place to rest. Six more villages do not allow us to leave without adding extra meat and acorn meal to our saddlebags. And, just before dark on our eighth day at the villages of the Mi-wuk in the Valle Grande, we arrive at the village of Paht-ki-yu.

The following day, the traveling men of the clan help us with advice and a simple map drawn in the wet sand. But just as we are about to leave, I hear a quick hiss, a bray, then a shout. I turn in time to see the burro bucking, Father Platon falling over a log and a rattlesnake slithering away toward the river.

"Arcadia!" he shouts.

Several Mi-wuk men run to him push the hem of his robe aside. One pulls a sharp shell blade from the thong at his waist, cuts into the skin on Father Platon's leg, puts his mouth to the skin and begins sucking and spitting out blood. Another rushes over, holding a long strip of animal hide, which both men tie above the wound. Then they carry Father Platon, now moaning in pain, into the nearest hut.

I convince Father Platon to drink the medicine the women bring, then help the woman cover him with a deerskin blanket. Then I take his hand and begin praying, just as I had done for Tuketu only days ago.

"It is serious, my wound?" he gasps as he reaches for his leg.

"No, Father. They have pulled the venom out."

He grabs my hand tightly. "A rattlesnake. Ah, I thought so."

I keep vigil with the women healers throughout the night. Though his night is restless and he occasionally cries out, by morning Father Platon is able to sit up to speak.

"Poor Arcadia. I'm afraid you must be on your way without me," he says weakly.

"I cannot, will not, leave you," I assure him.

"Child," he whispers, "God has spoken within your heart, and you have followed." He tries to smile. "And that serpent," he chuckles, "has given me a message: I am to stay with these people to teach them the word of God."

"But, Father—"

"The left pannier on the burro. My missal is there. And my compass. Bring them to me."

I run out and find the time-softened leather missal and the compass, then return to the hut. He instructs me to turn to the prayer to Saint Christopher. As he recites the prayer from memory, I read along with the book.

"Now, Arcadia. Take this missal with you. Teach the Awahneechee people about God, and our Savior, and how to pray. And"—he hands me the brass compass—"let this show you the way."

"But Father, what about Tuketu and me?"

"Have you confession to make?"

"No, only that…well, if we wish to marry…"

"Arcadia, if your heart is pure and your conscience clean, you will do the right thing. God will be your witness." He takes my hand in both of his, and manages a smile. "Do not fear."

. . .

At sunup, I say good-bye to Father Platon. As I depart, he tells me to take the burro along, for which I am grateful. Two of the tribe, Yu-wel and his wife O-hu-le, have volunteered to guide us to the next village. Though we now travel over low hills, we make good time, and arrive at the village two days later. The elders do their best, despite the language barrier, to help me find the correct route into the high mountains.

"Valley of the Awahnee?" I point to the place south and east on the map.

"*Wa-kah-la*," one says, pointing to an imaginary place on the map. "Awahnee, *koun*." Long way off.

Another man insists I exchange my horse for one of theirs. Since my mare has been showing signs of lameness, I agree and allow him to select a mesteño for me, a small, sturdy mare with, he assures me, an excellent temperament. Using a piece of charcoal, the Indians draw a map of their foot trail into the Valley of the Awahnee on the back of the letter from Tuketu. The next day I begin my journey upward, through the foothills and into the forest.

. . .

How can I tell of the harsh days that come? Rocks so large I sometimes climb over them not knowing whether I would fall over or step on the ground below. Two days without water as, temporarily lost, we stumble from one dry creek bed to the next. A strange night sleeping in what seems to be the collapsed cinder cone of an ancient volcano. At one point I must scare away a group of inquisitive grizzly bears with father's French cavalry pistol. I hunt with the pistol when I can. When I have no luck, I break open logs, as I've seen bears do, and throw grubs onto the fire for my only food. Each night, I wrap myself in my blanket and serape, as a mestizo might do, pull my big hat, now frayed and dirty, over my face and sleep, half-sitting up, against the trunk of a tree.

The mesteño tumbles down an embankment, breaking her leg, and I must shoot her. The pages of Father Platon's missal I tear out in desperation, one rainy night, to start a fire. And when my boots, never meant for walking over such harsh terrain, fall to pieces, I sit down and sob, wondering at my own foolhardiness, until I remember the soft Indian deerskin boots given me by a Miwok woman weeks before, find them and lace them onto my swollen feet.

Finally, bruised, scraped, and half-starved, I hear the sound of water rushing below. Suddenly, my aching feet have wings and just before noon the burro and I arrive just above the banks of the Rio Merced, which, the Miwok elders have promised, leads directly into the Valley of the Awahnee. I count my days and nights of travel. It has been just over a month since I left the rancho.

The next morning dawns cool and dry with only a few clouds brush-stroked across the sky. We thread our way out between oaks and pines and down to the riverbank below. Fat squirrels chip from their perches above. Two wolves drink on the opposite side of the river, look up, sharp faces questioning, then trot off westward.

As the burro nibbles at oak leaves, I eat the last bit of squirrel meat and berries from my saddlebag on a flat ledge facing the sun. My hips and knees feel raw and weak; I had no idea how much I had walked until last night. But with the sun high and bright, I begin again.

We travel with yet more care now, for even the footsure little burro is having difficulty keeping her balance on the stony riverbank. Soon, these rounded stones give way to stretches of radiant white sand. Clouds gather and thunder rolls down from the far peaks. The sky lowers, then the rain comes, great heavy drops that soon become a downpour. I lead the burro under a low oak. As quickly as the storm begins, it passes, and we are again on our way.

Without notice, the gorge flattens and the landscape seems to open around us. Now, the clear green river broadens as it travels around rocks and shoals. The anvil-headed birds scold us in huge numbers, then leave their high perches to join us as a noise-making escort.

And then, standing before me, is a gargantuan shoulder of gray stone, taller than the mast of the tallest ship, larger than any rock I have ever before seen, climbing into the sky ahead to snag the remnants of the clearing storm. Opposite rise three granite triangles from whose ramparts a waterfall plunges into a mist of lacy spray. At that instant, the sky before me clears and I find myself standing at the gate of a landscape so marvelous it must indeed have been pushed into place by the hands of a giant. On either side and ahead of me more massive rocks stand like stern sentinels, including one that resembles nothing less than a huge globe sliced perfectly in half. Beyond that and higher still, a wide bowl of treeless rock cradles clouds resembling stacks of burst featherbeds. Confounded by this open air cathedral, all I hear, oddly, is the dripping of the last rain from the pine needles, the chip of the squirrels.

I pull the burro along and she follows, eyes wide, as if she, too, is amazed by this grand new world. Soon, we come to an open meadow bounded by oaks. I see two little boys playing a stick game while their companion, a cinnamon-colored bear cub, swats at a bug.

I stand without moving in the shade of an oak. They look up, come over to me.

"Awahneechee?" I ask, pointing to one boy, then the other.

"Awahneechee!" One of the boys points to his chest and stands up straight. The burro, fearing the bear, backs up. I hold her firmly while I gesture toward the length of the broad valley, toward the campfire smoke rising in the distance.

"Tuketu, *hai-em?*" Nearby?

"Tuketu, *hai-em!*" The second boy motions to the little cub rolling on the ground, and they laugh together.

I try again, using my hands to indicate a creature of human size and shape. "Tuketu?"

"Tuketu!" they repeat in unison, and giggle. They come toward me and the taller one, taking my hand, leads me on a path along the shore of the river.

We veer off when we are deeper in, slightly away from the river and to the north side of the valley, toward yet another waterfall, dashing down the wall of rock from such height I cannot see its origin above. A village is ahead, a group of cone-shaped brush dwellings like the ones in the villages of the great valley, yet here seeming so much smaller for the vastness of the landscape all around. As we enter, people appear from behind the huts, boulders, and trees; old men, women holding babies, young men carrying bows and arrows in animal-skin quivers.

Then I see him. He is dressed as their men are, in a collar of brilliant feathers and a deerskin loincloth, his hair wrapped with a leather band. In a heartbeat, the glorious world around me fades and goes dark.

The roar of the great fall behind the village stirs me. It seems I am being carried in someone's arms. I try to refocus my eyes. "Tuketu? Tuketu?"

The arms lay me down on soft fur. A hand shakes gently as it caresses my brow, my cheek, holds me near. I feel warm tears falling through my hair, hear a voice, broken with sobs, murmuring "Oh, Arcadia. Oh, my darling Arcadia."

I reach out to him. His hand grasps mine and does not let go. An old woman brings a basket she says is medicine, and a gourd of tea; sharp, strong, herbal. Tuketu holds my head, helps me to drink. Someone covers me with an animal skin. And then I sink into sleep, a sleep more comforting than any

I have ever before known, from which I wake, only once in the night, to see the shape of the old woman chanting a low song as she sits nearby. I taste the sweet smoke from the campfire outside the door, see embers floating skyward. I am, momentarily, lost as to where I am then, remembering, my eyes, my tired eyes, close again. I am with Tuketu and I am home.

. . .

The next thing I know, sun is streaming through the doorway. Two women chat as they mend baskets off to one side of the hut. They look over at me.

One of the women puts her work aside, bends down and touches my arm as if to ask, "Are you better?"

I smile at her and sit up. I am, I discover, naked under the skin blanket. They bring me my rabbit fur tunic and a skirt of long grasses, which they tie around my waist. One of them braids my hair into a single plait around which they wrap a leather-and-shell band.

I am surprised at how well I feel; even my poor feet, which must have been tended while I slept, have stopped hurting. I emerge from the dusty cool of the hut into the brilliant autumn sun flickering through red and gold leaves. Tuketu is there and in an instant his arms are around me. We are that way for a long time, then we walk together to the hub of the village, where he introduces me to several of the clan. They smile welcome, motion me to sit with them by the fire. Tuketu and I share acorn porridge and a delicious fish. When we have finished, he helps me stand.

"I will be fine," I reply, smiling, to his anxious look.

"Come," he says, holding me close as he walks me to the river. There we sit on its banks, as the sun climbs above the valley, tipping the pines which stand like columns around us, with light like golden fire. I shake my head, a memory?

Tuketu runs his hand across my cheek, down my shoulder. "It is almost as if we had been together in a place like this before."

"Yes, yet different, too."

"Yet certainly with you."

"I would not have known of such beauty as this, without you."

"And I would not have known what beauty is, without you." He smiles, and takes my hand in his. "The village would like to adopt you, and would like you to have a Mi-wuk name. I thought Te-hey-ney, after a Mi-wuk woman honored for devotion to her mate."

"It is a beautiful name." I think of all the villages I have visited, all the kind people who have helped me find my way to Tuketu. And now, they wish me to be one of them.

We sit side-by-side, holding to each other with wonder. I rest my head against his heart. How much we have to learn about one another. How much we already seem to know.

"Arcadia, Te-hey-ney," he says, "I can think of no greater happiness for myself and I cannot imagine a world without you. Would you honor me by becoming my wife?"

"I feel I already am."

"Oh, Arcadia," he says, kissing me, "yes."

He lifts the turquesa and obsidian pendant from his neck and places it around mine. "May this memento be my testament: I promise to love none but you, even beyond this life, if it be granted."

I lay my hand against his cheek, and touch my lips to his. The river of mercy sings its joyful song as it journeys to the sea. The trees above us bend and sigh. He lays me back on the soft sand. And before we return to the village I am, with God our witness, his true and natural wife.

FOURTEEN

Emily

February-June, 2004

The Clare? For a moment I simply stared, uncomprehending, at the type on the card. Then, when my head cleared, I saw that it was a wedding announcement, which read:

CLARE NEWLAND

AND

PETER MACWAN

ARE PLEASED TO ANNOUNCE THEIR MARRIAGE

MAY 22, 2000

KANAPAALI BEACH, MAUI

with, at the bottom, a note: *"He is a Marine Archaeologist at the Center for Oceanographic Research in La Jolla. We are so happy! C."*

My entire body was literally buzzing inside as I reached down for the envelope underneath the card— an envelope with the name "Clare" scrawled across the top in Nick's handwriting. Were these items meant for the file I had come upon at Nick's home office? Had Nick forgotten them?

Inside the envelope were two pieces of paper. The first was a photo Christmas card of a young family on a beach, dated La Jolla, California, December 21, 2001. In the photo a woman who appeared to be in her early thirties sat on a beach chair with her arm around a bearded man of about the same age who looked to be East Indian. Between them sat a smiling baby with a head of sunny blond curls. It was signed "Clare, Peter, and Moira."

The second item was a letter postmarked December 20, 2001:

Dear Dr. Turner,

Merry Christmas! I can't begin to tell you how happy my life is now. The baby in the picture is our daughter Moira, who was born in July. We recently moved into a wonderful old house in the Mission District here and I have an amazing story I have to tell you.

As I was packing to move last spring, I pulled a box down from the top shelf of our bedroom closet and was suddenly smacked on the head by a small object wrapped in a square of shearling. I knelt down to pick it up and saw that it was a man's belt buckle, you know, the kind that fit with Western wear? It was incised with a modern design and had a big cabochon of turquoise set in the center.

When Pete came home that evening, I asked him where he'd bought it. "Oh, where'd you find that?" he asked. "I won it when I was a teenager in a raffle at a rodeo in Mariposa." He turned the buckle over in his hands and studied it and I could tell he was thinking of something. "I don't think I ever wore it," was the last thing I heard from him before he disappeared with it into the garage, where he kept a set of archaeological tools.

Just as I was starting to fix dinner I heard a sound behind me, turned around and saw him coming toward me from the hallway. He walked into the kitchen holding the stone out to me in the palm of his hand.

Just like the dream that brought me to you for help.

For a moment, all I could do was stare at him. Then, slowly, it came to me. Mariposa: Spanish for butterfly, the symbol for rebirth, you'd said. And the place, so near Yosemite, where Pete had lived for a time when he was a child. I was suddenly completely overwhelmed and burst into tears. Pete put his arms around me and said, "Clare, honey! What is it?" Then I had to ask, "Did you like living up near Yosemite?" "The Indians used to tease me about being a lost relative!" he said, "That's a strange question. Why?" I began to cry, but all I could say was this: "Oh, just something I remembered."

He held me for a long time then, and I held the cabochon close, as close as I could to the center of my heart. Someday, I may tell him what I discovered with you. For now, that turquoise stone is my most precious possession.

Warmest wishes for the holidays,

Clare

There are times in one's life—the birth of a child, a miraculous recovery—when the hallowed mystery of existence becomes manifest. Exactly how long I stood staring blindly at the paper I held, aware only of the racing of my heart and the sound of the sea whirling in my ear, I cannot say. But suddenly, my whole being stumbled against itself. I reached out for the desk chair and sat down heavily. Now Clare's regressions were more than just fanciful stories of the past. They had come to be echoed by the present.

I had my phone out even before I was out of the office. Information had no number listed for either Macwan or Newland anywhere in San Diego County. But they did have a number for the Center for Oceanographic Research. All I got was a recorded message. I left one of my own, asking if a Peter Macwan worked there, leaving both my home and cell phone numbers.

I received a call late the next morning from Dr. Macwan's assistant at COR. He was on an exploratory field trip in Crete with his wife and child. She was not sure when they would be returning to the States. I explained that I was a writer who was actually trying to reach Clare in order to interview her for an upcoming book. No, Dr. Macwan was not available by cell, she said, but they checked their e-mail as often as possible, if I would like the address.

All I could do was hope my message got through, or that they returned home before my story had to go to my editor. Meanwhile, I continued with my research on Clare's last story, if only out of curiosity, to see how much of it, as had the others, matched up with historical fact.

It sounded highly implausible that a sheltered young woman like Arcadia could walk across California and into the mountains without serious incident, until I remembered the stories of several young woman who had accomplished similar feats in various unexplored parts of the world during the last two centuries. Apparently, many Indians of mission-era California had in fact returned to their tribes inland although I also discovered, sadly, that wars had been waged by gold-seekers against the Awahnee Mi-wuk in the years 1850-51. As a result of these incursions, many Mi-wuk died, many more were removed to reservations and yet more simply assimilated, taking white names and dying in their time with nothing of their lives recorded, as may have been the case with people like Tuketu and Arcadia.

Likewise, my researches of Spanish California history disclosed several grants awarded in the area near San Juan Bautista, including one to the family Clare named, a family whose name had been taken from the mother's side, as was done at the time by American men who married Spanish women and became citizens of Spain. I could not locate any birth certificates for any offspring.

Going even farther back into Clare's stories, I discovered an amazing connection between Kalliste and California, a connection I discovered quite by accident while channel-surfing one night. Geologists and dendrochronologists had recently discovered that in certain species of long-lived trees, tree ring growth, the measure of age, is either absent or badly frost-scarred in the year 1627 B.C.

Some experts now attribute this anomaly to a dramatic lowering of global temperature due to a volcanic event, possibly the cataclysmic eruption of Santorini, Minoan Kalliste, whose blast was so huge it sent ash well into the stratosphere, preventing light and heat from reaching the earth's surface to an extent that frosts occurred throughout the summer of the following year in latitudes where frost is not commonly present. One source from which they have obtained this new insight? The famed bristlecone pine, native to the high country of Yosemite National Park in California.

Research completed, I had done as much as I could. And so I waited, trusting that the final gift within Clare's story, which was now a part of mine, would yet be revealed.

. . .

The last week of May, for some reason, seemed always hectic, with kids about to get out of school, and businesses working at top speed before offices became shorthanded at vacation-time. Tuesday the 28th had been an especially hectic morning for me, with two articles due on exactly the same day and the one editor I needed to speak to out with bronchitis. And my CR-V needing a new fuel pump. I had just finished a call on the hard line at around eleven AM when my cell went off.

I had already had such a morning I nearly screamed into it as I opened it. "Yes!"

All I heard was silence.

"Good morning," I said, more graciously, I hoped.

Finally I heard an amused female voice—a voice I had heard before. "I'm trying to reach Emily Wendell. My name is Clare Macwan."

The call I thought wouldn't come. For a moment, I was paralyzed. Then I sat down at my desk as I frantically shoved coffee mug, papers, and mouse pad aside in search of my notebook. All my neural circuits suddenly jammed, and the little speech I'd rehearsed so often for the past two months vanished instantly from my brain so I just plunged in with the truth, omitting any reference to my personal life with Nick.

"I'd be happy to speak with you, but it will have to be here. After being away from home so long and…well, I don't think I can deal with the freeways right now," she apologized.

Of course I would drive down. She suggested we meet at her home in June.

. . .

Clare's home was a white, 1920s hacienda-style with a well-tended garden, rosy bougainvillea traveling across the garage wall into the tiled courtyard and a solid, mission-style front door. I touched the bell button and an old fashioned chime rang throughout the house.

I heard small feet running in my direction, then heavier feet in pursuit. A child's voice shrieked with laughter. The door opened.

She was taller than I thought she would be. Her sun-bleached hair fell nearly to her shoulders in curls. She was dressed in a kimono-style batik wrap jacket and jeans. Although not classically pretty, she had a wide, gorgeous smile and nearly perfect teeth. And she was obviously several months pregnant, probably the reason she hadn't wanted the stress of driving long distances on the maze of the southern California freeways.

The little girl at her side had golden skin, amber-colored hair, and dark brown eyes, a striking mix, especially in a toddler. Her mother held her back with one hand. The other, she stretched out to me.

"You must be Emily."

The toddler looked up at me and mimicked, "Emiry!"

I followed her into the living room and moments later she returned with a cup of decaf for me. "Just give me a couple of minutes while I get Moira down for her nap."

The room was handsomely furnished: a chestnut leather sofa, deep armchairs, kilim rugs, commodious tables. I bent down to look at the framed photos next to the sofa. Clare and her husband, leis piled high on their shoulders, dressed in white cotton kurtas, laughing on a broad beach as they toasted each other with champagne flutes. Baby Moira, just hours old, in the arms of her smiling, but tired-looking mother. Group photos of East Indian and Anglo families, together and separately. And a more recent photo: Clare and her husband standing in front of a museum display case holding, if memory served correctly, the famous steatite bull head from Knossos.

Clare walked back into the room and saw me studying it. She looked down at the photo.

"I imagine you know more about me than most of my family," she mused. Then she smiled. "Please, sit down. Moira's asleep now, so we can have some quiet." She paused and looked at me. "Do you have children?"

"No, but I like them."

"We do, too."

"When's your baby due?"

"In about nine weeks," she said, smiling, and touching her stomach. "A boy."

"Congratulations."

"Peter wants at least four more children. I think we may be owed, don't you?" she asked, smiling.

I had been ruminating, on the way down, as to how to approach the stories on the tapes but it looked like Clare's natural extroversion would make it easy. "I'd say you were."

After a pause, she asked, "How's Dr. Turner?"

She was so happy. A wonderful husband, lovely home, a beautiful child and another on the way. This was no time to discuss death.

"Oh, well enough, I think." I heard my voice drop as I looked down into my lap.

"I must say, he was a lucky find. I must've gone to a half-dozen doctors before he helped me figure out that dream! But I'm so glad I pursued it. It's amazing, isn't it? Everything you need to know about yourself is in your dreams, and most people don't even bother to remember them."

And so we began. I took the manuscript of her stories from my bag and handed it to her. "I thought you might like a copy."

She opened it, thumbed through it, stopping to read at various points, then looked up. "You did all this yourself? This is wonderful! Thank you so much. I would have been happy to talk with you, if only . . ."

I held up my notebook. "Well, I do have a couple of questions, now that you mention it." In fact, the notebook was filled with questions, but Clare had already been so candid I turned the page and just began taking the occasional note as she spoke.

She'd finished her master's in Urban Planning, but wasn't working right now. It had been love-at-first sight with Peter, right on the breakdown lane of the freeway. ("It was so obvious," she said. "People were honking their horns as they drove by!") She'd never imagined herself married to a man of East Indian heritage, but she'd never imagined herself as a Minoan weaver, or an African-American slave, either. Her personal time-trip had been exhausting, and she'd frequently fallen into a deep sleep after returning home from the sessions.

She did not know why chunks of one era had come to her, then at other times her mind seemed to pick up one detail of one time and place, then another from others. The working of her mind in hypnosis had baffled even her. But from the first day of her hypnotherapy, she'd felt herself improving, and continued to improve every visit thereafter. It was, she said, the same feeling of release one might have as they were cleaning out dusty, long-forgotten souvenirs from a basement or attic.

Did she think the stories were "real"? Not as she was telling them, not real in the sense of being verifiable historical facts. But they felt authentic to her deep inside, almost, she said, as if at a micro-level of personal reality or belief accessed only in her altered states. In answer to my question as to whether she could remember ever having studied any of these historical periods she said no, except for what she might have picked up in art history classes: superficial knowledge of Bronze Age pottery, Byzantine tesserae, Angevin tapestries. Other than that, she admitted no deep interest in history as a subject.

How about travel? Had she been to any of the places she spoke of before her regressions?

"France. But only Paris and Chartres. Washington D.C., on a class trip, was as close as I've ever been to the Virginia Piedmont. Yosemite a couple of times. And"—she picked up the photo of the steatite bull's head—"the Cyclades."

"Santorini?"

"It was strange. We were on a small boat chartered by the Athens Dive Consortium, they're the Greek government's counterpart to COR, floating around inside that volcano. It was such a *déjà vu* moment. But I don't know if that came from the regression or from…" Her voice trailed off. For an instant, some confusion showed on her face, then she shrugged and smiled again. "Have you been there?"

I nodded.

"Beautiful, isn't it? Almost like someone's dream."

Had she had any dreams that referred back to her stories?

"Strange you should ask. I dreamed once last year that I was with a man who looked like Tuketu. That there was a war with the white gold-miners, which I guess happened. He and I were hiding out in the back country when we were ambushed. Then, the next thing I knew, we were down in a valley, in some kind of internment camp, it seemed. The man like Tuketu was sick with pneumonia. That was all. You know, sometimes dreams do seem more like memories."

She had read up on Bridey Murphy, but didn't think her own case was cryptomnesia. "At a hundred dollars an hour, I had no money to spare for games." But, bottom line, she couldn't explain how she knew what she knew, either. Only that, as she said, "The doctor taught me not to worry if they were true or not, just let them do their work."

Finally, I asked the one question which I myself could find no answer for: "So, how do you explain the appearance of the stone?"

Our eyes locked. Then, she smiled. "Should I?"

. . .

We talked for nearly two and a half hours, pausing only once to stretch our legs on a stroll through Clare's newly planted garden.

"I feel like I'm talking to an old friend," she said when we returned to sit down in the living room. "Have you been regressed?"

"Once, as an experiment."

"Did Dr. Turner do it?"

I started to answer, but suddenly the old pain rose up into my throat and my breath caught. Before I knew it, I felt one tear, then another, running down my cheeks. "Sorry." I reached into my pocket for a tissue.

"Did I say something wrong?" Clare sounded stricken.

I pressed the tissue to my eyes, wiped the mascara off, tried to steady myself. Clare had told me her innermost truths. After what she had done, I owed her mine.

"The doctor... Nick, died."

"Died?"

"It was sudden."

She stared.

"A car accident. A car hit him...near his office."

After a long moment she asked, as if she already knew the answer, "Were you close?"

"He died," I looked down, "five days before our wedding."

"God in heaven." She rose from her chair and sat down next to me. Her hand came lightly to my shoulder. "And all this time you were still able to work on my stories?"

Though I occasionally needed a fresh tissue, I gave her the details of Nick's death, told her how depressed I had become, told her about the rehab, then told her something that, perhaps, I'd been meaning to say all along: "It was the tapes that kept me going. I know they were your stories. But I found them in his desk drawer with my name and our wedding date on them so I knew he had meant me to have them. I stayed with them, and they've saved me, in a sense."

The room was still. All I could hear was my occasional sniffles. And a clock ticking on the fireplace mantel.

"A fortuitous legacy," she said, staring out beyond the room. She turned back, studied me, smiled, then put her hand over mine. "I'll be right back." She returned not more than five minutes later, holding something in her right hand. She sat down next to me again, gently pulled my wrist toward her and opened out my palm. I felt something cool and smooth drop into it, her fingers closing mine around it. I opened my hand and looked down.

A turquoise stone.

I looked back at her. "Is this . . .?"

"Yes. It is."

"No, I can't."

"You must." Her hands encircled mine and the stone in my palm.

"I hope—" I started to say.

"I do, too," she said, smiling through her own tears.

I now believed that, at last, Clare had found, and kept, her one true love; that she had, somehow, discovered an infinite past for herself; one that explained and validated the present. And the baby Moira seemed proof of the "divine child" of alchemical lore: divine because she had sprung from the *prima materia* of soul mates whose destined relationship had come to fruition by the grace of a heavenly hand.

The sun was filtering low through newly arrived rain clouds from the south. Evening traffic was picking up. It was time for me to leave.

Clare made me promise to stay in touch with her, gave me all the numbers and addresses where she could be reached. We hugged each other, and I wished her well with her pregnancy.

Halfway home, the rain began. Big warm drops splashed down, making radiant circles that appeared and disappeared in an instant in the ponding at the shoulder of the lane. I turned on the windshield wipers and listened to their beat across the glass. Sixty beats a minute. Galileo's measure of time. The steady rhythm of Nick's heart as I lay my head against his chest our last night together.

· · ·

The unseasonably wet weather kept me inside for two more days. Then the sun returned. That Sunday, after I'd filed away all my drafts and notes on Clare's tapes, I walked out to the beach, just below the park where Nick and I had first met. It was a panoramic afternoon made vivid by days of rain. There were others coming out to the strand: runners and skaters traveling the winding white path, volleyball players assembling teams, a pair of acrobats juggling bright wands.

I stood barefoot on the mirrored shore and, shading my eyes, looked out across the dark curve of Santa Monica Bay to Santa Catalina Island silhouetted in the distance, as Crete must have been once for Theion and Acasia. The surf-beat lapped softly against my feet. I curled my toes into the sand, those particles of earth that, the mystics say, are as many as all the lives we will ever live.

At that moment, in this realization, all the world around me seemed to dissolve and in its place, a vision, Clare's Priestess of the Goddess, appeared before me. I saw her arms stretch forward, the snakes of gold entwined around them and, with a snap of her wrists, I watched the snakes come to life, wind around each other as the Caduceus of Hermes, the sign of the medic, then curve again around, each clasping in the circle of eternal becoming, his tail with his mouth: the Greek *ouroboros*, doubled.

She laughed. The crystal beam from her dove headdress shone. And suddenly it was as if a shaft of light, a light of knowledge as penetrating as a second sun, touched the depths of my longing heart, and I understood the true meaning of my journey, that and more Nick could not have anticipated when he wrote my name on that envelope.

By fate or providence, it was not for me to know, Clare had come to Nick to tell her stories and be healed. Nick, in his calling as healer, had concentrated on helping her. Yet underneath the science he'd grasped the infinite truth conveyed through her stories, and believed. Now, by the simple act of writing my name on Clare's tales he had, without knowing it, given me his promise, even after his death, that he and I would meet and love again on earth. Clare's "healing fictions" had become my own.

Suddenly I felt a rush of joy. The wind came up and with it, a voice, one I knew well, calling "Emily…"

"I love you Nick—forever!" I shouted to the sun and sea, as I twirled and danced along the sand.

In how many lifetimes would Nick and I meet before we experienced one perfect life together? That was not a question I could answer. All I knew was that the ever-turning Wheel of Samsara had turned again for Clare and for me and, like a relay torch in some antique games we had each, in our turn, been given a promise of love, and life, never-ending. All because of one woman's dream—a dream of a turquoise stone.

ACKNOWLEDGMENTS

Straight-from-the-heart thanks to poet Mary Lee Gowland as well as to publisher Phil Wood for their kind interest in my writing during the many years of our friendship, and for their encouragement on this particular project. An equally large debt of gratitude is owed Rebecca Johns, Dorrie O'Brien, and Ross Browne and his staff at The Editorial Department for their invaluable editorial guidance. The Doe Classics Library at UC Berkeley, the Yosemite Research Library, Janet and Lionel Camut, Karl Fields, and Andrea Wild all provided research assistance at various stages of story development. Susan Wilson and Mary Levering offered important help with, respectively, business and legal aspects of publishing. Finally, all my love to my dear husband, patron and soul mate Bruce Webster, without whom this book would not be a reality.